SUCCOR ME!

Andromeda took the scenic route home—after all, when would she be able to talk Hermes out of his winged sandals again? She saw Scylla and Charybdis, there by the toe of the Italian boot, and they were as horrible as advertised. She flew over the Pyramids of Egypt. Next door, the Sphinx tried his riddle on her. "Oh, everybody knows *that* one," Andromeda said, and listened to him gnash his stone teeth.

Then she started north across the wine-dark sea toward Greece. When she got to the coast near Argos, she saw a naked man chained to the rocks just above the waves. He was a lot more interesting than anything else she'd seen for a while—and the closer she got, the more interesting he looked. By the time she was hovering a few feet in front of him, he looked mighty damn fine indeed, you betcha.

"I know it's the obvious question," she said, "but what are you doing here?"

"Waiting to be eaten," he answered.

"Listen, has it occurred to you that if I slap you silly, you can't do thing one about it?" Andromeda said indignantly. "Has it?"

"No, by a sea serpent," he explained.

"Oh. Well, no accounting for taste, I suppose."

ALSO IN THIS SERIES

Chicks in Chainmail,
Edited by Esther Friesner

Did You Say Chicks?!,
edited by Esther Friesner

Mathemagics
by Margaret Ball

BAEN BOOKS by ESTHER FRIESNER

Child of the Eagle

The Sherwood Game

Wishing Season

Chicks 'n CHAINED MALES

EDITED BY

Esther Friesner

A Baen Books Original

Baen Publishing Enterprises
P.O. Box 1403
Riverdale, NY 10471

ISBN: 0-671-57814-6

Cover art by Larry Elmore

First printing, May 1999

Distributed by Simon & Schuster
1230 Avenue of the Americas
New York, NY 10020

Typeset by Windhaven Press, Auburn, NH
Printed in the United States of America

Contents

Introduction

I know what you're thinking and I want you to stop it *right this minute*.

Don't try denying it. We both know the first thing that popped into your mind when you read the title of this book. I'd tell you that you really ought to be ashamed of yourself, but Who Am I To Judge? Besides, for all I know, you've already got a career in politics and my mama didn't raise any kids who like to pound sand down rat-holes.

Perhaps I should explain what this book is *really* about: It's about women rescuing men. There. Perfectly innocent. Wholesome and admirable, even. When I first came up with the title/concept for the Chicks in Chainmail series, one of my noble goals was to give the doughty Woman Warrior of fantasy fiction something *different* to do, a nice change from stomping around the landscape with a permanent grouch on, slaughtering any who dared oppose her (or worse, tried telling her to "Lighten up!"), and using her days off to go to the local tavern, get drunk, and have some out-of-work sailor tattoo the phrase All Men Are Worthless Scum Except For Breeding Purposes somewhere on her body guaranteed to upset her mother. (Unless, of course, she'd learned the whole stomp, slaughter 'n' swill routine from Mom herself.)

Here I must admit that when I was told that lo, the title of this book was to be *Chicks 'n Chained Males*, initially I reacted in much the same way as you did. (Yes, you did so too! 'Fess up and be done with it.) But how much greater was my startlement when I learned whence came the aforementioned title!

As those of you already familiar with these modest volumes may recall, the title of the first Chicks in Chainmail anthology (still available; buy many copies) caused a momentary access of trepidation on the part of Our Revered Publisher. This was understandable since, as he himself stated in the Disclaimer on the back of said book, he is a Sensitive, Nineties Kind of Guy.

Well, guess what? The Nineties are almost over. Maybe it's the approaching millenium, maybe it's ascribable to the ripple effect of the dreaded Y2K Bug, but for whatever reason, *he* is the one who came up with the title for the book you are presently holding in your dainty hands.

I think this is laudable, commendable, praiseworthy, and the rest of the synonyms in my on-line thesaurus for, as you may also recall from my introduction to the original *Chicks in Chainmail*, it was my desire to show the world that women can be strong and still be able to take a joke. (In fact, laughter when the joke's on you is a pretty good gauge of just how secure in your strength you are. Ever notice what happens to a whole lot of political humorists under certain military dictatorships? Ow.)

By giving us this title, Our Revered Publisher has demonstrated that Sensitive Nineties Guys can also own up to a sense of humor without relinquishing one inch of the moral high ground. Has the shining example of favorable public reaction to *Chicks in Chainmail* been instrumental in this epiphany? Have I, in some miniscule manner, been responsible for facilitating this cognitive evolution? Might we not interpret this consequence to signify that we have, in some fashion, rescued yet another man from the meshes of a misleading-if-well-intentioned ideology? (Oooh, I just *love* my on-line thesaurus!) I like to think so. It makes me quietly proud. In fact, there is one aspect above all others connected with this book and all associated therewith for which I am deeply, truly, and warmly grateful:

This time, *I* get the Disclaimer. It's mine, do you hear? Mine! Minemineminemine . . . *mine!*

Enjoy.

Harry Turtledove studied Greek in college and has a doctorate in Byzantine history. He's been selling fiction for over twenty years, won a Hugo, and has been a Nebula finalist. None of this has stopped him from "applying" the aforementioned knowledge and experience to creating the story that follows, for which I will be deeply grateful once I can stop laughing.

Myth Manners' Guide to Greek Missology #1: Andromeda and Perseus

by Harry Turtledove

Andromeda was feeling the strain. "Why *me*?" she demanded. She'd figured Zeus wanted something from her when he invited her up to good old Mount Olympus for the weekend, but she'd thought it would be something else. She'd been ready to play along, too—how did you go about saying no to the king of the gods? You didn't, not unless you were looking for a role in a tragedy. But . . . this?

"Why you?" Zeus eyed her as if he'd had something else in mind, too. But then he looked over at Hera, his wife, and got back to the business at hand.

"Because you're the right man—uh, the right person—for the job."

"Yeah, right," Andromeda said. "Don't you think you'd do better having a man go out and fight the Gorgons? Isn't that what men are for?—fighting, I mean." She knew what else men were for, but she didn't want to mention that to Zeus, not with Hera listening.

And Hera *was* listening. She said, "Men are useless—for fighting the Gorgons, I mean." She sounded as if she meant a lot of other things, too. She was looking straight at Zeus.

No matter how she sounded, the king of the gods dipped his head in agreement. "My wife's right." By the sour look on his face, that sentence didn't pass his lips every eternity. "The three Gorgons are fearsome foes. Whenever a man spies Cindy, Claudia, or Tyra, be it only for an instant, he turns to stone."

"*Part* of him turns to stone, anyway," Hera said acidly.

"And, so, you not being a man, you being a woman . . ." Zeus went on.

"Wait a minute. Wait just a linen-picking minute," Andromeda broke in. "You're not a man, either, or not exactly a man. You're a god. Why don't you go and take care of these Gorgons with the funny names your own self?"

Zeus coughed, then brightened. "Well, my dear, since you put it that way, maybe I ought to—"

"Not on your immortal life, Bubba," Hera said. "You lay a hand on those hussies and you're mythology."

"You see how it is," Zeus said to Andromeda. "My wife doesn't understand me at all."

Getting in the middle of an argument between god and goddess didn't strike Andromeda as Phi Beta Kappa—or any other three letters of the Greek alphabet, either. Telling Zeus to find himself another boy—or girl—wouldn't be the brightest thing since Phoebus Apollo, either. With a sigh, she said, "Okay. You've got me." Zeus' eyes lit up. Hera planted an elbow in his divine ribs. Hastily, Andromeda went on, "Now what do I have to do?"

"Here you are, my dear." From behind his gold-and-ivory throne, Zeus produced a sword belt. He was about to buckle it on Andromeda—and probably let his fingers do a little extra walking while he was taking care of that—when Hera let out a sudden sharp cough. Sulkily, the king of the gods handed Andromeda the belt and let her put it on herself.

From behind her throne, Hera pulled out a brightly polished shield. "Here," she said. "You may find this more useful against Cindy, Claudia, and Tyra than any blade. Phallic symbols, for some reason or other, don't much frighten them."

"Hey, sometimes a sword is just a sword," Zeus protested.

"And sometimes it's *not*, Mr. Swan, Mr. Shower-of-Gold, Mr. Bull—plenty of bull for all the girls from here to Nineveh, and I'm damned Tyred of it," Hera said. Zeus fumed. Hera turned back to Andromeda. "If you look in the shield, you'll get some idea of what I mean."

"Is it safe?" Andromeda asked. As Zeus had, Hera dipped her head. Her divine husband was still sulking, and didn't answer one way or the other. Andromeda cautiously looked. "I can see myself!" she exclaimed—not a claim she was likely to be able to make after washing earthenware plates, no matter the well from which the house slaves brought back the dishwashing liquid. A moment later, her hands flew to her hair. "Eeuw! I'm not so sure I want to."

"It isn't you, dearie—it's the magic in the shield," Hera said, not unkindly. "If you really looked like that, loverboy here wouldn't be interested in feeling your pain . . . or anything else he could get his hands on." She gave Zeus a cold and speculative stare. "At least, I don't *think* he would. He's not always fussy."

A thunderbolt appeared in Zeus' right hand. He

tossed it up and down, hefting it and eyeing Hera. "Some of them—most of them, even—keep their mouths shut except when I want them to be open," he said meaningfully.

Hera stood up to her full height, which was whatever she chose to make it. Andromeda didn't quite come up to the goddess' dimpled knee. "Well, I'd better be going," she said hastily. If Zeus and Hera started at it hammer and tongs, they might not even notice charbroiling a more or less innocent mortal bystander by mistake.

Just finding Cindy, Claudia, and Tyra didn't prove easy. Minor gods and goddesses weren't allowed to set up shop on Olympus; they lowered surreal-estate values. Andromeda had to go through almost all of Midas' Golden Pages before getting so much as a clue about where she ought to be looking.

Even then, she was puzzled. "Why on earth—or off it, for that matter—would they hang around with a no-account Roman goddess?" she asked.

"What, you think I hear everything?" Midas' long, hairy, donkeyish ears twitched. "And why should I give a Phryg if I do hear things?" His ears twitched again, this time, Andromeda judged, in contempt. "You know about the Greek goddess of victory, don't you?"

"Oh, everybody knows about *her*." Andromeda sounded scornful, too. Since the Greeks had pretty much stopped winning victories, the goddess formerly in charge of them had gone into the running-shoe business, presumably to mitigate the agony of defeat on de feet. Nike had done a gangbanger business, too, till wing-footed Hermes hit her with a copyright-infringement suit that showed every sign of being as eternal as the gods.

"So there you are, then," Midas said. "I don't know what Victoria's secret is, and I don't give a darn."

"That's my shortstop," Andromeda said absently, and

let out a long, heartfelt sigh. "I'll just have to go and find out for myself, won't I?"

Thinking of Hermes and his winged sandals gave her an idea. Back to the high-rent district of Mount Olympus she went. The god raised his eyebrows. He had a winged cap, too, one that fluttered off his head in surprise. "You want *my* shoes?" he said.

"I can't very well walk across the Adriatic," Andromeda said.

"No, that's a different myth altogether," Hermes agreed.

"And then up to Rome, to see if the gods are in," Andromeda went on.

"They won't be, not when the mercury rises," Hermes said, "They'll be out in the country, or else at the beach. Pompeii is very pretty this time of year."

"Such a *lovely* view of the volcano," Andromeda murmured. She cast Hermes a melting look. "May I *please* borrow your sandals?"

"Oh, all right," he said crossly. "The story would bog down if I told you no at this point."

"You'd better not be reading ahead," Andromeda warned him. Hermes just snickered. Gods had more powers than mortals, and that was all there was to it. When Andromeda put on the winged sandals and hopped into the air, she stayed up. "Gotta be the shoes," she said.

"Oh, it is," Hermes assured her. "Have fun in Italy."

As she started to fly away, Andromeda called back, "Do you know what Victoria's secret is?"

The god dipped his head to show he did. "Good camera angles," he replied.

Good camera angles. A quiet hostel. A nice view of the beach. And, dammit, a lovely view of the volcano, too. Vesuvius *was* picturesque. And so were Cindy, Claudia, and Tyra, **dress**ed in lacy, colorful, overpriced wisps of not very much. As soon as Andromeda set eyes on them, she started hoping the mountain would blow up and bury those three in lava. Molten lava. Red-hot molten lava. The rest of Pompeii? So what? Herculaneum? So what? Naples, up the coast? Who needed it, really?

But Vesuvius stayed quiet. Of course it did. Hephaestus or Vulcan or whatever name he checked into motels with locally was probably up at the top of the spectacular cone, peering down, leering down, at some other spectacular cones. "Men," Andromeda muttered. No wonder they'd given her this job. And they wouldn't thank her for it once she did it, either.

As Andromeda flew down toward the Gorgons with the spectacularly un-Hellenic names, Victoria flew up to meet her, saying, "Whoever you are, go away. We're just about to shoot."

Shooting struck Andromeda as altogether too good for them. "Some victory you're the goddess of," she sneered, "unless you mean the one in *Lysistrata*."

"You're just jealous because you can't cut the liquamen, sweetheart," Victoria retorted.

Andromeda smiled a hemlock-filled smile. "Doesn't matter whether I am or not," she answered. "I'm on assignment from Zeus and Hera, so you can go take a flying leap at Selene."

"Uppity mortal! You can't talk to me like that." Victoria drew back a suddenly very brawny right arm for a haymaker that would have knocked the feathers right off of Hermes' sandals.

"Oh, yes, I can," Andromeda said, and held up the shield Hera had given her.

She didn't know whether it could have done a decent job of stopping the goddess' fist. That didn't matter. Victoria took one brief look at her reflection and cried, "*Vae! Malae comae! Vae!*" She fled so fast, she might have gone into business with her Greek cousin Nike.

A grim smile on her face, Andromeda descended on

Cindy, Claudia, and Tyra. They were lined up on the
beach like three tenpins—*except not so heavy in the
bottom*, Andromeda thought resentfully. Had they been
lined up any better, she'd have bet she could've looked
into the left ear of the one on the left and seen out
the right ear of the one on the right.

They turned on her in unison when she alighted on
the sand. "Ooh, I like those sandals," one of them
crooned fiercely. "Gucci? Louis Vuitton?"

"No, Hermes'," Andromeda answered. She fought
panic as they advanced on her, swaying with menace—
or something.

"I wonder what she's doing here," one of the Gorgons
said. She waved at the gorgeous scenery, of which she
and her comrades were the most gorgeous parts. "I
mean, she's so plain."

"Mousy," agreed another.

"Nondescript. Utterly nondescript," said the third,
proving she did have room in her head for a three-
syllable word: two of them, even.

And the words flayed like fire. Cindy, Claudia, and
Tyra weren't even contemptuous. It was as if Andromeda
didn't rate contempt. That was their power; just by
existing, they made everyone around them feel inadequate. *Zeus wanted me*, Andromeda thought, trying to
stay strong. But what did that prove? Zeus wanted
anything that moved, and, if it didn't move, he'd give
it an experimental shake.

Andromeda felt like curling up on the beach and
dying right there. If she put the shield up over her,
maybe it would keep her from hearing any more of the
Gorgons' cruel words. The shield . . . !

With a fierce cry of her own, Andromeda held it up
to them. Instead of continuing their sinuous advance,
they fell back with cries of horror. Peering down over
the edge of the shield, Andromeda got a quick glimpse
of their reflections. The shield had given her and
Victoria bad hair. It was far more pitiless to Cindy,

Claudia, and Tyra, perhaps because they had further to fall from the heights of *haute couture*. Whatever the reason, the three Gorgons' hair might as well have turned to snakes once the shield had its way with them.

"Plain," Andromeda murmured. "Mousy. Nondescript. Utterly nondescript."

How the Gorgons howled! They fell to their knees in the sand and bowed their heads, trying to drive out those images of imperfection.

Still holding the shield on high, Andromeda drew her sword. She could have taken their heads at a stroke, but something stayed her hand. It wasn't quite mercy: more the reflection that they'd probably already given a good deal of head to get where they were.

Roughly, she said, "Stay away from Olympus from now on, if you know what's good for you. You ever come near there again, worse'll be waiting for you." She didn't know if that was true, but it would be if Hera could make it so.

"But where shall we go?" one of them asked in a small, broken voice. "What shall we do?"

"Try *Sports Illustrated*," Andromeda suggested, "though gods only know what sport you'd be illustrating."

"Been there," one said. Andromeda had no idea which was which, and didn't care to find out. The other two chorused, "Done that."

"Find something else, then," Andromeda said impatiently. "I don't care what, as long as it's not in Zeus' back yard." *And mine*, she thought. Thinking that, she started to turn the terrible shield on them again and added, "Or else."

Cindy, Claudia, and Tyra cringed. If they weren't convinced now, they never would be, Andromeda judged. She jumped into the air and flew off. That way, she didn't have to look at them any more, didn't have to be reminded that they didn't really look the way Hera's shield made them seem to. Plain. Mousy. Nondescript. Utterly nondescript. Her hand went to the hilt of the sword. *Maybe*

I should have done a little slaughtering after all. But she kept flying.

She took the scenic route home—after all, when would she be able to talk Hermes out of his sandals again? She saw Scylla and Charybdis, there by the toe of the Italian boot, and they were as horrible as advertised. She flew over the Pyramids of Egypt. Next door, the Sphinx tried his riddle on her. "Oh, everybody knows *that* one," Andromeda said, and listened to him gnash his stone teeth.

She admired the lighthouse at Alexandria. It would be very impressive when they got around to building it—and when there was an Alexandria. Then she started north across the wine-dark sea toward Greece.

When she got to the coast near Argos, she saw a naked man chained to the rocks just above the waves. He was a lot more interesting than anything else she'd seen for a while—and the closer she got, the more interesting he looked. By the time she was hovering a few feet in front of him, he looked mighty damn fine indeed, you betcha. "I know it's the obvious question," she said, "but what are you doing here?"

"Waiting to be eaten," he answered.

"Listen, garbagemouth, has it occurred to you that if I slap you silly, you can't do thing one about it?" Andromeda said indignantly. "Has it?"

"No, by a sea serpent," he explained.

"Oh. Well, no accounting for taste, I suppose," she said, thinking of Pasiphaë and the bull. Then she realized he meant it literally. "How did that happen?" Another obvious question: "And who are you, anyway?"

"I'm Perseus," he said. "My grandfather, Acrisius, is King of Argos. There's a prophecy that if my mother had a son, he'd end up killing Gramps. So Mom was grounded for life, but Zeus visited her in a shower of gold, and here I am."

"And on display, too," Andromeda remarked. Zeus

had been catching Hades from Hera ever since, too—
Andromeda remembered the snide *Mr. Shower-of-Gold*.
But that was neither here nor there, and Perseus was
definitely here. "The sea serpent will take your granddad
off the hook for doing you in?"

"You got it," Perseus agreed.

"Ah . . . what about the chains? Doesn't he think
those might have something to do with him?"

Perseus shrugged. Andromeda admired pecs and abs.
The chains clanked. "He's not *real* long on ethics,
Acrisius isn't."

"If you get loose, you'll do your best to make the
prophecy come true?" Andromeda asked.

Another shrug. More clanks. More admiration from
Andromeda. Perseus said, "Well, I've sure got a motive
now, and I didn't before. But I'm not in a hurry about
it. Omens have a way of working out, you know? I
mean, would you be here to set me free if I weren't
fated to do Gramps in one of these years?"

"I'm not here to set you free," Andromeda said. "I just
stopped by for a minute to enjoy the scenery, and—"

Perseus pointed. He didn't do it very well—he was
chained, after all—but he managed. "Excuse me for
interrupting," he said, "but the sea serpent's coming."

Andromeda whirled in the air. "Eep!" she said.
Perseus hadn't been wrong. The monster was huge. It
was fast. It was hideous. It was wet (which made sense,
it being a sea serpent). It had an alarmingly big mouth
full of a frighteningly large number of terrifyingly sharp
teeth. Andromeda could have rearranged those adverbs
any which way and they still would have added up to
the same thing. Trouble. Big trouble.

She could also have flown away. She glanced back
at Perseus and shook her head. That would have been
a waste of a great natural resource. And, no matter what
Hera had to say about it, Zeus wouldn't be overjoyed
if she left his bastard son out for sea-serpent fast food.

She drew her sword—Zeus' sword—and flew toward

the monster. One way or another, this story was going to get some blood in it. Or maybe not. She held up Hera's mirrored shield, right in the sea serpent's face. It might figure it was having a bad scales day and go away.

But no such luck. Maybe the shield didn't work because the sea serpent had no hair. Maybe the serpent had already maxed out its ugly account. Or maybe it was too stupid to notice anything had changed. Andromeda shook her head again. If Cindy, Claudia, and Tyra had noticed, the sea serpent would have to.

No help for it. Sometimes, as Zeus had said, a sword was just a sword. Andromeda swung this one. It turned out to cut sea serpent a lot better than her very best kitchen knife cut roast goose. Chunk after reptilian chunk fell away from the main mass of the monster. The Aegean turned red. The sea serpent really might have been dumber than the Gorgons, because it took a very long time to realize it was dead. Eventually, though, enough of the head end was missing that it forgot to go on living and sank beneath the waves. If the sharks and the dolphins didn't have a food fight with the scraps, they missed a hell of a chance.

Chlamys soaked with seawater and sea-serpent gore, Andromeda flew back toward Perseus. "I would applaud," he said, "but under the circumstances . . ." He rattled his chains to show what he meant. "That was very exciting."

Andromeda looked him over. He meant it literally. She could tell. She giggled. Greek statues always underestimated things. Quite a bit, here. She giggled again. Sometimes a sword wasn't just a sword.

She looked up toward the top of the rocks. Nobody was watching; maybe Acrisius' conscience, however vestigial, bothered him too much for that. She could do whatever she pleased. Perseus couldn't do anything about it, that was plain enough. Andromeda giggled once more. She flew a little lower and a lot closer.

Perseus gasped. Andromeda pulled back a bit and glanced up at him, eyes full of mischief. "You said you were here to be eaten," she pointed out.

"By a *sea serpent!*"

"If you don't think this is more fun . . ." Her shrug was petulant. But, when you got down to the bottom of things, what Perseus thought didn't matter a bit. She went back to what she'd been doing. After a little while, she decided to do something else. She hiked up the clammy chlamys and did it. Though she hadn't suspected it till now, there were times when the general draftiness of Greek clothes and lack of an underwear department at the Athens K-Mart came in kind of handy. Up against the side of a cliff, winged sandals didn't hurt, either. A good time was had by all.

Afterwards, still panting, Perseus said, "Now that you've ravished me, you realize you'll have to marry me."

Andromeda stretched languorously. A *very* good time had been had by all, or at least by her. She wished for a cigarette, and wished even more she knew what one was. "That can probably be arranged," she purred.

"First, though, you'll have to get me off," Perseus said.

She squawked. "Listen, mister, if I didn't just take care of that—"

"No, off this cliff," he said.

"Oh." Andromeda dipped her head in agreement. "Well, that can probably be arranged, too." She drew the sword again and swung it. It sheared through the metal that imprisoned Perseus like a divine sword cutting cheap bronze chains. After four strokes— considerably fewer than he'd been good for—he fell forward and down. They caught each other in midair. Hermes' sandals were strong enough to carry two. Andromeda had figured they would be. She and Perseus rose together.

After topping the rocks, they flew north toward Argos. Perseus said, "Can I borrow your sword for a minute?"

"Why?" Andromeda looked at him sidelong. "I like the one you come equipped with."

"It won't cut through the manacles on my ankles and wrists," Perseus said.

"Hmm. I suppose not. Sure, go ahead."

Divine swords had a lot going for them. This one neatly removed the manacles without removing the hands and feet they'd been binding. Thinking about all the times she'd sliced herself carving wild boar—those visiting Gauls could really put it away—Andromeda wished she owned cutlery like that.

Perseus said, "Can you steer a little more to the left?"

"Sure," Andromeda said, and did. "How come?"

"That's Acrisius' palace down there." Perseus pointed. "Who knows? Maybe I can make a prophecy come true." He dropped the manacles and the lengths of chain attached to them, one after another. He and Andromeda both watched them fall.

"I can't tell," Andromeda said at last.

"Neither can I." Perseus made the best of things: "If I did nail the old geezer, Matt Drudge'll have it online before we get to Olympus."

The wedding was the event of the eon. Andromeda's mother and father, Cepheus and Cassiopeia, flew up from their Ethiopian home in their private Constellation. Acrisius' cranium apparently remained undented, but nobody sent him an invitation. Danaë, Perseus' mother, did come. She and Hera spent the first part of the weekend snubbing each other.

Zeus dishonored two maids of honor and, once in his cups, seemed convinced every cupbearer was named Ganymede. After he got into the second maid of honor, he also got into a screaming row with Hera. A couple of thunderbolts flew, but the wedding pavilion, though scorched, survived.

Hera and Danaë went off in a corner, had a good cry together, and were the best of friends from then on out. A little later, Zeus sidled up to Andromeda and asked in an anxious voice, "What is this *First Wives' Club* my wife keeps talking about? Do you suppose it is as powerful as my sword?"

"Which one, your Godship, sir?" she returned; she was in her cups, too. Zeus didn't answer, but went off with stormy, and even rather rainy, brow. Before long, he and Hera were screaming at each other again.

And then Andromeda and Perseus were off for their wedding night at the Mount Olympus Holiday Inn. In her cups or not, Andromeda didn't like the way the limo driver handled the horses. Perseus patted her knee. "Don't worry, sweetie," he said. "Phaëthon hasn't burned rubber, or anything else, for quite a while now."

She might have argued more, but Perseus' hand, instead of stopping at the knee, kept wandering north. And, with all the gods in the wedding party following the limo, odds were somebody could bring her back to life even if she did get killed.

Ambrosia—Dom Perignon ambrosia, no less—waited on ice in the honeymoon suite. The bed was as big as Boeotia, as soft as the sea-foam that spawned Aphrodite. Out in the hallway, the gods and demigods and mortals with pull who'd been at the wedding made a deityawful racket, waiting for the moment of truth.

They didn't have to wait very long. Perseus was standing at attention even when he lay down on that inviting bed. Wearing nothing but a smile, Andromeda got down beside him. At the appropriate time, she let out a squeal, pretending to be a maiden. Everybody in the hallway let out a cheer, pretending to believe her.

After the honeymoon, things went pretty well. Perseus landed an editorial job at *Argosy*. Andromeda spent a while on the talk-show circuit: Loves Fated to Happen were hot that millennium. They bought themselves a little house in Syracuse. It was Greek Colonial architecture, right out of Grant Xylum, and they furnished it to match. When Andromeda sat down on the four-poster bed one night, she heard a peculiar sound, not one it usually made. "What's that?" she asked Perseus.

"What's what?" he said, elaborately casual.

"That noise. Like—metal?"

"Oh. That." Elaborately casual, all right—too elaborately casual. Perseus' face wore an odd smile, half sheepish, half . . . something else. "It's probably these." He lifted up his pillow.

"Chains!" Andromeda exclaimed. "Haven't you had enough of chains?"

"Well—sort of." Perseus sounded sheepish, too, sheepish and . . . something else. An eager something else. "But it was so much fun that first time, I, I . . . thought we might try it again."

"*Did* you?" Andromeda rubbed her chin. You don't find out everything right away about the person you marry, especially if it's a whirlwind courtship. Gods knew she hadn't expected *this*. Still . . . "Why not?" she said at last. "Just don't invite that damn sea serpent."

And a good time was had by all.

Aside from teaching high school English, Steven Piziks also teaches sex education. He assures me that this has nothing to do with the following story. Right. He also plays the folk harp and vanishes into the woods for hours on end. Coincidence? Check out his novels In the Company of Mind *and* Corporate Mentality.

Chain, Link, Fence

Steven Piziks

"What," the fence asked, "am I supposed to do with that?"

Kordel would have ground her teeth, but her jaws were already aching. "Buy it," she said evenly.

The fence merely snorted.

Kordel flared her nostrils and shot a glance at the statue on the table between them. The silver figure of a man about ten inches high was chained to a miniature table with gem-encrusted bonds. One improbably proportioned part of the man's anatomy speared skyward. His head was thrown back in what was either a shudder of ecstasy or a grimace of agony. Since he was alone on the table and his hands were chained down, Kordel rather imagined it was the latter.

"What'll you give me for it?" Kordel said through still-clenched teeth.

The fence barked a short laugh that echoed slightly about the spartan white walls of his seemingly empty shop; a wise fence kept his merchandise out of sight. Two heavy velvet curtains obscured the back room while a single window threw a hard square of light on the stone floor.

"Look, Kordel," the fence said, ignoring Kordel's glare, "you stole the statue of Sybaritus from the temple downtown. Very nice. A feather in your cap, and all that."

"Any temple with a back door deserves to be burgled," Kordel muttered.

"But," the fence continued, waggling a thin, bony finger, "this piece is . . . unique. If word gets out I have it, I'm going to have a bunch of murder-minded cultists on my hands." He steepled his fingertips. "Why don't you try pulling out the gems and melting it down?"

"I thought of that four fences ago," Kordel snapped. "But the thing isn't pure silver—only gilded. And the gems are barely semiprecious."

"Figures," the fence snorted. "A fake statue for a false god." He picked idly at the gilding, then noticed which part he was picking at and quickly dropped his hand. "I've never understood the Sybarites. Marks, all of them. They 'contribute' huge sums of money for a ritual orgy when they could get the same thing up the street for one-third the cost—and that without boring mumbo-jumbo to a god Anya Nightbond created for her own profit." He clucked his tongue. "I don't understand the attraction."

Kordel shrugged. "They think that sex with the presence of the god—drawn down into the statue—is better than without it. They also believe that without a weekly ritual, they'll become unable to have sex at all. Since they believe it's true, it becomes true. And Anya cashes in on their belief."

The fence lifted an eyebrow. "How do you know all this?"

"I attended their rituals," Kordel replied matter-of-factly. "Part of casing the job."

The fence gave her a sidelong glance and opened his mouth to ask a question.

"I wouldn't," Kordel warned. "I'm already in a bad mood."

The fence cocked his head, considering pro and con. Con carried the day. He picked up the statue instead and hefted it. "Whatever possessed you to steal this thing, anyway? You must have known it's a piece of junk."

"I made a bet."

"A bet?"

"I bet I could steal the statue of Sybaritus and make at least a hundred silver from it."

The fence snorted again. "I hope your stake wasn't valuable."

Kordel licked her lips and glanced away, fixing her gaze on the velvet curtains. "If I lose," she said quietly, "I have to turn myself over to the city guard."

"Uh-oh. Who did you bet with?"

"Bernard of Marthia. He bet his family jewel."

The fence made a face. "Old B.M.? What did he do? Trick you into drinking whisky?"

Kordel remained silent.

"Well," the fence said with resignation, "I think the city guard is going to be very happy in a couple days. And I'm going to lose a good client."

"Look," Kordel said desperately, "why don't you give me a hundred for the statue and quietly drop it down a deep hole? I'll pay you back later."

The fence's eyes went flat. "If it comes to that, why don't you just leave town to avoid paying up?"

"I gave my word!" Kordel flared back. "There are principles involved here."

The fence nodded. "Exactly. If anyone linked the sale

to me, my career would be over. Sorry, Kordel. The statue is valuable only to the cult. You've lost."

"You're wrong!" Kordel angrily snatched up the statue, stuffed it into a large pouch—it made an interesting bulge—and strode for the door. "There must be *someone* in this city who'll buy it."

"Not a chance," the fence called after her. "No one but the cult will touch the thing."

Kordel halted. She stared for a long time at the door in front of her. "You think so?" she said without turning around. "No one but the cult?"

"No one," he replied firmly.

Kordel grinned over her shoulder at him. "I think you're right." And she vanished into the street.

"What," the fence asked, "am I supposed to do with that?"

"Buy it," Kordel said gaily. "And stop sneering. It's an act designed to bring my selling price down."

The fence sighed and picked up the object, a large emerald this time. "What happened with your bet?"

Kordel grinned. "You're fondling the prize."

The fence looked up in surprise. "I'm holding Bernard's family jewel?"

"It's not a family jewel any longer," Kordel said.

"Obviously," the fence agreed, screwing a jeweler's lens into one eye and peering at the emerald. "This gem is flawed. How did you win? I would have sworn no one would buy that statue."

"Emeralds are always flawed," Kordel replied smoothly. "And I didn't sell the statue."

"You didn't?" Again the fence looked up in surprise, but the effect was rather ruined by the jeweler's lens. "Then how did you make a profit?"

Kordel leaned against the table. "Do you have any idea," she drawled, "how much money you can make holding a god for ransom?"

The fence thought about that, then laughed aloud.

"Nightbond tried to bargain with me, if you can believe it," Kordel continued. "But I told her if she didn't give me a thousand silver, I'd send her a pile of slag and her profitable little rituals would come to an end. I had her god by the—"

"I see, I see," the fence interrupted. "Now about this emerald . . ."

A sultry voice wafted into the shop as the fence peered out the window. "Is she gone?"

"She's gone," he replied.

The curtains to the back room rustled aside and a dark-haired woman slipped unctuously into the shop. A mail overlay clinked against her black leather corset, and a small cat o' nine tails rustled at her belt. "The emerald, please," she said, unfolding her hand.

The fence took up his customary place behind the table. "First my fee."

"Of course." Anya Nightbond reached into a black leather pouch and stacked several silver coins on the table with fluid grace. "Two hundred for the emerald and two hundred for your trouble."

"I like doing business with the clergy," the fence remarked as he dropped the emerald into Anya's supple hand. "Especially the wealthy clergy. Who's next?"

Anya toyed thoughtfully with the gem. "Gilroy the Smuggler takes dares if he smokes enough seer's weed. I'll give a bundle to Bernard of Marthia when I return the betting emerald to him."

The fence nodded. "Just out of curiosity," he asked, "Kordel demanded a thousand silver from you for the statue. How much did you tell your congregation she wanted?"

"How much would *you* pay to rescue your sex life?" Anya purred. Then she sauntered out the door.

Elizabeth Moon is a beautiful, brilliant, and incredibly talented SF writer (In My Humble Opinion) but she'd rather be rich. Her most recent book is Rules of Engagement. *She lives in Texas with her husband, son, cat and horse. She's supposed to be hard at work on her next book, but I'm glad she took the time to give us this story.*

Fool's Gold

Elizabeth Moon

"It's been done to death," Mirabel Stonefist said.

"It's traditional." Her sister Monica sat primly upright, embroidering tiny poppies on a pillowcase. All Monica's pillow-cases had poppies on them, just as all the curtains on the morning side of the house had morning glories.

"Traditional is another word for 'done to death,'" Mirabel said. Her own pillow-cases had a stamped sigil and the words PROPERTY OF THE ROYAL BARRACKS DO NOT REMOVE.

"It's unlucky to break with tradition."

"It's unlucky to have anything to do with dragons," Mirabel said, rubbing the burn scar on her left leg.

Cavernous Dire had never intended to be a dragon.

He had intended to be a miser, living a long and peaceful life of solitary selfishness near the Tanglefoot Mountains, but he had, all unwitting, consumed a seed of dragonsfoot which had been—entirely by accident—baked into a gooseberry tart. That wouldn't have changed him, if his neighbor hadn't made an innocent mistake and handed him dragonstongue, instead of dragonsbane, to ease a sore tongue. The two plants do look much alike, and usually it makes no difference whether you nibble a leaf of *D. abscondus* or *D. lingula*, since both will ease a cold-blister, but in those rare instances when someone has an undigested seed of dragonsfoot in his gut, and then adds to it the potent essence of *D. lingula* . . . well.

Of course it was all a mistake, and an accident, and the fact that when Cavernous went back to the village to dig his miser's hoard out from under the hearthstone it was already gone meant nothing. Probably. And most likely the jar of smelly ointment that broke on his scaly head—fixing him in his draconic form until an exceedingly unlikely conjunction of events—was an accident too, though Goody Chernoff's cackle wasn't.

So Cavernous Dire sloped off to the Tanglefoots in a draconish temper, scorching fenceposts along the way. He found a proper cave, and would have amassed a hoard from the passing travelers, if there'd been any. But his cave was a long way from any pass over the mountains, and he was far too prudent to tangle with the rich and powerful dragons whose caves lay on more lucrative trade routes.

He was forced to prey on the locals.

At first, sad to say, this gave him wicked satisfaction. They'd robbed him. They'd turned him into a dragon and robbed him, and—like a true miser—he minded the latter much more than the former. He ate their sheep, and then their cattle (having grown large enough), and once inhaled an entire flock of geese—a mistake, he discovered, as burning feathers stank abominably. He could not quite bring himself to eat their children, though his draconish nature found them appetizing, because he knew too well how dirty they really were, and how disgusting the amulets their mothers tied round their filthy necks. But he did kill a few of the adults, when they marched out with torches to test the strength of his fire. He couldn't stomach their stringy, bitter flesh.

Finally they moved away, cursing each other for fools, and Cavernous reigned over a ruined district. He pried up every hearthstone, and rooted in every well, but few were the coins or baubles which the villagers left behind.

Although the ignorant assert that the man-drake has powers greater than the dragonborn, this is but wishful thinking. Dragons born from the egg inherit all the ancient wisdom and power of dragonkind. Man-drakes are but feeble imitations, capable of matching true dragons only in their lust for gold. So poor Cavernous Dire, though fearsome to men, had not a chance of surviving in any contest with real dragons—and real dragons find few things so amusing as tormenting man-drakes.

'Tis said that every man has some woman who loves him—at least until she dies of his misuse—and so it was with Cavernous. Though most of the children born into his very dysfunctional birth-family had died of abuse or neglect, he had a sister, Bilious Dire, who had not died, but lived—and lived, moreover, with the twisted memory that Cavernous had once saved her life. (In fact, he had merely pushed her out of his way on one of the many occasions when his mother Savage came after him with a hot ladle.) But Bilious built her life, as do we all, on the foundation of her beliefs about reality, and in her reality Cavernous was a noble being.

She had been long away, Bilious, enriching the man who owned her, but at last she grew too wrinkled and stiff, and he cast her out. So she returned to the foothills village of her childhood, to find it ruined and empty, with dragon tracks in the street.

"That horrible dragon," she wailed at the weeping sky. "It's stolen my poor innocent brother. I must find help—"

"So you see, it's the traditional quest to rescue the innocent victim of a dragon," Mirabel's sister said. "Our sewing circle has taken on the rehabilitation of the faded blossoms of vice—" Mirabel mimed gagging, and her sister glared at her. "Don't laugh! It's not funny—the poor things—"

"Isn't there Madam Aspersia's Residence for them?"

"Madam Aspersia only has room for twenty, and besides she gives preference to women of a Certain Kind." Mirabel rolled her eyes; her sister combined the desire to talk about Such Things with the inability to *name* the Things she wanted to talk about.

"Well, but surely there are other resources—"

"In this city perhaps, but in the provinces—" Before Mirabel could ask why the provinces should concern the goodwives of Weeping Willow Street, her sister took a deep breath and plunged on. "So when poor Bilious— obviously past any chance of earning a living That Way— begged us to find help for her poor virgin brother taken by a dragon, of course I thought of you."

"Of course."

"Surely your organization does *something* to help women—that is its name, after all, Ladies' Aid and Armor Society. . . ."

Mirabel had tried to explain, on previous occasions, what the LAAS had been founded for, and why it would not help with a campaign to provide each orphaned girl with hand-embroidered underclothes for her trousseau, or stand shoulder to shoulder with the Weeping Willow Sewing Society's members when they marched on taverns that sold liquor to single women. (Didn't her sister realize that all the women in the

King's Guard hung out in taverns? Or was that the point?)

Now, through clenched teeth, Mirabel tried once more. "Monica—we do help women—each other. We were founded as a mutual-aid society for all women soldiers, though we do what we can—" The LAAS charity ball, for instance, supported the education of the orphaned daughters of soldiers.

"Helping each other is just like helping yourself, and helping yourself is selfish. Here's this poor woman, with no hope of getting her brother free if you don't do something—"

Mirabel felt her resistance crumbling, as it usually did if her sister talked long enough.

"I don't see how he can be a virgin, if he's older than his sister," she said. A weak argument, and she knew it. So did Monica.

"You can at least investigate, can't you? It can't hurt . . ."

It could get her killed, but that was a remote danger. Her sister was right here and now. "No promises," Mirabel said.

"I *knew* you'd come through," said Monica.

As Mirabel Stonefist trudged glumly across a lumpy wet moor, she thought she should have chosen "stonehead" for her fighting surname instead of "stonefist." She'd broken fingers often enough to disprove the truth of her chosen epithet, and over a moderately long career more than one person had commented on her personality in granitic terms. Stonehead, bonehead, too stubborn to quit and too dumb to figure a way out . . .

She had passed three abandoned, ruined villages already, the thatched roofs long since rotted, a few tumbled stone walls blacked by fire. She'd found hearthstones standing on end like grave markers, and not one coin of any metal.

And she'd found dragon tracks. Not, to someone who

had been in the unfortunate expedition to kill the Grand Dragon Karshnak of Kreshnivok, very big dragon tracks, but big enough to trip over and fall splat in. It had been raining for days, as usual in autumn, and the dragon tracks were all full of very cold water.

Her biggest mistake, she thought, had been birth order. If she'd been born after Gervais, she'd have been the cute little baby sister, and no one would ever have called on her to solve problems for the family. But as the oldest—the big sister to them all—she'd been cast as family protector and family servant from the beginning.

And her next biggest mistake, at least in the present instance, had been telling the Ladies' Aid and Armor Society that she was just going to check on things. With that excuse, no one else could find the time to come with her, so here she was, trudging across a cold, wet slope by herself, in dragon country.

They must really hate her. They must be slapping each other on the back, back home, and bragging on how they'd gotten rid of her. They must—

"Dammit, 'Bel, wait up!" The wind had dropped from its usual mournful moan, and she heard the thin scream from behind. She whirled. There—a long way back and below—an arm waved vigorously. She blinked. As if a dragon-laid spell of misery had been lifted, her mood rose. Heads bobbed among the wet heather. Two— three? She wasn't sure, but she wasn't alone anymore, and she felt almost as warm as if she were leaning on a wall in the palace courtyard in the sun.

They were, of course, grumbling when they came within earshot. "Should've called yourself Mirabel Longlegs—" Siobhan Bladehawk said. "Don't you ever sleep at night? We were beginning to think we'd never catch up."

"And why'd you go off in that snit?" asked Krystal, flipping the beaded fringe on her vest. "See this? I lost three strings, two of them with real lapis beads, trying to track you through that white-thorn thicket. You could just as easily have gone around it, rather than making me get my knees all scratched—"

"Shut up, Krystal," Siobhan said. "Though she has a point, 'Bel. What got into you, anyway?"

Mirabel sniffed, and hated herself for it. "Bella said if I was just investigating, I could go alone—nobody should bother—"

"Bella's having hot flashes," Siobhan said. "Not herself these days, our Bella, and worried about having to retire. We unelected her right after you left, and then we came after you. If you had just waited a day, 'stead of storming out like that—"

"But you're so impetuous," Krystal said, pouting. She pulled the end of her silver-gilt braid around, frowned at it, and nipped off a split end with her small, white, even teeth.

The third member of the party appeared, along with a shaggy pack pony, its harness hung with a startling number of brightly polished horse brasses.

"I needed a holiday," Sophora said, her massive frame dwarfing everything but the mountains. "And a chance for some healthy open-air exercise." The Chancellor of the Exchequer grinned. "Besides, I think that idiot Balon of Torm is trying to rob the realm, and this will give him a chance, he thinks. The fool."

Mirabel's mood now suited a sunny May morning. Not even the next squall off the mountain could make her miserable. Krystal, though, turned her back to the blowing rain and pouted again.

"This is *ruining* my fringes."

"Shut up Krystal," said everyone casually. The world was back to normal.

Cavernous Dire had subsisted on rockrats, rock squirrels, rock grouse, and the occasional rock (mild serpentine, with streaks of copper sulfate, eased his draconic fire-vats, he'd found). In midwinter, he might be lucky enough to flame a mountain goat before it got away, or even a murk ox (once widespread, now confined to a few foggy mountain valleys). But autumn meant hunger, unless he traveled far into the plains, where he could be hunted by man and dragon alike.

Now, as he lay on the cold stone floor of his cave, stirring the meagre pile of his treasure, he scented something new, something approaching from the high, cold peaks of the Tanglefoots. He sniffed. Not a mountain goat. Not a murk ox (and besides, it wasn't foggy enough for the murk ox to be abroad). A sharp, hot smell, rather like the smell of his own fire on rock.

Like many basically unattractive men, Cavernous Dire had been convinced of his own good looks, back when he was a young lad who coated his hair with woolfat, and had remained convinced that he had turned his back on considerable female attention when he chose to become a miser. So, when he realized that the unfamiliar aroma wafting down the cold wet wind was another dragon, his first thought was, "Of course." A she-dragon had been attracted by his elegance, and hoped to make up to him.

Quickly, he shoved his treasure to the back of the cave, and piled rocks on it. No thieving, lustful she-dragon was going to get his treasure, though he had to admit it was pleasant to find that the girls still pursued him. He edged to the front of his cave and looked upwind, into the swirls of rain. There—was she there? Or—over there?

The women of the expedition set up camp with the swift, capable movements of those experienced in such things. The tent blew over only once, and proved large enough for them all, plus Dumpling the pony, over whose steaming coat Siobhan labored until she was as wet as it had been, and so were half their blankets. Then she polished the horse brasses on Dumpling's harness; she had insisted that any horse under her care would be properly adorned and she knew the others wouldn't bother. Meanwhile, the others built a fire and cooked their usual hearty fare, under cover of the front flap.

They were all sitting relaxed around the fire, full of mutton stew and trail bread, sipping the contents of the stoneware jug Sophora had brought, when they heard a shriek. It sounded like someone falling off a very high cliff, and unhappy about it.

Scientific experimentation has shown that it is impossible to put on breastplate, gorget, helm, greaves, armlets, and gauntlets in less than one minute, and thus some magical power must have aided the warrior women, for they were all outside the tent, properly armored, armed, and ready for inspection when the dragon fell out of the sky and squashed the tent flat.

"Dumpling!" cried Siobhan, and lunged for the tent as the pony squealed and a series of thumps suggested that hind hooves were in use.

"No, wait—" Mirabel grabbed her. Siobhan, doughty warrior that she was, had one weakness: an intemperate concern for the welfare of horseflesh. "You can hear he's alive."

"Ssss. . . ." A warm glow, as of live coals being revived, appeared in the gloom where the tent had been. Dumpling squealed again. Something ripped, and hoofbeats receded into the distance. "Ahhh . . . sss . . ."

"A dragon fell on our tent," Mirabel said, with the supernatural calm of the truly sloshed. "And it's alive. And we're out here in the dark—"

Light flared out of the sky; when she looked up, there was a huge shape, like a dragon made all of fire. It was about the color of a live scorpion, she thought wildly, as it grew larger and larger. . . .

"That one's bigger," Sophora said, in her sweet soprano. "At least it's not dark anymore."

Mirabel had never noticed that dragons could direct their fire, in much the way that the watch commander could direct the light of his candle lantern. Silver threads of falling rain . . . a widening cone of light . . . and in the middle of it, their flattened tent held down by a lumpish dragon the color of drying slime along the edge of a pond. Its eyes—pale, oyster-colored eyes—opened, and its gray-lipped mouth gaped. Steam curled into the air.

"Is it a baby?" asked Siobhan. Then she, like the others, looked again at the expression in those eyes. "No," she said, answering her own question. Even Siobhan, whose belief that animals were never vicious until humans made them so had survived two years in the King's Cavalry, knew nastiness when she saw it.

"It's hovering," Sophora said, pointing upward. Sure enough, the bigger dragon, now only a bowshot above, had stopped its descent and was balancing on the wind. Its gaping mouth, still pointed downward, gave fiery light to the scene, but its body no longer glowed. Sophora waved her sword at the big dragon. "This one's ours," she shouted. "Go away, or—"

The dragon laughed. The blast of hot air that rolled over them smelt of furnaces and smiths' shops and deserts—but it did not fry them. It laughed, they knew it laughed; that was enough for the moment, and the great creature rose into the dark night, removing its light and leaving them once more in darkness.

With a live and uncooperative dragon on their flattened tent.

"We haven't seen the last of that one," Sophora said.

"My best jerkin is probably getting squashed into the mud," said Krystal.

"Shut up, Krystal," they all said. All but the dragon.

Cavernous Dire had never seen a dragon before he became one, and thus had only the vaguest idea what they were supposed to look like. Big, of course, and scaly, and breathing fire from a long, toothy mouth.

Long tail with spikes on it. Legs, naturally, or dragons would be just fire-breathing snakes. If he'd known that dragons have wings, he'd forgotten it after he became a dragon, and his own wings were, like those of all mandrakes, pitiful little stubs on the shoulders, hardly more than ruffles of dry itchy skin.

So when the real dragon swooped down the valley, he was amazed. She—he still thought, at this point, that the dragon was female—was an awe-inspiring sight, with the wide wings spanning the valley from side to side. She was so much bigger than he was. Crumbs of information about insects in which the male was much smaller than the female tried to coalesce and tell him something important, but he couldn't quite think, in the presence of this great beast. Dragons have this effect on all humans, but it's much stronger with man-drakes, and it amuses them to reduce their toys to mindlessness right before they reduce them to their constituent nutrient molecules.

The dragon flew past, and out of sight. Cavernous thrust his own long scaly neck out of his cave, trying to see where she'd gone. Nothing but wet rock, nothing but wet wind, nothing but curtains of fine rain stirred by her passage. She must be shy . . .

Strong talons seized his neck and plucked him from his cave as a robin plucks out a worm from the ground. The wings boomed on either side of him, and boomed again, and he was rising upward so fast that he felt the blood rushing to his dependent tail.

It is not for Men to know, or Bards to tell, what true dragons do to man-drakes in the high halls of the air, but it took several hours, during which time Cavernous realized how little he knew about dragon anatomy, his own or that of others, and how little he liked what he was learning now. Night had fallen by then, and soon he had fallen—was falling—and the glowing beast beside him rumbled warm laughter all the way down to the base of the clouds, then let him fall away into the wet night.

He didn't remember hitting the ground, but waking up was terrible. Darkness, cold, rain pelting his hide, and more pain than he had ever imagined inside him. His fire-vats had slopped over, burning other internal parts he hadn't known he possessed. Since it is the nature of dragons of all kinds to heal with unnatural speed, his broken bones were already knitting, but they hurt as they knit. Something was hitting him repeatedly, hard punches to the nasal arch, and squealing in his lower ear. He tried to draw in a breath, which hurt, and finally whatever it was quit hitting him and ran away. It was a long moment before he realized it had been a horse.

Light stabbed through his third eyelid, and he smelt the big dragon hovering above him. If he could have thought, he would have begged for mercy. Then darkness returned, and he closed his eye again, hoping that he'd wake up in his own cave and find it had all been a bad dream.

Experienced campaigners can light a fire in a howling wet gale, if sober and industrious. Those whose tents have been flattened by dragons, and whose last prior calories were derived from potent brew may have more problems.

Siobhan was off somewhere in the distance, calling Dumpling. It wouldn't do any good to call her back; as long as she was fretting over the pony her brain wouldn't work anyway. Krystal muttered on about her ruined wardrobe, but Mirabel heard Sophora give a gusty sigh.

"I suppose I'll have to do something about that dragon," she said. "And that means making a light—"

Experienced campaigners always have a few dry fire-starters in their packs, but the packs were inside the tent, underneath the dragon. Mirabel felt in her pockets and discovered nothing but a squashed sugared plum, left over from the Iron Jill Retreat some months back. Sophora had her Chancellor's Seal, with the crystal which could double as a lens to start a fire from sunlight . . . but not in the middle of the night. Glumly, they huddled against the dragon and sank into a state of numb endurance familiar from past campaigns.

Morning arrived with a smear of light somewhere behind the Tanglefoot Mountains. Eventually the sodden expedition could make out the shape of the fallen dragon, still lying on their tent.

Compared to the Grand Dragon Karshnak, it was a small specimen, not much larger than the tent it had flattened. Its color in this cold gray light reminded Mirabel most of a mud turtle, a dull brownish green. It lay as it had fallen, in an untidy heap.

But it wasn't dead. Even if thin curls of steam hadn't been coming from its nostrils and partially open mouth, the slow undulation of its sides would have indicated life within. Siobhan, returning with the mud-streaked Dumpling, eyed the dragon suspiciously.

Dumpling whinnied. At that, the dragon opened one gelid eye. Its mouth gaped wider, and more steam poured out. It stirred, black talons scraping as its feet contracted.

"We ought to kill it now," Siobhan said, soothing the jittery pony. "While we can."

"No," Krystal said. "If we kill it now, it'll bleed on the tent, and there go all our clothes."

"If we don't kill it now, and it wakes up and kills us, what use will our clothes be?"

Recovery from the dragon-change induced by eating a dragonsfoot seed, and then a leaf of dragonstongue, and then being slathered with Goody Chernoff's anti-wrinkle ointment (guaranteed to hold your present form until a certain conjunction of events) requires three unlikely things to happen within one day, as foretold in the Prophecies of Slart.

"Whanne thatte murke-ox be founde,
in sunlight lying on the grounde,
in autumn's chill to gather heate,
and when the blonde beautie sweete,
her lippes pressed to colde flesh,
and also dragons' song be herde,
then shalle the olde Man spring afresh,
and hearken to commandinge werde."

If the warrior women had known that Cavernous Dire *was* the dragon, bespelled into that form, and if they had known of the Prophecies of Slart—but they didn't. The Prophecies of Slart were only then being penned three kingdoms away by a young woman disguised as a young man, who had not been able to make a living as a songwriter.

Toying with the man-drake had been fun, but now the big dragon wanted meat. He could always go back and eat the man-drake—but if he did that, he'd be tempted to play with his food awhile longer, and his body wanted food *now*. He sniffed, a long indrawn sniff that dragged the prevailing winds from their courses.

Somewhere . . . ah, yes, murk ox. He sniffed again, long and low. It had been a long time—centuries, at least—since he'd eaten the last murk ox near his own lair. And he did like murk ox. Huge as he was, even one murk ox made a pleasant snack and a herd of them was a good solid meal, food for the recreation he rather thought he'd enjoy later.

The trick with murk ox was extracting them from the murk. They lived in narrow, steep-sided valleys too narrow for his great wings, where the fog lingered most of the day. The great dragon had learned, when much smaller, that flying into murk ox terrain, into the fog, led to bruised wings or worse. There were better ways—entertaining ways—to hunt murk ox.

The great dragon drew in another long, long breath and then *blew*.

For days a chill wet wind had blown down from the mountains. Now, in the space of a few minutes, it had shifted to the southwest, and then gone back to the northeast, then back to the southwest again. Back and forth, as if the sky itself were huffing in and out, unsure whether to take in air or let it out.

Then, with startling suddenness, the clouds began rolling up from the southwest, toward the mountains, the bottoms lifting higher and higher until the sun struck under them, glittering and sparkling on the drenched moorland. Higher still the clouds rose, blowing away eastward, and leaving a clear blue sky behind.

Mirabel squinted in the sudden bright gold light, but as far as she could see the land lay clear—wet but drying—in the sun, which struck warmer with every passing minute.

"It's certainly a break from Court procedure," Sophora said. "There every day's much the same, but this—"

"What's that?" asked Siobhan, pointing to a cleft in the mountains a few leagues distant. Little dark dots were moving quickly from what must be the entrance to a narrow mountain valley, out onto the moorland.

Sophora held up her Chancellor's seal, centered with crystal, and put it to her eye. "I had our guild wizard apply a scrying spell," she told the others. "Good heavens—I do believe—it's a kapootle of murk ox."

"Murk ox! But they never come out in the open. Certainly not the whole kapootle."

"Not unless they're chased," Sophora said. "Look." She pointed.

Mirabel recognized the flying shape without having to be told what it was. The big dragon, now gliding very slowly down the mountainside and aiming a stream of fire into the valley where the murk ox had been concealed until the clouds lifted.

Soon the last murk oxen had left the valley, but the great dragon seemed in no haste to snatch them. Instead, it floated low overhead, herding them closer and closer to the women and the smaller dragon. Then it dipped its head from the glide—not even swooping lower, they noticed, and snatched one murk ox from the herd. They could see it writhe . . . and then the lump sliding down the dragon's long throat, just like an egg down a snake.

Another jet of flame, and the murk ox kapootle picked up speed, lumbering nearer—those splayed hooves now shaking the boggy heath.

"That dragon," Mirabel said. "It's herding them at *us*."

"Oh, good," Sophora said. "I was hoping for some fresh meat on this trip, and hunting's been poor . . ."

"Not that much fresh meat," Mirabel said. The heaving backs of many murk oxen could now be seen quite clearly, though the curious twisted horns could not be distinguished from the muck they were kicking up.

Although it is well known—or at least believed—that a herd of horses or cattle will divide around a group of standing humans rather than trample them, the murk ox kapootle has quite another reputation, which explains why it has not been hunted to extinction by men. No one knows what the murk ox thinks as it gallumphs along, but avoiding obstacles smaller than hills isn't part of its cognitive processes. A kapootle of murk ox will trample all but the stoutest trees, and the mere human form goes down like straw before the reaper.

With the quick decision that characterizes the combat-experienced soldier, the warrior women bolted for the only cover available, that of the still-recumbent dragon on their collapsed tent. Siobhan dragged Dumpling along behind.

In moments, the lead murk ox overran their campsite. Emitting the strident squeaks of a murk ox in mortal fear, the lead ox galloped right over the dragon, digging him painfully in the snout and eye on the way up to his shoulder, and then staggering badly on the slippery scaled ribs, before running on down the declining tail. Only a few of his followers attempted the same feat, and all but one slid off the dragon's ribs, there to be trampled by their fellows. That one, unable to match its leader's surefooted leap down to the tail, launched itself right over the heads of the cowering warrior women, tripped on landing, and broke its neck.

"That was lucky!" shouted Mirabel over the piercing squeaks of the kapootle, now thundering past on either side.

"Yes," Sophora agreed. "Quite plump—a nice dinner for us." She started toward the twitching carcass, but a shadow loomed suddenly. They looked up. The great dragon lowered one foot and plucked the murk ox off the ground, meanwhile watching them with an expression which mingled challenge and amusement.

"You are a wicked beast," Sophora said, undaunted. Mirabel remembered that Sophora had been undaunted even by the Grand Dragon Karshnak, at least until she'd been knocked unconscious by a wing blow.

The dragon winked, and popped the murk ox into its mouth. Flames licked around it; they could smell the reek of burning hair, and then the luscious smell of roasting meat. Then, with a boom and a whirl of air, the dragon was up and away, chasing laggard murk oxen on with a lick of flame, and crooning something that might have been meant for music.

"Well," said Krystal, flicking dabs of muck off her vest. "Now *that's* over, maybe we can do something about getting this mess off our tent, so I can find out what's happened to my clothes."

Cavernous Dire had slept uneasily, with cold rain trickling down his ribs and under his tail, but each time he'd roused, he'd managed to force himself back to sleep. It hurt less that way. When sunlight struck his eyes in the morning, he clenched his outer lids tight to block it out and hoped for the best. He could feel that his broken bones were mostly mended, and the internal burns were nearly healed as well. But he did not feel like coping with the real world.

He had, however, sneaked peeks at the humans in his immediate vicinity. Four women in bronze and leather, with swords and short hunting spears. Cavernous Dire had not enjoyed human meat when he tried it before, and three of the four warrior women looked unappetizing in any form. The fourth, though, he might have fancied in other situations. She had silvery blond hair, peach-blossom cheeks, a perky nose, teeth like pearls, and a ripely pouting mouth. Years of solitude as a dragon, with a meagre and uninteresting hoard to guard, had given him time to fantasize about women, and this woman met all his qualifications except that she was carrying a very sharp sword.

If he just lay there and pretended to sleep, maybe the women would go away. His draconic scales dulled his tactile awareness enough that he didn't realize he was lying on their tent, and before he listened to enough of their conversation, he became aware of something else.

The ground was shivering. Then shuddering. Cavernous opened one eye just in time to see a dark hairy shape hurtling toward him, and snapped his eye shut. Sharp hard things hit the same tender parts of his snout which the horse had kicked in the dark, and then dented his scales on their way up his head, his shoulder, and along his ribs, where they tickled. And he could sense, with that infallible sense given to man-drakes, that somewhere in the sky the large dragon who had hurt him so badly was lurking, waiting for him to show life so he could be tormented again.

Better the tickle of murk ox hooves than the talons of a dragon. Cavernous hunkered down, feigning unconsciousness as best he could, as the kapootle squeaked and thundered past, though the moment when he sensed the great dragon close above him was almost impossible to bear. Then it was gone, and he dared open his outer eyelids again, just a tiny bit, to see what was going on.

"—And I say we butcher it now!" That was his diminuitive blonde, she of the perky nose and accouterments.

"You were the one who said it'd bleed on our gear," the tallest one said. "Besides, Krystal, you really should be grateful to it. It saved our lives."

"And if you say 'What's life without my embroidered nightshirt with the suede fringe?' I will personally roll you through that squashed murk ox," said the one with the crooked nose.

"I am grateful," Krystal said, sounding very cross. "What do you want me to do, Mirabel, kiss it and make it well?"

"Don't be silly," said the one petting the very dirty pony, whose harness was adorned with gleaming gold shapes. For a moment all Cavernous could think of was the treasure wasted on that stupid pony. "We all know you wouldn't kiss anything that ugly, no matter what it did for you."

"You—you—"

"Like when Rusty the Armorer fixed that helm for you, and all you did was wave at him—"

"Well . . . he's *old*. And he has only three teeth."

The one named Mirabel grinned suddenly. "Come on, Krystal—I dare you. Kiss a dragon. Maybe it *will* cure it."

"Eeeeuw!"

"Scaredy-cat."

"Am not!"

"Just think, Krystal, how your . . . mmm . . . special friends will be impressed . . . if you do dare the dragon's breath, that is. If you don't—are they going to respect you, even if you do have that fancy mask?"

Krystal glared at them, shrugged, and twitched the twitchable parts of her anatomy. Then, with a pout the dragon was finding increasingly adorable, she shrugged. "All right. But only because I know you'll make up some horrid story about me if I don't. And not—*not* on the lips."

She sauntered toward the dragon's mouth. Cavernous had to roll his big man-drake eye down to watch her. She leaned over his snout, lips pursed.

From the man-drake's point of view, the kiss was an explosion of sensation unlike anything he'd ever felt, and the strange feelings went on and on. No one had told him he could turn back into a man, so he hadn't bothered trying to imagine what it would feel like. His eyes opened very wide, but all he could see was whirling colors.

From Mirabel's point of view, Krystal put her lips to the dragon's snout, and the dragon collapsed like a bagpipe's bag, with a sort of warm whooshing noise, and almost simultaneously, the moor burst into spring flower. Where the dragon had been, a scruffy-looking naked man hunched against the cool air. Although Mirabel knew nothing about physics, she had just observed that the energy released when a large form condensed to a small one could generate enough heat to activate seeds and accelerate their growth.

Krystal, who had had her eyes shut, stepped back and opened them. When she saw that the tent was no longer covered by a dragon, and that lumps within the wrinkled canvas suggested the remains of their gear, she made straight for the collapsed entrance. A dirty old man didn't interest her at all.

Mirabel had gone on guard instinctively, as had Sophora, and the appearance of Cavernous Dire did not reassure them. Decades of life as a man-drake had left him no handsomer than when he had chosen misering over marriage. Now his greasy hair was stringy gray instead of black, and his lanky form even more stooped. A dirty-looking gray beard straggled past his chest no farther than necessary . . . in fact, not quite far enough.

He looked like the sort of man who would lurk in dark alleys to accost the sick or feeble.

"Who are you?" Sophora asked, in her Chancellor voice.

"Cavernous Dire," the man said. His voice squeaked, like an unoiled hinge.

"You're Cavernous Dire?" Mirabel asked. Her mind boggled, then recalled the shape and expression of Bilious Dire, made a quick comparison, and knew it must be true.

"You were a dragon . . ." Sophora said.

"They tricked me," the man said. "Just because I was getting rich and they wanted my money . . ." He sounded peevish, like someone whose neighbors would trick him every chance they got.

At that moment the big dragon returned. They had not heard it gliding nearer, but they heard the long hiss as its shadow passed over them.

"Nooooo!" wailed Cavernous. "Don't let it get me!"

"He's Cavernous Dire?" Krystal said, crawling out from under the tent. "He's the one we were supposed to rescue? Eeeeuw!" Nonetheless, she struck an attitude, peering up at the big dragon with conscious grace.

Mirabel and Sophora both had swords in hand, but Mirabel knew that they hadn't anywhere near the force necessary to tangle with a dragon this size. But they also had nowhere safe to run. The dragon smiled, and let its long, thin, red tongue hang out a little, steaming in the morning air.

What might have happened next, she never knew, but Cavernous Dire suddenly snatched her belt knife, and lunged toward Siobhan and the pony Dumpling.

"Here's treasure!" he screamed, hacking at the horse brasses on Dumpling's harness.

"Hey—stop that!" Siobhan tried to grab his arm, but Dumpling interfered. The pony backed and spun, fighting Siobhan's hold and cow-kicking at Cavernous. The dragon seemed to be amused, and let another yard or so of tongue slide out. Cavernous quit hacking at the brasses individually, and slid Mirabel's knife up under the harness, which parted like butter. Two more slices, and he'd cut it free, all the while dodging Siobhan's angry swats and Dumpling's kicks. He snatched it from the ground, dropping Mirabel's knife, and turned back to the dragon, holding the harness at arm's length.

"Treasure! Gold! Take it! Go away!"

"Yesss. . . ." The long tongue lapped out, and gathered it in—but Cavernous did not let go, and the tongue wrapped round him too, snatching him back into the dragon's toothy maw as a lizard might snatch a fly.

A gulp, and the bulge that had been Cavernous Dire disappeared into the dragon's innards. A flick of the wings, and another, and the dragon was gone, sailing low over the heather, back toward the distant kapootle of murk ox.

Dumpling squealed and bucked, landing on Mirabel's knife, which shattered.

"My best knife—!" Mirabel said.

"I hope he hasn't cut his hoof," Siobhan said.

"My best shirt, ruined!" Krystal held up a nightshirt with a wet stain down one side.

"Shut up Krystal," they all said.

On the way back to the city, they agreed that Bilious Dire need not know the whole story, only that at the end Cavernous had sacrificed himself for others, and been eaten.

Mirabel's sister had things to say about the outcome which left a coolness of glacial dimensions between them for more than a year. At Monica's instigation, the Weeping Willow Sewing Circle paid for a plaque commemorating the Dauntless Courage of Cavernous Dire, in saving the life of four of the King's Guardswomen from a dragon. Every May-morn, they lay a wreath beneath it. Mirabel Stonefist won't walk by that corner at all anymore. Siobhan Bladehawk narrowly escaped punishment for defacing the plaque as she tried to correct "Four of the King's Guardswomen" to "Three of the King's Guardswomen and One of the King's Cavalrywomen."

In the belly of the dragon, Cavernous Dire remains undigested, a situation acceptable to neither him nor the dragon. Neither of them knows that it is Cavernous's miserly grasp of the pony Dumpling's horse-brass which maintains this uneasy stasis.

Meanwhile, the Chancellor of the Exchequer had a very satisfactory chat with Balon of Torm, whose arms, dyed orange to the elbow, proved he had been dipping into the treasury. Sophora Segundiflora may be the only person satisfied by the expedition.

Despite repeated association with Bad Companions (i.e., he had stories in both previous "Chicks" anthologies and he co-wrote Split Heirs *with me), Lawrence Watt-Evans has authored over two dozen novels (*Touched by the Gods *is the latest) and over a hundred short stories including the Hugo-winning "Why I Left Harry's All-Night Hamburgers."*

And now, welcome to the dog-eat-dog world of politics.

In for a Pound

Lawrence Watt-Evans

The moment she was absolutely sure they were out of earshot of anyone else, she hissed at him, "Are you *nuts?*"

He smiled at her as he held open the car door. "I don't think so," he replied.

"But *running for mayor?*" She stood beside the car, not willing to interrupt the discussion even long enough to take her seat.

"Why not?" he asked, still smiling that toothy smile of his. "Seriously, Jen, do you see anyone better suited to the job? I'm an upstanding member of the

47

community, I've had a good education, I have a career in public service . . ."

"Dave, you *know* why not!" She pointed at the sky. "You're going to have a *demonstration* of 'why not' in another hour or so!"

His politician's smile vanished, and he looked at her with an expression that just reeked of sincere concern— an expression she was quite sure he had practiced for hours in front of the mirror.

"And why should that disqualify me from serving as mayor? Surely you realize it's just an occasional inconvenience. So I'll be unavailable a couple of nights each month . . ."

"*Inconvenience?*" She stared at him, astonished. "Dave, you're a *werewolf*, remember? You inherited a genuine gypsy curse. That's a bit more than an inconvenience!"

"Why?" he asked mildly.

Her jaw dropped.

"Really, Jen—it's not as if I'm running for president. It's just mayor of Eltonburg. So I'll want to spend a couple of nights a month in private; so what?" He patted her on the arm, urging her into the car.

Stunned, she sat. She watched through the windshield as he walked around and climbed in the driver's side.

"Dave," she said, "suppose there's a City Council meeting on a full moon? Suppose there's a disaster— a blizzard, say—on the night of a full moon?"

He shrugged. "I'll be ill, or unavoidably detained. These things happen; people will understand. It hasn't been a problem for me before."

"Before you were just a police lieutenant, not the mayor!"

"Detective lieutenant," he corrected her—he was touchy about the distinction between the two sides of Eltonburg's police department, enforcement and investigation. He started the car and looked over his shoulder to be sure the street was clear.

"Whatever. Don't you think that, even in Eltonburg, some reporter might stumble across the truth? Old Bill Beasley isn't going to give up his job without a fight, despite the indictments--he's going to have his people checking up on you all through the campaign, just looking for some little flaw. What if he notices you're never around at the full moon? How are you going to explain that? Suppose he says you spend a couple of nights a month at the strip clubs down on Route 8—how are you going to prove you *don't?*"

Dave frowned as he swung the car around the corner onto Main Street. "He couldn't prove I *do*."

"He wouldn't *have* to prove it—what are you going to say instead? That you grow fur and go running through the streets on those nights?"

"Well, why not?" Dave asked. "I've never hurt anyone. Sure, I'm not quite myself when I'm a wolf, but I'm no ravening monster. Even real wolves aren't, and I never *completely* forget who I am. I've chased a few cats, sure, but I never bit or clawed anyone—not even the cats. Not even that damned spitting Persian down on Third Street."

"So you'd just admit the truth? And you think people will vote for a werewolf? You know how old-fashioned some of the people in this town are—and they're Mayor Beasley's biggest supporters. You don't see Beasley standing up in front of the congregation at Calvary Baptist and getting them worked up about the spawn of Satan?"

"I'm not the spawn of Satan . . ."

"Tell Reverend Henry that!"

He settled into an angry quiet for the remainder of the drive home.

When they were out of the car but still in the garage he burst out, "Damn it, Jenny, I *am* running for mayor, because *somebody* has to to get that crook Beasley and his weasely flunkies out of office! Yes, I'm a werewolf, and it *is* a drawback, and an inconvenience, and we don't want anyone to find out, but I don't think it's going to come out—maybe Beasley will find out I'm never around at the full moon and will try to make something out of it, but who'll believe him? I'll just say it's private business, all in the family, and you'll back me up, and my mother will, and the voters'll believe us. Why shouldn't they?"

"Because they're human, and they want to believe the worst of any politician they hear about." She sighed. "But if you want to risk it, I won't stop you. You're right, you'd be the best mayor Eltonburg's ever had, and *someone* has to run against Beasley. But I don't *like* it, Dave!"

"No one's asking you to like it," he muttered. He twitched and stumbled as he reached for the door to the house.

Jenny knew the signs. "Get those clothes off," she ordered. "We don't want them torn. That suit cost six hundred dollars."

He sighed. "Right," he said, pulling off his tie. "I guess I cut it closer than I meant to." He slipped off his jacket and handed it to her.

His fingers were already shrinking by the time he started on his shirt buttons, the nails thickening into claws. Jenny hurried to help.

Undressing him was a lot more fun the other twenty-odd nights of the month, she thought—he'd be returning the favor, and when the clothes were off he wouldn't drop down on all fours and run off howling.

He might howl a little, or drop to all fours, but he wouldn't run off. And he wouldn't be furry and wagging a tail.

By the time his pants were entirely off he was more wolf than man, and a moment later he was *all* wolf. He trotted to the overhead door and glanced back at Jenny expectantly.

"Oh, all right," she said. She pushed the button, and the door lifted. She stopped it once it was high enough for him to slip out.

"Don't be all night, okay?" she called. "I'd like to get to sleep at a reasonable hour."

He didn't answer; instead he ran off, tongue lolling, down the street.

She sighed, pushed the button to close the door, then stooped and scooped up his clothes. It would serve him right if she *didn't* wait up, and he turned back on the front porch.

Of course, then the neighbors might see him out there naked, which would be hard to live down—and his mayoral hopes would be completely dashed. She trudged into the house and up the stairs, the bundle of clothes in her hand.

An hour later she was in the kitchen, treating herself to a glass of wine, when she heard the growl of a truck's engine and glanced out the front window.

She froze, and set the wineglass down carefully. Then she rounded the corner to the foyer and stepped out the front door onto the porch.

The Animal Control van was cruising slowly down the street; as she watched it stopped under a streetlight, and a man in a gray uniform jumped out, holding a pole with a loop on the end.

A second man came around the front of the van. "There he is!" he called, pointing at the Rosenthals' bushes.

Her heart sank. Dave had been careless, and had been spotted.

She tried to think what she could do. If she claimed he was her dog . . . well, they had discussed this. He had no collar, no registration, no vaccination tag, and the Animal Control people would insist, quite reasonably, that she take her dog in and get him a license and get his shots taken care of.

Except he couldn't come in for a rabies shot unless the full moon was in the sky, and the vets weren't generally open then.

The two men were rushing for the bushes, one to

either side, trapping their prey between them. She saw a flash of gray fur, and the two men dove, pole sweeping around, and then the three were all in a heap on the Rosenthals' lawn, and a moment later the two men were dragging a snarling, struggling wolf toward the van.

"Hey!" she called, stepping down from the porch—she'd find a way around the problem with the shots; maybe she could claim religious grounds for not having it done. "Hey, that's my dog!"

The two men ignored her as they heaved Dave into the cage in the back of the van and slammed it shut. She hurried toward them.

Once the cage was locked, one of them turned to face her.

"That's my dog," she said, pointing.

"He hasn't got a tag," the uniformed man said.

"We hadn't got around to it yet."

"Well, you can't let him run loose with no tag, lady. Eltonburg's got a twenty-four-hour leash law."

"I know, I know, I'm sorry—we've just been so busy . . ."

"The law's the law, lady. You want him back, you can come down to the pound and claim him, first thing in the morning. And bring your checkbook."

"In the *morning*?" A vision of Dave waking up naked in a cage at the pound appeared before her. "Can't I have him back now? I . . . I don't feel *safe* without him watching the house!"

The man shook his head. "Sorry, lady. We got rules—we find a dog running loose with no ID, we take it to the pound. No exceptions. Look, it's just one night."

"But . . ." She stared at Dave, who stared back at her with frightened yellow wolf-eyes.

The other man slammed the van door. "No exceptions," he said.

The first man said, a bit more kindly, "Look, lady, we used to cut folks some slack on this, but we just got tired of people who let their dogs run around wild, and

promised every time oh yeah, we'll be down first thing
tomorrow and get a license, we'll put a collar on him
right away . . . and then nothing, and two or three days
later we'd pick up the same dog chasing someone's cat
up a tree, or digging in someone's lawn, still with no
tag. So now we have to be tough about it—some people
ruined it for the rest of us, y'know?"

"I know, but . . ."

"I'm sorry, lady." He turned away.

She watched helplessly as the two men climbed into
their vehicle and drove away.

This was a nightmare. They were taking her husband
away! And tomorrow morning, when the moon set, he'd
turn back to himself there in the dog pound, stark
naked, and they'd find him there, and it would be in
all the papers, and they'd assume it was a prank, or that
he'd been drunk, and any chance he might actually be
elected mayor would be gone . . .

And besides that, it would just be so *embarrassing!*

She couldn't let that happen. She had to get him out
of the pound *tonight.*

But how? She supposed there must be someone there
at night, but it would just be a guard, and she wouldn't
be able to claim Dave—the night watchman, or whoever
was there, would just tell her to come back in the
morning.

She'd have to *force* them to free Dave.

And how was she going to do *that?* Walk in there
with Dave's service weapon and order them to free her
dog?

She blinked as she stood on the lawn, watching the
Animal Control van round the corner onto Armistead
Avenue.

Why *not* just walk in with the gun and demand her
dog?

Well, for one thing, they would recognize her, and
the night watchman probably had a gun of his own.

But she could get around that . . .

She stood, thinking hard, for a moment, then turned and went inside.

A few hours later, somewhere between 2:00 and 3:00 in the morning, she cruised down the deserted streets and parked the car in an empty lot two blocks from the pound; she didn't want anyone getting her license number. Then she got out and opened the trunk. She was trembling; it took three tries before she could get the key in the lock.

It opened at last, though, and she reached in and pulled out Dave's bulletproof vest.

She'd never worn it before, and it was too big for her, but she got it on and tied it in place, the kevlar panels pressing uncomfortably on her breasts—it was meant for a man, not a woman, and she was big-chested.

Then she pulled on the old black raincoat, to further hide her figure—she was already wearing black jeans and a black T-shirt, to make it as difficult as possible to see any distinctive details about her. Her feet were in old deck shoes with black stockings pulled up over them, to blur any markings or footprints.

Then came the motorcycle helmet with the dark visor, hiding her face and hair completely—and making it hard to see; it was like wearing sunglasses at night.

It *was* wearing sunglasses at night, really—the tinted visor was meant to serve the same purpose, as well as keeping bugs out of a motorcyclist's teeth.

And then came the scary part, as she lifted Dave's pump-action twelve-gauge out of the trunk.

She had fired the gun exactly three times. The first time she had started at the bang when it went off, but the other two she had been ready for it. She had still completely missed the target Dave had set up for her, and the next day her shoulder had been sore from the recoil, but she had fired it.

Her hands trembling again, she loaded five rounds of birdshot into the magazine. That wouldn't kill anyone, she was pretty sure, but it should be enough to hurt and to scare away anyone who got in her way.

Thus equipped, she marched toward the pound.

There were lights on—not very many, but at least two. That was a good sign; she needed there to be someone in there she could frighten into opening Dave's cage. She reached the main entrance without serious incident, despite being almost blind with the helmet's visor down; she had to lift it to peek now and again. Once she reached the entry she held the shotgun in one hand, and pounded on the door with the other.

Nothing happened; she pounded again.

She was starting to think about what she would do if the night watchman refused to answer when a surly voice called, "Who the hell is it at this hour?"

"It's an emergency," Jenny called. "I need to use your phone."

"Oh, Christ . . ." The door started to swing open.

Jenny thrust the barrel of the shotgun into the crack, then pushed herself after it, stepping into the building.

She found herself in a narrow hallway, on a scuffed linoleum floor between green concrete walls, lit by bare bulbs in wire cages overhead. Backing away from her was a young man in a dirty T-shirt and torn jeans.

The lights at least let her see through the confounded visor. "Put up your . . ." she began; then she stopped as she realized he already had both hands raised high.

"Oh god oh god oh god," he said, stumbling backward down the hall. "Listen, there's no money here, I swear there isn't, if there were I'd have stolen it myself."

"I don't want money," Jenny growled, trying to lower her alto voice to a tenor—she had hopes that her disguise hid her sex as well as her face.

"What, did Uncle Bill do something again? Listen, I swear, I didn't have anything to do . . ."

"Shut up," Jenny growled, aiming the shotgun at the man's nose.

The man—a kid, really—shut up and froze where he was.

Uncle Bill?

"Who are you?" Jenny demanded. "Who's Uncle Bill?"

"I'm Rafe Hayes," the kid said. "Uncle Bill's the mayor. My mom's brother."

"Mayor Beasley is your uncle?" She stared for a moment; yes, there was a resemblance. "He got you this job?"

Rafe nodded eagerly. "You don't want to hurt me," he said. "My uncle would get really pissed."

"I don't care what your uncle wants!" Jenny roared—aware as she did that her bellow was not up to Dave's standards; she didn't have a man's lung capacity or a cop's experience in yelling. "I'm here for my . . . for the animals." It had occurred to her at the last instant that revealing she was after a particular "dog" might not be wise. She didn't want to attract everyone's attention to that one specific canine, especially not when she'd told the animal control crew that Dave was her dog.

"Oh!" The kid looked suddenly relieved. "You're an animal rights activist? Which group?"

"Uh . . . Free Our Furry Friends," Jenny improvised hastily.

"I haven't heard of that one . . ."

"We're new."

"So, like, do you have a specific agenda? Have you got a truck here, or something, to take 'em away?"

"That's not your problem. You just open the doors I tell you to open and keep your mouth shut and your hands where I can see 'em." She jabbed with the gun; Rafe's hands, which had started to descend, rushed back up toward the ceiling.

"Okay," he said, staring at the gun.

"Good. Now, where are the cages?"

Rafe led the way down the corridor and through a door into the depths of the pound. Jenny found herself surrounded by dogs of all sizes and varieties, most of them asleep, a few stirring at this unexpected intrusion. A Great Dane whined at her, and a Pomeranian yapped.

She didn't see Dave.

"Where are the newest ones?" she asked. "The ones they brought in tonight?"

"Oh, they're in the other room," Rafe said. "We don't put 'em in here until the vet's okayed them."

"Show me," she growled. An Alsatian growled in response. "Shut up," Jenny told the dog. Then she gestured with the gun.

Rafe led the way to the holding area; here half the cages were empty, several held cats—and crammed into one of them was a big gray wolf, wide awake and watching them silently.

"Let that one out first," Jenny said, pointing. "That cage is too small for him; it's inhumane."

"Yessir," Rafe said. He fetched a ring of keys from a peg by the door and unlocked Dave's cage. Dave bounded out the instant the door opened, then hesitated, looking at Jenny and Rafe and Jenny's gun.

"Good dog," Jenny said. "You're free now." She waved at the room's open door, and Dave trotted out into the passageway, out of sight.

Now Jenny found herself facing a dilemma; to maintain her cover story of being an animal rights activist she needed to let more animals go—but she didn't particularly *want* a bunch of strays roaming the area.

She hoped they wouldn't do any real harm.

"Let out the others," she said.

Rafe hurried to unlock the cages, releasing the half-dozen cats—and while he was doing that, Jenny stepped back out into the hallway and closed the door.

Dave was waiting there; he looked up at her expectantly. Obviously, he thought she had a plan.

She didn't; she was making this up as she went along. She needed some way to get out of here without making a mess of it all. She wasn't a detective like Dave, with lots of police training . . .

Police. She looked at him, and then smiled.

"Is that a siren?" she shouted. "Damn it, did you call the cops?"

"No, I swear . . . !" Rafe called back. A cat yowled and hissed, and Rafe muttered something Jenny couldn't make out.

"You stay in there until I tell you to come out, you . . . you untrustworthy person, you!"

Lame, Jenny, she told herself. Really lame. "You untrustworthy person"? She giggled. "Come on, Dave," she said. "The car's that way."

Together, woman and wolf ran for the door.

They were almost there when Rafe burst out of the room with a pistol in his hand and fired at her.

The first shot went wild, chipping concrete from the wall, but the sharp bang startled Jenny; she stumbled, but caught herself without falling.

The second shot hit her square in the back and felt like she'd been kicked.

"Ow," she said, as she turned around and raised the shotgun.

Dave had already spun around and was charging down the hallway; Rafe fired again, this time at the animal plunging toward him.

"No!" Jenny shouted, raising the shotgun—but she couldn't shoot; she might hit Dave.

Dave didn't seem to be hurt. Rafe fired again, at point-blank range, and then Dave's teeth closed on his wrist. Jenny heard something crunch horribly, and the pistol fell to the floor. Then Rafe went over backward, the wolf on top of him . . .

"No!" Jenny shouted. "Da— Don't! Get off him!" She raised the shotgun again and pointed it directly at her own husband.

The wolf turned and glared at her, those big yellow eyes almost glowing. For a moment they stared at each other—and Jenny realized she was staring along the barrel of the shotgun, the sights aimed directly at Dave.

She lowered the gun, and Dave leapt off Rafe and ran for the door.

Jenny hesitated until she heard Rafe groan—he was alive and conscious, so she didn't think he could be *that* badly hurt. She turned and yanked open the door; Dave bounded out, with Jenny close behind.

A moment later they were in the car, Dave in the back and Jenny driving. She pulled out of the lot with tires squealing.

They made it home safely, and Jenny staggered inside. She dropped the shotgun, peeled off her black raincoat and her Kevlar armor, tossed aside the motorcycle helmet, and then leaned against a wall, panting. Utterly exhausted, she let herself slide down until she was sitting on the floor.

Dave came to her, tongue lolling from his mouth, and put his head in her lap. She petted him once before falling asleep, sprawled there in the foyer.

She was awakened by the transformation; dawn's light was streaming into the house, and the head in her lap had changed from a wolf's to a man's. Dave's eyes, human once again, looked up at her.

"That little bastard shot you!" he said.

"I had your bulletproof vest on," she said. "He shot *you*, and you weren't wearing anything!"

He still wasn't, she noticed admiringly. Her husband was unquestionably a fine-looking man—when he was a man at all.

"Just fur," he said. "I guess the stories are true, though—you need silver bullets to kill a werewolf."

"I would rather never have tested that," she said, stroking his hair.

"Would you really have shot me if I'd done what I wanted to and ripped his throat out?" Dave asked.

"I don't know," Jenny admitted. "And I *really* don't want to test *that* one!"

"Same here," he said. "But I'm glad you aimed— helped me get my temper back under control. I mean, the little bastard *shot* you!"

"I'm fine," Jenny insisted.

Dave sat up. "Let me see your back," he said.

She was too tired to argue; she turned and let Dave pull up her shirt.

"Nasty bruise," he said. "Skin's not broken."

"Told you," she muttered.

"Yeah, you did," he agreed. "And you told me I was crazy to run for mayor, and you were right about that, too." He shook his head. "I probably broke that kid's wrist tonight, and I might've killed him. And . . . and if the silver bullet part is true, then maybe the contagious bite is true, too, and he'll be out there running around on all fours next month, same as me. That's *bad*, and we'll have to do something about it. This whole werewolf thing— I was kidding myself, Jen. It's not just an inconvenience. It'd never work, me being mayor."

She twisted around to face him. "You're not going to run?" she asked.

"No, I'm not," he said.

She remembered Rafe Hayes talking about his uncle, Bill Beasley. She remembered Rafe making threats and promises and firing that gun wildly. She remembered a dozen other things about Bill Beasley and his family, and she considered what might have to be done to ensure that Rafe Hayes didn't become a public menace at the next full moon.

"Then *I* will," she said.

Russian-born Marina Frants's first Baba Yaga story, "A Bone to Pick" (co-authored with husband Keith R.A. DeCandido) appeared in Did You Say Chicks?! *She's back with a tale which demonstrates that any quest requiring you to kill someone known as "the Deathless" is going to be, well, a Learning Experience.*

Death Becomes Him

Marina Frants

"Someone's coming," Baba Yaga announced from the kitchen. "A man on a horse."

Vassilisa put aside the stocking she was darning, got up from her chair, and walked over to the window. She saw no sign of a rider, and heard nothing but the usual forest noises. But if Yaga said someone was coming, then someone undoubtedly was. Vassilisa turned away from the window.

"Is this good news or bad news?" she asked.

Yaga looked up form the stewpot she was stirring to aim a gap-toothed grin at her apprentice.

"Depends on what you consider good, doesn't it?"

Vassilisa rolled her eyes. "Are we going to talk to him, hide from him, or add him to the stew?"

The last suggestion was only half-serious. In the six

61

months Vassilisa had known her, Baba Yaga has shown no taste for human flesh, no matter what the stories said. She did, however, use human bones for some of her more powerful spells, and if their visitor had hostile intentions, he stood a good chance of ending up in pieces in the pantry.

Yaga looked mildly annoyed. "I suppose we'll talk to him. He's bringing a gift."

Once again, Vasssilisa took the statement on faith. Yaga always knew what was going on in the forest. She could talk to the dead trees, the dry leaves, the bones in the ground. Vassilisa was slowly learning to do the same, but it still took her a great deal of painstaking, exhausting, and often smelly ritual to perform spells that Yaga could cast with a thought.

She returned to her sewing, resisting the temptation to pester Yaga with questions. If the rider was bearing a gift, then he was probably going to petition for a favor, which meant he was very desperate indeed. Favors from Baba Yaga tended to come at a high, and often unexpected, price. Vassilisa had found that out six months before, when she came seeking a way to save her village from the Tatars, and ended up leaving that village forever to become Yaga's apprentice. Not to mention housemaid, gardener, and general errand-girl.

Outside below the windows, a horse snorted nervously and stamped its hooves on the ground. A man's voice called out, "Hello? Anyone in the house?"

He repeated his call four times before Yaga poked her head out the kitchen door to glare at Vassilisa.

"Well? Are you going to go out and speak to him?"

"I'm pretty sure he's not looking for me," Vassilisa grumbled, but she put down her sewing again, and went to fetch the ladder.

She caught a glimpse of the visitor as she opened the door—a tall, broad-shouldered young man in a shabby cloak, riding a chestnut horse. He was looking up at the hut's windows, one hand shielding his eyes against the sun. Vassilisa felt terribly self-conscious as she climbed down, presenting shabby skirts and faded stockings to his view. Most of the time, she rather liked living in a hut that stood on chicken legs. It kept most of the forest critters out—the legs simply shook off and stomped anything that tried to climb them. But at times like this, she really wished she could teach the damn things to *squat*.

By the time she reached solid ground, the rider had dismounted. He stood at the gate, watching Vassilisa with a puzzled frown.

"Baba Yaga?" he asked in a tone of shocked disbelief.

Vassilisa fought down a snicker. It had to be a bit disconcerting, she supposed, to come searching for a legendary ancient sorceress, and be presented with a freckle-faced young woman in a homemade dress.

"No," she said, and didn't know whether to be amused or insulted by the expression of relief on his face. "I'm Vassilisa, Yaga's apprentice. You can tell me what you need."

He hesitated for a moment, then swept off his hat and bowed to her, just as politely as if she'd been Yaga herself.

"Thank you. My name is Aleksei. I need your—Yaga's—help. I've brought payment . . ." He turned to untie a bulging sack from his saddle. The sack looked heavy, and rattled when he dropped it to the ground. Aleksei dug inside it, and pulled out an oversized gold goblet with a green enamel base and a circle of emeralds around the lip of the bowl. He held it out to Vassilisa, who nearly dropped it. She had never held anything made of gold before. The goblet was much heavier than it looked.

"I have more," Aleksei told her earnestly. "As much as you want. You can have this whole bag if Yaga helps me."

Vassilisa turned the goblet over in her hands,

frowning. She couldn't imagine what they'd do with it. It was much too large and heavy to actually drink from. Sell it, maybe? They'd need to travel all the way to Kiev to find a buyer who could afford such a thing. Vassilisa shrugged. It hardly mattered. Knowing Yaga, the price would end up being something else entirely.

"What do you need?" she asked.

Aleksei hesitated again, staring down at the ground and shifting from foot and foot. Finally he opened his cloak to reveal a knee-length coat of chainmail underneath.

"It's this armor," he said.

"What's wrong with it?" It looked like very good armor, well-made and brightly polished, much finer than the rest of Aleksei's clothes.

Aleksei looked at Vassilisa with pleading eyes. "I can't get the cursed thing off!"

Vassilisa bit her lip. She *wasn't* going to laugh. Aleksei didn't strike her as the brightest person she's ever met but he was, presumably, capable of undressing himself. So there had to be a real problem there.

"Tell me all about it."

Aleksei, it turned out, had discovered an abandoned castle about a week's ride to the north, and gone in to explore it. He had found mice, bats, spiders, dust, and a great deal of treasure lying about, but no people. No living people, anyway.

"There was a skeleton on the floor in one of the treasure chambers," Aleksei said. "Buried under a pile of gold. The bones were scorched, and his clothes were all burnt away, but the armor was still bright and shiny. Not even dust had settled on it. I figured it *had* to be enchanted, so I . . ."

"So you robbed him."

Aleksei gave her a defensive look. "He didn't need it anymore, did he? I thought it would protect me in battle."

"It didn't protect the previous owner," Vassilisa pointed out. Aleksei blinked.

"No, I suppose it didn't. I hadn't thought of that. So can Baba Yaga help me?"

Vassilisa tucked the jeweled goblet under her arm and returned to the ladder.

"I'll see what we can do."

"Hmph." Yaga lifted the goblet in her gnarled hands, and tapped one crooked nail against the stem. "Useless piece of junk. Still, the boy did bring a gift. I guess you'd better help him."

"Me?" Vassilisa sputtered. "What am I supposed to do? I don't know how to get that armor off him!"

Yaga fixed her with a narrow-eyed frown, the kind she usually got when Vassilisa bungled a spell, or forgot a lesson, or didn't get the dishes clean enough.

"And what do you do when you don't know?"

That was one of the earliest lessons. Vassilisa sighed. "You find someone who knows, and ask."

"And who would know, in this case?"

Vassilisa opened her mouth to answer, and quickly closed it again. Her first impulse was to say *the wizard who enchanted the armor*, but they didn't know who it was, and had no way to find out. She thought about it for a moment.

"The previous owner?"

"Good girl. The man's bones are still in the castle, aren't they? Go and talk to him."

"But—" Vassilisa began, then stopped. Why was she arguing? Yaga wasn't asking her to do anything she hadn't done before. Doing it for practice in the warm safety of the hut might be more comfortable than doing it for real, but the process was the same, wasn't it? "All right. I'll go get ready." She headed toward the small closet where she and Yaga kept the dried herbs used in their spells.

"Take the flying mortar!" Yaga called after her. "I can't spare you for two weeks, you know! There's spring cleaning to be done."

"I don't know how you managed before I came along," Vassilisa muttered, busily sorting through rows of little jars on the closet shelves. "Which reminds me—what are you going to demand for payment?"

"Payment?"

"Well, you're not going to take that silly goblet, are you? As you said, the thing's useless. So what will you take?"

"When you came to me, did I tell you the price in advance?"

"No."

"Then don't ask stupid questions now."

"Are you sure Baba Yaga cannot come herself?" Aleksei asked for what had to be the hundredth time. "It could be dangerous, after all . . ."

"The castle is abandoned," Vassilisa snapped. "You said so yourself. Nothing there but bats and mice and a dead man with no armor. That much, I think I can handle."

"But—"

"She's *busy!*"

It was clear that Aleksei did not think that Vassilisa could help him. It was getting to be insulting. All right, so she wasn't a great sorceress who knew everything and could cast spells with a thought. She could do this . . . couldn't she?

Sighing, she hiked up her skirt and climbed into Yaga's mortar—a narrow waist-high bowl carved from a single oak stump—which she'd dragged from its little shed in the back of the garden.

"Hand me that bag, will you?"

Aleksei handed her the tattered sack where she'd packed the herbs she would need for the spell. Vassilisa resisted the urge to dig through it again. She had already gone over it three times. Everything was there. And this endless checking and rechecking would only serve to convince Aleksei that she didn't know what she was doing. Vassilisa clutched the sack to her chest and leaned forward as far as she could to make room for Aleksei behind her.

"Climb in," she ordered.

It was a tight squeeze. The mortar really wasn't made for two people. Vassilisa wrinkled her nose as Aleksei's chest pressed against her back. He smelled like . . . well, like someone who hadn't taken his armor off for a week. She tried to take shallow breaths as she recited the activating spell on the mortar.

They lifted into the air with a lurch and a wobble, and a startled yelp from Aleksei. Vassilisa ignored him, and concentrated her thoughts on guiding their flight. The wind whipped her hair back and lifter her shawl off her shoulders, so that she had to clutch the ends in one hand to keep it on. She *loved* this. All the hours spent cleaning Yaga's dishes and scrubbing Yaga's floors were made worth it by these moments of magic.

The forest rushed by below them in a green blur, flat at first, then sloping upwards as they entered hillier country. Aleksei's arms were wrapped tightly around Vassilisa's waist, but she barely remembered he was there. She almost missed his cry of "There!" but caught herself in time and guided the mortar down.

It was a strange place to build a castle. No towns nearby, not even a village. Just trees. The castle, with its moss-grown walls and crumbling towers, looked as if a giant hand had picked it up somewhere else, and dropped it carelessly in the forest. Vassilisa brought the mortar down in the central courtyard with only a slight jolt. She climbed out, and hopped up and down a few times to work the kinks out of her knees.

"All right, Aleksei. Lead the way."

The inside of the castle was dim and musty. Most of the wooden doors had rotted away, and all the windows were broken. The ceiling of was lost in shadows. Vassilisa could hear scurrying sounds in the corners. Every now and then, a dark shape fluttered overhead—birds or bats, she couldn't be sure.

It was easy to retrace Aleksei's steps from the foot-prints he'd left in the dust on his first visit. They walked through wide, echoing corridors, brushing aside the occasional cobweb as they passed, until they reached an arched doorway. The door hung at an angle, one hinge rusted all the way through, the other barely holding. It squeaked ominously as Aleksei pushed it open. Vassilisa followed him in and froze, staring.

She'd never seen that much wealth in her entire life. She'd never even imagined that much. There were mountains of coin, piled higher than Aleksei's head. There were gems of all colors, strewn about like pebbles. Jeweled belts and necklaces lay tangled in the dust, rings glittered on the stone floor, surrounded by rat droppings and dead bugs.

Vasilisa had never given much thought to possessing great riches, but the sight still held her transfixed for a moment. She imagined herself draped in velvet and brocade, with jeweled slippers on her feet, dancing at the Prince's court in Kiev. She picked up a diamond necklace from the floor and held it to her throat.

The sight of the gems glittering against the faded linen of her dress restored her perspective. She shook her head, and let he necklace fall from her fingers. This wasn't what she came for.

"Show me the bones."

The skeleton lay atop a glittering spill of gold and silver. It must've been there a long time. The bones had faded to a dull white, except for the parts that were scorched black. A dented helmet, tarnished with age, adorned the skull.

"I didn't realize he'd be so long dead." Vassilisa knelt at the skeleton's side. Most of the dead man's clothes had been burned to blackened shreds, but a few small tatters remained. She could see a glimmer of gold thread on the brittle fabric, indicating that the dead man had been more than just a wandering peasant. "It'll make the spell harder."

"Can you do it?" Aleksei looked dubious. Vassilisa glared at him.

"Of course I can do it!" *I think.* "Clear me some space on the floor, will you?"

She poured a handful of tinder into a shallow clay bowl and lit it, nursed the spark to a steady flame, then poured on the herbs from her jars, one pinch at a time. The flame turned yellow, then blue, then green. A bittersweet smell permeated the air. Vassilisa closed her eyes, clasped the piece of cloth in her fist, and leaned forward to breathe in the smoke.

Yaga always claimed that this part wasn't necessary. Useless trappings, she said, a prop for the weak-willed. The power in the spell came from the caster, not from dead plants and smelly smoke. That was all very well if you were as old as the forest, and could speak to rocks and raise the dead with a thought, but when most of your life had been spent tending a vegetable garden and raising chickens, and magic crept up on you unawares, your will needed a prop. Vassilisa took another deep breath, and chanted the spell.

The words floated upwards on wisps of scented smoke. Vassilisa's eyes remained closed, but white sparks danced across her vision, like afterimages of lightning. The piece of cloth in her hand felt hot. She let the heat flow through her, and out into the air again, searching for any remnant of the dead man's spirit, demanding that he speak.

"What?!" The voice rang in her head, startling her into gasping in too much smoke all at once. Vassilisa fell back, coughing, but kept her eyes closed.

"Who are you?" she demanded.

"You're the one who dragged me back from the dead, you tell me!" The voice sounded ill-tempered. The dead often were. Vassilisa's instinct was to apologize, to offer an explanation, but Yaga had warned her not to try.

Arguing with the dead was a fruitless task, she said. They had all the time in the world, and would keep you talking until the spell wore off, just for spite. You had to command them, not convince them.

She let more power bleed into her, then sent it after the voice, repeating her question with more insistence.

"Who *are* you?"

There was a short, resentful silence before the answer drifted into her thoughts like the smoke.

"Ivan Tsarevitch."

A tsarevitch? Vassilisa bit back another apology, this time for speaking out of turn to royalty. She needed to get to the point before the flame in the bowl burned out and the spell wore off.

"You were wearing an enchanted coat of armor when you died. What does the spell do?"

"Nothing bad." This time, the voice held a note of exaggerated innocence. "It's a protection spell. Go ahead, put the coat on."

Spiteful bastard. "Someone already has. How does he get it off?"

Silence. Vassilisa opened her eyes just long enough to throw another handful of herbs on the fire.

"How?"

"Kill Koschei the Deathless."

"What?"

"You heard me." Now Ivan sounded smug. Vassilisa was beginning to get an image of him, a golden-haired, blue-eyed, arrogant fellow in fine clothes, smirking at her with his arms folded across his chest. But she had no idea if this was really him, or just the image he wanted her to see, or simply her own imagination putting a face to the snide voice. "This is Koschei's castle. I came here to kill him, for he was threatening my father with sorcery. I didn't want to go." The smirk changed to a scowl. "He's a sorcerer, what was I supposed to do against him? So Father had this armor made for me. It will turn any blade and deflect any arrow. It also wouldn't come off until I either died, or spilled Koschei's blood."

Vassilisa decided that she didn't blame Ivan for being ill-tempered. That was a rotten thing to do to someone. She suspected that Ivan had been a troublesome younger son.

"What happened?" she asked.

"He killed me, of course. What need does a sorcerer have for blade or arrow? He threw a ball of flame at me."

"I'm sorry."

"Good. I'm glad somebody is. Can I go now?"

Vassilisa released the spell, and watched Ivan's image fade from her mind. It was a waste of time feeling sorry for him, she told herself. He'd been dead for decades, there was nothing she could do for him. Better to concentrate on Aleksei.

He was squatting a few feet away, watching her with concern.

"Are you all right? You were talking to yourself."

"I'm fine." Vassilisa's mouth felt sticky, and her eyes stung, but it was only a side effect of the smoke, and she was used to it. "You, on the other hand, are in trouble."

Aleksei's face grew steadily paler as Vassilisa related her conversation with Ivan Tsarevitch.

"B-b-but," he stammered when she was done, "Koschei hasn't been heard from in years!"

"That's because he's dead," Vassilisa said with a sigh.

"He is? How do you know?"

"Yaga told me. And don't ask me how she knows. But Koschei the Deathless is now Koschei the Dead, which makes it difficult for you to kill him, doesn't it?"

Aleksei's shoulders slumped. "What do I do then?"

"I don't know. Let me think." Vassilisa stood up and paced. The sensible action would be to go back and ask Yaga for advice. But that would mean admitting defeat in the first independent task Yaga had ever assigned her.

She couldn't do it. It was too embarrassing. "Blood. Ivan said *blood*."

Aleksei blinked at her. "What about it?"

"At first he said you must kill Koschei to get the armor off. But later, he said you must spill his blood. There's a difference."

"What difference? He's *dead!*"

"Then there must be a body somewhere." Vassilisa stopped packing, and stooped down to repack her bag. "Let's go find it."

Finding a single dead body in an empty castle proved daunting. There was no crypt in the castle, and nothing on the grounds that looked like a grave. Vassilisa and Aleksei trudged up and down the corridors, checking every room as they went.

"What will we do when we find him?" Aleksei asked, as they climbed yet another flight of stairs.

"I can cast a spell to restore his body. Then you spill his blood, and we'll see if that helps."

"You're going to bring Koschei the Deathless back to life?" Aleksei looked as if he wasn't sure which one of them had gone mad.

Vassilisa rolled her eyes. "Of course not! I couldn't, even if I wanted to. But I can bring his body back to the way it was before it rotted. It won't last long, without a spirit to keep it together, but you only need a few seconds to spill blood."

She stopped, because the staircase had come to an end. They stood at a long, narrow landing with a single door at the far end. Vassilisa gave it a push, but it wouldn't budge. "Locked. But it looks—"

"Let me try." Aleksei launched himself forward, slamming his shoulder against the door. The boards promptly shattered to splinters. Aleksei, caught by surprise, fell through the opening with a cry and a crash.

"—rotten." Vassilisa finished, coming in after him.

The room proved to be yet another treasure chamber, they'd seen a dozen like it in their search. Vassilisa found that the sight of gold and jewels no longer impressed her. The body in the center of the room, on the other hand, impressed her a great deal.

Koschei had not been dead quite as long as Ivan Tsarevitch. Parchment-dry skin still covered his bones, and a few wisps of white hair clung to his skull. His fur-trimmed boots and long coat of sea-green brocade were mouse-chewed and moldy, but still holding together. He lay curled up in a narrow space between two chests full of gems, one hand buried among the glittering stones. Vassilisa shuddered. He must've died there alone, counting his wealth as life slipped away . . .

She shook off the image, and helped Aleksei to his feet.

"Have your sword ready. A body this old won't stay restored for more than a few seconds."

Aleksei looked slightly ill, but drew his blade without comment.

This was a simpler spell, which was just as well, because Vassilisa was running low on herbs. There would be no need to drag an unwilling spirit into a conversation. All she had to do was convince a pile of long-dead bones that they weren't all that long dead. She didn't even bother to close her eyes as she chanted the spell.

As she spoke, the corpse began to twitch. The withered hands stirred, dislodging a fall of precious stones onto the floor. The skin bulged and swelled in odd places as layers of flesh reappeared over bone. Aleksei made a gagging noise, and crossed himself with a shaking hand. Vassilisa, lost in the feel of the power flowing through her, barely spared him a glance.

"Get ready," she muttered.

And then the flame in her bowl exploded in a blinding red burst that nearly scorched her face off. Vassilisa fell back with a cry. The spell spun out of her control, twisting into something new, something too powerful for her to hold on to. The force of it sent her sprawling to the floor. She lay there breathless, blinking the fireburst's afterimage from her eyes. Her vision cleared just in time to see Koschei rise to his feet.

"Why, thank you, girl." His voice was a soft rustle, like dry leaves in the wind. "I was hoping someone would do that."

Vassilisa tried to suppress a whimper, and failed miserably. What had she been thinking, casting a spell on a sorcerer's body? She must've been delirious. She should've known he'd be there, waiting for a way back.

Koschei advanced on her with shuffling steps. His movements were slow and jerky, his body obviously still trying to remember how to walk. Vassilisa scrambled away from him. Koschei raised one hand. A ball of fire coalesced in his cupped palm.

"Leave her alone!" Aleksei lunged forward. Koschei seemed mildly surprised to find there was another person in the room. He turned, and threw the fireball at Aleksei instead of Vassilisa.

Aleksei proved better at ducking than Ivan Tsarevitch had. He fell flat on the floor, somehow managing to hold on to his sword as he hit. The fireball struck the wall behind him, leaving a black smear.

Vassilisa felt the shimmer of magic in the air as Koschei cast his spell. She tried to grasp it, but it was too wild, and she was too frightened to concentrate. She watched Aleksei climb to his knees and then drop again, just in time to avoid a burst of flame that melted a pile of silver nuggets into slag.

"Look what you did!" Koschei sounded peevish. "You made me spoil my treasure." He lifted his arm again.

Vassilisa grabbed the first thing that came to hand—a gold candlestick—and threw it. It hit Koschei's arm, spoiling his aim and giving Aleksei a chance to take shelter behind a tall stack of gold bars. Unfortunately, it also focused his attention on her once again.

Vassilisa scrambled back in time to avoid being cooked, though too late to keep her skirt from getting singed. She could barely see or breathe from the smoke, but now that she had survived the first few seconds of Koschei's attack, her fear was receding. The sorcerer was powerful, but he was also slow and clumsy. And every time he cast a spell, the maelstrom of magic in the air grew calmer, more manageable.

Vassilisa clambered over to where Aleksei was squatting behind his golden barricade. He gave her a grim look, frightened but not hysterical.

"Distract him," Vassilisa whispered.

Aleksei's eyes widened. He opened his mouth to object, closed it again, gave a resigned shrug, and moved into the open.

Vassilisa crouched low on the floor to keep out of Koschei's sight, and closed her eyes. She had never tried this sort of spontaneous magic before, but Yaga insisted it could be done, and now was certainly a good time to try. To help herself concentrate, she imagined her little bowl of herbs in front of her, the tiny spark of flame in the center, the smell of pungent smoke in her nose. The presence of real smoke in the room actually helped. She touched the magic swirling about her, and waited for the lull that signaled Koschei's latest attack. When it came, she reached out with her mind and began, ever so slowly, to reverse her earlier spell.

She knew it was working when she heard Koschei scream. The air seemed to tremble as he struggled against her spell. Vassilisa groaned. He was so strong, she felt like she was trying to push a mountain from its base. But his body was weak, still more used to death than to life, and it gave her something to work with. Vassilisa held on to the spell, despite the growing pain in her head, knowing that her advantage grew with every passing second.

Koschei's scream turned into a whimper, then a groan. There was a thud as something soft and heavy hit the floor. The mountain of magic that Vassilisa was pushing against suddenly gave way, then vanished. Vassilisa opened her eyes.

Koschei's body was sprawled facedown on the floor, motionless. Vassilisa did not need a closer look to know that he was dead again—the flesh was already beginning to rot. Aleksei knelt a few paces away. His sword was on the floor next to him, and he was holding an oversize gilt platter in front of him as a shield. His hair and clothes were singed, but he seemed unharmed.

"Hurry up!" Vassilisa shouted at him. "Spill his blood while he still has some!"

Aleksei dropped the platter, snatched up his sword again, and shuffled over, still on his knees, to Koschei's side. He lifted the blade with a grunt, and brought it down in a sweeping arc, striking the dead sorcerer's head off his shoulders with a single blow.

"Just making sure," Aleksei muttered as a stream of black blood oozed across the floor.

For a few moments, the two of them just sat there. Vassilisa felt as if she'd run all the way across Russia. Aleksei looked no better. Talking seemed like more effort than either one of them could manage.

"Well," Vassilisa wheezed after a while. "Can you get it off now?"

"I'm afraid to try," Aleksei said, but he reached to undo the first fastening.

It came apart easily. Too easily, in fact. The heavy chainmail tore like the flimsiest fabric. Aleksei looked startled at first, then broke into a wide grin as he ripped the coat off in pieces.

"Yes!" He jumped up and danced a wobbly jig around the room, tossing scraps of armor in all directions. "It worked!"

Vassilisa picked up one of the scraps. It felt like ordinary chainmail, heavy and not at all fragile. But then she pulled at one edge, the rings came apart like strands of cobweb. Vassilisa shrugged, and let the piece fall.

"Well," she said, "I guess we can call the trip a success then."

"I hope you know how lucky you are," Yaga grumbled as she smeared burn ointment on the spots where Vassilisa's eyebrows used to be. "Koschei at the height of his power would've turned you into dust without breaking a sweat."

Vassilisa glared at her. "I said I was sorry. Stop lecturing me."

"I'm not lecturing. I'm talking sense. But do you listen to me? Some apprentice you are." Yaga stoppered the ointment jar and put it back on the shelf. "There. You're done."

"Thank you. Are you going to go talk to Aleksei now?"

"No."

"Oh. Should I ask him to come in here, then?"

"No."

Vassilisa blinked in confusion. "But . . . you were going to tell him your price. For helping him."

"*I* didn't help him. You did the work, you name the price."

"Me?" Vassilisa's voice rose in a squeak. "But I—"

"But nothing. You've earned it. Go claim your reward."

Something in her voice, and in the thoughtful way she looked at her, made Vassilisa bite back any further objections.

"I can ask for anything I want? And you'll let me have it?"

"Me? What do I have to do with it? It's your reward. And your decision."

Vassilisa's head was spinning as she climbed down to the yard again. *My decision.* Had she imagined it, or did Yaga put an extra stress on that last sentence, as if she'd meant more by it than what she actually said. *My decision.* But what did she want?

Aleksei had just finished resaddling his horse, and was tying up the saddlebags. He stopped when Vassilisa approached, and turned to watch her with a nervous expression.

"Is Yaga coming down?" he asked.

"No." Vassilisa shifted from foot to foot, feeling awkward and nervous. What did she want? What did Yaga want? What did Aleksei have to give? She didn't know. But she suspected that if she asked for half his treasure and a ride to Kiev or Novgorod, that he would give it. And Yaga would let her go.

No more living in a forest, away from the world. She could be a rich woman in a big city, and never darn another sock or scrub another pot. She could dance at the Tsar's palace in jeweled slippers.

And trip over my own feet, most likely.

Vassilisa leaned against the fence and looked around at the hut, and the vegetable garden, the cat asleep in a sunny spot, the chickens milling around the coop. She remembered what it had felt like, to fly the mortar above the forest. She remembered the power coursing through her as she defeated Koschei.

"Well?" Aleksei prompted.

Vassilisa closed her eyes and took a deep breath. "The cup. The one you offered earlier. Yaga's changed her mind. She wants it now."

"Oh." Aleksei looked relieved and disappointed at the same time. "All right."

Vassilisa climbed back into the hut, not waiting to watch him ride away. Yaga was in her rocking chair, sipping tea from a mug, looking insufferably pleased with herself.

"So?" she demanded. "What did you get?"

"Here." Vassilisa thrust the goblet at her. "We can use it for a flowerpot or something."

*After multiple nominations for the Nebula, Hugo,
Edgar, and World Fantasy Awards, plus a gig on the
TV ad (Would you buy a used Borg from this woman?),
not much scares Susan. Not even when I told her I was
going to subtitle this story "Xenadoon" (You'll see why!)
Her most recent books are* Vulcan's Forge *(with Josepha
Sherman) and* Cross and Crescent.

Straight Arrow

Susan Shwartz

It wasn't just life flashing before Lt. Kyria Mavricos'
glassy eyes as she punched out of her crippled fighter,
but a veritable mountain range of clouds. Below them
was probably the nastiest part of what used to be
Yugoslavia. And some very hostile hostiles. And it was
all coming up to meet her way too fast.

One instant, her F-15 had been on a high, fast
overflight; the next, every instrument had gone dead,
she'd lost control, and she'd set off that damned
explosion underneath her butt and prayed the canopy
would blow before she blasted through it.

Air-to-air couldn't have taken out her F-15 before
something registered on her screens. Surface to air?
Here, where Serbs fought Croatians, Greeks fought

Macedonians, and everyone hated Albanians and Turks and dreamed of terrorists, you had to be prepared for Scud-like flying objects, but, in the instants before power died, nothing had shown up.

EMP? She wouldn't have thought the locals had any technology left, let alone anything good enough to mess with an F-15's electronics.

What was left? Wind shear? Those gray critters with the big eyes? What about a Bosnian branch of the Bermuda Triangle that chowed down on F-15s?

She drew in arms and legs and plunged through the clouds. Maybe lower altitude would clear her head.

Her chute erupted with an impact like whiplash. *If this doesn't kill me, my CO will.* Any time a female pilot ejected—let alone bored a hole in the ground—the Air Force didn't just conduct an investigation, it threw a collective fit. And just let CNN sniff it out, or Rush . . .

It wasn't as if her squad had called her Little Ms. Congeniality before. Even if the fact that she'd grown up speaking Greek at home let her translate some of the menus and local papers. Some of the other NATO types were Greek, but they all spoke English. Regardless, some of the pilots—the other pilots—nursed attitudes that could charitably be described as Neanderthal studying to be Cro-Magnon without the blessings of Ayla and her posterity.

I don't want to be a poster child for Affirmative Action. I just want to fly.

Kyria jerked as something holed her chute not a meter from her helmet. Dammit, even if it didn't violate the rules of war to shoot down people who had to eject from planes, it still was lousy manners.

The ground was coming up fast now. She tried to peer through the mist at the spinning landscape, hoping to spot possible hiding places she could use, the nearest source of water, maybe an easy route out, though "easy" was a misnomer in these mountains.

The whine in her ear made her whip her head

around. Another hole in the chute. And what had made it hadn't sounded like any bullet she'd ever heard.

Look out for that tree!

The last thing she saw before the tree clobbered her was two small figures standing in a clearing, bows slung over their backs.

Why was some imbecile was singing "George of the Jungle" in a peculiar hoarse voice here on a Serbian mountainside? If one of those damn archers was the comedian, that was *two* reasons the bozo deserved to die.

That couldn't be right. Any locals would be singing in Serbo-Croatian or whatever. So she had to be the one trying to sing. *Trying.* She spat a mouthful of blood and one tooth.

Testing, she thought. One . . . two . . . three. Arms and legs ached but were otherwise in working order.

So was the rest of her, even if her helmet felt like she had the brain bloat that Boomer in her wing declared women got once a month, cancha take a joke, har har har.

He'd never made that joke around the CO or anywhere else he could be nailed for it. *So help me, I'm going to make it back and wipe his face with it.*

But the chain of command wouldn't help her now. What would?.

Her survival vest held drugs, a knife, a radio, maps, matches, a First Aid kit, tools, and a side arm. And face paint for camouflage. Really gorgeous with a bloody nose and probably shiners, but the regs said to apply it right away. Her hands were hardly shaking at all now.

Her parachute billowed overhead, caught by the tree that had braked her fall and damn near broken her.

First, secure her chute. Then, look around for a place she could hide out in while she sent a message. *Come on, God. You helped get Captain Scott O'Grady out of the soup and into a book contract. How about me?*

The folds of her parachute jerked. More arrows, dammit. No guns?

In that case, I've got the bastards outnumbered. Sure.

She drew her side arm, then wriggled into some covering underbrush just as someone jerked the chute down from the tree.

Voices again. My God, they were speaking Greek. Not *demotika*, but something close, more old-fashioned sounding than even her grandfather, who'd liked to pretend they were still living in the age of Pericles, which also had been a lousy age for ambitious women.

A branch snapped, and she whirled round. Standing over her was a tall woman dressed in leather, if not much of it, a curved bow slung across her back, high-laced boots, and holding a very businesslike-looking hunting knife. If the woman hadn't stepped on that branch deliberately, she could have slit Kyria's throat before Kyria heard her coming.

"The mists have brought us another one!" she called.

A wordless, high-pitched shout of triumph answered as Archer Number 2 strode forward. Not as tall as the first woman, she was fair, as some Macedonians had been, time out of mind. She carried a long staff, not a sword. And, as she folded Kyria's parachute into a bundle, her hands lingered on the fabric as if she wondered at its smoothness.

Oh shit, Kyria thought, *I've waked up in the Xenaverse.*

Before she could even try playing Quick Draw, the tall woman's long staff slammed out at her head. The explosion of pain, followed by blackout, was almost a relief.

Red light erupted, ejecting Kyria back into consciousness the way she had been hurled out of her cockpit. She flailed against whatever it was tied her down.

Blankets. Coarse wool blankets and fleeces.

Rainbows erupted in Kyria's field of vision. What had Doc Dworkin said about concussion? Keep awake. If you're dizzy or you vomit, get help. She glanced about. They'd settled her in some sort of shelter, but what passed for a door flap was open, and the noise in the camp made it unlikely she'd be getting any sleep. So did the idea of what a bunch of primitives could do with her gear.

I'm not doing very well, am I? she thought. *First I punch out. Then I black out. Now I'm a prisoner.*

"She's awake." Again, that curiously old-fashioned Greek. A woman's voice. Maybe she wasn't hallucinating. This region had a history of female guerrillas.

"See if she'll drink something."

The blond woman crouched at her side, holding a steaming cup. Good thing she'd had all her shots.

The cup pressed against her bitten lip. She swallowed so it would go away.

"I'd hate to take a urine test right now," she muttered to herself. "Where's my gear?"

The woman was wearing her belt knife, she observed. Damn. That Marine-issue Bowie knife had been a gift from one of the friendlier men in her outfit, who'd scrounged or traded for it.

"Until we got your clothes off, we thought you were male," said the blonde.

She sounded disappointed. *You, my drill instructor, and half my flight. You'd think women warriors, at least, would be half civil . . .*

"We know of no Amazons who wear such garments," the woman continued. "Or carry such gear."

Kyria blinked and took a quick look south. If this woman was any example, it was a myth that Amazons mutilated themselves so they could shoot better. This woman had the complete set . . . Encased in the proverbial bronze bra.

Okay, so this is the uplift war, not ethnic cleansing. I still want out.

I'm nuts, right? Maybe it was better than reality, considering that reality in this part of the world consisted of ethnic cleansing, meaning genocide, rape, and anarchy.

A child holding something olive-colored with trailing straps ran toward the central fire.

"No!"

Before Kyria realized what she was doing, she was on her feet, out of the tent, and heading unsteadily and quite bare-ass toward the blaze. If the kid threw that thing on the fire, they were all in trouble.

The blonde caught her round the ankle and brought her down. Someone else cuffed the child and whirled it—him—around before returning him to the circle of women and children.

"What can you expect of a boychild? He's almost old enough to be sent to his father's tribe, and if you ask me, he's enough trouble that I say we set him loose before the mists arrive!" the blonde said.

"I am Demetria," her benefactor said. "And your name?"

"Mavricos, Kyria," she rapped out. "Lieutenant, US Air Force . . ."

Demetria's voice interrupted the recitation of her serial number and birth date. "This 'air force' is your tribe? From your name, you would be of the ruling line?"

If "Kyrios" meant "lord," then "Kyria . . ."

Long-lost princess. Right. Kyria resisted the temptation to tug the goatskins, which didn't stink as badly as she'd expected, over her head until Demetria stopped asking questions.

Demetria held a second cup to her mouth. "Drink. This will steady you."

"My tribe, yes," Kyria agreed as soon as her head stopped spinning. "But I am not in line to rule." What Intel would say about any of this was another thing not to think about. Section 8 would be the least she could expect.

"You may feel better if you dress," said Demetria. "Certainly, you will feel warmer. The clothes I brought will do for now, but we must find you better before you meet the queen."

That bronze bra was cold! Kyria discovered as she wriggled into it. She pulled on the rest of the garments—a dark leather tunic, a skirt of those metal-tipped strips her military history prof had said were called *pteruges*. Or something. No boots. These women might be low-tech, but they weren't stupid.

"Can I have my stuff?" she asked again. If she could just get to her gun, her radio, her medical supplies, maybe she could make a break for it. *A prisoner's first duty is to escape.*

Demetria was six inches taller than she and had that staff. Right.

"The queen will decide when to return your possessions to you. Meanwhile, you will be well treated, as befits your rank."

Lieutenant? Or princess of the tribe "US Air Force"?

"When can I speak with her?" Kyria asked.

"Now that the mists have lifted, she is out hunting." Demetria emphasized the last word and smiled thinly. "She will not return until tomorrow. I know she will want to confer with you in the absence of your queen. For now, rest."

Kyria emerged from her shelter the next morning to respect and curious whispers. She had the mother of all headaches, and if she didn't find a bathroom soon . . .

Well, at least she didn't have cramps. Thank heaven for small mercies.

She gestured urgently, and a hand pointed the way to a Bronze Age equivalent of a latrine. Two very young women leaned on trees nearby, pointedly allowing her privacy, while still letting her know she was under guard. They carried businesslike knives and staffs like the one that had put Kyria out of action the day before. Two against one, even if they weren't much more than kids. Better not, she told herself.

At least, not till after breakfast.

"I don't suppose you have a shower nearby," she asked, as she readjusted the leather garments Demetria had handed her. *Don't even* think *about asking if there's coffee.*

"There is a hot spring, Kyria, if you wish to bathe." The way they spoke her name, it sounded like a title. "We will alert the guards."

"After breakfast," she decided. "You do have breakfast around here, don't you?"

Demetria hailed her on her return and gestured her to a seat by the fire. Suspended from a tripod was a heavy pot in which bubbled what looked like oatmeal or some sort of boiled grains with dried fruit mixed in. She ladled out two bowls and handed one to Kyria, who took it with as much grace as she could, considering how hot it was and how hungry she suddenly found herself.

Demetria clapped her hands. Kyria's guards of earlier that morning disappeared into one of the shelters, then emerged.

"My gear!" Kyria got the words out despite hot porridge that damned near scalded her mouth. She had more attention for the sage-green and gray vest with its many pockets, pouches, and straps than she did for the pain.

One of the young guards had parked Kyria's helmet on top of her mop of hair and was trying hard to swagger. The other carried her vest and was trying just as hard to peek into it without being caught.

Demetria barked laughter. "Quite the warriors, now that they have passed their women's trials. Patience, cousins. The queen should return this evening, and I will wager you a dozen arrows that she does not return alone."

The girls blushed identically.

"Are they twins?" Kyria asked. "They look a lot alike."

Unobtrusively, she checked the nylon holster in its innermost pocket: yes, the automatic was still there. Her headache lightened. She sorted through her First Aid kit to make certain no one had mistaken pills for the coffee-flavored candy that her survival gear also contained, popped two painkillers anyway, along with a broad-spectrum antibiotic, and waited for the headache to subside.

She offered some of the hard candy to the twins. Nice-looking kids. Come to think of it, they had a marked resemblance to Demetria. Who looked a lot like the other women who emerged from various huts, from the woods, and from the bank of a nearby stream to watch Kyria. *I may be the first person some of these women have ever seen who doesn't resemble them.*

Demetria snapped something in Greek too fast for her to follow.

"Your pardon. We do not see many strangers here."

That returned her to the question that dogged her all day, persistent as her young guards. Where was *here*?

Bosnia? Macedonia? Some time in the past? Maybe this was a sort of branch office of the Bermuda Triangle, and they were all stuck. What were these mists that seemed to determine when they could hunt and when they could leave?

If they were all stuck here, maybe the ethnic cleansing that had been going on since the breakup of Yugoslavia had accounted for some of the locals . . . the locals . . .

. . . from whom these Amazons had drawn their breeding stock. *Maybe the gene pool's getting a little shallow.*

The girls had flushed when Demetria had assured her the queen would not return alone. "I've bagged another one!" Demetria had called when she'd found Kyria. So that was what the queen was hunting.

Kyria suppressed a grin. *Guess who's coming for dinner?*

If she'd just wandered into an Amazonian version of the Dating Game . . .

My God, talk about fraternization.

Light was glinting off the mountains when a brighter light erupted into the center of the camp. A heliograph?

"The queen's coming." One of the younger women started smoothing her hair. Another bit her lips to redden them.

Kyria raised an eyebrow at Demetria. "Do we dress for dinner around here?" she asked. Her project for the day had been washing out her flight suit. She'd had to shoo away a number of eager helpers, all with that same family resemblance. If she had to meet a foreign dignitary, she preferred to do so in some semblance of uniform.

"Five . . . six . . . seven . . ." came a cry from the outskirts of the camp. "The guards are bringing up the rear."

"Only seven?" asked a girl slightly taller and darker than the others.

Demetria shrugged. "We take what the fates send, little sister," she said. "Now, run along." The girl wavered visibly. "Go on! They won't bite . . . I think . . ."

She made shooing motions. Finally, the girl ran off, laughter trailing after her like a bright scarf.

A child ran to Demetria and whispered in her ear. "The queen has summoned you."

No time to change, then. She followed Demetria past the campfire, where only children and older—meaning more than twenty—women sat efficiently butchering something—a deer? A sheep? A goat while another roast sizzled on a spit. Her nose wrinkled at the scent of rough wine. A feast, Amazon-style. Might be fun. She heard a skirl of flute music, a clash of chords and drumbeats interrupted by a shout that sounded like a bawling-out.

She'd hoped to get a look at the queen's . . . trophy males? She managed not to grin. If, as she suspected, these mists let the warrior women reach through time, they'd probably be drawn from a number of times and places. Genetic diversity, after a fashion, but, judging from the look-alikes, the system was breaking down, had been breaking down for generations.

She glanced around, but Demetria led her and her guards walked past a number of shelters, their doors already firmly tied shut (Demetria chuckled), and toward a cave. Stuck into the earth outside it was a spear, a helmet and plumes swaying on its point. *The equivalent of a flag over Buckingham Palace. Her Majesty is At Home*, Kyria determined. A red fire—one of her flares burned outside it in a brazier. So they'd seen flares before.

Demetria and the wannabes—great name for a rock band—led her into the cave toward another fire. A tall figure, her head covered in a huge mask, reclined on a pile of furs that would have given PETA spasms. Half-covering them was some of the fabric from Kyria's parachute. Fastened to the rock walls, glinting with crystals, were—an M-16, a Lee-Enfield, a scimitar that had to be four hundred years old, and a collection of helmets and other trophies she couldn't identify.

The mists had obviously been going on for a long time.

Demetria came to what clearly passed for *tenn-HUT* among the Amazons.

If this woman says her name is Gabrielle, I'm dead. No way I won't crack up.

The queen removed her heavy mask. She was taller than Demetria. Her hair, before the gray streaked it, had been as black as Kyria's own. "Greetings, sister," said the queen. "I am Hippolyta."

You are not going to say you are Lieutenant Diana Prince, Kyria told herself. *This isn't a comic book. And you'd better come up with a matronymic damn fast.*

She drew herself up and inclined her head formally like British soldiers did in all the movies. Field-grades got charm school; lieutenants made do with movies and TV.

"I am Kyria," she said. "Daughter of Eleni." Her mother had preferred to call herself Elly, but that didn't sound Greek. Or regal.

The queen gestured Kyria to another pile of furs. She gestured, and one of the girls poured wine into . . . that wasn't a beaker, Kyria's mind gabbled. A rhyton. Did that mean these Amazons had trade with Scythia or the equivalent at some point in the past? The cups that the girls handed her and Demetria were heavy silver; she would have bet that Hippolyta's was gold.

Kyria sank down onto the furs, which felt surprisingly comfortable after a day of goatskins, stumps, and rocks, and took a cautious sip of . . . *a charming little wine with overtones of violence and delusions of grandeur.*

"We saw you," said the queen. "You leapt in fire from a chariot that flew across the sky. You grew wings, easing your fall. And then your chariot fell with a noise like unto Hephaestus' anvil . . . One of my huntresses found me and brought me—this!"

She handed Kyria a scorched, torn metal shard to which fragments of paint still clung. What had ever possessed their squad leader to pick a sea lion as insignia anyhow? Scott always had had a weird sense of humor. Maybe she could say she was under Poseidon's protection or something and they'd take her to the sea. Right.

The woman leaned forward, expectantly.

"Yes, this is from my . . . my chariot."

"I would learn more of it," the queen said, as if the idea that information would be withheld was unthinkable.

Sorry, I can't violate the Prime Directive, Kyria's mind gabbled.

"I have equipment in my ship," was what she actually said. "Metal you could work into useful tools." *Not to mention the radio and the black box that I need . . .*

The queen raised her winecup and sipped. "We saw where your . . . your 'ship' landed," she said. "A good thing the snows had melted, or we would have had fire."

"Can you take me there?" Kyria asked.

Uh-oh, never rush in a bargaining session, she warned herself.

"We could," said the queen. "But the land is tricky if you do not know it, and we have enemies who would not be as gentle captors as we."

Outside the music skirled up. Kyria heard raucous singing. *Must be some party.*

"My daughters are trained from birth in the ways of this land. You . . ."

Better pay attention. This woman wants something of me, or she wouldn't have led with the news about my plane.

The second attendant brought in a steaming platter.

"From the feast," she said.

"For luck!" Demetria threw a piece of meat into the queen's hearthfire. "My queen, you will excuse me? I must make sure order—such order as may be—is kept." The queen nodded.

It was impolite to talk business while eating. Kyria noted the presence of bread and salt with relief and went light on the unfamiliar meat.

"Our garments look well on you," Hippolyta complimented Kyria once the food had been taken away by the two attendants. "Now, you look like a proper woman warrior . . ."

"Your Majesty is too kind." *God, I didn't know people ever said things like that, even in the movies.* She stifled a grin. "Demetria told me they thought I was a man until they got my flight suit off."

Sounded disappointed about it too. Guess I know why, now.

"Demetria longs for a daughter," said Hippolyta. "She has had three sons, all of whom have been sent to their fathers, except for the last one, who was malformed and whom she decided not to rear." The woman took a sip of her wine. Attempting protocol, Kyria reached for the pitcher and poured, first for the queen, then for herself.

Hippolyta nodded approval.

Exposure of the unfit. Disappointment when the queen came in accompanied by so few men. And that family resemblance—*there's more inbreeding around here than in Boomer's family*, Kyria thought.

Outside, the music rose. She heard laughter—men's voices as well as women's.

"How many daughters do you have?" asked the queen suddenly.

Oops! That one came right out of left field.

"None," she replied. "None yet," she corrected herself fast.

The queen raised an eyebrow. "Is it prudent to wait so long?" she asked. "I mean no discourtesy, but even with the mists' blessing, we have found fewer tribes that will be willing to . . . exchange with us each year . . . As Demetria knows, the opportunities must go to younger women, best able to give the tribe healthy daughters."

Just what she didn't need: a wake-up call from a Bronze Age biological clock!

Kyria looked down, a merchant hoarding her bargaining chips. Inbreeding. Declining fertility. Fewer available mates. "There are many healthy people where I come from. Many men. Many healthy men."

This time, the queen leaned over to pour wine for both of them.

Kyria toasted her, then drank cautiously. This was going to be a *long* bargaining session.

"You realize your people may have abandoned their search for you." Hippolyta stifled a yawn. My God, she had staying power!

Outside the cave, the sky was pale. In a little while, the women who'd feasted that night would be going about their morning chores with Amazon-size hangovers. *I bet seven of them are praying for morning sickness in the near future.*

"What of the men you caught in your hunt?" she asked the queen.

"Once the mists return, we shall blindfold them, take them away from here, and release them, together with the boys who are old enough to leave us, and let them return to their tribes."

"Will they be expected?"

Hippolyta laughed. "They are not the first we have taken since the Goddess brought us here to protect us after Troy. The mist is the veil she cast down to protect us."

So that was the story? Well, some Afghans claimed to be descended from Alexander the Great's warriors. And it was as convenient an explanation for the mist as she was going to get right now.

She nodded respect at this alleged goddess, and Hippolyta proceeded. "These new prizes will not be the last. Their tribes will be glad of them and of new sons. Perhaps they too wait for the mists. Perhaps they will come looking for them—or for us, to punish us. They have tried before and failed, but now our numbers grow less."

"My tribe will be looking for me," Kyria insisted. "At least, they will mount a search for the plane."

"For your equipment, but not for you?" asked the queen. "This is no way to treat a warrior and a princess of your tribe. Is it because you are a woman? In that case, why not stay with us?"

One more woman's genes aren't going to solve your problem, queen.

Kyria shook her head, wishing for strong black coffee. She'd tried to be moderate, but she had had a lot of wine. "I can't. That would be desertion. No, let me get to my plane, and I can radio . . . I can call . . . for help. They will come pick me up and drop off whatever supplies we agree on."

Knives, warm clothing, simple tools, probably MREs to help them get through the winter. *Hell, if we could fly in Pampers and Tampax, we'd make a killing. And I'd love to see how Amazons with PMS react to chocolate.*

Queen Hippolyta had sat, gazing into the fire. "You have said that we—my sisters and I—are a story out of legend. Will you be believed when you tell them of us or how we found you?"

"Probably not," Kyria said. *If they don't throw me out, I'll be flying a desk from now on. At worst, well, they say counseling isn't all that bad. Kind of like root canal.*

"Will this bring you trouble?"

Lady, you can't begin to imagine.

"But you plan to tell them."

Kyria sighed, leaned forward, and threw a stick on the fire. "You are an archer, Majesty. Among my people, we call a person who behaves with honor a 'straight arrow.' I will tell my people the truth though they would more easily believe a lie because an officer does not lie nor tolerate those who do."

"Those who come for you, will they be men or women?" Hippolyta asked.

"More men than women, I should think," Kyria answered with the straight truth.

"Could they be persuaded, do you think, to stay for awhile? We would gladly entertain them."

Kyria's eyes met the queen's. She tried to keep her face straight, but failed.

That would be the mother of all shore leaves! Think of it, she imagined some morale officer saying, *as diplomatic relations. Applied diplomatic relations. Close your eyes and think of USAF?*

"You could always ask," she said.

Kyria paused, leaning against a tree, and tried not to think of how quickly an F-15—always assuming the mists didn't materialize and bring it down—could overfly the ground that had taken them days to cover, always with scouts out and an eye to the weather.

Apparently, those damn mists were picky about when they appeared. If you were in the right place at the right time, you lucked out. The Amazons' collection of trophies drawn from across centuries showed they had been consistently lucky. If not, you waited around for the next attack of the mists and hoped your local enemies didn't pick you off first.

I still don't know what we're up against.

Did it matter? Waving aside the offer of a filled wineskin—*unpurified water, wine, and badly tanned goatskin's not my drink of choice*, she had a sip from her canteen. For her, the mists had acted like an electromagnetic field, sufficiently powerful to bring down a high-performance, high-altitude jet. How did the men snatched out of time see it? As a flying carpet? A pillar of cloud?

With luck, I won't have to stick around long enough to find out. At least, the past few days, she hadn't been useless. Her survival vest carried snares as well as weapons and medical supplies: she'd earned her keep.

I could make a place for myself here, I know it. But it would be desertion. My first duty is to get home.

"Hurry!" Demetria urged them on. "The mists are coming. Can't you smell them?"

All I can smell is me. Hope any hostiles out there have stuffed noses.

From the youngest girls to pass their warrior trials to the gray-haired, scarred veterans, these women made Special Forces look like the Junior League. She'd like to have turned them loose on Special Forces, let alone the pilots in her wing. Now, if they only remembered what she'd told them a radio looked like.

Two of the Amazons gestured, *Come on!*

"We climb up to that spur next." A gray-haired veteran pointed to a rock spur that looked to be a thousand meters away, most of it straight up. "There's a clearing beyond it."

Kyria crouched in the cover of the rock spur, hearing searchers crunch through debris. The ground was blackened here. In some places, the rock was fused, glassy. She drew in a gulp of air that burned. They had climbed high enough that she could see clouds floating below her. Clouds that, with any luck, would form the mists she needed to get herself out of this.

Hope the radio survived impact, she thought. Hippolyta's hunting party had brought in sizable chunks of fuselage and said that the rain had prevented a total burnoff. It didn't make sense, but what around here did?

Past the rock spur, the ground flattened out to form the "clearing" she had been promised. She didn't think much of it. Granted, the helo pilots she knew bragged they could set down on a dime, but . . .

What's the difference between a fairy tale and a pilot tale?

A fairy tale begins "Once upon a time." A pilot tale begins "And there I was at 20,000."

They weren't at 20,000, thank God. Kyria thought she'd heard a story once of some Nepalese maniac in a chopper evacuating people off Everest at that kind of altitude, but she wouldn't want to try it herself.

She thought of taking something for her headache, then thought again. She had face to maintain. And supplies to conserve, in case the mist took its sweet time about showing up.

Damn. She didn't remember having altitude problems at the Academy.

We didn't have to worry about drill instructors with swords in Colorado Springs, she remembered.

"Alexa brought this in. Is it what you need?" Demetria, with her usual soundlessness, had come up around the rocks—what's a traverse of a hundred meters or so among friends?—and dropped down beside Kyria. She reached around and unstrapped the Amazonian equivalent of a backpack. What emerged from the swathings of scarred hide was . . .

Her radio.

Grabbing was rude. More than that: grabbing might antagonize Demetria, and that was counterproductive. Not to mention potentially suicidal.

"Two of the scouts brought this in," Demetria said. "Is it the talisman you wanted?"

"Point them out to me this evening," Kyria asked. "I'd like to thank them myself."

There must be something in her equipment she could spare: a knife, maybe, or maybe the penlight.

Or—the idea struck her the way the sunset struck the valley below, with the force of revelation: if I'm picked up, there's no end to the things I can give these people!

Unless, of course, her rescue party had heard of the Prime Directive. Which, considering the number of Trekkies in the Air Force, was all too likely.

She bent over the restored equipment, testing it out. Once she got it working, maybe she could lay out a landing field—or some kind of X-marks-the-spot—for a rescue helo.

And then, it would be time to hurry up and wait. For the mists.

Or for anyone else dependent on the mists to arrive.

It could be rescuers for her.

But it could also be hostiles. Bosnians. Croatians. Albanians. Or, seeing that the mist respected time as little as it respected persons, they might have to watch for anything from stray soldiers from Alexander the Great's time to crusaders to Ottoman Turks.

The more the merrier, or the more genetically diverse.

As long as the Amazons could continue to take them.

In, of course, a manner of speaking.

✧   ✧   ✧

The fire had died to a memory of smoke. Frost had formed on her sleeping bag. By the time the Amazons emerged, appallingly alert, from their sleeping pelts, dampness in the air had wakened Kyria. You never did get much sleep at altitude, she recalled. Just as well. It would keep the guards awake and slow any potential attackers.

She gazed out over the rock lip. The sky was lighter, but if she was expecting a spectacular sunrise, she could forget it.

Already, the bowl that was the valley had filled.

With mist, ruddy from the sunrise.

Was this the condition they'd been waiting for?

She heard Demetria whisper a prayer. Odd to find that, at this end of time, the Amazon was as big a straight arrow as she.

How long would the mist last? The best Kyria had been able to get was: it lasts as long as it lasts.

Apparently, the weather-wise—mist-wise?—among the Amazons could sense when the mist was due to arrive.

Demetria lifted her head and nodded. *Go*. The Amazon gathered her own gear and soundlessly dressed.

She reached over and tested the radio one last time. It had survived impact. Would it survive this too? She checked and loaded the flare gun.

Last night, she'd marked the clearing herself for a helo landing. She was running on a lot of assumptions here: assuming the mists held long enough to call in a recovery mission. Assuming it could see the landing field, such as it was.

Assuming it was an Air Force helo.

Hippolyta had taken one hell of a risk sending her up here. A risk she'd been glad to take in the hope that Kyria would be able to do something for the tribe that had taken her in.

And that might be the rashest assumption of all.

"Let's do it," she muttered to herself and began transmitting.

She sensed when the number of women at her back began to diminish. There'd be hunting parties out today for certain. Amazons hunting men; men hunting Amazons.

Over the centuries, they'd had to have built up a certain amount of blood feuds that made twentieth-century backlash look like a love-in.

From the corner of her eye she could see Demetria slipping from point to point, talking to the various scouts. Which ones were set to watch her?

Possibly none, Kyria thought. *Hippolyta trusts me, after her fashion. And I gave my word.*

And I'm just going to go off and leave these people, aren't I? Hardly seems right.

Neither did involving the Air Force in their survival strategies—or the Amazons in twentieth-century style ethnic cleansing.

I'll think of this tomorrow. Tomorrow is another day. And possibly, another century.

She bent over the radio, searching from frequency to frequency. From time to time, she picked up noise . . . chatter . . . something . . . but nothing that told her that this clearing on a desolate mountain peak in ex-Yugoslavia had any connection to her own time and place. The mist thickened below them, reaching up to lap about them. Damn! How could a chopper spot her in this kind of limited visibility, let alone make pickup?

It would have to wait until the mist started to dispel. Assuming she could raise an Air Force unit. Assuming they hadn't called off the search. Assuming . . . oh damn.

What was that?

Electricity crackled across the miles, accompanied by crisp words, made almost incomprehensible with static. She could take those words, take them and twist them into a rope, a lifeline.

Swiftly, she bent, whispered her own message in answer to the demand she heard.

"They're coming!" she hissed at Demetria, who had returned from briefing her scouts. She nodded. And checked the positions of her staff, her bow, and her arrows. At least the sword was sheathed. For now.

A scout, scarcely more than a girl, rushed up to them, crouched over. Demetria hissed something that brought the scout's eyebrows up in surprise.

"We've got visitors," the warrior said.

"How're they armed?"

Demetria shrugged. "The usual. Bows. Arrows."

Kyria supposed that was better than, say, a detachment of Serbs.

Still, arrows had been known to pierce plate armor. A lucky arrow—and a particularly strong archer—might be able to puncture a helicopter's fuel tank. She could hear an icon out of her childhood intoning in the familiar deep voice, "I would calculate the odds against that at . . ."

How do you like those odds, Kyria?

Not one damn bit.

She glanced down at the valley. The mist was thinning. Ominous sign, really. If she could see out, people could see in.

Could see her, and attack.

She had a few spare clips for her side arm. After that, she was down to the local weapons—bows and arrows, knives and swords.

And after an endless time of waiting, of eating whatever was put into her hand, preferably without looking at it, of nature calls, and watching the mist evaporate as the sun climbed toward noon, she heard the *thwock-thwock-thwock* of a helicopter. What was that painted on the fuselage? A sea lion? It wasn't just rescue, then, but some of her own come to bring her home.

She fired the flare gun before Demetria could grab

her wrist. Fire launched into the sky, signaling her presence.

Demetria pushed her down. Maybe Hippolyta hadn't been that trusting after all.

"Those are my people!" Kyria protested. There was no way she could reach her revolver.

"That doesn't look like your chariot," Demetria observed.

How could she tell, from a crash site?

"It's mine. Same emblem, see?" Right now, that helicopter couldn't have been any more beautiful if it had carried the Angel Gabriel.

Click your jump boots together three times and say: There's no place like home. There's no place like home. There's no place like home.

"It flies lower, yes. And can land here."

Now came the part that was really risky.

She stood, dressed again in her flight suit rather than something out of a sword and sorcery epic, scurried into the center of the improvised landing strip, and semaphored her arms. Her instructors at the academy would kill her—if the archers didn't. She suspected the Amazons gave points for bravado. Or, if the had phrase applied, sheer ballsiness.

An arrow whizzed by her, damn near bouncing off her helmet.

Just the way I came in. Damn!

Now, she could hear more arrows—the bronze age version of covering fire—and battlecries. She drew, dropped, and set off the smoke end of another flare to confuse things thoroughly, and wriggled back to the rock spur the way she'd learned—knees, elbows, chin (ouch!) in basic training. Granted, there was no barbed wire and no one was using live ammo.

But you could get just as dead from an arrow, and the idea of one hitting her in the . . .

By the time she got back under cover, the radio was squawking hysterically.

"Yes, that was me. And we've got ground action," she said. "I don't think they've got guns."

The squawk rose in pitch.

"Bows and arrows!" she cried. "No, I'm not seeing things. And I don't inhale."

She spared a look into the valley. The air was clearing fast now; she could make out individual trees. Yes, and individual fighters emerging from the forest to engage each other. Ugly. Even as she watched, four Amazons tackled what looked like a warband and brought them down. She threw another flare, gushing orange smoke, to break things up.

Unfortunately, up above the treeline, far too close for her comfort, someone wearing what looked like boiled leather had an Amazon down on the ground, was raising a sword overhead . . .

Kyria snapped off a shot. Lucky! The man fell with a howl, clutching his leg.

The *thwock-thwock-thwock* grew louder. The air darkened as the helo broke through what remained of the cloud cover and loomed overhead.

God, it made one gorgeous shadow! Kyria thought—then flinched as arrows ricocheted off.

Some of the women had broken cover, were standing looking up in amazement. The idea of vulnerable people, approaching before that chopper's rotors had come to a full stop . . .

"Get back!" she screamed. "Demetria, tell your people to get back."

She ran forward, knowing the chopper would hover, and she'd have a matter of minutes, if that, to race toward it and in.

Demetria screamed something and gestured. Away from the chopper, the land began to glow. The sun grew brighter.

The mist was fading fast now.

Thwock . . . thwock . . . thwock . . .

Coming in for a landing.

Unfortunately, it looked as if the infantry had arrived too. Good God, what had the mist dragged in this time? Were those actually hoplites?

Men were gesturing, urging her forward, shouting just as if she was making an eighty-yard run for a touchdown at the Superbowl . . . she was throwing herself at the hatch . . . someone had grabbed her arms . . . the chopper started to lift . . .

A gust of wind blew a patch of the mist right at them, enveloping the chopper.

Damn. The chopper's engines choked, then stalled. Its rotors ground slowly to a stop.

"Now what?" demanded the man who had boosted her into the chopper. She recognized him from base: Lieutenant Tony "Mad Anthony" Wayne.

"I told you," she said. "There's a local condition. Works like EMP—oh, I don't know, call it an obscure application of Clarke's Law."

"You got brain bloat but good this time?" Why in hell had Boomer come along on this one? She had a moment's vision of him, surrounded by Amazons, and managed, just in time, not to grin.

"Haven't got time to explain. I suggest . . . allies over here . . . let's GO!"

She turned in time to watch the Amazons sweep past the chopper and intercept the remaining archers and a stray hoplite or two.

Oh, there'd be a hot time in the old town tonight.

She waved at Demetria, who emerged from around a rock, cleaning her sword. She sheathed it, put her hands to her throat, and shrieked a victory cry, throbbing up and down on two shrill notes.

"I see you brought us guests!" she hailed Kyria.

"These are my friends," she said. "Men of my unit." Yes, and there was Kathy Banks, too, the other female pilot in her wing. Under her helmet, Banks was all eyes—and a smile that gradually expanded into a seriously evil grin.

"This is a joke, right?" Banks asked.

"You'd better tell me what's going on, Lieutenant," Wayne snapped at Kyria. In a minute, he'd draw, and she'd really be up the proverbial creek.

"You won't be able to take off in these weather conditions. It's like EMP. Shorts out everything. But these are friendlies . . ."

Very friendly.

She leapt from the chopper—no one was going anywhere, at least not till the mists came up again— and ran toward the Amazons. Now, she could grin. Demetria met her halfway.

"When do you think we can expect the mists to come again?"

Demetria raised her head and sniffed the air.

"A couple of weeks," she said.

So. They'd think the chopper had broken off radio contact, had crashed in the mountains. She wondered if they'd send in a search party, much good it would do them until the mists arrived. And meanwhile . . .

She turned to the helo pilot. A captain. Humph. She rated. Well, F-15 pilots were expensive to train. And female F-15 pilots were a PR nightmare, his sour expression seemed to indicate. *And thank you very much, sir, only "thanks" isn't quite the word I had in mind. I suspect the Amazons will express their gratitude too.*

Everyone into the gene pool!

"Sir," she said, "I suggest we get this craft under cover. Camouflage. The local friendlies say it'll be at least two weeks before we can fly out."

"How the hell do they know?"

Kyria shrugged. "They know local conditions, sir."

"And what do they expect us to do until then?" the man demanded.

His eyes rounded as Demetria and several of the scouts came up, bows, swords, bronze bras, and all. Not an ounce of cellulite on any of them anywhere. Banks and Kyria covered their mouths at the same time to conceal smiles. *I believe the technical term is "relax and enjoy it,"* Kyria thought.

"They're very friendly, sir," Kyria said. "I'm sure they'll think of something."

There was some satisfaction in knowing that she wouldn't be leaving the Amazons in the lurch. And at least as much in watching Boomer's face as the Amazons gave him the once-over. Maybe he'd stop preening soon.

And best of all, since all of them were in it, there wouldn't be any scapegoating. Talk about unit cohesion.

Or maybe the best thing to say would be: Don't ask. Don't tell.

As an infant, Rosemary Edghill was discovered
floating down the Amazon in a hatbox and was raised
by the Lords of the Middle Terraces in downtown
Zinderneuf. Though a dead ringer for the Crown Prince
of Ruritania, she has found time to write over a dozen
novels in several genres and far too many short stories
like this one.

No, I have not been drinking; that's the bio she sent
me in its entirety. So there.

Bad Heir Day

Rosemary Edghill

> For, lo! Whosoever pulleth this swordeth out
> of the stoneth, shall, all things being equal,
> probably be King of Britain, more or less, if
> everything works out okay.
>> From the *Prophecies of Geoffrey
>> the Equivocal*, Sixth Rev. Ed.

It's not my fault how things turned out. My brother
(he's not really my brother, but that's another story that
the bards don't like to sing) says it's only what anyone
could expect, but Mo has a much lower opinion of
people than I do. Probably that comes from having

studied magic in his misspent youth, although if you ask me, growing up on a farm with three older brothers like Ingrate, Aggravating, and Garish would be enough to sour anyone's disposition. By the time I was old enough to get to know them, I was glad, believe me, that Mother'd had the foresight to dress me as a boy. Not that this alone would have been enough to save me, but I could run fast, too. Faster than the sheep, anyway.

But you'll be wanting to hear about the prophecy, and my parents, and things like that. I would like to stress that I neither planned nor expected how things turned out. Maybe Mo did. You could always count on Mo for things like that. Complicated plots and really spectacular revenges, that's my brother.

Well, step-brother, anyway. And it isn't as much his fault as it was the old king's. Rules are rules and prophecies are prophecies, and people should understand that what they say is what they mean, no matter what they intended to say instead. But the person whose fault it *really* was, was Ambrius' merlin. You'd think people wouldn't go around annoying wizards, wouldn't you? But kings are all the same, Mo says. He keeps wanting to tell me this long story about somebody named Saul who was king a long way east of here, and I tell him, "Mo, what is your *point*? Does this guy have a sword?" And Mo tells me that no, but there's a harp mixed up in it somewhere, which is not much of an inducement as I've never been really musical. The *zakpjip* sounds like a pig caught in a gate, if you ask me, and Orkney's too damp for harps. The bards are always complaining.

Anyway, I suppose you want to know about King Ambrius. The main thing to know is, he was one of these guys who put everything off until way beyond the last minute, and so the bottom line is, he's eighty, he's dying, and he hasn't got an heir. What he does have is a War Duke named Uther, and guess who's the insiders' pick for the next king? (This is the point at which Mo always wants to tell me about some people named David and Adonijah and Solomon and Abishag. I ask him, doesn't he know any stories about people with *normal* names?)

Anyway, what Uther didn't know when he hustled Ambrius off that mortal coil was that the king had gotten an heir on a girl named Nimhue, a serving girl of the blood of the Old Line who had been brought to Ambrius' bed to give him heat. You can get away with a lot if you're king, as I intend to prove. I came into the world while Uther, now High King of Lochrin, was still piling stones on Ambrius' tomb in blessed ignorance of my mother's interesting condition.

I was smuggled from the palace on the night of my birth by the king's merlin, who was a lot fonder of my mother than he was of Uther, especially considering Uther had gone secretly to the Druids to be named Pendragon and King, and so much for the King's Royal Companions, a.k.a. the hostages Ambrius had exacted from all the noble families of the realm with the promise that, failing further developments, one of them would be King.

It sounds complicated, but it's not. A few murders, some betrayals, a clandestine alliance or two . . . of course, by the time Uther was hitting his stride in the backstabbing department, Nimhue was long gone. Uther had done a major prereign housecleaning and parceled out the old king's women to whoever would take them. Mom got Lot, Orkney, and four stepsons. Uther got the throne. The merlin got the gate, because Uther didn't want him around when he was breaking his latest set of campaign promises. He'd promised the Druids that he'd drive out the followers of the Chrestos who'd come in on a "One God—One Vote" platform and were annoying everybody. What the Druids had failed to note was that the Chrestians were like *that* with the Roman legions, and Uther thought that a Roman legion might be more good to him later on than a few sprigs of mistletoe and some sacred snakes, but by the time the

Druids had worked that out for themselves Uther was already on the throne *and* anointed with the Dragon's Blood, and they were pretty much stuck with him.

Nobody in Orkney paid much attention to this at the time. If it didn't come in a dragon ship waving torches, no one up north really cared. Still it was always amusing to hear what fools the *sassenach* were making of themselves, so when the merlin came to visit (usually arriving just before the first hard snow of the season, necessitating his staying the winter; the man had a marvelous sense of timing, ask anyone) and tell us what was going on down in Lochrin, we listened. Ingrate, Aggravating, and Garish (Lot's three eldest, in order of annoyance) never were sure he wasn't going to turn them into toads (a vast improvement, it would be, but not really a *stretch*, in my opinion) so they were marginally better behaved while he was here. Mo and I were the youngest, so we got most of his attention.

I think he would have liked to take Mo as his successor, but Lot was real down on the whole castration thing (Mo wasn't too big on it either, truth to say), so most of what the merlin knew would die with him.

At least, I thought so at the time. Now I'm not so sure. Being King changes your perspective.

Meanwhile, by the tenth year of Uther Versus Practically Everybody (the Tribute Kings of the Royal Kindred being really sore losers who could carry a wicked grudge), Uther was pretty desperate for some Peace In Our Time. The Druids weren't talking to him, the Legions were staying put in Armorica, and the Chrestians were proving to be a pretty weak reed—the White Priest might talk a good fight, but he couldn't bring Uther alliances and he couldn't bring him luck.

So when Ambrius' merlin floated a rumor that he had one last great magic to perform for the right person and the right price, Uther jumped at it like a gaffed trout. What the merlin did then did not bring Uther luck either, though it took Uther some time to figure that out. He was too dazzled by this fairy tale about a magic sword known only to the merlins' college, which lay in a cave in the hills to the west and upon which Ambrius had sworn his vows of kingship.

And which, the merlin let it be known, he was willing to give Uther as a free gift, owing to how he was the last of his line and all. Uther, never a subtle man, believed him.

And so the merlin went off with the White Priest, a cohort of soldiers, and two teams of double-yoked oxen to fetch Guenhwyfar the Shining, the merlin's magic sword. They found her right where he said she'd be, only there was a slight catch: Guenhwyfar was sunk to the hilt in two sword-stones.

One was an iron anvil such as swords had been forged on since my grandfather's day, and the one below that was a heavenstone such as the old bronze swords were poured out on. And written upon them both in large friendly letters was the merlin's final judgment upon Uther: that anyone who might draw the sword forth from the stone and anvil was the true and rightful overlord of the land, accept no substitutes.

Anyone, mark you.

Well, you probably know the rest of the story as well as I: that everyone—starting with Uther—tried to pull the sword out and nobody could, which was way too bad because Uther, like Ambrius before him, did not have an heir. Uther had gone through six Queens in all (divorced, beheaded, died, divorced, beheaded, left with no forwarding address), with the interval between the weddings (and the beddings and beheadings) getting shorter as Uther lost patience, until there was absolutely nobody in all Lochrin willing to date the man, let alone marry him.

This was the main reason that Uther didn't simply sink the whole mess (sword, stone, anvil, inconvenient prophecy) in the River Tame and let the fish try to draw the sword. While the merlin's travelling wondershow was sitting in front of Caer Londinium, Uther could at least pretend he was taking the whole succession thing seriously. (Mo says Uther thought he'd live forever. I tell Mo I'm not as stupid as he'd like to think I am. I think Uther thought that the last time a king had named an heir, look what happened to that king. Better to keep them guessing.)

This was mainly the period during which Uther turned the place upside down looking for the merlin, who had made himself a very scarce fellow indeed, as who could blame him? Looking for him, though, ruined Uther's health, and after twenty-one adventure-fraught years of reign, Uther was dying, and *still* no heir in sight. People were talking, even up in Orkney.

Naturally there was a fair held in the City of Legions down South. A sort of a hiring fair, because with the sword stuck firmly in the stone, and Uther having done such a good job of weeding out importunate claimants in his salad days, any man's claim to the throne was by now as good as any other's (though, *entre nous,* the Duke of Cornwall's was better than most, plus he had an inexhaustible supply of Eirish mercenaries who'd work for cheap *usquebaugh* and some hot dance tunes). Claims needed armies to back them, and my step-father had an army for sale. Having learned from Uther's example, he didn't leave anybody behind in Orkney who might have the least interest in the throne. We all went, even Mother.

And certainly Mo, since Mo was easily bored and dangerous therewith and nobody knew it better than his father, especially after the affair of the sheep, the Archbishop, and the traveling portrait painter. If Lot went to war, I knew that the Three Stooges were going to draw lots to see who got Mo as squire, since, face it, would *you* want *him* to be the last person who'd handled your armor?

But I digress.

While Uther or his spies would probably recognize

Mother, he didn't even know I existed. So Mo and I had the run of the town, while Mother stayed put inside the tent and Lot went around trying to drum up business. Naturally, the first thing Mo and I wanted to see was the merlin's sword—me, because it was probably the last piece of magic anyone would ever see, Mo, because the last piece of magic anyone would probably ever see could probably be used to cause trouble.

It's much better to stay on his good side, really. But he was my best (and only) friend and I'd always liked him. Besides, he has a strong appreciation of how long I can carry a grudge.

Anyway, we got to the courtyard in front of the White Tower, which was the king's residence, and there Guenhwyfar was, surrounded by bored guards and gold-painted iron chains.

"Do you think it's true?" I asked Mo, after I'd puzzled out the inscription on the stone and the anvil. The merlin had taught me to read, but it wasn't like there were any books in Orkney to practice on and I was a little rusty.

"You mean, do I think somebody can pull the sword out of the stone and live past the point Uther's chief steward Gaius slips something into their wine? No," he said comprehensively.

"But it says that whoever draws the sword gets to be king."

"Don't believe everything you read," Mo advised me kindly.

"It isn't fair," I said, kicking at a stone. Mo rolled his eyes, then grew thoughtful. "No," he said reflectively, "it isn't, is it?"

Lot's first mistake was bringing Mo, and his second was in giving Mo enough free time to reflect on how much he'd hate going to war as squire to one of his brothers. This meant that by Friday everybody in Caer Londinium had heard a shocking new rumor that Uther was going to give everyone one last chance to draw Guenhwyfar the Shining out of the stone—*everyone*, not just knights and nobles and well-connected types like that. It was either the exciting new rumor (three guesses on the source) or the sight of his vassals preparing to carve him like a roast out of sheer boredom and uncertainty; either way, Uther geeked and set a date.

By the next Holy Day of the Chrestos a tent city stretched along both sides of the River Tame for half a league and the line to try Guenhwyfar was nearly as long. Uther made an impressive speech for a man who had to be carried out in a litter and swore that he would abide by Guenhwyfar's choice . . . and that any man who wouldn't do the same had better ride for the border, because his lands were forfeit.

It was exciting policy decisions like that which got Uther where he was today: no matter which way the cat jumped, all the kings were sworn to peace and mutual assistance. Mo said that Tyndareus had made all the Greek Kings swear a similar oath about somebody named Helen. My opinion is nobody would go to war over a girl. I don't know where he gets this stuff.

The princes had finished up by noon, and second sons and landless men were trying now, equally without success. Uther had gone back to the White Tower, but there were enough bored guardsmen and White Priests around to make sure he was informed of anything interesting.

"You try it," Mo said to me.

"Yeah, right," I answered. Mo's brothers were in the queue waiting for their turns, and if Guenhwyfar could be wooed by brute force and stupidity, we'd have a new king by tea-time.

"Let me list the reasons," Mo said, and proceeded to tell me a bunch of things I didn't know he knew, ending up with: "and since the inscription says '*whomsoever*,' and Uther says he'll abide by her choice, you've got it taped."

Assuming I could pull the thing at all, but Mo never let minor obstacles like that stand in his way.

"And what's in it for you?" I asked suspiciously, because Mo did not generally exert himself for nothing.

"To be your chancellor," he said promptly. "And not Gawain's squire."

I guessed they'd already drawn the lots. So to speak.

"If I can be King," I said, "you can certainly be Chancellor, Modrat."

We had to wait until Ingrate, Aggravating, and Garish were out of the way, drowning their sorrows in the nearest ale-butt, but by the time they were well gone the only people who approached Guenhwyfar did so for sport, and it was easy enough to usurp their place. While the sun still stood a good handsbreadth above the horizon, I stood on the platform and clasped Guenhwyfar.

I knew at once that the merlin had left her for me and that Mo'd probably had inside information. One might suggest that if the merlin had wanted me to have Guenhwyfar, it would have been better just to bring her to Orkney, but that wasn't how his mind worked. And besides, his way had led Uther into a most inconvenient pledge (never piss off a wizard, remember?), and as I have said, rules are rules and prophecies are prophecies, and Uther had been very explicit: who pulled the sword would be king, and king hereafter.

So I did.

Wouldn't you know that one of my step-brothers would pick *then* to be thrown out of the tavern? Ingrate—or, to name him properly, Gawain—staggered to his feet, took one look at me, and bawled out for all the world to hear:

"That's my sister Vivane! She can't be King!"

So I'm a girl. Sue me. I was amazed he knew, actually. Most people don't look past the hair and the clothes.

I'd been hoping to put the moment off a little longer—but Gawain has a voice that can stun a sheep at sixty paces (which explains much about his love life), and soon enough Agravaine and Gaheris had joined him, telling anyone who would listen that *their sister* had just pulled Guenhwyfar from the stone and what was somebody going to do about it, eh?

I found out then that cold steel is a better argument than all the words in the world, because I managed to defend my position beside the anvil until Uther could be summoned back from the tower. By then three of my brothers (guess which) were sitting at the foot of the platform bleeding and howling, and an enormous crowd had gathered to stare at me as if I were the two-headed pig at St. Audrey's Fair.

Uther's litter was ringed with torches. He stared at me, and at the sword, and did not say anything for quite some time.

"Well," he finally said. "Well, well, well, well, well."

("That's a deep subject," Modrat muttered. I elbowed him in the ribs.)

"What am I to do with you?" Uther said.

The crowd—and my foster brothers—had a number of suggestions, none of which I thought it would do me any good to hear.

"This woman Vivane is the daughter of Nimhue, last wife of King Ambrius, and your heir," Modrat bellowed loud enough to be heard in Oxford. "And by your law and your oath, she who has drawn Guenhwyfar from the stone and the anvil must rule Lochrin when you are gone."

Mo was speaking for the broadsheets, needless to say. He never talked like that at home.

Uther smiled as if his face would crack, because Modrat was right, and if he went back on his word now he'd be cold potroast by morning and Cornwall would be on the throne.

So the king beckoned us down to him and the crowd cheered and we all set off for the White Tower—a place a good deal safer to be than *Chez* Orkney this particular evening, by my reckoning. Modrat walked beside the king, the torches glinting off his fox-red hair, and I carried Guenhwyfar upraised for everyone to see.

"I'll have to be sure to find her a good husband," I heard Uther muttered as he was carried off.

"Did I happen to mention," Modrat asked him, "the ancient Druidic prophecy that states the wielder of Guenhwyfar cannot marry anyone except a man who has defeated her fairly in battle . . . ?"

Yeah, right, and the ancient prophecy was dated about fifteen minutes ago. I didn't think Uther would go for it, but tomorrow is another day, as the bards say. I had the sword. I'd be king. Simple.

Besides, possession is nine points of the law, and now that I had Guenhwyfar what were they going to do, write me out of history?

So she's had over two dozen stories published in places like Amazing *and* Asimov's *and* Playboy *(!), and she's co-edited an anthology* (Ripper) *with Gardner Dozois, and she's one funny lady. Yet for all that, there's one thing I fear I'll never let her forget: "Under Her Skin," her story about a vampire that doesn't drink blood but . . . fat.*

Wish fulfillment: It works for me.

Why Do You Think They Call It *Middle* Earth?

(or how I slew a dragon and found myself a mate)

Susan Casper

I bet that most of you believe the earth is right side out, solid all the way down, at least until you hit that molten core, and hotter than blazes in the middle? I did too. That is, I did until I fell through a crack one day.

Oh, yes, I did. There I was walking down the street, minding my own business and not really bothering anyone, when . . . Well, actually, I can't really say what

117

happened. I was walking down the street when this guy comes up to me and says, "Lady can you spare some change?" Can you imagine? I mean, I know I am considered a large woman, but do I look like a bank or something? But hey, I'm not an ungenerous soul. I took a minute of my time to tell him how to get out of his situation, starting with a bath and maybe some clothes, and I was just getting to the part about a job when whammo. I think the earth opened right beneath my feet, but maybe the hole was there all along and I just didn't notice. I do know I was falling. I was so startled that I didn't even notice what I passed on the way down, which pissed me off when I landed on account of I wouldn't know who to sue. It got dark kinda fast and after that I couldn't see anything until I hit the ground with a thud.

Fortunately, the ground was soft, and after a moment I saw some stars . . . not in the hitting your head kind of way, but actual points of light in the sky. It took a minute to realize what they were. It was morning when I started and I knew I hadn't been falling all that long, but it was night when I landed all right. The moon was yellow enough to pass for a giant lemon, and after a moment other lights were visible a long way off. Wherever I was, I was damned upset. I was gonna be late for work, for starters. I pulled out my cell phone and tried to call the office, but there must have been some heavy interference in the area. I couldn't connect to anyone. I tried then to stand up and fell back again, the heel of my shoe twisting right off underneath me. I took them off to look at them. That's what I get for shopping at Payless. I shoved them into my purse. They would fit if I didn't zip it, but that meant my stockings were gonna be ruined. I took them off too, sliding them down under my dress, then, shoes sticking half out of my purse, and thank heaven I carried the big one that day, I picked what I thought was the closest of the lights and headed off in that direction. There wasn't a path, so far as I could tell.

Whatever it was I was walking across, it wasn't any kind of grass my feet were familiar with; it crackled and crunched with every step. I had the horrid feeling that if I stopped for even a moment, I'd feel it moving underfoot.

My name is Emily Prentiss, by the way, and if I do say so myself, I'm one of the best corporate traders in the business. The guys hate the fact that I've got more kills than any two of them. I know what they call me behind my back. "Super-bitch," "Dragonslayer," and "She-Wolf," are some of the milder terms they have for me. But the point is, when I set out to do something, I get the job done, which is why I kept walking, lawsuit in hand, ready to take the head of the first person I came across.

"By God, somebody's gonna pay for this!" I muttered over and over again whenever a rock or thorn caught my tender skin. The light turned out to be from a little wooden shack. I couldn't see anything through the window, but the light meant someone was there. Boss or worker, I didn't care. I meant to find out just what the hell was going on. There was no bell or knocker. I pounded on the rough wooden door with my fist, noting how it bent inward with every blow. I'd have it off the hinges if that was the only thing that would work, but after a moment it opened.

"Are you in charge here?" I asked, intending to go on with my tirade until I noticed that no one was there, and then my eyes lowered. A child. Damn! Why on earth would a little boy be answering the door in what was obviously the middle of the night? No, not a child. A small man, maybe a little over three feet tall. He had a short beard and straight blond hair that had probably been cut using a soup bowl.

"Lady, have you been drinking?" The voice was deep and gruff; not at all what I'd been expecting. His jacket was leather, and made him look like a diminutive thug until you looked further down and saw that instead of the usual jeans, he wore green tights that stretched up out of soft, silver boots. I could feel my mouth working, though no sounds were coming out. On his part, he seemed as puzzled as I was.

"Drinking!" I said. I got as far as "Listen, you little . . ." then stopped myself mid-sentence. No point getting into it here and now. That's what lawyers are for. Besides, the handicapped are *so* touchy. Fishing under the shoes, I found my organizer and slid the pen out of its sheath. "Just give me your name and then take me to your boss." I almost said "leader," there being something about the place that felt so alien.

"Lobish, son of Frobish, at your service," he said with a short bow that told me he felt free to make fun of me. He wasn't gonna get away with it. I made a quick note. "Now tell me, pray, where are you from and how did you get here?" he went on.

"How did I get here? I fell through a damn crack that somebody left in the sidewalk. Now if you will be kind enough to tell me who is in charge here?" I asked him, pleased to see the worried look come over his face. Now we were getting somewhere.

"The Prophecy," he said. Odd sort of name, but I duly wrote it down. "This isn't good." I had to agree. "You'll have to come with me. It's a bit of a walk, I'm afraid."

The nerve of some people! "Oh no," I said. "I've already ruined my shoes. Look at them. And they were expensive imports, too. I'm not walking anywhere in my bare feet. My tootsies are killing me."

"Tootsies?" he asked. I lifted a foot and pointed. "Ah," he said, "just a minute. I think I have something here." He went back into the room. I wasn't invited, but I followed anyway. It was a strange little room. A slab of wood in the center must have doubled as table and bed, for the only other furniture was a small chair and a large elaborate chest. That chest was a beautiful piece of work, inlaid with light and dark woods and decorated with tiles of marble, it seemed out of place in such spartan surroundings. It opened without a sound; the inside seemingly crammed with more than that small space could possibly hold. With a carelessness that belied the neatness of the tiny room, he tossed objects one at a time over his shoulder. Pots and pans, a pick, a few items of clothing—the pile behind him grew into a mound before he stood triumphantly holding what looked like a pair of small silver socks for a child.

"Those things won't fit me," I said, but he had me seated before I could finish my thought, and, with a single motion, slid them onto my feet. I had to admit, to myself at least, they were comfortable. I stood, and the hard-packed earth felt very different than it had when I first walked in. Soft, it felt, almost springy, like fine pile carpet. They probably wouldn't do much about rocks and stones, and they sure didn't go with my suit, but I was anxious to get this over with. Besides, they might let me keep them.

It was still quite dark when we started out and for the first hour we didn't talk much. The only sounds we heard were our own footsteps and the occasional beat of large wings . . . bats maybe, or some very big bird. I didn't want to know. As the sky started to lighten, I turned to Lobish.

"Hey, isn't there somewhere to stop," I asked. I was in pretty good shape, or so I thought, but this overweight gnome had me panting to catch up. "I could really use a cup of coffee."

"Coffee?" he asked. Was it really possible to live without the stuff? "I don't know what coffee is, but there's no time to stop now, my lady," he said. "The situation is most urgent." He offered me a flask and I warily wiped the rim and took a sip. Something warm filled my mouth and burned the back of my throat. I spat it out on the grass.

"Getting me drunk won't help," I shouted, upending the flask. He made a desperate lunge and managed to pull the flask from me before I'd gotten rid of much of it.

"You may need this later on," he told me as he screwed the lid back in place and handed it to me. "It's elvish wine, and it may burn going down, but it will never affect your sense," he added. "Come, it's not far now."

"Finally!" I said as we neared a glade and I could hear talking through the trees.

"Yes, m'lady, please wait here," Lobish said.

"I think I've waited quite long enough." I pushed past him and entered the clearing. I am ashamed to admit that what I saw there actually stopped me for a moment. Several men stood around in a circle and all were as short as Lobish. The fat ones all had red or dark gold curly hair, the thin and willowy ones were blond, and I swear their ears came to points. Inbreeding at its finest. "Must be rednecks," I said, to which Lobish's only reply was "Huh?"

At this they all turned and looked in my direction, and suddenly, every one of them looked nervous. A rather tallish woman—well, tallish for this group, she came up to my nose—walked forward from the crowd. She might have been a model, for her face was beautiful, except for her height, or lack of it, and of course those unfortunate ears. She was wearing a floor-length silver dress, most inappropriate for such a meeting.

"M'lady," she said, extending her hand. I shook it.

"Oh no! This can't be right!" one of the short, round, bearded men objected. "*She* can't be the one!" He was shouted down by an even smaller man, this one not quite so out of shape, and, thank heaven, beardless. As he stood to speak, I noticed that he seemed to be wearing a pair of furry slippers.

"Sit down and let the lady have her say," the toddler-sized man shouted.

"Why must I listen to an elf?" the first man sputtered as he sank back to his seat. A fine one he was to mock her lack of stature. Why, he was even shorter than she!

"The Lady Laurelwind speaks for all peoples," her defender replied in a likewise subdued tone.

She held up her hand for silence, and when it came I heard, off in the distance, a continual banging sound, like a child playing with pots. Laurelwind paid it no notice. "It's not up to any one of us to say. Our path is clear. It was written in the stars."

"But she's a *woman*," he protested. "She shouldn't even *be* here."

"The stars are never poor scribes," Laurelwind said without raising her voice. "We are but poor interpreters,"

All this time I waited quietly to hear what offer I would be given. If there was anything I learned from my years in the business world, it was to wait and let the other guy make the first move. You'd be amazed how often you discover you can jack your price up even higher than you thought. Besides, I was still a little confused which of these factions was going to be more favorable to what I wanted. Nevertheless, the longer this discussion went on, the angrier I got. No one here seemed to care in the least how much trouble they were putting me through. I was gonna soak them for a bundle. There was personal injury, at least a bruise or two, a pair of shoes (expensive Italian pumps, I'd decided), and by now a whole day's pay into the bargain. But this whole argument was gonna heap a lot of digits onto the pain and suffering claim. The lady seemed to be the one in charge at the moment. I had to hide an evil grin as I made my move.

"Lady," I said, as it seemed to be their general form of address, though I let my voice make it clear as to my doubt of her claim to that status. "I've about had enough here. I want you to tell me, right now, what you're gonna do about getting me home."

"Home? But you cannot leave. I cannot send you back until you've done a service," she said as if she were offering me tea and cookies.

"You want me to do WHAT?" annoyed to hear my voice growing shrill. This was just great. Now they wanted me to go to some stupid church before they took me back? I wasn't gonna do it. No way!

"You must do a service," she said again, her voice still quite calm. "An act of bravery. Oh, I do hope you're up to it."

"Hey," I said, finally realizing what she wanted. "You can't do this to me. It's kidnapping or extortion or something." I spotted an empty log and sat with a gesture meant to show I wasn't gonna take any more of this nonsense. "I won't do it," I said and folded my arms across my chest.

"See, I told ya," the fat guy said, with all the grace of a six-year-old. I half expected to see his fingers waggling at his ears.

"You must do as it suits you," Laurelwind said, waving him off with a gesture that I wasn't meant to see. "I'm sure we can find shelter for you until you can build accommodations of your own. I'm afraid you will find ours a bit cramped for your needs, but Mantown is far to the other side of the badlands. Those of your race mainly live there, or in the Nicthalene far to the south."

I felt my eyes roll upward as my head shook from side to side. "Look, I don't want accommodations, cramped or otherwise. I don't want to go to the Nickline or whatever you called it. I just want to go home. Home. Back to my own little cramped apartment with my own little cat and my own little bed. So, just put me on a bus, or call a taxi for me—or wave your magic wand if that's how things work around here—and get me out of here."

"I know not of what you speak," she said, doing her best to look puzzled. Not a bad job of it, either. "But I do know that you can not be sent back to your world until you have done a service. It's not because I wish it this way. It's simply the way things are. The magic simply will not work unless you prove yourself worthy."

"Okay, you can be sarcastic too. Now let's get down to business. I want to go home *now*," I said, using the tone that always closed deals for me, "and I don't want any nonsense. How dumb do you think I am?"

"That I cannot answer," she said, sounding as sad as a Miss America contestant who'd just been asked how to achieve the world peace she longed for. "I only know that if you come from the world above, then magic is the only way back."

I don't know how long my jaw hung open. However silly it sounded, she was serious. "What do you mean, 'the world above'? Look." I pointed up. Above us the sky was blue. The sun, partly covered by clouds, was already halfway through its climb toward noon.

"The world above, your world, is invisible to us, just as we are invisible to you. Once, long ago, there was free travel between the two and some of your people came here to live. Then, one of your kings tried to involve us in his war. A great Elven sandcaster named Vitalix closed the gap between the two worlds to keep us safe. Travel through is only possible at times of need, and none may return until the need is removed."

"Oh," I said, nodding. I let more than a touch of sarcasm creep into my voice. "You're an elf, then." She nodded. "And I suppose *he's* a dwarf?" She nodded again. I threw my hands into the air and stood up. "And where, pray tell, are the fairies?"

"Fairies?" She blinked a few times then suddenly blushed, looking down at the ground to hide a smile. "Oh dear. Fairies were just a little joke some of our boys cooked up one day. The wings were just some leaves attached with glue. They really flew through magic." She sounded so apologetic that all I could do was stare up at the heavens and silently ask for help.

"Please sit and let me tell you why you were called here," Laurelwind said. She dusted the log with her long, flowing sleeve and the two of us sat down. "Several years ago now," she began with a deep breath and a look on her face that told me this was gonna be a long story, "a man of your world stumbled into ours, just as you have. He was a tailor named Steinberg. We'd had no prophecy to predict his arrival and so we scried to see just what our need for him was. Oh, many goats and chickens were sacrificed as we checked and double-checked, but all answers were the same. Steinberg the tailor would sire a man child who would become a great king of men, and one day, this child would lead us all to greatness. Poor Steinberg. He was not happy here. He told us much of the place whence he came. A great metropolis. So great that even our crystal cities and the great gold and marble mines of the dwarves could not match its grandeur. Oh, to one day see such a place! My thoughts are of thee, oh Newark," she said bowing her head reverentially. Heaven help me, I actually patted her hand.

"Steinberg moved into the Nicthalene, but so few are the human women there, and most of those already taken to wive, he could not find anyone to love. Eventually, he grew so lonely that he decided to make the long journey to Mantown. I suspect he thought his luck would fare better there. Leaving naught but a note behind, he left his home one morning, a pack of goods on his back. We might never have known any more of him, but when he reached the Kra Dunah Di, the dwarves living there took him in. They fed him a great banquet, and clothed him in proper attire for such a journey, and unable to keep him with them, sent four of their best and bravest along to see that he came to no harm. For their sin in allowing him to pass, they have been banished from their mountain home until he is restored to us." A tear dripped slowly and gracefully down her face, but she sniffed and went on.

"The badlands are a dangerous place. The home of dragons. Dragons are kept out of these lands east and south of the mountains by a powerful spell, but in their own lands they reign supreme. How the party thought to pass those lands, I'll never know. It was a great fire dragon, the largest and fiercest of all, that came upon them. Steinberg he took prisoner. The dwarves fought bravely, but three of them were killed. The fourth he spared with a message. The dragon wished to meet a man at the Spider Bridge in the mines. Together they would duel in single combat. If he lost, we would get our Steinberg back. If he won, we would cede the dragons all the lands southeast of the mountains, and all the humans and animals therein would be fair game. We would retain all the northern lands, of course. It was just as this message was delivered that the sky split with a great stroke of lightning, and meteors filled the sky. Other omens too, foretold your coming."

"I am *not* a man," I told her, belaboring the obvious.

"But in your tongue man is used for any human, is it not? It was only in our interpretation of the dragon's word 'man' that we were fooled. So, before I can send you home, you must meet this dragon, Bloodsport, his name is, meet him in single combat," she said.

That stopped me. I don't think I even took a breath for several minutes. Me fight a dragon? What on earth could she be thinking? I simply stared at her. Finally, I sighed.

"Me, fight a dragon?" I said. "What on earth could you be thinking?"

"But you are called 'Dragonslayer', are you not? I saw it in the signs. The stars never get such things wrong." Everyone was looking at me expectantly. Boy, were they gonna be disappointed! Not as disappointed as I was, though. I had a feeling I was gonna be here a long time.

"Um . . ." I said, then, "err . . ." I noticed that she blinked a lot. It made her look rather vapid. "Well . . ." I went on. "Yes, and then again, no."

"Well, have you killed a dragon or haven't you?" she asked, getting right to the heart of the matter.

"You mean a *dragon* dragon . . . big as a house,

scales, huge wings, breathes fire, that kinda thing?" I asked. This had to be the most ridiculous conversation I'd ever had in my life. She had the nerve to look confused. "I'm not even sure I believe there *are* such things as dragons," I said to break the stalemate.

"Oh," she said. She looked bleak. "There are such things as dragons, m'lady.

"Even so, what makes you think this Steinberg guy is still alive? Why wouldn't the dragon simply eat him, then whether you send someone to fight or not, it's all the same thing?" I asked, trying to be reasonable.

"Never!" she answered, shocked. "Dragons are perhaps the most honorable creatures that ever lived. Far more concerned with honor than men are, or even elves."

"Kidnapping is honorable? Killing people and taking their homes, that's honorable?" I asked.

"But yes, don't you see? This is their way. They've thrown down the gauntlet, but they will not do any damage until we pick it up. If we refuse, then we are without honor and they may do as they wish," she told me. I shook my head and let this pass. I didn't think I was ever gonna understand it.

"Anyway, assuming for the moment that dragons do exist, just how would I have seen one?" I asked. Logic didn't seem to be a big thing here. "Look Laurie, Dragonslayer's just a nickname. It means that the people I work with think I'm good at taking on the big guys."

"But that is exactly what we need," she said, brightening. "Someone who is good at . . . taking on . . . the big guys." She gave me the kind of piteous look that would have gotten her almost anything from most of the guys on staff. That's one of the reasons I'm so good. Stuff like that doesn't get to me.

"Show me someone I can argue with and I can get you almost anything, but a dragon? No way! I didn't live thirty-four years just to get incinerated now. I don't *do* dragons," I said firmly.

"Then we're doomed," she said, hanging her head sadly.

"I'm sorry for ya," I told her.

"Be sorry for yourself!" This came from the small man with the fuzzy feet. "You'll be living in Mantown. You'll go before the rest of us do."

Laurelwind reached out and took hold of my hand. "Please don't worry about that," she told me. "It's true I cannot send you home as you wish, but we will not send you to live in Mantown to your doom. We'll make a place for you in the Crystal City, and you can live among the elves."

I thought about this. It sounded exciting for all of about twenty seconds. I could see the lively conversations with people whose response was to blink repeatedly when you talked about business. No TV, no radio, at least I didn't think there was. Not even a cup of coffee. And from what I could see in this group, their idea of high fashion was a bathrobe. How could I face the day without my morning latte? And then there was the idea of living somewhere where no one came up higher than my nose. Who would I dance with?

"Okay," I said with a heavy sigh. "What do you want me to do?"

That banging I'd heard in the distance turned out to be my coffin being prepared. Well, not strictly a coffin. It was mail, woven links surprisingly light, with metal plates to cover my breasts, loin, elbows, and knees. I assumed, being metal, that it was fireproof, but I didn't think it would do much for its contents in the face of extreme heat. I expected to look like a comic book heroine. It fit over my clothes the way that a melon fits over an orange. I'd had easier times getting into a wet bathing suit that was two sizes too small, but when it was on, it was even less comfortable. With every step, I rattled like a sleigh at Christmas.

"Your sword, m'lady," Lobish said, and kneeling before me he held out an elaborate jewel-encrusted pommel. I think he lost a finger as I slid the sword out of his grip, but he stoically said nothing, gripping his hand and bleeding quietly. I tried to offer him a handkerchief but my pockets were inaccessible at that moment.

We were to meet with Bloodsport at the Spider Bridge inside the cavern. Assigned to accompany me were one from each of the four dragon food groups.

"Barish, son of Garish at your service," the dwarf introduced himself with a deep bow. The fuzzy-footed fellow with the big mouth was Ordlow Longdinger, and the representative of the humans—who actually surprised me by being taller than I was—bore the romantic handle Chuck of Grand Rapids. All of them were dressed in armor much heavier than my own, which made me wonder if maybe there wasn't some benefit to being roasted rather than char-grilled. The last member of the party was an elf named Longshanks, a definite misnomer if you ask me. He wore no armor at all. I guess this was so he could run fast when the time came. Each was just chock-full of dragon-fighting wisdom, which they cheerfully imparted as we made the trek to the mountains.

"My grandfather knew someone who heard about a dragon-killing once, and he said the best place to go for him was right under the chin," Barish told me.

"Who on Earth told you that?" Chuck of Grand Rapids asked, his voice dripping with scorn. "It's the eye, you know," he added to me. "I have it on the highest authority."

"You've . . . got . . . to go. . . in . . . through . . . his . . . mouth," Ordlow panted as he trotted to keep up with the rest of us.

"Now that's a good way to get roasted," Chuck of Grand Rapids said.

Longshanks just smiled to himself and let the others argue.

"Oh, you know something better?" Barish asked him.

"*My* grandfather actually killed a dragon once," Longshanks said.

"Really?" Ordlow puffed. He sounded like a heart attack on the hoof. I stopped to let him catch his breath, fishing out the canteen that Lobish had given me and gave it to Ordlow for a sip. His eyes bulged for just a moment and then a broad smile came over his face. I hooked it onto my armor rather than fighting to put it back inside, then turned to Longshanks.

"Well?" I said.

"He got someone to distract it with an argument, and while they were shouting he climbed the cliff and dropped a huge boulder on it," Longshanks said smugly. I thought about this for a moment.

"This solution does sort of depend on there being a cliff and a boulder nearby, doesn't it?" I asked.

"Oh, yes," Longshanks said after a pause. "I never thought of that."

We made our way to the bridge without incident. Leaving my party at the opening, I walked out to the middle and looked around. No dragon, but at the other end of the bridge a man stood by himself. He was tall and slender, almost too thin, with huge, brown, puppydog eyes. He wasn't handsome in any movie star way, but there was something sensitive and tender about the way his mouth trembled, and a beautiful resonance in his voice as he squeaked "help!" when he saw us. Something odd came over me. Something I'd never felt before. It was quite disturbing. My stomach felt suddenly as if it was crawling with bugs and my knees went decidedly weak.

"Please help me!" he said again, this time in a barely audible whisper. It sent a rather pleasant shiver through me.

"Steinberg," I called, and was so pleased at the way his beautiful name tumbled from my lips that I said it again. "Steinberg!" I smiled at him. He smiled back and licked his dry lips. That did it. My body began to vibrate. Time seemed to slow like in one of those dreadful movies other people always make you watch, and I found myself running toward him, arms outstretched, as if there was no one else there in the world. I was halfway there when I heard the voice.

"Stop right there!"

It seemed to come from everywhere at once, bouncing off the cavern walls, totally surrounding me. I froze in mid-step, half expecting to see the world's largest amp when I turned my head into the sudden breeze I felt coming from the right. It was blowing right under my helmet. Most annoying.

"Stop that!" I demanded. "You're messing up my hair."

"All right," Bloodsport boomed. He seemed incapable of making sound any other way. He was huge and red with a very dragony face, an enormous body, and two great wings that were orange underneath and looked like flames when he flew. His belly was covered with yellow and orange scales bigger than my bathroom floor, with bits of gem and gold and the odd foot or hand caught in the cracks between.

He floated down delicately to land right next to his prize and put a wing around him almost affectionately. "Do you wish to challenge me for the life of this mortal?" he asked. With each word a small belch of smoke escaped his mouth and I saw Steinberg recoil in pain. "And, of course, the mortal too has the right to object."

"Ouch," was all Steinberg had to say.

"Now cut that out!" I shouted. I could feel myself getting really pissed—something I almost never allowed myself to do since it blurs your judgement and makes you an ineffective arguer—but somehow I couldn't help myself, watching poor Steinberg rub the burned spots on his arm. "You dragons are supposed to be so honorable. Feh! Scorching that poor man like a tidbit on a pu-pu platter! What's the matter with you, anyway?

Didn't your mother ever teach you any manners?" I found myself walking toward him, pulling my sword, and using it to emphasize my gestures.

He blew a jet of fire toward me, heating up the metal of my armor. It merely counteracted the chill of the cavern; besides, the warmth of the breastplates felt good against my nipples. For some reason I couldn't fathom, I threw a smile at Steinberg and felt my insides turn to jelly. I pulled myself together and turned my attention back to the dragon.

"See," I said. "That's just what I mean. How childish. What you need is a spanking. I mean, I've had indigestion myself. I know it's uncomfortable, but you don't have to take it out on everyone else. Take some bicarb, for goodness sake. Have an Alka-Seltzer. Down a couple of Mylanta and take a nap. It'll be gone by morning. But noooo! *You*," I said, pointing with the sword. It caught him between two scales, dislodging a large gold crown and something that looked like the head that had been wearing it when it was collected. "Oops, sorry. My bad," I said with a shrug, kicking the items aside. "Did I hurt you?"

Bloodsport lifted his head, pulling it way back against his neck, and I could see that he was getting ready to unleash a really big one. This was intolerable! I reached up and smacked him across the mouth with the flat of the sword, just as his mouth began to open. "Stop it this instant!" I said.

Surprised, the dragon sucked in his breath, pulling the gout of fire down into his throat. His eyes bulged, almost popping off his face. His mouth opened, and billows of dark gray smoke came pouring out, but instead of a roar, the sound that accompanied it was a mere hiss. I thought I could make out the cry of "Water!" buried in there somewhere. Shaking my head, I unhooked the flask and handed it to him. He snatched it from my fingers with two little claws at the end of his wing and sucked the contents down, cork and all.

"Yeeeeoooowww!" he shouted, backing away until his feet no longer had ground underneath him and, as he fell into the chasm, opened his wings and headed off somewhere far below.

"Wow," Steinberg said. "You saved my life. Cool!"

I put my arm around him and we headed back to the wildly cheering men I'd left at the foot of the bridge. Touching him I felt sparks jump between us. No man had ever made me feel this way.

"Come on, Steinberg of Newark. Let's go home," I said.

"Oh please," he said as we neared the party, "call me Oswald." He put his arm around my waist and I leaned into him.

"Okay, Oswald," I said. "What do you know about making coffee? I think the Nicthalene could use a coffee shop. And if we're gonna be raising kings, I'm gonna need a *lot* of it!"

Author of the mystery novel, St. Oswald's Niche, *Laura has also had her work appear in* Analog *and numerous anthologies including the first two "Chicks" books. Talk about curtain calls! She challenges the Gentle Reader to find all twenty theatrical allusions hidden in this story.*

Leg Irons, the Bitch,
and the Wardrobe

Laura Frankos

"Your Highness, you've missed your mark *again!*" snapped Cammek.

Princess Louizza of Leffing glanced at the stage. "Oops," she giggled, and hopped backwards. "Sorry. Let's start at Jeckie's line about the costume ball, all right?"

"No, it's not all right!" Cammek said, throwing the script to the ground with such force that the princess' bodyguard emerged from the wings, her hand tightening around her sword hilt. "*I* am the director here and I shall decide . . ." Cammek let his voice trail off, not so subtly reminded of his position by the bodyguard's steely glare. Barking at King Pennilvath's favorite daughter was Not The Thing To Do. Louizza wasn't really a bad sort. She *was* trying. Often very trying.

Cammek ran his hands through his curly, prematurely graying hair—which undoubtedly would be grayer still assuming he lived to see *Away We Go* debut at the Combined Kingdoms' Dramatic Festival. "Break time," he said at last. "We'll resume at the top of scene three."

The actors scrambled to the rear of the theatre, where the king had assigned two flunkies and a cook with a magic hot cart. Having a royal in the cast gave certain advantages; Cammek had never eaten so well in all his years in the theatre.

Jeclyn, the male lead, obviously agreed. "What's on the menu today?" he asked in a resonant baritone. "Yummy! Stuffed mushrooms!"

The princess chuckled. "I've seen you in a dozen plays, Jeckie, reciting wonderful lines, but somehow 'Yummy! Stuffed mushrooms!' was never one."

"Well, Princess," said Polsiee, the second female lead, "even actors have to eat."

"Especially actors," said Clim-bor-pon, heaping his plate.

Polsiee turned to Clim-bor-pon. "I'd have thought you would have said actors had to drink, not eat."

The comic from Leffing's far western border did like the bottle. But Polsiee should have known better than to try trading barbs with him. Cammek waited for the sky to fall. Clim-bor-pon licked chopped green onion from his thumbnail. "It is said some wine and some dine. And some *whine* and dine." Clim-bor-pon's western accent made the "h" all the more noticeable. "Speaking of that, my dear, aren't two mushrooms plenty for a figure like yours? Got to watch the waistline."

Everyone laughed, even Polsiee, though Cammek was convinced it was merely good acting on her part. Princess Louizza laughed the loudest and helped herself to more mushrooms, neither action designed to endear her to Polsiee's heart.

A sudden crash made everyone jump. The princess' bodyguard rushed to her side, sword drawn. A flunky peered cautiously from behind the lighting tower. "Sorry," he stammered. "I dropped the tea tray."

Louizza put a hand on her defender's armored shoulder. "Calm down, Tipsy. I'm not under attack from teacups. Why don't you help the fellow clean up?"

The bodyguard's eyes raked the cast members standing near Louizza, searching for trouble. Finally she muttered, "Very well, Princess," and went to assist the flunky.

"Isn't it absurd calling such a sober young woman 'Tipsy,' Your Highness?" asked Polsiee.

"Her full name is Tip-lea-pon," Cammek said. "From the west, obviously."

"Of the Pon clan," said Jeclyn. "Relative of yours, Clim?"

The comic shook his head. "Maybe a distant cousin."

"She's never talked about her family," said the princess, "and she's been with me for years. Cammek, I'm off to the necessary before we resume."

Clim-bor-pon murmured, "Even actors have to eat, even royals have to . . ."

Cammek watched Louizza walk towards the privy. Tip-lea-pon saw her, too. She immediately abandoned the servant to his teapotsherds and followed her charge.

Polsiee shuddered. "It's creepy. She's always watching the princess. I couldn't live like that."

"It's her job," Cammek said. "I've gotten used to having her around. In fact, if it weren't for Tip-lea-pon, I suspect I'd be in hot water—literally—for spending so many hours alone tutoring Louizza." He sighed. "Hours and hours."

"Don't you enjoy late evenings with a beautiful, young, *thin* woman?" Clim-bor-pon said, with a wicked side glance at Polsiee, who, while still beautiful and female, could no longer lay claim to the other two adjectives.

"Two beautiful women," Cammek corrected him. "I find Tip-lea-pon stunning."

"Even though she could break you in two?" asked Jeclyn.

"Maybe because of it," Cammek said. "Not that I'm likely to find out. She never takes her eyes off Louizza. Besides, I'm not her type. The only sword I've ever brandished is a stage prop."

"Leaving aside the romantic predilections of western warrior women," Polsiee said with a sniff, "do you feel your tutoring is paying off?"

"What do you think?" Cammek countered. "Louizza's not . . . impossible. Her timing's improved. Knows the play cold."

"She's good in the funny bit she has with me," said Clim-bor-pon.

"But she's not cut out for the romantic lead, is she?" Polsiee asked bluntly.

Cammek sighed. "No, she's not." Of course, Polsiee wasn't right for it, either, no matter what she thought. Twenty years ago, certainly. But that was neither here nor there. "We'll keep rehearsing. If I truly feel we shouldn't go on, I'll tell the king. I'll resign."

The others stared. "You're mad," Jeclyn finally said. "Pennilvath will never stand for it."

Cammek drew himself up to his full height, which wasn't much. "King or no king, I have a reputation to uphold. Meanwhile, back to work."

Ten days later, Cammek scrawled his signature across the bottom of a paper that had taken him longer to write than some one-act plays. It expressed, in rather oblique terms, why he felt *Away We Go* could not open in time for the Combined Kingdoms' Dramatic Festival and was therefore resigning. He mentioned Louizza's hard work and that he sincerely hoped her eventual stage debut would be the success she deserved. That done, he summoned a delivery boy. "Take this to the palace," he said.

"Quick as a wink, sorr." He tucked it in his pouch.

"Um. Take your time with this one. Really. Here's a tenner. Have a drink first. Maybe two. It's hot today."

The delivery boy stood at attention. "Can't do it, sorr. Delivery in thorty minutes or less. If one of my supervisors saw me downing a cool one with a hot message in my bag, I'd be out on my ear."

"Gods above, I should have packed first," muttered Cammek. "Tell you what: hand the message over and I'll call you again, in an hour."

The messenger's hand moved to the pouch. "Against regulations, sorr. You entrusted this message to our services and it is now officially the property of the re-cip-i-ent. If I gave it back to you, I'd be interferin' with the post." He pulled out his watch and exclaimed in horror. "Twenty-seven minutes to go! Good day, sorr!"

Cammek hastily packed a satchel. His cherished possessions were few: his two Perrie awards; two miniatures of his parents; the collected plays of Ghoti; and a cravat that had once belonged to his idol, famed director Father Abbot Jorj, who left a monastery for the theatre. Nearly everything else was replaceable. He wouldn't have an entry in the C.K.D.F. for the first time in seven years, but better no entry than a ruinous entry.

Twenty minutes later, he was on the coach heading for Ruspecalton. A uniformed guard threw open the door at the border and snapped at him: "You are the award-winning director, Cammek? You are under arrest, sir."

A bevy of guards—well, a half dozen, anyway—escorted him back to the palace. "What's the fuss?" he asked. "I'm not a criminal. Shouldn't you be chasing ax murderers?"

"Some would say cutting the king's favorite daughter out of her chance to debut at the Festival is worse'n cutting off somebody's head," the head guard said. "Like, the king himself would say that. He *did* say that, in the message he broadcast over the crystal links to all the border stations. So I guess that puts you with the ax murderers, now don't it? Logical, like."

Cammek assumed he would be tossed into a dungeon, but the guards dragged him to the throne room. They dumped him in front of Pennilvath, Louizza, and Tip-lea-pon, who stood at attention behind the princess. *Let's work on that entrance again*, Cammek thought. *The audience is not amused*.

Pennilvath scowled ferociously; Louizza was teary-eyed and red-nosed; but was that a hint of sympathy in the bodyguard's gray-green eyes? *Nah, couldn't be*.

The king tossed a parchment to the floor in front of Cammek's nose. Cammek caught a glimpse of his own handwriting before Pennilvath pointed his scepter at the parchment. The air filled with magical energy; the parchment burst into multicolored flames.

"Resignation denied," the king snarled.

Louizza stepped forward, evidently afraid her father planned to toast a Perrie-award winning director next, and not with the best bubbly. Like a shadow, Tip-lea-pon moved with her, making sure the royal skirts did not come in contact with the burning parchment. "Daddy, don't hurt him," Louizza said. "He's a genius."

"Why was this 'genius' sneaking across the border?" asked Pennilvath. "I should flame him now. He is guilty of bringing anguish to a royal personage."

"May I explain?" Cammek asked.

"No, you may not. I am issuing a royal decree. I, Pennilvath of Leffing, hereby order the prisoner, Cammek, son of Orrnun, to eight weeks' hard labor."

Cammek glanced up, barely believing his good luck. Eight weeks' breaking rocks. He could survive that. Better him breaking rocks than guards breaking his bones. Then Tip-lea-pon shook her head ever so slightly. Pennilvath wasn't done.

"The labor shall take place within the confines of the Royal Theatre, where the prisoner shall direct Her Royal Highness, Louizza, in the play, *Away We Go*, and open that play at the Combined Kingdoms' Dramatic Festival. Furthermore, sirrah, you shall make my baby a star! A star the likes of which the C.K.D.F. has never seen!"

Cammek privately reflected that the king's dialogue got noticeably undecreelike there at the end. "If I fail, Your Highness?" he asked.

The king loomed over him. "If you think you've been savaged by critics before, you ain't seen anything yet!"

Cammek looked around his prison. Leg irons let him roam most of the building, but he couldn't get to the exits. He'd been told someone was coming later with bedding and that he could dine on leftovers from the cook's hot cart. When the cook arrived for morning rehearsals, he would bring a supply of Meals Recently Ensorcelled for Cammek to eat; prisoners don't deserve palace cooking.

Cammek had been too busy fleeing to grab lunch, so he investigated the hot cart's contents. The glacial unit held leftover mushrooms, meatballs, sliced carrots (what Polsiee usually ate, except when the chef tempted her, which was fairly often), and a rack of beer bottles. He assembled a plate and stuck it in the slot for the micro-dragon to heat. The puff of heat that radiated from the cart gave him an idea. He opened the hatch and removed the micro-dragon, which blinked at him.

"Here, boy, blaze that for me," he said, pointing its snout at his chain. "Come on, heat it up, that's a good boy." The micro-dragon stared in perplexity.

"That won't work, you know," said a voice from the doorway. "They only blaze *inside* their carts. Safety-sorcery—so children won't burn their houses down. Besides, even on that little fella's highest setting, he couldn't do much more than toast bread. You need hotter flames to melt iron links."

Cammek peered into the darkness. "Tip-lea-pon? What are you doing here? Is Louizza here, too?"

"No. I'm off duty. I brought your bedding. My

apartment's nearby, so I offered to deliver it. Where do you want it?"

Cammek put the micro-dragon away and picked up his dinner. "Doesn't matter. I won't be sleeping anyway. Care to join me in a bottle? I'm tempted to drink myself into a stupor."

"I don't advise it," Tip-lea-pon said. "You have no idea how much pleading from Louizza it took to let you keep your head. That was really inept, you know, sending your resignation before you were out of the kingdom."

"I never dreamed Pennilvath was so blasted efficient, even if he did win the last two wars." Cammek studied the warrior woman as she opened her own bottle. "Something . . . seems different about you. What?"

"You're used to seeing me glued to Louizza's side."

"Must be. I didn't think you ever got time off."

Tip-lea-pon snorted. "Since the rehearsals started, I haven't had much, but that's my own choice. I'm officially on from dawn to dusk, but when Louizza's stayed late here, so have I."

"Why? Can't be much fun for you."

Tip-lea-pon's muscled shoulders shrugged. "I'm . . . interested in the theatre." She finished her bottle. "Well, I must go. But I thought you could do with a cheering word. Things will work out. I'll burn an offering at the temple of the gods of drama for you."

"Thanks, but to get out of *this*, I'd probably need to build them a new temple."

After she left, Cammek arranged his bed on a couch from Act Two. As he drifted off to sleep, he realized why Tip-lea-pon looked different: she wasn't wearing her armor.

She looked good without it, too. Cammek had pleasant, if wildly improbable, dreams.

Unfortunately, Tip-lea-pon's offering must have offended the gods. The morning rehearsal was ghastly. The veteran actors were furious with Cammek for abandoning them, and Louizza had cried herself into a bad cold.

Cammek ate his M.R.E. accompanied only by his leg irons. Suddenly, he heard a faint whisper. "Cammek. Listen; and don't be alarmed. I'm here to help."

He whirled, trying to see who was talking to him. No one was nearby. Tip-lea-pon stood about ten feet away, but she was staring, tight-lipped, at the princess, who was blowing the royal nose.

"Don't say anything," the voice continued, allowing Cammek to determine where it was coming from. The ground? No, *his leg irons were talking to him.* "I shall explain my plan in full tonight, but you must cancel the evening rehearsal."

"Cancel it?" Cammek hissed. "It's eight weeks until the festival!"

"Cancel it," the irons said firmly. "If you make Louizza sick through overwork, the king won't stop at putting you in chains."

"All right," Cammek said. "I didn't have much enthusiasm for working late myself. Are you a magical spirit?"

The irons hesitated. "Yes, it must be magic. Or something," they said finally.

Cammek began walking—clanking noisily—to the stage. He paused as he passed the warrior woman. "Did you, er, hear anything just now?"

"Hear what?" she asked.

"Never mind." If people knew he was hearing voices, he'd be in more trouble. "Listen, folks, I'm canceling tonight's rehearsal."

Scattered applause and rude cheers met his announcement. "Big of you, Cammek," said Jeclyn. "Most generous." Sarcasm dripped from his dulcet tones.

"Let it be, Jeclyn," Cammek said wearily. Of all the professionals, Jeclyn had given him the most grief over his aborted resignation. It made sense: he was best suited for his part; no matter what kind of reviews the rest got, his would be good. Clim-bor-pon was doing his usual outstanding work in the comic role, but there wasn't much to it, and Polsiee was, in Cammek's opinion, definitely inadequate as the second lead.

After everyone left, Cammek ate his dinner and waited for the magical spirit or whatever it was to return. Hours passed in silence. He even tried talking to his leg irons. They didn't answer. Disgusted, he opened another beer.

"Cammek!" came a harsh whisper from backstage.

Chains in one hand, beer in the other, he hurried behind the curtains. "I'm here," he panted, "Where are you?"

"Nowhere and everywhere. Isn't that the conventional answer?"

"Uh-huh," he said. "So why does it sound like you're coming from the wardrobe?" He flung open the door, revealing nothing but costumes.

The voice continued to come from inside the wardrobe. "Shut up and listen. You have to produce a successful play in two months or die. Moreover, you must make the princess a star. You can, if you'll take a chance."

Cammek coughed. "I'm under a death sentence. What's chancier than that?"

"Good. We think alike," said the wardrobe. "I've known this for some time. Now, what would you say Louizza's main talents are? You must capitalize on them."

"She's too funny for the part. And though she's pretty, she doesn't act it, if you know what I mean. Not the type heroes fight over."

"She can also sing and dance splendidly. She started at the age of three."

Cammek swigged his beer. "So? This isn't opera."

"Bear with me," said the wardrobe. "Now, what's wrong with the play?"

"The king's cousin wrote it. It's a sweet frothy piece about the opening of the frontier province and whom the local baron's daughter will take to the costume ball: the handsome dragonrider or the evil minister. There's a funny subplot with one of the ladies-in-waiting and the captain of the pegasus cavalry. Not much to work with, considering my competition. I mean, Prince Harrold puts on bigger productions every year. His budget for magical effects is ten times mine."

"I agree, it's too bland. But you don't need gimmicks like wyverns swooping out of the sky. Here's what you do: put every major dramatic or comic scene in *Away We Go* to music. Have them sing and dance."

"That's crazy. I told you, this isn't opera."

"Of course not. It will be something new. Not quite an opera, not quite a revue. If people accept that a bard or an opera star can sing of love, why not a dramatic actor?"

"Because it's never been done!" Cammek drained his beer and wished for more. Maybe if he drank enough he'd see pink mastodons and stop hearing voices.

"You admitted the play needs pumping up. By making it into a musical play, you emphasize Louizza's best skills. Recast her as the lady-in-waiting; build the part up a bit to play off Clim-bor-pon better."

"What?" Cammek yelped. "She's supposed to star. How can I bump her into the second lead?"

"Because she'll shine there and she won't as the dreamy daughter. Trust me, she'll get rave notices, far better than Polsiee would have. Polsiee's getting too long in the tooth to play man-hungry flirts, no matter what she thinks."

Cammek began pacing, no easy task in leg irons. "But . . . singing actors?"

"Clim-bor-pon's a natural—he started out in the western theatrical revues, doing eight shows a week. Put him in charge of the dance numbers, too. Jeclyn's got good pipes. Did some bardic concerts for charity in Ruspecalton. The only problem's Polsiee. She can't sing and she's way too old to play the lead."

"Oh, she'd just *love* seeing the lady-in-waiting role increased and lose it to Louizza! But what could I do with her? Cast her as the baroness?"

"Yes, and cast little Benasbiee as the lead. She played opposite Jeclyn in *Prosciutto,* and she can sing, too."

"They'll never buy it. They'll walk out, led by Polsiee."

"They can't. Check the fine print on that decree— your 'death sentence.' It endows you with all powers, fully backed by the throne, to make this play a success and Louizza a star. If they squawk, throw 'em in the dungeon for disobeying a royal decree. All legal."

"Ooh, when I think of the actors I wish I could have jailed in past productions! But you're forgetting something." He peered into the wardrobe, still hoping to find a living presence among the sequined gowns. "I can't direct a musical play without music! How about *that?*"

The wardrobe chuckled. "Oh, I've been thinking about that for some time. You'll have your music."

Cammek yawned. "Listen, spirit, it better come soon. There's not much time."

"Go to bed, Cammek. You'll need your strength."

Late in the night, a soft noise woke Cammek. He clanked backstage to find a sheaf of papers bound with a silk ribbon and adorned with a single red rose lying in front of the wardrobe. "My angel of music!" he cried. The wardrobe didn't answer. Cammek glanced heavenward—presumably the best direction in which to address angels, even if they did speak from leg irons and wardrobes—and noticed the covering on the skylight was ajar. Angels didn't need to use skylights, did they?

Cammek spent half the night poring over the music, the other half rewriting. When the cast arrived, he bluntly told them of the changes. As he predicted, some immediately wanted out. Polsiee was the noisiest, especially upon learning she'd been recast as the baroness. "This is demeaning to an actress of my stature," she said.

"You'll play it," Cammek said. "Or you can reprise your role in that tawdry women's dungeon drama. In a real dungeon this time."

Clim-bor-pon, however, waxed enthusiastic. "This is exactly what this play needed. We of the west have a tradition of musical revues. In fact, a couple of these songs have a distinct western air, especially that one of Jeclyn's about the carriage with the tasseled trim. I like it. And I'm going to like playing opposite you, Your Highness."

Louizza, Tip-lea-pon at her side, was studying one of the songs. The angelic spirit had been right: the princess *could* sing. "This one's so funny: 'I'm Just a Maid Who Can't Say Nay.' What do you think, Tipsy?"

The bodyguard stifled a yawn. "Promising. Palace scribes should make copies of the songs and rewrites, and arrange for musicians."

Cammek clapped a hand to his head. "Of course!" He scribbled a note, had the princess seal it with her signet ring, and sent it off with a flunky.

That first day, Cammek spent a lot of time with Clim-bor-pon, discussing dance in the show and how to use other traditions from the western provincial theatre circuit. The cast, accompanied by a royal pianist, began learning the songs. By day's end, everyone felt much better about the play—everyone except Polsiee, who kept shooting Cammek deadly looks.

"I'll make sure everyone in the Combined Kingdoms knows what you've done," she said as she left.

Cammek shrugged. "I had no choice. Either I try this or I die."

"You've ruined my career! No one will ever see me as anything but a matron after this!"

"At your age, wasn't that inevitable?" Cammek asked bluntly.

"I had a few more good years, but no more, thanks to your stupid musical play!" She stormed off, brusquely passing the princess and Tip-lea-pon, who came on guard the moment the older actress approached.

"She's upset," Louizza observed.

Tip-lea-pon said, "I can't blame her, but the play is definitely better."

"Er, yes," Cammek said. "Tip-lea-pon, might I have a word with you? Alone?"

The bodyguard looked to her mistress for permission.

"Go on." Louizza giggled. "He doesn't bite. I'll wait at the hot cart, with Jeclyn."

"Very well, Princess," Tip-lea-pon said. She still kept one bloodshot eye on Louizza as she walked away. "How can I help you, Cammek?"

Cammek pointed to the rose he'd been wearing in his vest pocket. "You already have. Where'd you learn to write songs like this?"

"I don't know what you mean."

"Clim-bor-pon's been telling me about the traveling shows in the west. Said the players rarely specialized, but learned a host of skills. Acrobatics, fencing, composing, and . . . ventriloquism." Cammek had the satisfaction of seeing six-feet-one of fighting woman warrior blush. He pressed on: "These songs are western in flavor—just what we need, given the setting of the play—and you're from the west. Only a palace insider would have known about Louizza's singing ability *and* the details of the decree that locked me in these chains—and you're a palace insider. Finally, only somebody in great shape could scale this theatre to speak to me from the skylight." He looked her over, most appreciatively. "Baby, that's definitely you."

If anything, Tip-lea-pon blushed more deeply. She also wasn't watching Louizza, Cammek noted with pleasure. *Wow, I've distracted her!*

"I grew up in one of those western troupes," she said at last. "I've made it a hobby to take scenes or plays I've enjoyed and write music for them. I've got about a dozen scores in my apartment."

"If I survive this —" Cammek shook his leg irons "—I'll want to see those."

Louizza skipped over. "Jeclyn says you have to try the fried tomatoes. Whoops, am I interrupting something?"

Tip-lea-pon coughed delicately. "Master Cammek is trying to invite himself over to my apartment."

Louizza grinned. "Hey, that's a *great* notion! Take him up on it."

"I may, Princess," Tip-lea-pon said, "if you shine brightly enough to get those chains off him."

"Aw, leave them on," Louizza said. "Sometimes it's fun if they can't get away."

As she walked off, Cammek fixed a quizzical gaze on Tip-lea-pon.

"Royal Bodyguards are sworn to secrecy," she said. "And a good thing, too."

Pennilvath didn't trust Cammek, for the director remained chained (muffled with velvet cloth to prevent clanking backstage) on opening night. But by intermission, they felt as light as a feather: the audience had cheered every song and the cast oozed confidence. The princess, in particular, got a huge hand. Pennilvath bellowed delightedly from the royal box: "Sing out, Louizza! Smile, baby!"

Then, just before the second act curtain, a worried Tip-lea-pon approached him. "Polsiee's disappeared. I'm afraid she may be out for revenge, since Louizza's stealing the show. Find the understudy; I'll keep an eye out for Polsiee."

"Gods save me from temperamental actresses!" muttered Cammek.

Act Two opened with the costume ball, a romantic exchange between Jeclyn and Benasbiee, then a comic one between Clim-bor-pon and Louizza. The audience was roaring with laughter when a creaking noise drew Cammek's eyes to the flies above the stage. A great enameled ostrich, emblem of the western province, hung over the actors. It swayed slightly, once, twice . . .

Before Cammek could shout a warning, one of the tall noblemen in the chorus, Sir Borstler, plucked Louizza out of harm's way as the bird crashed to the stage. The cast members stood, stunned. The audience watched in confusion, unsure if the action were part of the play.

Sir Borstler peered at Louizza through his helmet. "You're not my gel," he ad-libbed in a terribly snooty eastern accent. He handed her back to Clim-bor-pon. "Terribly sorry. Thought that buzzard was about to smash me best gel to bits. You know, I'm only visitin' here, but I thought your ostrich-birds were flightless."

"And that one proves it," Clim-bor-pon ad-libbed. "We of the west need a new emblem, something more aerodynamic. An albatross would be dandy, if only we weren't a land-locked province. Meanwhile, let's clean up and get back to dancing!" He gestured frantically for the curtain.

"Get Louizza's understudy!" Cammek said as the crew swept away the debris. "She's *not* going back out there while Polsiee's on the loose."

"Oh, yes I am!" The princess writhed in the protective grasp of the nobleman. "Let go, Tipsy! My big number's in the next scene."

"Your father would never permit it if he thought you were in danger," said Tip-lea-pon, tugging at Sir Borstler's ill-fitting stage armor.

"If I cower like a rabbit, I won't get any notices, and my father will fry Cammek," Louizza said. "Besides, if you try to stop me, I'll have you arrested for violating Father's decree ordering Cammek to make me a star. The show must go on!"

Cammek and Tip-lea-pon gazed at each other in confusion. Clim-bor-pon clapped the princess on the back. "That's the spirit. Gods, you're a born trouper. I'm sure Polsiee's long since fled, but to be safe, we won't go on until we've searched backstage and alerted the guards at the doors. Sound good?"

"Yes!" Louizza said enthusiastically.

Tip-lea-pon waggled a finger at her. "I'm sticking to you like glue, even if we have to rewrite scenes so 'Sir Borstler' is onstage every time you are."

The search turned up nothing. Polsiee had vanished. Knots in his stomach, Cammek prepared to resume the second act as soon as the enameled ostrich fragments were removed from Louizza's gown. Tip-lea-pon kept guard at the dressing room door. Cammek whispered to her, "This is madness. If Polsiee tries again, Louizza will be dead as an act of revenge; I'll be dead for not following the decree; and you'll be dead for not protecting the princess."

"But you can't argue with Louizza's logic," Tip-lea-pon said. "If you put in the understudy, you're a dead man anyway. And frankly —" she looked down on him fondly "—I'm damn glad Louizza's got guts. I've gone to a lot of trouble to save your hide. Wouldn't want it to go to waste. Besides, if the princess chickened out and her father zapped you, she'd feel guilty forever and end up a rotten queen."

"So the future of Leffing is at stake. That makes me feel worse." He kicked at his chains. "None of this would have happened if I'd managed to leave the kingdom."

"Hey," she said softly. "It hasn't all been bad, has it? Some things are worth taking a chance on."

He gulped as she slid an arm around him. "You're right. But in the meantime, I'm still the king's prisoner and we've got to get through the second act without anyone getting killed. How can things get worse?"

Tip-lea-pon grimaced. "Guess who I saw in the sixth row?"

"A frustrated, homicidal actress?"

"Worse. It's that renowned scribe, Creek, son of Attkins. Isn't he one of the judges for the Perrie awards?"

"Swell. Pennilvath might as well blast me now and save all the bother. Creek's hated four out of my last five festival entries." Cammek rested his head against Tip-lea-pon's chest. True, it was covered with Sir Borstler's pasteboard armor, but Cammek always had great powers of imagination.

Louizza opened the door of her room. The pair jumped apart, Cammek falling backwards over his chain, Tip-lea-pon instantly at attention. "Come on, Cammek," the princess said as she swept past him, her bodyguard hot on her heels. "Time for me to go out there and knock 'em dead."

"Let's hope that's all," Cammek said weakly.

Much to everyone's relief, the second act went as smoothly as the first, in spite of "Sir Borstler" popping up at odd times. Cammek dared to peer out at the audience a few times. Pennilvath thumped his royal seat with glee every time Louizza appeared; even dour Creek was seen grinning.

The only hint of trouble came during the curtain calls, when the enchanter in charge of lighting botched the spotlight several times. Louizza got a standing ovation, but didn't stay on stage to enjoy it very long; Tip-lea-pon whisked her into the wings as soon as possible.

Cammek stepped out to deliver a few closing words. He normally would have relished the resounding cheers he got—especially those from the royal box—but he was unconscious of any other feelings than profound relief. Then something *whooshed* by his head. He hadn't had an audience pitch things at him since that brilliant but unpopular thriller he did about the demon Berber and his companion, the mad cook. A second *whoosh* and his chained legs were yanked out from under him and his face slammed into the stage. He heard screams from the audience and caught a glimpse of Tip-lea-pon slashing at the curtain ropes. The curtain fell with a thud.

Dazed, he slowly sat up. His nose was bleeding all over his best shirt and Abbott Jorj's cravat. Clim-bor-pon knelt by his side and offered a hanky.

"Whad happened?" Cammek said.

The comic spread his hands. "If I had to guess, I'd say Tip-lea-pon just saved your life. Somebody—care to wager who?—started shooting crossbow bolts from the lighting tower. Not to worry: our multitalented composer is storming the tower even now."

Cammek struggled to his feet, intent on following. Clim-bor-pon stomped on his chain with his heavy boots and brought him to a complete stop. "Stay here, you twit," he said. "Let the girl handle it. She's the expert. Listen: I think things are settling down."

The ear-splitting roar of confusion in the house was indeed dimming. Jeclyn, among the tallest in the company, was peeking out and delivering a running commentary: "Tip-lea-pon's coming out of the tower. She's got Polsiee. There are guards everywhere. The king's standing in his box, shouting and pointing. Polsiee's screeching. Gods, here come the scribes! I don't know about you, but I'm not going to wait for the chronicles to record what she has to say. Maybe I can get quoted a few times myself."

Following the male lead's lead, the cast stampeded in search of publicity. Cammek wearily trudged after. Polsiee, in the grip of three guardsmen, held forth on her injustices, with the scribes hanging on every word. When she saw Cammek near, she hissed, "He had it coming! He had it coming! The Festival is no place for wild innovations!"

"Don't know about that," said Prince Harrold. "I've been quite inspired by the novelty of *Away We Go*. I'm considering an aquatic musical for *my* next entry. My kingdom has many sea legends, and I have this fabulous merman with a big brassy voice for whom I haven't found a spot in a traditional play."

"I agree: a most impressive experiment," said

Creek. "I shall give it my highest approval, especially the debut of a new comic star." He actually smiled at Louizza.

"Your Highness!" Tip-lea-pon dashed to the princess, sword drawn. "What are you doing out here, unprotected?"

"Mingling with my public," Louizza said. "You've caught Polsiee. What do I have to fear?"

The naiveté of her question, offered up in a crowd of often-vicious scribes and fellow actors (many of whom were known backbiters), made Cammek laugh, though it hurt his nose. The princess had a lot to learn about show biz.

A fresh group of royal guards cleared a space in the mob for the king. Everyone bowed, which set Cammek's nose off again. The king pointed at Polsiee. "I'm not sure what went on there at the end, but I hear you had something to do with it. I never did like you; always posturing instead of acting. Take her away, men, and we'll get the details later."

A group of scribes chased after her, intent on getting further details *now*. The rest waited to hear what the king would say.

"Well, Cammek," Pennilvath said, "tonight, old man, you did it. My Louizza was a joy to behold. Loved the play. A glorious victory. Can't wait for the Perrie awards." With regal nods to everyone, he departed.

"Uh, he does realize that we mere directors have nothing to do with the award process, doesn't he?" Cammek asked. "It's up to esteemed judges like Master Creek here. Otherwise, I may *never* get out of these leg irons."

Louizza frowned. "You should be out of them right now! Silly Daddy, always leaving others to tidy up after him. I'll send word for the dungeon officials to unlock you."

Tip-lea-pon reached into her boot and withdrew a small leather pouch. "No need. I came prepared."

"Lock-picks!" Clim-bor-pon exclaimed. "Another talent you developed while touring in the west?"

Tip-lea-pon nodded while she manipulated the thin lengths of iron in the locks. "I can escape handcuffs, leg irons, *and* a locked trunk while submerged in a glass tank in less than two minutes. There, Cammek, you're free."

Cammek looked at her equipment. "I can't imagine a pouch like that is standard gear for Royal Bodyguards."

"No," she said. "I must confess I brought it in case the show flopped. I wasn't going to leave you in chains to await your death."

"What?" Louizza cried. "You'd desert me for him?"

Tip-lea-pon looked from the princess, still resplendent in her sequined costume, to Cammek, rumpled and blood-stained, with his nose feeling (and no doubt looking) three times its normal size. "Yes," she said in tones that permitted no arguing, not even from royalty.

Louizza clapped her hands together. "Wonderful! How fabulously inspiring! You ought to make that the subject of your next musical!"

"Too controversial," Cammek said. "Only members of a royal family can get away with writing about real royalty, the way my colleague Hal did."

Prince Harrold grinned. "Dad wasn't too pleased about my portrayal of him in *The King and Me*, but as I'm next-in-succession, he couldn't do much without bringing the family line to an abrupt halt."

"Still," Cammek said, "this evening was certainly full of dramatic tension. I keep thinking about that falling ostrich. Naturally, an ostrich is too absurd. But if you had something more elegant, more romantic . . ."

Tip-lea-pon caught on. "Yes, something hanging up there that you wouldn't expect to put the characters in dire peril. And then—boom!—it crashes and scares the audience out of its wits."

"A jeweled clock?" suggested Louizza.

"A famous painting?" said Jeclyn.

"An anvil?" said Clim-bor-pon.

"A crystal chandelier?" said Tip-lea-pon.

Cammek spun around (so easy without leg irons) and caught his new lady love by her strong, capable hands. "A falling chandelier? Hmm . . ."

As one, they turned to look at the stage, all their fertile, creative imaginations working feverishly. Then Cammek shook his head. "Nah, it would never work. Might be a good effect, but what possible reason could we have for one character to drop a chandelier on another?"

Tip-lea-pon nodded. "No motivation."

"On the other hand, *I'm* motivated to see the other scores you've written," Cammek said. "Thanks to you, I can do that." He shook his unchained leg for emphasis.

Tip-lea-pon put her arm around him. "Yes, indeed. I'm looking forward to . . . collaborating with you. Come on, let's go home."

Since she's the author of Xena: All I Need to Know I Learned from the Warrior Princess, *by Gabrielle, as Translated by Josepha Sherman, I was rather ~~relieved~~ surprised by the one-word title on this tale of rescue, romance, and horsing around. She is also known for* Merlin's Kin, Son of Darkness, Vulcan's Heart *(with Susan Shwartz), and forgiving puns.*

Shiftless

Josepha Sherman

The sign on our door reads discreetly, "Tartin and Tartin, Solutions and Investigations," and underneath that, "Licensed Shifters," together with the government seal. But here and now, the sign might as well have been invisible, for all the business we were getting.

"Hey-yi, Jazi, look at this."

I glanced up from my record-keeping in time to see Kerrik shift into the shape of an improbably large, rainbow-feathered, and very silly-looking bird.

People are always wondering what it's like being married to a shifter, forgetting when they ask me that I'm one myself. And of course what they mean is, what's it *like*, nudge, nudge, wink, wink. I'll say only (when

I'm not telling them to mind their own business) that
yes, we have fun, and that's due more to the fact that
we love each other than to any . . . shall we say . . .
magical maneuvers.

"Don't moult on the carpet," I muttered. Then,
relenting as he drooped his wings sadly, "Very pretty."

Kerrik turned back into himself with a shrug. "Come
on, love, smile. Business is going to pick up, I feel it.
Any day now, we're going to have more jobs than we
can—"

A knock on the door interrupted him. With a "told
you so" wink, Kerrik flung open the door. "Ah, Ser
Warkan. What may we do for you today?"

Warkan comes direct from Royal Security, and is one
of those somber, solid, honest types of no certain age,
the ones whose job it is to see that everything runs
smoothly and legally. We'd worked for him before, quiet,
no-publicity but nicely paying jobs. "There's a mage,"
he said with no preamble. "Flashy sort, wealthy. Name's
Garrith Kundin, or at least that's the name on the
records. He bought the old Renten place outside the
city, and he's been busy restoring the estate and rebuild-
ing the horse breeding facilities."

Kerrik and I glanced at each other. "Let me guess,"
I said. "He's gained too much wealth too quickly."

Kerrik finished, "And you think that he's into something dark or you wouldn't be coming to us."

Warkan frowned. "We *know* he is: Just haven't been
able to prove anything, that's all."

Of course all magicians in the kingdom must be
licensed, the same as with us shifters, and no honest
Practitioner complains about it. Ever since the Power
Wars pretty much wiped out the Lartai Fields back in
'81, there have been strong legal bans on the dark side
of magic.

"I see where this is leading," Kerrik said, as casually
as if we weren't hurting for a job. "You want us to get
in there and find you that proof."

"Exactly."

Sitting around our desk, khaffik mugs in hand, we got down to details, terms, risks. And with every word, I began to get more and more uneasy. Contrary to public belief, shifters can't just shift out of injuries; if you've been stabbed as hound and shift back into human, the wound's still there. And yes, we certainly can be killed, just like anyone else. This Kundin sounded like a nasty type, the sort who would think nothing of using magic to enslave or torment others. According to what Warkan was telling us, Kundin had an alarmingly high rate of employee turnovers—or downright employee vanishings. And rumor had it that he was getting money from certain sources in exchange for not harming said sources.

Ah yes, and rumor also said that shifters, as well as Kundin's employees, had been disappearing, though that didn't mean anything too serious, let alone that he was involved. We do tend to be a peripatetic lot, mostly because shifters tend to learn some awkward secrets, not always by chance. Still . . . there's always this danger: Stay shifted too long in another form, and you may forget your rightful shape. The thought of a human ending up as a hawk or bear, with no remembrance of any former life . . .

Rumor, after all, is sometimes based in truth.

But before I could voice my objections, Kerrik said, "Can do." Utterly ignoring my frantic signals, my dear husband leaned back in his chair, smiling. "Ser Warkan, you've got yourself your shifters."

That's Kerrik for you: In a word, reckless. Oh, his heart's in the right place, even when he's literally someone else, and I do love the man. But a little forethought added into his makeup really would be nice.

As soon ask for the wind to be a rock.

When we were alone, I exploded, "Are you out of your—we have a partnership—how could you—"

"Money, love. Remember it? That pretty, shiny stuff we're almost out of?"

"Don't get cute, Kerrik." As his face instantly became a child's wide-eyed face, I snapped, "I mean it!"

He dropped all silliness. "And I mean it. Jazi, I'm going there—and I'm going alone."

"You can't! Dammit, the danger—"

"Horses," was all he said in reply, tapping me on the nose with a forefinger.

Right. Kundin was breeding horses. And I . . . I have an allergy that won't let me go anywhere near the beasts without starting to sneeze madly.

"See, Jazi? Has to be me alone."

I wasn't buying that. Turning away, I pretended to be very busy shuffling papers. Kerrik's arms closed about me from behind, but I went boneless and slipped out of his embrace.

"Hey, love," he cajoled, "I'm not an amateur! I'll be careful."

And I was a garden snake.

I mean that literally. I was getting so angry at his cockiness that I needed to cool off a bit outside, sliding out the window into the garden below.

Wrong move. While I was out there, slithering through the grass and fuming, something large flapped away overhead.

Kerrik.

Come back to me, love, I thought, along with some less printable things. And then I added, *Alive, and in your rightful shape, dammit.*

I waited.

The day passed, and I waited some more.

Another day passed, and finally I sighed to hide my uneasiness, and went down to the market square to see if there was any news.

Oh, there was news, all right: Kundin had just bought himself a brand-new horse, a shining black stallion like none anyone had ever seen.

I bet.

He'd bought the beast from Ashaqat the Horse Trader, a stocky more-or-less honest little man. Ashaqat, when cornered by me, admitted that yes, he'd known it was no true horse he was selling, but that Kerrik had sworn him to secrecy. "Kundin didn't argue," he said. "Just paid my price right off. Didn't like my rope halter, though: Threw his own onto the, uh, horse."

Oh. No. "His own halter didn't have iron in it, did it?"

Ashaqat blinked in confusion. "Yes. Think so."

Damnation! Iron's the one metal that plays havoc with shifters, blocking their powers. Kerrik was chained up in horse shape as long as that halter stayed on him—and Kundin, by that deliberate use of iron, showed that he knew perfectly well he'd just caught himself a shifter. And if he kept Kerrik trapped in that form—

Not for long, I told the sorcerer silently. *Not my husband, curse you.*

But how was I going to get Kerrik out of that mess? I couldn't just shift my way onto the estate; Kundin had made it clear that he was sensitive to a shifter's magic.

But nonmagical folk managed travel without shifting. So after a bit of thought, I put on the guise of a warrior woman, no great champion, just someone in battered leather armor. Not an unusual disguise in these days of peace for a warrior to be wandering about looking for work. I could more or less use the worn sword at my side, though I really, *really* didn't want things to come to that. I wasn't too happy about having iron at my side at all, but hey, couldn't play the role without a sword.

And so, acting on the theory that the simplest alibi was often the best, with no other disguise than this, I set out for Kundin's estate.

Now, just because I'm allergic to horses doesn't mean that I can't enjoy looking at the lovely creatures, and I stood at the sight of the first fine green pasture of them, sniffing and wheezing just a touch, watching the mares and geldings grazing their way along, and all the while hunting for one special black stallion.

Nary a one. Not necessarily alarming, since stallions aren't generally pastured with mares. And none of the horses wore iron-studded halters, so none of them were anything *but* horses.

I hoped.

Kerrik, I thought.

Standing here wasn't getting him back. I marched on as though I were nothing more than a disgruntled warrior determined to find a job, right up to the main house, a rambling thing of white walls and a red-tiled roof, and rapped on the door.

Of course I got the should-have-been-expected, "Trade and servants around back."

Right. *Good move,* I told myself. *Blow your cover right from the start.*

But matters were about to get even more interesting. As I turned to stalk with proper warrior indignation to the servants' entrance, I all but collided with a tall, distinguished figure, dark hair touched so charmingly with gray at the temples—Garrith Kundin himself.

Distinguished, yes. But just then, I wouldn't have cared if he had looked like the King of the Serpent Isles, because I was too busy trying not to show my sudden burst of sheer panic. Surely he knew right off? Surely he sensed I was a shifter?

No, you idiot!

Not even the mightiest of mages could sense magic that wasn't being used.

"My lord." I dipped my head to him in what I hoped was convincing warrior respect. "Forgive me."

A hand under my chin (and me trying not to flinch or, for that matter, bite) forced me up again. "For what, lady? Surely you *are* a lady, judging by your tone. Lost, perhaps, and hiding in warrior guise? Or *are* you a warrior, perchance, a noble one whose horse has thrown her?"

"My lord jests." Oh, hell, that's what had started this.

Roughening my voice, I continued, "'M a good worker, lord, a hard worker. And, well, you know what things are like out there for warrior-types these days." I shrugged. "Could use a job."

He drew his hand back as though wishing for soap and water. "I have no need."

"Please, m'lord. I'll do anything to get a new stake."

Kundin was already bored with me. "Go find the head groom. He can always use someone to help out. I trust you have no objection to hard work?"

"No, m'lord." *I'll be too busy sneezing my fool head off to mind the work.* But at least I'd be nearer Kerrik. "Thank you, m'lord."

Kundin didn't even bother to acknowledge that with a wave.

Too easy, I thought, *far too easy.*

But there are times when you just don't want to argue about it. I went to the Head Groom, a bleak-eyed fellow like the spear carrier for Depression, and told him I was the new girl (all hands in stables are "boys" or "girls," no matter the age), then set to work raking out manure and carrying heavy pails of water and, yes, sneezing like mad. Rubbing my watering eyes, I pretended to merely be admiring the stock.

Not a stallion in the barn. Great.

So I, feigning utter ignorance and a brain the size of a pea, asked one of the under grooms, a scrawny, lank-haired young man with weasely eyes, "Where are all the stallions?"

He, predictably, snickered. "Right here, sweetheart, right here."

Cute. I let my hand fall to the hilt of my sword as though by chance, and said, "Must be a mistake. I see only mares and," the slightest of pauses, "geldings. Where are the stallions?"

"Where the hell do you think?" That remark about "geldings" had gotten to him. "In the stallion barn, the other side of the farm. You keep away from there, if you understand what's good for you." Clichés, too. The boy was a walking wonder. "Woman goes near a stud—hell, you know."

Uh-huh, sure.

That night, of course, I left my musty little cubicle and set out for the stallion barn. Not quite as easily as all that. Nights are *dark* when you don't dare shift, and I couldn't take advantage of those nice patches of mage light coming from the globes set on poles; I had to stay safely in shadow—stubbing my toes, tripping over rocks and thinking, *Kerrik, you owe me for this, I mean, you really owe me.*

Shathal the Silversmith, maybe . . . maybe even Eri the Goldsmith . . .

The dimly lit stallion barn loomed up before me. There would be guards, but I could deal with those. With the sword, if need be. It was the magical shielding that was worrying me.

But hey, I was passing as an ordinary, non-magical warrior woman: The shielding shouldn't react to me. Shouldn't.

Kerrik, I reminded myself, and slipped into the barn, instantly surrounded by the warm, hay-and-horse aroma, my hand firmly over my mouth to stifle sneezes. The guards, two of them, were huddled at the far end of the barn, lost in what looked like a fevered game of Roll the Sticks, as fiercely as though they were at war with each other, and I tiptoed forward.

Oh, hell. Hell and all the demons.

There were no less than six stallions in the barn. Each and every one of them was black without a single distinguishing white mark. And each and every one of them wore an iron-studded halter.

I risked the softest of whispers, trusting to keen equine hearing, "Kerrik?"

Right. Keen equine hearing, all right: All six pairs of ears twitched in my direction. Stifling a sigh and another sneeze, I set about doing this the hard way.

Each stallion was, as I saw, almost absolutely the same as the next, so I gritted my teeth and, as the first horse gave me a wary sniff, I gave him one, too.

Hastily smothered sneeze: True horse.

Second horse, same reaction.

Third horse tried to bite me. Kerrik? No. Horse.

Fourth horse—

I sniffed, sniffed again. No sneeze. I damned near rubbed my nose against his: Nothing! Not even the slightest of eye-waterings. This was Kerrik!

"Kerrik!" I whispered. "Do you know me?"

Was that a nod, or merely a horsey head-toss?

"Wait, wait, let me get the halter off—"

No. The sudden blaze of broken magic would surely bring Kundin rushing in here. Warily, warily, I slid open the latch on the stall door, praying that it wouldn't squeak, then warily, warily pulled the door open, praying that it wouldn't groan. Kerrik worked his careful way out, placing each hoof delicately so that it wouldn't clop, following me as closely as a dog. The guards were still engrossed in their game . . . we were going to make it . . .

No, we weren't. As we left the barn, every mage light in the vicinity blazed into life. And there, dramatic as an actor, stood Garrith Kundin, dark cloak like a shadow about him and eyes amused.

What could I say? "You knew."

"Oh, from the beginning. Don't!" he added sharply to Kerrik, who was edging forward, teeth bared. "Move, and she's dead. In fact," the sorcerer added with a thin smile, "she's dead anyhow."

And with that, he was a great brown bear, and lunging. I had no time to drag off Kerrik's halter; he was still stuck in horse form. So I drew my sword and slashed at him. Ha, yes, got him—

No. No, not with that thick ursine pelt. I'd just cut off some fur, which would probably translate only to a scrape on human hide. And he, with an equally quick slash of claws, tore the sword from my hand.

So much for that. I abandoned all pretense of being a warrior woman and shifted away from him, leaving my clothes and leather armor in a heap on the ground and racing off as a slim-legged doe. Sure enough, the bear followed, swiping at me with claws like knives.

Damnation! There were sorceries like this, allowing the non-shifters to change shape—keep their clothes in the process, too, curse it—but the spells took power, a lot of power. Where Kundin was getting so much strength . . .

Those missing employees. Yes, and the dull anger of everyone here—he was slowly draining their lives!

Ridiculous time for a revelation. The bear's teeth clashed shut, almost on my haunch, and I put on a new burst of speed. We raced over the ground—ha, yes!

A little closer, I told him. And I—

Shifted to cat, going flat to the ground. Sure enough, the bear rushed right over me, then stopped so suddenly he went head over heels. I leaped up, shifted to wolf, lunged for his exposed throat—

And found myself face-to-face with a great serpent, the type that crushes its prey. He did his best to crush me, a loop of his muscular body coiling about me and squeezing, but I—

Shifted to bird, flapping frantically free. He followed as a hawk, talons snatching for me, and I—

Shifted to human, dropping with a thud, right at Kerrik's hooves. As the hawk desperately backwatered his wings, I snatched up that discarded leather armor and swung it with all my force. I connected with the hawk so hard I heard him give a human "oof," and knocked him sideways out of the air. As the sorcerer fell, Kerrik reared, and his jaws snapped shut on the hawk's tail feathers. The hawk gave a very human yell and—

Suddenly was Garrith Kundin again, hanging ignominiously by the seat of his finely cut pants. A stallion's jaws are strong, and his neck muscles are like rock: without much effort, Kerrik held the sorcerer dangling helplessly.

"Give up, Kundin?" I asked, scrambling back into my warrior's garb. "All Kerrik has to do is shift his grip just a little bit to the front, and close his teeth with just a little bit more force, and—"

"Don't!" he gasped. "I surrender!"

"Wise," I said, and went hunting for rope. Iron does a fair job of binding magicians' powers, too, so I used two of those iron-studded halters to bind Kundin. "All right, Kerrik, drop him."

Kerrik did, snorting and trying his best to spit. Kundin lay in a furious heap.

"I won't forget this," he snarled.

Beyond us, his workers were gathering and, for a moment, my heart lurched. But the expression on all their faces was hardly that of love for their employer, so I merely smiled. "That's good, Kundin. You can think about this night all the time that you're in prison. Bend your head a little, Kerrik . . . ah, there."

I pulled off the cursed halter. The stallion blurred, vanished, and my husband stood, stark naked, in its place, looking dazed, relieved, and damned chilly. I snatched Kundin's cloak from him and wrapped it about Kerrik. His arms closed about me, and for a long, long while we could do nothing but cling to each other as though we'd never let go.

But Kundin was raging. "This is criminal! Criminal! You have no grounds—"

"Oh, I don't know about that." Letting go of Kerrik for the moment, I ticked off the sorcerer's crimes on my fingers. "Wrongful imprisonment. Imposing of unnatural shape on a shifter. Draining of life force from employees. Yes, and I suspect that if we nosed about a bit, we'd find a few bodies, too. . . ."

We didn't. Warkan's forces did. They didn't find any more shifters being held against their wills; I don't want to think about how many of the horses on that farm might not have been born as such.

Well now, you can't shift the past. It's comforting to know that Kundin's former employees testified, as did the families of the deceased. He's not going anywhere again. Not in human form, anyhow: The punishment for what he did is permanent shifting into . . .

He makes a very pretty frog.

Now, back to Kerrik and me. Back to our happy little home, and me raging at him. "And what if I hadn't gotten there in time? You would have been a horse forever!"

"Oh, I would have found a way—"

"No, you would not!"

"I would."

"Would not!"

I'll spare you the rest of that. In fact, even I couldn't stand it, and flounced off to bed.

But Kerrik . . . well now, my infuriating, incorrigible and utterly dear-to-me husband shifted into a coverlet.

And what happened after that, dear reader, I leave to your imagination.

What is an editor to do with a writer who reports having studied "too much Sanskrit, not enough Hindi, and just the right amount of Telugu"? I don't know if there's much call for any of the above where he now lives (New York, with his wife and no kids, pets, or plants), but my word, does this man know how to shop! All is forgiven.

May/December at the Mall

Brian Dana Akers

Katya crouched under a palm tree in the food court of the Mall of Alternate Americas. She had picked a two seater with an excellent field of view. Her triple cheeseburger was history; just a few fries left. It was lunchtime and the court was filling up. Someone would be asking for the other seat soon. She merely had to pick the right wildebeest.

A teenage boy with a hopeful smile wearing a leather jerkin approached. Katya glared at him and dropped her hand to her hilt. He wisely pivoted ninety degrees. A fat abbess got the same treatment. Then Katya saw a tall, thin, older man—not an *old* man, just suitably older than Katya—holding his little orange tray and looking for a seat. She gave him a big smile and motioned him over.

"Have a seat," said Katya.

"Thanks." The man sat down. He had a veggie burger, salad, and some kind of fruit drink.

"Wow," said Katya. "Veggie burger and salad. You really live on the edge." She crinkled her nose.

He gave a little shrug. "There are old travelers, and there are bold travelers, but there are no old, bold travelers."

"A traveler? You're sure you're not an accountant?" asked Katya.

"I'm a survivor. Only the prudent survive."

"Oh, let's all be prudent. That sounds like lots of fun!"

He frowned and bit into his burger. Travelers from every era were filling the court: knights in self-shining armor, damsels distressed by impossibly thick sandwiches, samurai discussing hara-kiri techniques, and Aztecs preparing to sacrifice combination platters to their own personal stomach gods.

Katya slowly bit another fry. She tried not to be too obvious. "I'm sorry. Here I am teasing you and we haven't even introduced ourselves. My name is Katya."

"Reimann."

"Where are you from, Reimann?" She batted her eyelashes.

"Just got back from seventeenth-century China. Picked up some incredible silks. A few paintings. Statuary. Vases."

"Are you a merchant?" Katya could practically see the words "sugar daddy" tattooed on his forehead.

"I'm a . . . conservator," said Reimann. His shoulders sagged. "Some time streams get the hell pillaged out of them. They're not healthy. I'm trying to save some of it." He stared at his burger. "I'm just one person."

She paused to process that. "You're very dedicated."

"Mm," said Reimann. He glanced at her and forked his salad.

"No, really. A lot of people wouldn't shoulder that

burden. They would just go with the flow. People like me." She winked and laughed.

"It's hopeless. I just feel way out of it. Too much looping through time. I'm out of phase and time-lagged." Reimann frowned and stabbed his salad again. His eyes got that thousand-year stare.

Katya looked down and concentrated on her fries. This was a bad turn. She had dealt with guys in futures shock before. They became so distant and detached that they weren't good for *anything*. She would have to snap him out of it, quick.

"You know a great time to kick ass? The late Roman Empire. Tops. They're all a little slow from the lead poisoning." She pulled her short Roman sword out of its scabbard and clanged it down so hard on the table that Reimann jumped in his seat. The food court went dead silent for a moment as everyone assessed the risk of a fight. Katya's face flushed. She fixed Reimann in the eye.

"You old guys keep thinking it's going back to the way it was. It's not. Loosen up. Have some fun."

Reimann focused on her and gave a dry laugh. "Girls just want to have fun."

"Now those are words to live by!" said Katya. "Want to hear a few more? Let's go shopping!"

Reimann laughed louder. "Okay, kiddo, whaddiya say we go and buy you some new chain mail?"

Katya's eyes sparkled. "Kiddo? Kiddo? You're calling *me* kiddo? You're not *that* much older than me. At least, I think you're not."

Katya popped the last fry in her mouth. Both stood up, dumped their trays and stacked them on top of the trashcan. She grabbed his hand and squeezed it playfully.

"Just follow me. You're not married, are you?"

"No, I'm young and virile and on the prowl." Reimann laughed again. Katya laughed too. It was such a cute thing for prey to say. "And you're a blonde with brains, boobs, baby fat, and ebullience. Just my type."

Katya laughed. This was more like it.

"Which store?" asked Reimann.

"Definitely Cleopatra's Closet. Definitely." Katya waited for him to object. Either he didn't know the store, or he had money.

They strolled through the mall, getting to know each other. The kiosks that used to sell flight insurance now sold temporal insurance. Reimann growled that it was a scam—time-line arbitrage that was helping screw everything up. When they passed a T-shirt store, Katya had to stop and read each shirt.

"Hey, this one's for you: 'OLD AGE AND TREACHERY WILL TRIUMPH OVER YOUTH AND INEXPERIENCE.'"

"I'm not treacherous. I'm sweet." He grinned.

She smiled and held his hand. "This is great. 'When the going gets tough, the tough go shopping.' That's my philosophy."

Reimann laughed. "You and everyone else. That's why this place is a neutral zone."

"Neutral zone?" asked Katya.

"For R and R. For shore leave," said Reimann. "Agora . . . bazaar . . . market . . . mall. There's always some place like this in every time stream. Always someplace to shop."

Katya had never heard it put quite that way before. The Muzak just made the mall seem so ordinary. "Do you understand how it all happened?" she asked. "Every explanation I've heard sounded like a lot of arm waving to me."

Reimann looked thoughtful. "Not really. What's the first cause of anything? Somehow temporal streamers weakened the tensegrity of our old unitary space-time and frayed it into all these strands." Katya let him talk. Maybe talking would help him get it out of his system.

"Sometimes I can almost feel immense loops of time coming into the mall, like the ribbons of Earth's magnetic field. For these few decades, Minnesota is important. For other times, other places.

"Oh, you know, speaking of other places, someone from the twenty-fourth was telling me Da Lat is a cool little town."

"Never heard of it. Where is it?" asked Katya.

"Vietnam. Central Highlands. During the American phase of the war, all parties had a tacit agreement to spare the town. In fact, officials from both sides, from time to time and without knowing it, rented villas side by side. I want to check it out sometime. Come with me?"

"Da Lat. Right. I'm sure." She rolled her eyes.

"Hey, here we are. Cleopatra's Closet. Isn't it cool?" said Katya. They admired the window displays.

"Very authentic looking," said Reimann. "Hell, it probably *is* authentic."

"The real thing? Great! Let's go!"

The store wasn't exactly Egyptian—more like the boudoir of a Moorish princess. Clothes were tucked away in a fantastic collection of armoires and chests. Browsing there was like rummaging through her private affairs. The atmospherics simulated a late afternoon in Spain. It was elegantly done.

A saleswoman sized up the situation instantly. "Welcome to our store. My name is Serafina. What would the young lady be looking for today?" She lowered her voice. "When not in Rome, don't do as the Romans do. You *need* new chain mail."

"Don't I know it!" said Katya. "Which way to the heavy-duty battle stuff? I want a complete suit." Serafina was thrilled to oblige.

Katya squealed when she opened the giant armoire. "They have everything here! Everything!"

"I can put together some very attractively priced ensembles for you, too," said Serafina. "We have all the major patterns—birdcage, oriental six-on-one, Persian three-on-one—and most of the minor ones as well. It's all done in the latest synthetics. Strong and very light." Reimann sighed and sank into an overstuffed leather armchair.

Katya darted into the dressing nook with a chain-mail brassiere. The cups were a little small, making her look quite ample. She tucked and jiggled and bounced and wiggled. She threw her hair back. Time to give Reimann a quiz.

She stepped out and asked (in all apparent innocence), "Do I look fat in this?"

Reimann fixed her in the eye and said, "Absolutely not. That one looks great on you. If anything, you're too thin. You're ravishing. You're stunning."

"Oh, you're *so* sweet, Reimann."

She kept turning around in front of the mirror, undecided.

"I think, though," added Reimann, "that if you're going back to, oh, the eleventh or twelfth, you'll want something with more protection."

Katya left the brassiere on and started hefting the swords.

"That rapier," said Serafina, "has a matching dagger with a hidden cavity for poisons. It's an exquisite set. I'm sure I can do something on the price. Trade-in for your Roman stuff, something."

"I think the rapier clashes with the brassiere," said Reimann. "They're from completely different eras and countries."

Serafina leaned over and whispered in Katya's ear. "Purists. Can't stand them. We'll send him away in a few moments. Make sure he leaves his credit card." She straightened up and told Reimann, "Excellent observation. I recommend we begin with the body armor and accessorize afterwards."

Katya went nuts trying on different pieces of armor. Reimann cautioned her about helmets that were too bulky or poorly ventilated, warned her how finicky the joints could be in French armor, and generally tried to speed the decision-making process. Katya beamed when she had, at last, selected an ensemble.

"Some people say money can't buy happiness. I say they just don't know where to shop."

"Jesus, you're deep," said Reimann.

Serafina looked thrilled. "I have some wonderful lingerie that would set off that armor quite nicely. You know, for after the battle. One mustn't forget that you're a woman, as well as a warrior."

"Oh God," moaned Reimann. He looked at his watch and sagged deeper into his chair. He looked like a broken man.

"Oh, you poor thing," said Katya. "You don't have to sit though this, too. Just leave me your card, and I'll come find you afterwards."

Reimann reached into his wallet and handed her one of his credit cards. "Really? Can I go? Really? You won't mind?"

Katya plucked the card away. "Of course not. Why should you have to suffer?"

Reimann's sudden reprieve seemed to give him a burst of energy. He gathered his limbs and made a beeline out of the store. Katya flourished his card and grinned.

"Let the games begin!" she cried.

After Katya was accoutered, accessorized, auxiliarized, generally armed to the teeth (and such good friends with Serafina), she left the store to look for Reimann. She strolled past Missile Gap, Missile Gap Kids, and Baby Missile Gap. She peeked into Krazy Katapults, searched Dragons for a Dollar, and scoped out Onagers R Us.

She was starting to worry when she heard girls' voices coming from a men's room. That ain't right, she thought. Katya looked up and down the hall, but didn't see anyone who looked like mall security. She checked that her armor was secure, gripped her shield and drew her rapier.

Then she kicked the door in.

There was Reimann, chained spreadeagled to a bathroom stall. His mouth was gagged and his feet dangled above the floor. Five teenage girls, smoking cigarettes and wearing heavy makeup, looked toward the door.

"Be gone, you little mall rats!" cried Katya.

She weighed into the gang of girls, splitting them into two groups—two to her right, three to her left. She spun to her right and grazed the first girl with the tip of her rapier. The girl backed to the wall and started sidestepping to the door.

"Where are you going?" screamed the second girl. She turned her head toward the first and Katya butted her with her shield. Girl number two crawled for the door.

Katya instantly wheeled to face the remaining three. She crabstepped toward Reimann, so they couldn't harm him or hold him hostage. The ringleader tried to look tough by swinging her chain. Katya looked down.

"I think you'll find oversized jeans a liability in combat—besides looking incredibly stupid."

When the ringleader glanced down at her baggy jeans, Katya caught her chain with the tip of her rapier and flung it aside. The ringleader lunged for it. Katya smacked her in the ass with the flat of her blade and sent her flying. The remaining two girls broke and ran after their friends.

"And smoking is prohibited in all restrooms!" Katya yelled after them.

Katya turned to Reimann. Her face was flushed with the excitement of battle. Sweat trickled down her forehead. Her breasts heaved. She grinned with relief and ungagged him.

"Reimann, what happened?"

"Mall chicks in chains."

He gasped for breath. "I was lost in thought when I walked in here. Then I heard the door latch behind me and looked up and there they were. I knew I was in trouble. I said, 'You can't do this. This is neutral territory.' And they said, 'We ain't time travelers, jerk.

We're locals.' Then they gagged me and chained me up and debated the pros and cons of various indignities. I couldn't believe I had stumbled into this mess. I didn't know what I was going to do. Then you burst in the door like an avenging angel. God, you were magnificent!"

Katya loosened the chains and lowered Reimann to the floor. She wet a paper towel and wiped his face.

"I have you to thank for the armor, you know."

"Money well spent." He smiled.

"You know what you were saying about the time streams not being as healthy as they should be? I shouldn't have laughed at you. You were right. This shouldn't have happened."

Katya looked into his eyes. They lost their thousand-year stare and gazed back into her eyes. The eons, the centuries, the hours evaporated away until only this moment existed, and Reimann was in it and no other.

"I . . . I feel young again."

Katya couldn't fight back a small sob. She gave him a close hug and then snapped her head back.

"You do!"

Jan's another of our Repeat Offenders in the "Chicks" series, and we're happy to have her back. She lives with husband Steve Stirling in Santa Fe, New Mexico, where the prairie dogs roam wild and free, mugging passersby. So far all of her publications are fantasy, but she's declared her intentions to write a romance.

Yo, Baby!

Jan Stirling

Wheezing like a broken bellows Alzira shuffled along, sandals scooping pebbles at every step. Pure white hair clung to the sweat on her face getting into her dry mouth; she coughed. Her heart pounded so fiercely it was a wonder she wasn't bouncing down the street with every beat.

Velops, too small to keep up with her, was all but swinging from the end of her arm, but Alzira had grown too weak to carry him. He fell, scraping both pudgy knees badly.

Dark eyes filled with tears, he bit his lower lip and made no sound. Alzira's heart swelled with pride, Velops understood so little of what was happening. Yet her Lopy held on, fought to behave like the warrior he was.

Gasping for breath, Alzira knelt and lifted him; then

felt as though rising was beyond her strength. Desperately she looked down the alleyway, expecting to see their jailer, a snarl on his thick face.

But there was no one.

"Ready?" she asked Velops. He nodded.

Panting still, her rising accompanied by a symphony of creaking and popping, Alzira took Lopy's hand and led him onward. She clenched her free hand, aching from the impact of the slop bucket against the head of their erstwhile keeper. He wasn't dead—the blows she'd struck had been too weak—it had taken three strikes just to knock him out. And the knots binding him were nowhere near as tight as they'd have been when she was young.

A little over a week ago.

At the end of the alley Alzira stopped, staring in puzzlement at the slap-dash, gypsy look of the place before them. Wagon backs, or rickety tables with awnings of old canvas had been turned into shops. Accents strange to the ear, scents foreign and exotic abounded.

She should know this place; memory teased her, danced out of reach. Then her aging brain sparked— they were at the Itinerant's Market, where peddlers, tinkers and entertainers of all sorts plied their trade. She knew this place, they could hide here.

Feric sat behind the small table in his tiny blue tent attempting to look mysterious. Symbols hung about outside informed the passing public that here was a soothsayer, a diviner, or more forthrightly, a fortune teller; prices adjusted accordingly. Feric's highest price was cheap, too.

Just not cheap enough to tempt the hard headed citizens of Sarna.

The young mage stifled a sigh as yet another potential customer passed without making eye contact.

An old woman stumbled into sight, a child of perhaps

two years clutching her hand. Turning to Feric the expression on her face became one of relief. She looked all around, then dragged the child into the tent.

Feric's graceful gesture made the tent flaps swing closed, giving them privacy of a sort.

"Welcome, madame," Feric murmured unctuously, deepening his voice for effect. "How may I serve you? Have you come to discover what lies in store for this fine . . . young . . . person?"

The child was so young Feric couldn't tell the gender without a peek into its diapers; best not to risk annoying the client by guessing wrong. Not to mention ruining the illusion of omniscience he was trying to build.

"No," the hag snarled in a growling purr that must have been alluring in her younger days. She flashed a look at the closed tent flaps. "You can do magic." Her eyes narrowed. Then, "Me. I want to know what's in store for me."

She snapped him a look that all but grabbed his neck and smacked his head against the tent pole, demanding *So you're not gonna give me any trouble, are you boy?*

He knew she'd call him boy. If she was twelve she'd call him boy. All Terion's friends did when they got that look in their eyes.

The woman sat on one of the cushions with an audible crackling of her knees, gently guiding the child to the one beside her.

She looked around the tent the same way Terion, Feric's soldier sweetheart, would when entering a new place; the swift, efficient sizing up of a professional warrior. Her wrists were thick, the hands muscular and calloused, like Teri's.

"As you wish," Feric said, his voice like expensive oil. *Why doesn't she want to know her grandchild's future? She can't have all that much future left to worry about.* "Cards, crystal, or shall I read your palm, warrior lady?"

"What?" She straightened, big hands groping at her

hip for a sword. "What makes you think I'm a warrior?" she demanded. Then thrust her hand at him. "Palm," she snarled.

As he took her hand, the child made a sound, almost a whimper and the woman turned her head. She seemed to be listening to the sounds of the street outside.

"My . . . friends are warriors," Feric said, "their hands all have calluses like these." He touched the rim of thickened skin that extended from her thumb to near the end of her index finger.

The woman gave him a measuring look.

"You're honest," she said musingly.

He smiled his best professional smile.

"Of course. A soothsayer who lies isn't . . . " *Honest? Very soothful? Where are you going with this, Feric?* "Very wise," he finished lamely but with relief.

He cleared his throat, straightened her hand and began.

"You're in danger," he said, touching her palm. He frowned. "You may escape this danger by your own actions, aided by friends."

The hag turned her hand and clasped his with an astonishingly firm grip, dragging him forward until their noses almost touched. Her eyes **bore**d into his as she said, "I have *need* of an honest man."

Feric blinked. *Oh, please,* he thought, *don't let it be the kind of need I think she means.*

She put the toddler's hand in his and, smiling, said, "Thanks for your advice." Then, rising to the sound of snapping bones, she scuttled from the tent.

Magician and child gazed at one another with mutual expressions of wide eyed horror.

"Madam!" Feric bellowed, leaping over his low table, cushions and the child. He swept the blue curtains aside to find her gone. "*Ple-eea-se!*" he shouted. "Come back! You've . . . forgotten something."

The mage looked at the child, baby really, who was managing to look noble and mysterious. Exactly the look that Feric practiced in front of his mirror, but with more conviction.

"Granny will be back," he assured the toddler cheerfully. Praying that granny would indeed be back. And soon.

The child sighed and laid its head on one of the cushions, apparently meaning to take a nap.

Feric bit his lip as he watched the baby settle.

Teri's going to kill me, he thought.

"You accepted a *baby* in payment for telling a fortune?" Terion's brow was deeply furrowed as she gazed at the sleeping child. "I can't believe you did that."

"I didn't *accept* the baby, she left it," Feric said. "She moved so fast, scuttled out like a lizard—I couldn't believe . . ." At his partner's arch look he stammered, "But . . . it . . . I . . . she . . . I was in *shock!*"

"I think you still are," Teri said, kissing him lightly. "Well." She stood back, arms folded across her chest. "Did she say anything that made you think she'd be back?"

"She said she needed an honest man," Feric said miserably.

Terion cocked her head, looking at his drooping figure with sympathy. She gave him a gentle pat, he staggered slightly.

"So . . . what're you gonna do with it?" Teri asked, gesturing towards the sleeping baby. She kept her eyes and posture noncommittal because she sure as blazes didn't know what to do.

He glanced from Terion to the sweetly sleeping child. "I . . . guess I'll keep it until she comes back," he said.

Teri covered her mouth, hiding her smile. She loved his soft heart. But adopting a child wasn't the same as picking up a stray cat or dog.

"You'll have to take care of it," she warned him. *Well, I'd be saying that if it was a cat.* "And it'll cost you."

"Oh, surely not," Feric said cheerfully. "If two can

live as cheaply as one, then surely three can live as cheaply as two. Especially when the third's as small as this little person."

With a grin, Teri threw a brawny arm around his narrow shoulders and hugged him to her.

"Your economic theory stinks, but your heart's in the right place." She pursed her lips, sighed and said, "All right. I'll check through the market and surrounding neighborhoods to see if someone's missing a baby. Y'know, if she was senile this might not be hers. She might've just picked it up and carried it along until she was tired of it."

"She didn't *seem* senile," Feric said doubtfully.

Teri gave him a squeeze and shook him gently.

"She gave an infant to a total stranger. That doesn't argue for stability, my dear."

Feric looked thoughtful. "I didn't get to read much," he said, "but she was in danger."

With a sigh and a roll of her eyes Terion let him go.

"She was!" he insisted. "Real danger, too, not like she was going to stub a toe or something. Bet she left the baby with me to keep it safe. She was preoccupied— not listening to me at all, really. Like someone was after them and she feared to be found."

"Oh, Feric, you're making up a whole history for her. You know fortune telling's not your best thing."

"I'm getting better," he muttered.

"She's probably some dotty old granny who is right now wondering if she's forgotten something." Terion leaned down and lifted the child, cradling it in her arms. "Let's go have supper," she said, putting a stop to his sputtering. "Then I'll start looking around. I'll get some of the squad to ask questions too. We'll soon have this little one back where she, or he belongs."

Terion walked along, thinking hard. She'd been to city guard headquarters; no missing child to match their found one had been reported.

The baby's healthy, despite the dirt and rags, so someone's been looking after it, she mused. *Granny? Then why dump the child on the first stranger she met?* Maybe she'd found it beyond her strength or means to care for it. *If so Feric's the perfect mark.* Teri's mouth quirked at that. No way would her sweetie throw the baby out with the bathwater.

None she'd questioned in the Itinerant's Market knew of a wandering granny or missing baby.

But that's the nature of the place, Teri thought glumly. *People leave. Who'll notice you're missing when you're expected to disappear.*

Shrieking! Howling—an angry, unending cry. The source; the room occupied by Feric and herself. Alarmed, Teri ran for home, leaping upstairs two at time. She flung open their door, then slammed it shut behind her.

"Feric! What happened? I could hear that baby screaming all the way down the street!"

"I don't know!" He wrung his hands. "He just started and nothing I can do will shut him up."

"It's a he?" she asked.

"I *don't* know!" Feric snapped.

Terion sniffed. "Well, you're about to find out," she said. "It needs changing." She went to the wash basin intending to toss him a linen towel.

"You do it!" Feric said in a panic. "You're the woman."

There was a silence. Like that following a deafening peal of thunder. Even the baby was silent, its mouth open, staring at the young mage. Feric cringed and put his hand to his mouth, as if, too late, he'd stuff the words back in.

Slowly, Terion turned.

"The crying," Feric said in a rush, pointing at the baby with both hands. "I wasn't thinking, I was panicked."

She raised one brow, glanced at the child. The baby looked positively indignant.

"If you want a pet, my boy, you have take care of

it *and* clean up after. I have nothing to do with it." She flung him the towel. "I will, however, get you some hot water." She picked up the pitcher and left the room.

Feric and the baby looked at one another.

"That was close," the magician said.

He could have sworn the baby nodded.

A few moments ago, when the market shut down, Feric had closed his curtains, resolved to find out something about their little boy. Taking the cards the baby had played with, dry now, he dealt them, then blinked at the pattern the cards formed.

"This *can't* be," Feric whispered.

Reaching out he touched a card indicating royal blood.

Suddenly Terion swept aside the tent flap, a peculiarly pleased expression on her handsome face.

"You won't *believe* this!" she whispered. She turned and held the curtain aside.

Feric shot to his feet when he saw the gold coronet glittering in the man's dark hair. His visitor's robes were embroidered with the royal crest of Sarna. Standing, the man's head touched the blue ceiling; so broad were his shoulders he literally filled the tent. A smile beamed out of his black beard like a crescent moon.

"I hear you've found my nephew," he said.

Feric bowed. "I found *a* baby, Your Grace. Hopefully it will be your missing child."

"Well, where is he?" The Duke looked around the small tent, a frown quickly replacing his smile.

"Our neighbor happened by, Your Grace, the baby was restless, so she volunteered to take care of him for a few hours. He's at our apartment." Feric was nervous about the Duke's reaction to this news. Teri, he knew, would be appalled. He avoided her eyes.

Terion had all she could do to keep from shouting, *Are you crazy? You gave the Duke's nephew into the care of a woman who gives spankings for a living!* Teri knew this was unfair, Feric couldn't have known they were coming. And she liked Lustra, who'd been a good neighbor and friend to both of them. *Besides she's too professional to spank somebody without being paid for it.* Especially someone who wouldn't enjoy it.

They could only hope the Duke, in his joy at finding his nephew, wouldn't notice the babysitter's true profession.

"I'm sorry, Your Grace," she said aloud. "We never dreamed we'd find the child's family so quickly."

"Of course," he said coldly. "In any case this is no place for children. Shall we go?" he asked Terion, Feric having disappeared upon being unable to supply what was wanted.

"Yes, Your Grace." Teri bowed. *If he does notice Lustra's a . . . well, I don't want my sweetie within arm's reach.*

Feric sat down with a "Woof!" *The Duke's nephew! That explains the cards.*

An arm snaked around his neck dragging him backwards, a knife dug into his neck. Feric prayed that whoever it was would strangle him because the knife was as dull as air.

"Where's my Lopy?" a voice growled in his ear.

What in the cold hells is a lopy? Feric asked himself. *A shoe, a doll, a breakfast food?* Sounded like food. *A big bowl of lopy,* he thought frantically.

"I don't have any," he gasped, pushing at the arm around his narrowing windpipe.

There was a pause, then a hard hand smacked his head.

"The boy, you idiot! Where's the baby I gave you to care for?"

"Oh. Ah. The Duke . . ."

Another slap.

"I saw the Duke. Where's the baby?"

Alzira let Feric go. He sat up, rubbing throat and head as he turned to stare at her.

"Are you mad—running away with the Duke's nephew?" he asked.

"The king's his only relative and Velops has no children!" she snapped.

"Well isn't it possible the Duke knows something you don't. I mean, perhaps the king . . ." instinct warned him not to say it. "You know."

"Velops—has—no—children," she said through the teeth she had left. Alzira stood staring haughtily down at him. "If the Duke gets the child first he'll be dead in days."

"How can you say that?" Feric asked.

"Because the babe is King Velops, and *I* am Queen Alzira."

Feric stared, she couldn't be who she said she was. The Queen was a blooming young warrior of twenty-two. And yet, he *felt* she was telling the truth, sensed the tickle of magic now he was this close to her.

Alzira grabbed Feric by the front of his robe and pulled him up, very slowly, arms trembling with the effort.

"You *will* help me," she told him. "Where—is—Velops?" Alzira watched his eyes, sensed him wavering. "Take a chance!" she demanded.

"Follow me," he said.

Lustra waited as long as she could, then changed into her working clothes, telling the landlady she was taking the baby with her to the cook shop where she ate so that Teri or Feric would know where to find them.

Now, while she sipped her after dinner wine, the baby rested his rose petal cheek against one ripe, white breast, his chubby hand slowly stroking the other.

"Vel-Lops!" an old woman squawked.

The baby sat bolt upright, exactly the same expression on his face that Feric might have worn had Teri caught him in the same situation.

"Ah!" the infant shouted ecstatically and slid off Lustra's black satin lap. "Ah!" he repeated, toddling rapidly towards the hag.

"Pffft!" Alzira gave a dismissive wave and turned her back on him.

"Ah?" he said sadly. Then began to cry, mouth opened wide, with no sound coming out. Red-faced the child danced silently, caught his breath and an ear-shattering shriek burst forth.

"Please, Lopy! Don't be such a baby!" Alzira snapped. "And don't try to tell me you didn't know what you were doing."

Feric and Lustra exchanged glances. She frowning, he shrugging sheepishly.

"Ah!" Velops said passionately and threw chubby arms around her leg.

"We've no time for this," Alzira said, snatching him up. Cold shot through her as she realized he was now light enough for her to carry.

"You didn't see me," Feric whispered to Lustra, then led Alzira and Velops through the grease-stained curtain that mercifully hid the kitchen from the customers.

Lustra shook her head and took another sip of wine. Teri and Feric were certainly an odd couple.

Terion entered the cook shop, stopping short at the sight of a childless Lustra.

"Mmmwhere's the baby?" she managed to ask casually. She felt the Duke looming over her like a tidal wave looking for a village to drown.

"Ohhh," Lustra drawled, "his little old lady showed up and he fairly *flew* into her arms." Never glancing at the Duke she made a little moue in response to Terion's horrified expression. "You should be pleased," Lustra scolded. "He's back where he started and happy to boot. If you didn't want me to give him up, you should have said so."

Irritated, Terion gestured to the Duke.

"Turns out our waif belongs to the royal family. He's Duke Allu's nephew."

Lustra glanced up at him through her eyelashes.

"You naughty man," she purred. "You should be punished for losing your nephew." She gave him an assessing look.

To Teri's surprise the Duke bowed low, hand to his heart.

"Beautiful lady," Allu murmured, "the blame is all mine."

"Yesss," Lustra hissed, eyes glittering.

The Duke moved to take the other seat at her table. A long, pale leg snaked out to claim it. The cross gaitering on Lustra's sandals went all the way to the top of her leg and so did the Duke's eyes, to where the delicate skin of her inner thigh plumped out against the black leather.

I can almost see his eyes leaping out of his head and running up and down her leg yelling "Yippee!", Terion thought. She'd never seen her neighbor slip into working mode and was impressed, also astonished to see the Duke responding like this.

"You should go find your nephew," Lustra said, flicking her fingers at him in dismissal.

Terion felt her eyebrows rise.

"Of course, Lady." Allu bowed again, gestured for his people and Terion to leave with him.

"Not her," Lustra said, touching Terion's wrist. "I want her to stay."

The Duke's eyes flared, then lowered. He touched his heart.

"Lady," he said. "Until we meet again."

This time Lustra's eyes flared.

Teri rolled hers, but was relieved to see the Duke and his people leave.

"My *dear*," Lustra enthused, "I must take you and Feric to dinner as a reward for introducing me to the Duke! I've dreamed of something like this, but never imagined it could really happen. *Oooooh!*" She clasped her hands to her ample bosom. "I'm going to be sooo rich!"

Terion gestured toward the door.

"Um . . . he left."

"Oh," Lustra stretched luxuriously and smiled, "he'll be back. I can *smell* it." Her eyes went round. "Oh, you'd better go home. I can't imagine where else Feric would take them."

"Feric? Feric was with them?"

Lustra cocked her head and shrugged. "He said he wasn't."

Terion chuckled. "Maybe *we* should take you to dinner."

Lustra decided to accompany Terion home.

"I want to find out what this is all about," she explained. "I was too busy flirting with His Grace to ask him any questions."

"What makes you think he'd tell you anything?" Teri asked, eyeing her neighbor dubiously.

"Oh, if you handle them right the clients will tell you anything you want to know," Lustra said smugly. She flicked her hand. "It's all in the wrist."

Teri rolled her eyes and said, "Pfff."

She unlocked her door to find Feric leaning over an incredibly old woman on the bed, a tiny infant cradled in her arms. Lustra, coming in behind her, gasped at the sight and threw herself backwards until she hit the wall.

"It just happened," Feric said, straightening. "Her Majesty must be about ninety now."

"Her Majesty?" Terion repeated.

"This is King Velops," he said, indicating the baby.

"That isn't the baby we've been taking care of," Terion protested. "He's, what, nine months old?"

"It is!" Lustra hissed, eyes wide. "*I* put that ribbon on his ankle, and that woman . . . in the cook shop was *much* younger!" She put her hand to her mouth, bit her knuckle.

"Magic," Feric explained. "They're under an aging spell. Queen Alzira says it's Allu's doing. He presented them with a "very special vintage" and when they woke they were locked in a cellar, she was years older, he was just a child. They were prisoners for about a week, then they escaped, but Alzira couldn't manage the King and seek help. As for help," he shrugged, "she tried, but no one believed her."

"Naturally," Terion murmured. If Feric hadn't vouched for the old woman's story she wouldn't have believed it herself. Now that she looked at the baby more closely Teri thought there was a resemblance to their own waif. She shook her head. "What do we do?"

"Oh!" Lustra suddenly said, ducking into the hallway. "Are you looking for me?" she asked of a page, who'd knocked on her door.

The boy took her in, satin—cleavage—long legs and swallowed hard.

"Are you M-m-mistress Lustra, madam?" he asked.

"I am." Lustra held out her hand with a sultry smile.

He fairly floated to her, presenting a roll of fine vellum, sealed with the Duke's ring.

"Thank you, madam," the boy said as she accepted it.

"Aren't you sweet," Lustra gushed and gave him a kiss on the cheek.

The boy vanished. Only the sound of a moose falling downstairs told them he hadn't used magic.

"They're so adorable when they're that age," Lustra said as she returned to Teri and Feric's room. "What a pity they grow up."

Feric felt as though he should apologize.

"From the Duke," Lustra said with a lilt of her well-shaped brows. She broke the seal. "Ah ha!" she said. "I'm invited to dine with His Grace, and to wait upon his pleasure this very night. Immediately." She pressed the letter to her bosom. "You've no idea what this means to me! I'll be introduced to the aristocracy. I shall achieve respectability! Of a sort," she continued in a less rapturous tone. "I must prepare." She spun towards the door.

"Wait!" the old woman said.

Lustra turned back at the tone of command in the cracked voice.

"You can get us in to the Duke." Alzira looked at Terion. "We might be able to force him to give us an antidote."

"Unlikely," Lustra said with a pout. "Even if the spell could be reversed you'd need the mage who cast it. And I promise you, *he* won't be there tonight."

"It's their only hope," Feric said.

"Look at them," Teri agreed. "They're almost out of time. You have to help."

"Oooh!" Lustra said, shaking her fists and stamping her feet. "This was my one big chance! Don't you know that?"

"Woman," Alzira croaked, "I assure you, if you help us, you'll only gain by it."

"Of course I'll help. The Duke's very attractive, but he'd make a terrible king."

"My child is ill," Lustra said to Duke Allu's chamberlain. "This is his nanny, this is his wet nurse and this is my physician." She must have said this to forty different people on their way here. "Find them an anteroom nearby where they can be comfortable."

"Yes, Mistress," the chamberlain said with blatant disapproval.

Can't really blame him, Terion thought. *It is a little eccentric to bring the family to an assignation.*

"Stay here," the man snapped at them, then bowed to Lustra. "If madam will follow me."

Lustra smiled haughtily, walking behind him as though she owned both palace and chamberlain.

The adults smiled at one another. The baby began to smell. Again.

✦   ✦   ✦

They'd heard the Duke dismiss the last of his servants half an hour before. Now they crept out of the room where they'd been waiting and tiptoed to Allu's bedroom door. Terion pressed her ear against the panel.

Lustra was speaking, then there was silence. The Duke made . . . a very interesting noise. Teri stood straight, gave the door a disapproving glance then tried the knob. The door opened soundlessly and Terion blinked at what she saw.

The Duke was bound to a padded drying rack, bent double in a way that put his muscular bottom uppermost. Lustra stroked his back with a whip made from ribbons and strips of fur.

"Oh! Yes!" the Duke cried.

Lustra noticed them and put a finger to her lips, then placed a rather complicated gag in the Duke's mouth.

Teri and the others came openly into the room. The Duke began to struggle in his bonds.

"Oh, no no no," Lustra cooed. "This is for your own good, my sweet." She kissed her fingertip and tapped his nose. Then she went over and made sure the door was locked.

"You're going to tell us how to restore the King and Queen to their natural state," Terion said.

Allu murfled something through his gag. Tightening her lips Teri unbuckled the thing and dropped it.

"I'll tell you nothing," the Duke snarled. "You'll never get away with this!"

Teri picked up Lustra's little whip.

"You forget," the Duke sneered, "This sort of thing . . . entertains . . . me."

Raising one eyebrow Teri dropped the toy and, reaching beneath her cloak, brought out what her sergeant called the unit's "attitude adjustment device." Ten thick, four-foot-long knotted rawhide strips attached to a wire-wound wooden handle. Teri shook it out, listening to the dry sound of the knots against the stone floor.

"You forget," she said with a grim smile, "I'm . . . not an entertainer." She raised her arm for the first stroke.

The door burst open to reveal a helmeted and chain-mailed figure, standing in a cloud of mist.

"I warned you," said a sepulchral voice.

Alzira, cradling Velops in her arms fell to her knees and bowed her head.

Feric stood between the Queen and the figure in the doorway as Lustra crawled out from under the collapsed door.

"Who're you?" Terion demanded.

"She's Baza, shaman of my warrior order," Alzira croaked. "She warned me of my brother-in-law's scheme to overthrow us. "You were right, Lady," she said to the shaman. "Please help us."

The shaman took off her helmet and the Duke's laugh cracked out.

"She's the one who sold me the spell that's killing you," he told Alzira. "Don't look there for help! Or to me either." And he laughed again, until he began to cough.

"You're in no position to laugh, Your Grace," Baza said, entering the room. She took a vial from her pouch and gave it to the Queen.

Alzira poured half of it into the reluctant baby's mouth. Velops began to weep and fuss. Then she drank the rest of it. She clutched her throat and looked askance at the shaman.

"Yes, it tastes terrible," Baza said, "and will feel worse, but that can't be helped." Reaching down she removed the king's diaper, then placed her own cloak over him.

"Why?" Alzira asked.

"Because His Grace was going to try to kill you," Baza answered. "This way I could control the circumstances and so convince you of his sincere desire to murder you."

As they watched Alzira transformed into a young

woman and Velops was now a man. They both looked at the bent Duke.

"He's my only brother," Velops said sadly. "Though he's a traitor, it would break my heart to kill him." He shook his head. "Somewhere in his life, who knows where, he might have been turned from this path."

"You can't trust him!" Baza and Alzira said as one.

"Yet, I'd give him another chance if I could," Velops said.

"Um." All eyes turned to Terion. "He could start again," she said, making a drinking gesture. "From the beginning."

Baza smiled, then began to laugh. She took a vial from the pouch at her waist and rose, walking towards Allu.

"A truly splendid idea," she said.

Ever since Chicks in Chainmail *many folks have mentioned the Obvious Pun as a story tie-in. Of course I would never resort to puns (and I have a lovely bridge in Brooklyn to sell you), but I'm glad Jody did. For a woman who lists her main career activity as "spoiling cats" she's also managed to write twenty books, the latest being* Waking in Dreamland *with the sequel,* The School of Light, *coming in July.*

Don't Break the Chain!

Jody Lynn Nye

"Messages for you, my lady," the pink-cheeked page said, falling to one knee beside her.

Lady Doretia reached eagerly for the scrolls. Eighteen years old, with a curious mind underneath her black silk tresses, and a burning intelligence looking out of her bright blue eyes, she was a voracious reader and an avid correspondent. Luckily for her, most of her friends were of the same bent, and the muddy roads that led between their several fathers' fiefdoms were daily filled with pages carrying pages from one of them to another. She popped the wax seal on the first. Lady Zoraida was holding a masked ball at the end of the month. Oh, good. That would give Doretia a chance to wear that strange gown that Great-Grandmama had left her in the will that was open at the sides and showed a daring hint of undergown. Lady Promese had dyed her hair with henna, but the color had come out more purple than red and, "of your courtesy, sister in arms, if you have knowledge of anything that will reduce the color to a mere glow, I would be grateful unto death." Doretia put the letter aside with a mental note to bring it up to the family sorceror, an ancient man who lived in the tallest tower on the castle walls, and who could be depended upon to keep Promese's mishap a secret. Lady Goana's father was holding a tournament in the first week of spring, and would she like to take part? Doretia certainly would. She scribbled a note of thanks, and sealed it hastily.

The sixth missive she unrolled made Doretia frown. More chain mail. How annoying. She had *begged* her friends not to involve her in any more! She felt so guilty when she realized she would have to pass the scroll on to another unsuspecting friend, or worse, copy it and send it to several friends. She always thought about throwing chain letters into the fire, even when the instructions promised dire magical consequences. Of an enquiring turn of mind, Doretia wondered what would really happen if she did destroy the letter, and decided her father and six brothers would be irked if she managed to get killed by a mere piece of paper, when they were doing their best to train her to be a proper shield-maiden, so she could get killed in the field of battle beside her future husband. Whoever he would be. Doretia had no prospects as yet, though she dreamed of being wooed by the handsomest warrior, who would shower her with jewels. She picked up the note to put to one side when words on the page caught her eye.

"Please, fair lady, will you not bend all of your efforts unto the freedom of an Unfortunate gentleman? It behooves you to pass along this missive to assist him in gaining his liberty. Do not let the Missive fall to Earth without sending Relief. I pray you, do not Break the chain, upon your Honor. Send it Onward to the next brave lady of your Acquaintance, but add Thy name to the list, so I may know whom to Thank when I have my deliverance. All of these things are vital Unto my Release. Of your Grace fair Lady do not fail!"

Such an entreaty made this an interesting nuisance, though, Doretia thought, reading the words through again. Instead of the usual plea for her to offer a prayer in the name of the first woman on the list (they were always women) or to send a groat to a particular charity, this read rather as if it had been written by a man, a gentleman, in fact, and in extremis. She could almost hear the voice of the writer. It would be deep, resonant, and very cultured. But was the peril true? Doretia had heard of Urbano legends. Those were stories passed along from person to person that were not true but so exciting and so near to the edge of plausibility that one wanted to believe in them. They were named for the Duke of Urbano, of the southern duchy of Bongiovi, whose tall tales had been charted traveling almost all over the world. Like all of her friends Doretia had shivered with delight hearing the compelling stories, like the one about the old woman who came to the door of a cottager woman who was in desperate need of help with her child. The old woman coddled the babe all day while the mother finished her work. The mysterious visitor stayed for dinner, then left. In the morning the mother discovered the babe had been switched for a changeling.

Everyone swore he or she knew someone who had known the person on whose land the cottager actually lived, but Doretia wasn't satisfied about the veracity of the story. Oh, it made good telling, but it was too circular, too perfect. Out of curiosity she had personally sent out an interesting legend de Urbano she had made up herself, about demons that hid within the privy, and had the satisfaction of it coming back to her no less than eight months later, during the Christmas celebration in the Hall. Everyone also knew an Urbano legend about somebody who had been cursed because he or she had failed to pass on a chain letter. But what if this "piteous gentleman" wasn't real? Most likely he was the brother of one of her correspondents' correspondents, prevailed upon to write out a letter at his sister's dictation to give verisimilitude to a heartbreaking story that would get them all talking.

Still, it was a chain letter, which carried with it the possibility of a curse. But to whom could she send it? The list at the bottom of the fraying parchment contained the list of nearly every friend Doretia had. Almost with relief she saw that Lady Fomentia du Ryott, her best friend, hadn't seen it yet. Doretia picked up her shaved quill and prepared to address a wrapper to Fomentia. She stopped and chewed at the top end of the pen. Should she? It was a temptation, to get it fairly out of the castle and into the hands of someone who would appreciate it, but she hated to promote these wretched things. The words at the bottom caught her eye again.

" . . . Of your Grace fair Lady. . . ."

This wasn't at all like the other chain letters she had received over the years.

Doretia stuffed it into the tapestry bag hanging among her bed curtains with her other correspondence, but that didn't put it out of her mind. She couldn't stop thinking about it. The plaintive tone of the missive stayed with her through the day's sword practice, through siege-breaking exercise, and through her cooking lesson, causing her to burn a pastry case and collect a scolding from the castle cook. The oddest thing was that the gentleman pleaded for help, but didn't give her any directions for finding him.

Her six brothers laughed at her for lending any credence to a nonsense letter. Doretia laughed along with them, but as soon as she was finished with her education for the day she set out to find the sender. After dinner she dispatched pages with urgent queries to all the ladies on the list who were her acquaintances. All of them came back with puzzled replies. They could be of no help. Well, best to go back to the earliest person to pass it along. The first name on the list was Princess Radamanta of Hermetica, the next kingdom west of her home realm of Oligarch. Doretia had never been there, although her elder brothers had. It was a wealthy nation, but rumored to be cruel. Perhaps there really *was* a gentleman in distress. There was no harm in asking the princess if she knew anything more about the letter she had sent on its way.

Doretia's father had smiled gently upon his dreamer of a daughter, but more importantly had given his permission for her to go on quest for the gentleman in peril. She strapped on her new chainmail, with the lioness worked into the breast, and the sunburst on the back of the coif in bronze links, got her squire and a few of her friends together, and rode westward toward Hermetica.

The journey felt more of a riding party than a serious enterprise. The fall weather was very fine. At the manor house in the fiefdom that marched beside Doretia's they picked up Lady Delia Catisson, who guided them on a color tour while they rode through the western forests. It was so nice Doretia was nearly distracted from the object of her quest. The friends caught up on gossip, laughing over their various romances, travel, and hobbies. About two years before Zoraida had bought a Junior Enchantress's kit. She was very keen on making progress as a wizardess, and read their futures in the runes whether they wanted to hear them or not.

"Here's yours, Dory," Zoraida said, holding up a handful of ivory plaques in her small palm. "You will marry a mystery man."

"They're all mysterious," laughed Lady Goana Fitz-Ansarts, who was wed to a burly redhaired northerner.

Doretia shook her head. "I'm not ready to fall in love," she said.

"No one's ever ready," Zoraida said. "It just hits you like a ton of bricks."

"That's not a very mystical observation," Promese protested. Her very purple hair was carefully covered by a hood.

"I'm only at the fourth portal," Zoraida said, mildly. "I guarantee I will become much more obscure in my line of patter sometime in the next twenty-six lessons."

In spite of her will telling her firmly that the fortune was only a guide to what could happen in her future, Doretia's imagination insisted on creating a mysterious gentleman whom she would save, and would be so grateful that he would share his throne with her, and shower her with gifts and praise. She snorted. Ahead lay her real future, riding into Hermetica after a fantasy.

"Border crossing," she alerted the others.

At the border between Oligarch and Hermetica, two sets of guards faced one another over the dashed line painted on the road. Recognizing the distaff arms of several Oligarchical houses, the green-and-gold-clad guards on Doretia's side of the line stood aside and saluted them with honor. The black and red livery of Hermetica marched forth to block their path.

"Names?" the taller guard boomed, his voice coming from all the way inside a barrel chest. Doretia was almost knocked off her horse by the force of it.

"Lady Fomentia du Ryott, Lady Promese Bro Cann, Lady Zoraida Stouffe, and I, Lady Doretia Tortia, request permission to enter the fair land of Hermetica," Doretia replied.

"And you wish to pass into these lands in search of *what*?" the human hurricane asked.

"Well, I received this letter," Doretia said, reluctantly. It sounded silly now that she said it out loud. She had to show it, then wait while the two guards sounded it out between them. Soon, they returned it to her.

"You're welcome to look for your missing gentleman," the guard boomed, as if he couldn't believe it. His companion snickered into his collar. "Although I think you're looking in the wrong place. You'd be better off down south in Bongiovi. You know," he said, nudging his comrade hard in the ribs, "Duke Urbano's place?"

He thought he was witty. Doretia stiffened her back and kept her chin up as she rode forth at the head of her party friends.

"I want to know how it comes that I didn't get this letter," Fomentia appealed to the other women behind her. "If Dory doesn't like them, send them to me! But I don't understand: if she doesn't believe in them, what are we doing here?"

The castle of Hermetica loomed up out of the forest before them, great towers of dark gray stone blocks with dark red pennants fluttering from the walls and turrets.

"Nice color scheme," Promese exclaimed. "Now, my father has paid no attention to me when I tell him that gold is no color to wave above yellow aggregate. Go for orange or green, I begged him. But, no-oo-oo," she said, glumly. "Monochrome."

"I am so glad that my mother understands color theory," Caramelle said, sympathetically. "Red granite and white—so classic."

"But it always looks as though you're waving a flag of truce," Goana giggled.

"This place looks as though it's always in a state of war," Doretia said, frowning. But she chided herself not to make something out of nothing. The castle didn't really feel sinister, more forbidding and remote, like church at Christmas.

"I wonder if her parents are really strict," Fomentia whispered as they rode into the well-kept cobbled courtyard.

The hilarious discussion rang off the walls. The guards in smart maroon jupons saluted the women, and sprang forth to help them dismount.

"Her Highness, Princess Radamanta, will be pleased to receive you," the steward informed them, and escorted them with dignity up the stairs between the heavy-based towers and through the black, iron-banded doors.

"A gentleman in distress, here?" Radamanta asked, throwing back her head and letting out a tinkling laugh. Doretia noticed the merriment never got anywhere near her eyes. She disliked her on sight, but forced herself to listen politely to the princess of Hermetica. After all, their countries were not at war, and had not been for decades.

No one would ever have thrown the insult "monochrome" at Radamanta, for all that it suited her appearance. A tall, elegant girl in her early twenties dressed in ochre damask to suit her light golden-brown hair and a golden skin, she looked like she knew how to handle herself in a dining hall or a battlefield. "I doubt that there is a gentleman in distress anywhere within my father's kingdom. We are a happy people."

"But," Doretia said, producing her scroll, "isn't this your signature here on this letter? Don't you remember sending this on?"

Radamanta reached for the letter and read it. Her eyes flashed dangerously, but she tossed it back to Doretia with a dismissive smirk. "I've never seen that. That is not my signature. I have so much correspondence I have a scribe who handles all unimportant documents for me," she said, flicking a careless hand toward a meek, little, balding man who sat near the window at a writing desk. He favored the visitors with a wan smile. "Doubtless he signed it and passed it along. It's nothing. I had the prayer to St. Expedita last month."

"So did we," Lady Zoraida said, with a longsuffering grin. Radamanta nodded.

"As you see, it's but a tall tale someone thought up and decided to pin my name to, to give it an air of truth."

Doretia felt her cheeks burn red. "I am so sorry to have troubled you, Your Highness."

"Not at all!" Radamanta said, smiling kindly upon her with a haughty air that made Doretia's hand itch for the pommel of her sword. "I'm happy to meet shield-sisters from our neighboring kingdom. Perhaps since you have come all this way you will stay with us this evening for dinner and entertainment. Our cooks are very good, and we are expecting a peddler who sells magic crockery! It should be most amusing."

Fomentia's eyes gleamed. "Oh, do let us stay, Dory. I should like to see such wares."

"Come and meet my friends," Radamanta said, stepping down from her throne. She led them to another grand chamber lined with tapestries, where several young women sat, doing embroidery, polishing armor, and talking. Their shrill voices rose to the beamed ceiling. "Daddy and Mummy have been up at the north border fighting the barbarian hordes for three months now, so we have the castle all to ourselves."

"Isn't that nice?" Zoraida said, rolling her eyes at Doretia.

Under the vaulted ceiling of the great hall Radamanta introduced them to her friends one by one. Doretia found herself thinking as she shook hands, 'I can take her. And her. And her. Not her, though.' She wished she had brought her brothers along to back her up, then was ashamed. A Tortia afraid of a brawl?

"This room would be wonderful for a brawl, I mean, ball," Doretia stammered.

"It's been used for both," Radamanta said, placidly.

"I had heard some three months ago you were engaged to be married, Your Highness," Doretia said, sitting down on a bench near the fire. She hoped it sounded as if she was pumping for an invitation. Radamanta took the bait and smiled in that superior way of hers.

"Indeed, yes. Well, there's some things to be settled yet that are not to my satisfaction," the princess said, her hazel eyes flashing. "The engagement ball will be held when my betrothed and I come to certain terms over the marriage. I'll be sure to send you all a scroll."

"Thank you," Doretia gushed.

"We'd be pleased to come," Fomentia said.

For all Doretia's misgivings, Radamanta was a good hostess. The food was superb and was well served. Over the dinner the ladies gossiped as if they had known one another for years, talking about betrothals, parties, battles and travel.

"I was engaged last year," said Lady Trapezia, a muscular lass with long blonde braids, "but he had these old-fashioned ideas about my not fighting any more. It took a while, but we came to an arrangement."

"How droll," Radamanta said. "I always believe in maintaining my advantage, and I insist upon agreement."

"Who is your affianced, Your Highness?" Goana asked, from her end of the long table. The Oligarchans were, Doretia noticed, not near the fireplace. Radamanta's hospitality extended only so far.

"Prince Felxin of Catania," Radamanta said, proudly. "Catania is just south of here, you know."

"What's he like?" Fomentia asked. "Is he handsome?"

"How about you, Lady Doretia?" the princess asked, skirting the question. "Are you wed?"

"No, not yet," Doretia said, with a smile that hid her discomfort. "Half my friends here are married, and half are engaged. I am the lone holdout. Lady Zoraida was recently married. Her wedding was quite marvelous. All the décor was green, just fancy!"

Radamanta looked pitying, which made Doretia like her even less. As a welcome relief to the intrusive line of questioning, the peddler arrived. Touper showed off his goods, handling each urn and jar to its best advantage in the torchlight. The well-scrubbed peddler was most persuasive.

"See here, ladies, how well these containers close," Touper said. "Each of these crocks will keep a mort of meal or grain fresh throughout the winter. An there be no weevils in the grain to begin with, there will be none able to gain access through the seal at any time." Doretia and the others giggled at the rude noise the flexible wax-and-leather seal made when it clamped onto the top of the sample jar.

"The journey need not be a total loss," Doretia told Fomentia as she paid over three coins for several crocks. "This will be a good present to help our cook forget what an awful pupil I am."

"Isn't this nice?" Radamanta asked, bearing down on them. With her long bronze hair falling over the shoulders of a gown the same color, their hostess gave the impression she was wearing armor even though she wasn't. "You will find these of good value. My father's cook swears by them."

"It is kind of you to let us stay," Doretia said. She toyed with a container small enough for unguents or cosmetics. "How cunning the design, intended to keep in what one wanted to keep in, and keep out what one wants to exclude. Almost like a . . . prison for freshness."

"Indeed," said the princess, with a haughty smile. "It is our intention to promote modern designs. We also hosted a smallclothes party here last month. It's a shame. I don't think the peddler will be back. He didn't seem satisfied with our order."

"You should invite the tapers and candlestick trader," Fomentia said. "*He* was good fun."

"He is to come next month," Radamanta said. "I believe in encouraging modern conveniences and luxuries."

The exhausted potter left with an emptied cart and a well-filled money pouch. As it was well past midnight, Doretia and her friends were invited to stay in the guest chambers. The Oligarchans sat together for a while in the grim stone chamber assigned to Doretia, combing one another's hair. The only window was an arrow slit high on the wall, and no exit but the door, which had locks on both inside and out. The second door she thought led to the next room was the privy. The chamber would make a good prison, Doretia thought, and probably had.

"Keep alert," she warned her friends, when they bid her good night.

"Oh, for what?" Fomentia asked, cheerfully. She was *so* young, Doretia thought. But Zoraida and the others knew what she meant. The ladies of Hermetica seemed friendly, and yet Doretia didn't like the place at all. Perhaps it was bad magic affecting her mood. In the dark she thought she heard the cry of a soul in torment.

"And now you are sure there is no gentleman in distress lurking here, you can be on your way," Radamanta said, bidding them farewell the next morning from the front stairs. "How nice all the same that chance brought us together."

Doretia was now feeling stupid that she had dragged everyone along with her for a fool's errand. "Well, I had to find out for myself," she said, hiding her face in her horse's mane. "Sometimes there's magic in these things, and I didn't want to let it drop . . . you know, maybe a curse . . . ?"

Radamanta laughed at her more than with her, she thought. "Oh, you just fell for a Legend de Urbano, didn't you? Pity. Well, how nice of you to come. Goodbye."

Doretia couldn't look at her friends. They said nothing as they readied themselves to go. She busied herself strapping her purchases into her saddlebags. Their departure from Hermetica would be quiet and subdued, not at all like their noisy arrival.

In fact, it was so quiet that when Radamanta, her friends and servants had gone up the stairs and shut the great black doors, a small voice at their feet could be heard.

"Ladies? Of your courtesy, ladies, I beg a moment of your attention . . ."

Doretia froze. It was the voice from the scroll, without a doubt, just as resonant and cultured as she had imagined it. But where?

"Over there," Fomentia said, pointing to a low grille no more than six inches high at the base of the castle wall.

Doretia stared at it in amazement. She hadn't seen it when they'd first ridden in, but they—or Doretia had—been impressed by the height of the towers, not their foundations and, if truth be told, the lot of them had been making enough noise to drown out an invasion.

With a glance at the stairs to make certain the princess really was gone, Doretia sidled over to the wall. She could just see a shadow in the low room. A slim shadow, with a heroic profile and a strong jawline that momentarily clove the darkness. Doretia gasped as she felt her heart turn over. She heard the clank of chains as the figure raised his hands to the window. They were long, beautiful, strong hands.

"If you could see your way to assisting me, ladies?" the warm voice asked.

"It's the gentleman from the scroll!" Fomentia shrieked with delight. "Why, he was here after all!"

"Sh!!" Doretia hissed. "Yes! And we're going to get him free." She pulled her chainmail coif up over the back of her head and drew her sword. "First I'm going to have a word with Radamanta for lying to my face and making me feel like a fool. Onward and upward, ladies!"

Zoraida grabbed her sword and spell book. The others followed with weapons drawn, their faces grim. Doretia just thought they might take Radamanta by surprise. But the princess had a few words prepared for them as well.

The door flew open, and Radamanta stood at the top of the stairs in full bronze mail. She pointed her sword at Doretia and her friends.

"Take them all! I don't want any of them getting word out to Catania!"

"Hermetica!" her warrior friends shrilled.

Oh, well, after that, what was there to reply but, "Oligarch!" Doretia rushed upward into the fray.

And was immediately beaten halfway down the stairs. The clash that followed was virtually out of a textbook. Radamanta was every bit as terrifying a fighter as she was a hostess. She was several inches taller, had the longer reach, and her skills as a swordswoman were unmistakable. It looked as though Doretia's quest would end not only in failure, but defeat in battle at the hands of a woman who not five minutes before had been her hostess.

Then, Doretia realized with a shock that Radamanta *had* been trained by the numbers. Every move came straight out of books, with no variation. Doretia's attempt at a Valvlol undercut was answered by the Bellatrix thrust and riposte. Any Fermor hack attack was followed by the Rancour spin and parry. Radamanta did it all perfectly, as did her muscular friends. But that was their downfall. Doretia felt for the first time as if her six brothers *were* there behind her. Assuring her battles never went the way the teachers told her they would, they constantly threw every alternate situation they could at her during sword practice, until she stopped reading the manual, and started reading her opponent. Radamanta was an only child. Doretia felt sorry for her.

Backing in a circle around the cobbled yard, Doretia began to throw in variations in her attack. After a Drakeney thrust she stepped left instead of right, or double-thrust before leaping back. Her ploy flustered Radamanta. The princess's perfect golden complexion flushed with an unpleasant red hue, rendering her orange. She began to make mistakes.

To Doretia's left and right, her friends were catching on to the same tactic. Goana screamed the war cry that had made her house feared throughout the known kingdoms.

"Scar their faces!" she screamed, leaping with sword held high at the large blonde maiden, who recoiled, throwing a mailed arm up before her face. Fomentia's sword licked out like a snake. The Oligarchans formed a solid line of flashing metal that drove the Hermeticans backward, up the stairs, into the castle, and on up toward the guest room. Zoraida hurried up and stood behind the door. As soon as Radamanta and her warrior women were safely inside, she threw the lock and spelled the door shut. At once the Hermetican women started pounding to be let out, and Doretia heard a voice behind the door begin a weird keening. Zoraida cocked an ear. The hasp started to slide.

"They've got a Junior Enchantress in there, too," she exclaimed. "Hurry." She started chanting. The lock slid back, just in time.

Doretia didn't waste a moment. "Find that scribe," she shouted.

The little man came out of his hiding place in the audience chamber without hesitation. Doretia thrust the letter at him.

"Did you send this?"

"Yes, madam," the wretched man said, jumping at the sound of the banging from above. "The prince was so kind."

"Prince?" Fomentia asked, opening large eyes at the scribe. "Prince Felxin of Catania. They'd be betrothed by now if it wasn't for her greediness. It was all very unfair." He lowered his voice to a whisper. "She's very unreasonable. I knew she wouldn't ever let him go. So he wrote the note and I sent it. Was that wrong?"

"Not at all," Doretia assured him. "Take us to him."

The gaoler did not need a sword at his throat to open the cell door in the noisome prison beneath the castle tower. The sound of chains clanking began when the gaoler preceded them in with his lantern. The captive prince had risen to greet his rescuers.

Felxin was a head or more taller than Doretia, with smooth black hair, green eyes like a cat's, broad shoulders tapering down to a slim waist, and a smile as bright as a cathedral full of candles. In his prison he had still kept himself in shape, neat and clean, no easy task when burdened with a hundredweight of iron chain fastened to his neck, wrists and ankles. He was more handsome than Doretia could ever have dreamed. She staggered backwards, feeling like she'd been hit in the stomach by the arm of the family quintain.

"A ton of bricks?" Promese asked, shaking her purple locks knowingly.

"Two tons," Doretia breathed. The handsome prince knelt at her feet.

"My lady, thank you for your courage. Not everyone has the fortitude to face down Radamanta."

"Oh, he's dreamy," Fometia squealed. Indeed he was, Doretia thought, and wrenched her mind away to the matter before her.

"Why is Radamanta holding you prisoner?" she asked.

Felxin shrugged his broad shoulders, causing the hanks of gray chain to clatter a protest. "She wanted to rule my country as well as her own, and yet would not allow the same courtesy to me. I can admire independence in a woman, but she must have all or nothing. I am prepared to stand side by side with my queen, not a step below her." Doretia regarded him curiously. He sounded almost too good to be real. A man with whom she didn't have to fight for equality. He made a sour face. "She not only wouldn't break off the engagement, but locked me up until I should give in."

"But couldn't you fight free of her?"

Felxin looked abashed. "She's by far the better sword, and you don't have to know her long to find out how underhanded she can be. She tricked me. Now she holds me by stealth, by chain, and by magic." He shook his bonds. The crowd of ladies keened in sympathy.

"We'll free you right away," Doretia said. She seized the chain hanging from the collar around his neck and started searching along its lengths for the locks. It had none. The bad magic she had suspected was here. She drew her sword. Cold iron would dispel an evil charm. She took aim, preparing to strike. The prince's cry arrested her. He clasped his hands.

"No, fair lady, don't! If you break the links the magic backlash will kill me. It's a chain of logic, and cannot be opened by force."

Doretia frowned but dropped the links. "We can't break them. We can't unlock them. What will free you? It said nothing in your letter."

"The letter!" Felxin exclaimed. "Do you have it?"

It was still in her belt pouch. Doretia took it out.

"Complete the conditions of the letter, I beg you." Felxin looked around at their faces. "Has anyone got a pen?"

"A pen!" said Delia. "You need a locksmith."

"In this case, a pen is mightier, and less fatal," Doretia said, suddenly understanding.

"Take mine," the little scribe said, holding out a quill dripping black at the tip. Doretia hadn't even seen him take out a bottle of ink. She made a mental note to take him with her—someone who was a quick draw like that would be of value in her menage. With a flourish she wrote her name beneath the last one on the list, Promese's, and waited. Nothing happened.

"Nothing happened," she said, disappointed. "What did I do wrong?"

"It's a chain letter!" Felxin said urgently. "You must pass it along."

"But there's no one else . . ." Doretia began, then smiled. But there *was*. She thrust the document at Fomentia, who seized it happily.

"At last!"

There was a flash and a boom in the small cell, as all the chains binding Felxin burst apart and fell to the floor in a rain of individual links. Felxin flexed his wrists and stretched his shoulders.

"At last!" he exclaimed. "Thank you, thank you, good lady."

A yelp came from above, accompanied by the sound of metal falling on stone. Zoraida came running down the stairs.

"You will enjoy this," she said, a catlike smile on her face. "Radamanta and all her gang are now clapped in chains. It just happened."

"The curse recoiling," said the prince. "How perfectly apt." He took Doretia's hand and kissed it. "My lovely rescuer, I owe you my life. How can I thank you?"

"Um," said Doretia, looking up into his shining green eyes. Her brain seemed to have frozen. "I, uh, liked your letter. You write so nicely. Perhaps you could write to me again someday?"

"She's not affianced," Fomentia called over her shoulder, teasingly. Felxin's beautiful eyes widened with interest.

"No?" he asked. "Then, first I might write to your father, to ask if I might call upon you."

"Any time," Doretia told him, wondering why she felt so breathless, as if her perfect-fitting mail was suddenly too tight. Felxin swept her into his arms and kissed her warmly on the lips. She fell back, gasping in surprise, but not at all displeased.

"I am so sorry, fair lady," the prince said, with a twinkle in his eyes. "It was a chain reaction."

This one is for all of those women out there who have ever had to juggle career and family, to say nothing of what happens to the juggling act when the nest empties out and there's a hole in your resume big enough to drive a dragon through.

Cross CHILDREN Walk

Esther M. Friesner

"And how was your work day, dear?" Garth asked his wife. He meant well.

"You *know* how it was!" Zoli flung her spoon down into the dish of Seven Berry Surprise pudding. Sugary globs splattered everywhere. "Nothing's the same since the water-dragon disappeared. No excitement, no adventure. I spend my days hoping someone will fall in, just so I could rescue them, but the Iron River's so sluggish it'd be as thrilling as fishing kittens out of a washbasin. I *hate* my job!"

"For Gnut's sake, Zoli, it's not like anyone's *forcing* you to be a crossing guard."

As soon as the words escaped his lips, Garth regretted them. He clamped his hands over his mouth, but too late. He'd done the unthinkable: He'd spoken his mind to his wife. He was doomed.

Zoli rested one still-muscular arm on the dinner table and leaned towards him with *that* look in her eye. He knew *that* look. It was the same one he'd seen when they'd first met, right before she decapitated the Great Ogre of Limpwater, thereby saving Garth's bacon.

"Well," she said in a deceptively soft voice. "And have we, perhaps, forgotten *why* I became a crossing guard in the first place?"

"No, dear," Garth mumbled. "It was the only job for you in this town." He did not add *Besides keep house.* He knew better. He'd been married to Zoli for twenty years, but he still recalled how she'd dealt with the Great Ogre, and he was still very much attached to his bacon.

"Oh, so you *do* pay attention. And why is it that I, Zoli of the Brazen Shield, have no other job opportunities?"

"Because—because you scare people hereabouts."

"So I do. Which means no one in this dratted little backwater will employ me for labor befitting a grown woman. I've seen the blacksmith and the carter and the rest all eyeing the strength of my arms and back, but I know what they're thinking: 'I'd love to have her toil for me, but if it doesn't work out, where will I ever find the balls to *fire* her?' That *is* what they say of me, isn't it?"

"Nearly." Garth had indeed overheard his fellow townsmen discuss Zoli's unexploited strength in those very words, with one exception: They didn't worry about where to find the balls to fire her so much as where they'd find *their* balls *after* they fired her. So far the most popular theoretical answer that had come up during open debate at the Crusty Boar was "Up a tree." "Down your throat" ran a close second.

Zoli tilted her chair back and swung her feet up to rest among the dinner dishes. Old habits died hard, and most of hers had been formed in the barrack room, the war camp, and the forbidden temples of half a dozen assorted snake gods. "So I am a crossing guard, for want of any better employment, because I fell in love with you and *you* insisted on retiring *here*."

"It's my home town," Garth defended himself. "Anyway, you *made* me retire and settle down when you got pregnant!"

"Are you saying it's *my* fault I'm unhappy?" Zoli had *that* look in her eye again. Garth shut up fast. "It was different when the kids were small," she continued. "But now they're grown and gone it's either mind the ford or go mad with boredom." She sat up straight and began chunking her dagger into the tabletop slowly, methodically, and with a dull viciousness born of deep frustration. "Why did the dragon have to vanish? While he was here, the townsfolk respected me because I protected their brats. But now? Kids learn from their parents. Some of them lob spitballs at me, others make snide remarks about how tight my armor fits. Which it does, but they don't have to say so."

Garth came around the table to stand behind his wife, his hands automatically falling to the task of massaging tension from her shoulders. "You know, sweetheart, maybe the problem isn't that you're a crossing guard, but that you're a *school* crossing guard."

"Tell me about it," she grumbled.

"I could have a word with Mayor Eyebright, get you a transfer to the toll bridge."

"Like *that* would be so much more exciting." She shrugged off his kneading hands impatiently and stuck a heaping spoonful of pudding in her mouth.

Garth frowned. "I'm *trying* to help. On the bridge, you wouldn't have to deal with those snotty kids."

Again Zoli slammed her spoon into the pudding, this time splattering herself and her husband, except she was too worked up to notice. "When have you ever known me to run from *any* battle?" she demanded. "Even one for these yokels' respect? I may have let my membership in the Swordsisters' Union lapse, but I've still got my professional standards. *I will not surrender!*" This said, she flopped back down into her chair and ate what little Seven Berry Surprise pudding was left in her dish.

And I will never again ask how your day was, Garth thought as he too resumed his seat and tucked into his dessert. They finished their meal in silence.

Meanwhile, at the far end of town, Mayor Eyebright was enjoying his own dinner while at the same time doing what he did best, namely ignoring his wife and seven children. His evening monologue droned on and on, not only between mouthfuls of food but straight through them.

"Oh, what a day I've had!" he sighed, stuffing half a slice of bread into his cheek and keeping it there while he talked. "There was a terrible dust-up at the Overford Academy, a faculty meeting that ended in a scuffle and eviction. They actually summoned the town patrol! Why a bunch of wizards can't police themselves . . . I mean, we're paying them more than enough to teach our children, so why can't they hire their own security force instead of coming running to *me* every time there's a body wants booting into the cold-and-cruel? Do they think the patrol works for free? Those bloodsuckers charge the council extra for hazardous duty, which includes ejecting wizards. They *claim* that it takes five men working as a team to subdue one wizard. *Five!* A likely story. And what was it all about, I ask you? *Tenure.* Bah! Why should a frowzy bookworm be guaranteed a job for life? *I* say that the more of 'em get yanked off the academic titty, the better men they'll be."

"Master Porfirio's not frowzy!" little Ethelberthina objected.

A gasp of astonishment gusted from the other members of Household Eyebright. An octet of horrified stares fixed themselves on the youngest daughter of the house, a pert, plump lass of twelve summers. Ethelberthina met her family's collective gawk with the same cool self-possession that had caused all of her teachers to write

"A young woman who exhibits many potential leadership qualities. If you don't beat them out of her, I will," on her progress reports.

"Ethelberthina, how *dare* you interrupt your father!" Goodwife Eyebright exclaimed.

"Oh, poo," said the unnatural child, crossing her arms and looking for all the world like a tax assessor. "Dad should know the *real* story about the fuss at school. Those old buzzards *said* they fired Master Porfirio for inapt morals, but the *truth* is he talked back to the dean."

"If he talked back to someone in authority, he got what he deserved," Mayor Eyebright opined, giving the girl a meaningful look. What it meant was: *Don't push your luck.*

"Poo," said Ethelberthina a second time. "Our philosophy master taught us that authority without virtue merits no obedience. Anyway, it all depends on what he talked back to the dean *about*, doesn't it?"

Mayor Eyebright had long known that Ethelberthina was nothing like her two elder sisters. Mauve and Demystria were normal females, properly deferential. The closest Ethelberthina ever came to deference was knowing how to spell it correctly. Still, a father's duty was to make all his girls into proper women. He had to try.

"You know, Ethelberthina," he said slowly, "you are a very *exceptional* girl."

Ethelberthina knew what that meant. She stood up from the table with the weariness of *Here we go again* upon her. "Another trip to the woodshed?"

Mayor Eyebright shook his head. "Not this time. No sense beating a dead horse. Thus, instead, I will be removing you from Overford Academy soonest."

"*What?!*" For the first time in her young life, Ethelberthina was actually attentive to her father's words.

"No need to thank me. I'm merely correcting an honest mistake for which I blame no one but your mother. *And* her meddling old Granny Ethelberthina. It was *that* woman who insisted we put you to school." Here he gave his wife a reproving look.

Goodwife Eyebright, pregnant with Number Eight, murmured almost inaudibly into her vanished lap, "You didn't *have* to do what Granny said, dear."

Her husband scowled. "Of course I did; she was rich! I refused to risk offending her until she was safely dead and our inheritance secured." His scowl shifted to his youngest daughter. "Sneaky old cow."

"Daddy, I *did* say I'd share Great-granny's money with you as soon as I'm old enough to get it out of the trust fund," Ethelberthina said sweetly. "And so I will . . . *if* I remember. Master Porfirio once taught that a broken heart affects the memory, and I would be *so* heartbroken if you took me out of school!"

"There," Mayor Eyebright said bitterly. *"That's* what comes of educating females: Flagrant displays of logic at the dinner table! Well, my girl, you may be your great-granny's sole heir, with the money held in trust until you're sixteen, but the *king's* law says that if you marry before then it becomes your husband's property when you do. Perhaps you follow my reasoning?"

Ethelberthina's face tensed, but she maintained a brave front. "You'd force me to wed some local lout, except *first* you'll make sure he signs you a promissory note for most of my trust fund."

Her father smiled. "You *are* a smart child."

"Smart enough. The king's law still requires a *consenting* bride, and I *won't.*"

Mayor Eyebright looked casually up at the ceiling. "Dear," he said, "how much more is sixteen than twelve?"

"Four," she answered, suspicious of this arithmetical turn in the conversation.

"Four years, four years . . ." he mused, tapping his fingertips together. "Four long, exhausting, years. Four empty years just waiting to be filled with all *sorts* of things that can make a young woman—even a young woman of your feminine shortcomings—more than a little eager to become a bride. *Anyone's* bride, as long as marriage means escape." He leaned forward with a wolfish smile.

Ethelberthina's lip trembled, but in a wobbly voice she still defied him: "I'll run away!"

"I doubt it. You're wise enough to scrape away the rind of romantic folderol from the harsh facts of existence. I needn't tell *you* what sort of life you'd lead in the wide world at your tender age with neither money nor skills."

Ethelberthina lowered her eyes and bowed her head over her plate. Her father allowed the full impact of this sudden quiet to settle in securely over his family. When he was satisfied with the depth and immobility of the subservient hush, he announced, "You will finish out the semester—only a week left, no sense in wasting tuition—but when that's done you will return to a young woman's proper occupations. That's all." With that, he resumed his dinnertime discursion as if the exchange with his daughter had never occurred. The girl herself ate her dinner a little more slowly and quietly than usual. This added weight of silence on Ethelberthina's part was duly noted and pleased her father no end.

As many an equally thick soul before him, Mayor Eyebright had decided that silence meant surrender. He did not know his daughter well at all.

To anyone else it was a nasty, huge, stinking, half-eaten corpse of *draco aquaticus*, or the common water-dragon. To Master Porfirio it was a welcome diversion from his own dark thoughts. He had discovered the body quite by accident, as he wandered aimlessly downstream along the riverbank, kicking at clumps of reeds and muttering many curses against the faculty of Overford Academy. No one was more surprised than he when he came eye-to-empty-socket with the deceased monster, despite the fact that the fumes of its dissolution were strong enough to peel the paint from passing rivercraft. Like most wizards, Master Porfirio had destroyed his sense of smell over the course of hundreds of alchemical experiments gone awry.

There was nothing wrong with his sense of sight, however. "So *that's* what became of you!" he exclaimed, scrutinizing the sad remains.

There was nothing apparently extraordinary about the body. Like others of its kind, the late water-dragon of the Iron River consisted of a disproportionately large, horse-like head attached to a long, sinuous, finned body. It was not an attractive creature, barring the scales which were the shimmery green of summer leaves. Master Porfirio tugged one loose with surprising ease and scrutinized it closely.

"Not even a hint of silvering," he told the corpse. "You were a very young monster. Whatever you died of, it wasn't age."

He tucked the telltale scale into his pocket and ambled along that portion of the body which did not trail off into the river. "Incredible," he said, noting the way in which the soil had been churned up around the creature's corpse. "You beached yourself before you died, and it looks like you were in a lot of pain. But pain from *what*? There's the question."

He paced up and down one side of the body, then leaped over the beast's back to check the other. It no longer seemed to matter to him that he was unemployed and as badly beached as the dead dragon, with only a few coins in his purse and no letter of recommendation for a new position. A dedicated scholar, Master Porfirio was easily distracted from his own troubles when confronted with an intriguing mental puzzle such as this.

"Not a mark on you. Nothing except for these old scars the crossing guard gave you, and that was over two years ago. I guess she scared you, too. Gnut knows, she scares everybody. Loud sort of female, I think her daughter Lily studied Advanced Alchemy with old Master Caromar before he died and Dean Thrumble gave his own idiot son the post. Over *me*. As if that incapable clod could complete even *one* experiment without botching it horribly! At least *I* know better than to dump my mistakes in the river. I don't care if it did get me fired, I'm *glad* I took a stand against him at the faculty meeting! Someone had to."

The burden of bitterness on his soul elbowed out Master Porfirio's scholastic interest in deducing the water-dragon's doom. Taken up by his own words, he leaned against the creature's flank and relieved his spirit to an audience of one, and that one dead. "I suppose that when that moron graduates to blowing up parts of the school, someone else *might* object to his inept antics, but I doubt it. Not with my fate such a fresh example of the price one pays for truth-telling. Bah!"

In his wrath, Master Porifirio brought his fist down hard on the water-dragon's back. To his shock, the scales crumbled on impact and his hand sank up to the wrist in deliquescing flesh. Uttering an exclamation of disgust, he shook off most of the goo and hastened to wash the rest away in the river.

"How very odd," he murmured as he knelt by the water, scubbing his hand. "Dragon scales are the hardest substance known, resistant to all save the keenest blades, and then only when wielded by expert hands. Perhaps they turn brittle when the beast dies? Hmm, no, if that were so, there wouldn't be a waiting list seven leagues long of king's guardsmen ready to pay top price for dragon-scale armor, to say nothing of the ban on selling it to—ouch!"

The disemployed mage yanked his hand out of the river and stared at it. The skin, once the pasty hue favored by pedagogues everywhere, now looked as dark as if its owner had soaked it in walnut juice. It had also developed a number of ugly boils of a size not seen this side of a troll's rump. His other hand, however, retained its original aspect. His glance darted from one to the other with a growing expression of bafflement and dismay.

Master Porfirio was no slowcoach. On the great chalkboard of his brain an alarmingly simple equation was rapidly being posted and solved. He looked from his hands to the dead water-dragon to the water, then upriver, to where the thatched roofs of Overford Academy and its attendant town bided in unsuspecting peace.

"Oh dear," he said. "I suppose I should go back and inform the authorities. I'm sure they'll do the right thing."

Ethelberthina Eyebright was on her way to school when she happened across the battered body of her former alchemy teacher in the alley behind the Crusty Boar. "Goodness," she told the corpse. "When Dean Thrumble terminates someone, he doesn't fool around."

She was about to continue on her way when the corpse groaned and rolled over, sending a pair of honeymooning rats scurrying off. "Master Porfirio?" Ethelberthina knelt and gently touched his shoulder.

"It's me; I wish it weren't." The banged-up wizard pulled himself to a sitting position against the alley wall. "Is that you, Ethelberthina? Hard to see after one has been punched in both eyes more than necessary."

"Yes, sir," the girl replied dutifully. "What happened? I thought you'd left town."

"I almost left existence." Slowly and painfully he got to his feet, groaned, stretched his battered bones, then asked, "Child, do you love your father?"

Ethelberthina was taken aback by this unexpected question. "I—I suppose I do. I don't *like* him very much at the moment, though. Why do you ask?"

"Oh, just the passing hope that I might prevail upon you to slip a little powdered toadstool into the old pus-bag's supper some fine day, as a favor to me."

"My *father* did this to you?" Being bright, she quickly

amended her question to: "I mean, he was the one who ordered it done?"

The wizard's face looked like a ravaged berrypatch, purple and blue and crimson with a medley of bruises, cuts, and abrasions, yet he still managed to force his pummeled features into a sarcastic expression. "Just his little way of letting me know that so long as the town of Overford continues to collect taxes from and sell supplies to Overford Academy—to say nothing of how many locals the place employs—his official policy towards all school-related complaints will be one of proactive disinvolvement."

Ethelberthina gave him a hard look, "D'you mean *Hands Off?*" she asked.

"*Hands Off* the school and all who sail in her, *Hands On* anyone with a grievance against them."

"It seems like an awfully extreme reaction, even for Dad, having you toughed up just for complaining about your dismissal."

"That was not the substance of my complaint," Master Porfirio said primly. (A bit *too* primly; pursing his lips made him wince with pain and resume a less haughty expression.) "Ah well, never mind. Your father would not heed me. His punishment will be upon his own head."

"You're not going to hurl a vast and awesome spell of destruction against Dad, are you?" Her question was more by way of detached scientific inquiry than filial protestation. Although she did love her father—perhaps sincerely, perhaps out of inertia—she was still deeply hurt by his decision to remove her from Overford Academy.

"Who, me? Mercy, no; I'm just a member of the junior faculty—*was* a member of the junior faculty. We can do you some really impressive illusions, but initiating vast and awesome spells of destruction requires tenure." He shook his head. "Your father's punishment shall be no more than the natural result of his do-nothing attitude. A pity that so many innocent souls will likewise suffer. Were you not a mere slip of a girl-child, I would encourage you to leave town while yet you may. However, since you are still too young and female to take any effective steps towards self-preservation, I can only advise you to be a comfort to your poor mother and say your prayers diligently until inevitable eradication finds you. Good day."

With that, Master Porfirio attempted to depart the alley. He almost made it. What stopped him was an unexpected yank at the back of his robe which half throttled him, pulled him off balance, and made him sit down hard on the garbage-slicked cobbles. No sooner did he hit the pavement than Ethelberthina stood before him wearing an innocent smile that was anything but.

"I beg your pardon, dear Master Porfirio, but would you mind one last question from an unworthy girl-child?" she asked sweetly.

The wizard glared at her. "You yanked my robe! How *dare* you lay hands upon me?"

"Me, sir? When I'm only fit for making prayers and pastry?" Her childish simper hardened into a disturbingly adult sneer as she added, "*And* predictions. And I predict that you'll get no peace until you tell me what's going on. I refuse to wait docilely in ignorance for some unknown doom to land on my head. I'll see you and Dad both sewn up in a sack and pitched into the Iron River first!"

Master Porfirio stood up a second time, keeping a newly respectful eye on Ethelberthina. "Well," he said, "if you've any sort of grudge against your father, tossing him into the river will afford you the sort of all-in vengeance that is at once convenient, efficient, and grisly."

"I doubt that." Ethelberthina crossed her arms. "Dad knows how to swim."

"I admire your practical nature. Yet ere long, surviving immersion in the Iron River will require more than keeping one's head above water." He held out his transformed hand for her inspection and told her how the repulsive changes in it had come to pass. "The water itself's bad enough—killed a whole dragon, after all— but now there's more and more of the beast's poisoned innards leaking into the river every instant, to say nothing of the fresh muck Junior Thrumble's adding to it daily."

"You mean young Master Thrumble?" Ethelberthina asked. "Is he really *that* evil?"

"Not at all," said Master Porfirio. "But then, he needn't be. The efforts of one dedicated bungler can outdo the evils of a hundred archvillains without breaking a sweat. So far he's only killed a dragon."

The girl shivered. "Something must be done."

"I tried. You saw where it got me. Too bad; I rather liked this town, but what with Dean Thrumble's purblind attitude towards his son's blunders and your own father's refusal to wake up and smell the dead water-dragon, it will take a better man than I to save the place."

"Oh?" Ethelberthina grew thoughtful. "In that case, I know just the person." And she told the wizard a name.

Master Porfirio frowned. "Is *that* your idea of a better man than I?" he asked. She nodded happily. "Ethelberthina, has anyone ever told you that you're a very *exceptional* girl?"

"Often. Usually I can't sit down afterwards."

"Can't sit . . . ?"

"Oh, never mind. Now, shall we save Overford?"

"What's all this?" Garth demanded. It wasn't every day he came home to find his wife entertaining a strange wizard and the mayor's youngest daughter.

"A godsend," Zoli replied. "These good people have finally offered me something *interesting* to do. It's a dark plot involving corruption in high places; more than usual, that is. If you stay, you help us; if you don't want to get involved, clear out."

Garth made no move to go. Instead he stood by the door, giving his wife's guests the mother of all hard stares. Finally he pointed at Ethelberthina and blurted: "Shouldn't you be in school?"

"Not according to my father," she responded calmly. "He thinks it's a waste of time, educating females."

"*What*?" Garth's face went red with indignation. "A waste, is it? Our Lily graduated from Overford Academy and went on to become Duke Janifer's senior resident alchemist! She earns *twice* your father's pay, bribes included. You tell your daddy *that*."

"I believe he already knows," said Master Porfirio. "Why do you think he hates educated women so much? He doesn't want to face the embarrassment of any more Lilys."

Garth hoisted a chair and slammed it down backwards at the table, straddling it like a horse. "Whatever this is about, count me in."

"Good," said Zoli. "We'll be needing a babysitter."

In the Swordsisters' Union Hall at East Prandle, Pojandra Foeslayer glanced from her caller to the papers on her desk and said, "A favor? Favors for union sisters only. Your membership lapsed ages ago. Can't say whether you still meet our qualifications."

"Bugger 'em," said Zoli, sitting on the desk. "I don't want to re-up. Why feed dues into an organization that no longer meets my professional needs as a mercenary guard?"

"'Mercenary guard?'" Pojandra echoed sarcastically. "*School crossing* guard. Everyone knows it!"

"That's still guard duty, and I still get paid," Zoli replied.

"So do we," Pojandra snapped. "Go 'round to Customer Service, put in a work order, pay up like everyone else."

"Impossible," Zoli said. "I can't afford to hire as many of you as I need."

"If you can't afford to pay for us—" Pojandra stopped short, her words cut off by the point of Zoli's dagger as it tickled the underside of her chin.

"Tsk," the former Swordsister remarked. "And you with a *young* woman's reflexes. Tell you what, love: *I* promise not to tell your captain about how an old relic like me got the drop on you, and *you* tell her why it's a good thing to loan me the services of ten Third Rank warriors."

"T—ten?" Pojandra swallowed hard. "But—but minimum wage for Third Rankers is—It'd mean tapping the warchest. We can't afford to—!"

Zoli brought her face very close to Pojandra's and smiled. "As long as East Prandle's downriver from Overford, you can't afford *not* to."

The water-dragon attacked the toll bridge at mid-morning on Market Day, when traffic was heaviest. The beast reared out of the river with a mighty roar, sending the crowd into a blind panic. Draft animals snorted and stampeded, pulling their wagons after them willy-nilly, blocking both lanes of the bridge and preventing an orderly evacuation. Farmers and merchants abandoned their wares and scrambled over the blockading carts, but fat times made for fat men and few of them could haul their bulky bodies over a kitchen table, let alone an oxcart. They collapsed in despair against one another, yammering for rescue.

To its credit, the town patrol came running up to the bridge as soon as word reached them, but one look at the rampaging water-dragon petrified them in every limb. (Later, in the Crusty Boar, they spoke of this as "assessing the situation." Their drinking buddies amended it to "close-order wetting yourselves.")

"Is *that* our old water-dragon?" one of their number gasped. "It looks bigger than I recall."

"Can't be our old 'un," said his comrade. "I heard as ours died."

"Died, hey?" a third remarked. "Don't look dead to me. You ever see the body?"

"No, but a friend of my wife's brother-in-law's cousin told us that—"

"Maybe it did die, and that's why it's bigger," said the first man. "Dead things swell up bad, in the warm weather."

"That accounts for the size, but what about all that thrashing about and roaring?" his companion countered.

"Rigor Morris."

Their discussion was polite but impractical. For his part, Mayor Eyebright would have preferred less debate and more decapitation. His position in the crisis was most unenviable, for at the instant of the attack he was smack dab in the middle of the bridge, manning the toll station. Banning all wet-wheeled vehicles from Overford Market (thus forcing all commercial traffic to use the bridge) had been his idea. For this lucrative inspiration, he got the right to man the booth one Market Day per month, plus the town council's promise to take his word about that day's receipts. Mayor Eyebright would sooner miss his father's funeral (and had) than his assigned stint at the toll booth.

This day, he found himself actively wishing to be anywhere else. The water-dragon loomed over the bridge, mouth gaping wide, fangs dripping. Mayor Eyebright knew that he was going to die, a fact which he resented deeply. Rancor swallowed terror and he came storming out of the toll booth, shaking his fist and shouting, "Unnatural monster! You're supposed to be *dead!*"

"I am," the water-dragon answered.

Mayor Eyebright dropped his upraised fist to his chest and staggered backward. "That's my Ethelberthina's voice!" he exclaimed.

"Yum," the dragon agreed.

"How dare you devour *my* daughter?"

The water-dragon shook with laughter that sounded decidedly nonreptilian. "She was too delicious to pass up. As were the other children."

"Other—?" The mayor's jowls looked like slabs of calf's-foot jelly.

"Every last one of 'em as they were on their way to school."

"How's that?" A fat merchant came waddling up to the mayor and poked him in the chest, dragon or no dragon. "All the toll revenue you Overforders gouge from us and you can't spare your own kids the hire of a crossing guard?"

"We *do* have a crossing guard," Mayor Eyebright sniped back. "Where *is* she? I'll have her salary for this!"

"You won't have much, then," the resurrected water-dragon chuckled.

Just then there came a thunderous cry of "Halt!" as a cloud of purple smoke erupted from one of the decorative pillars flanking the townward side of the bridge. The people's eyes turned towards the sound.

Looking more than a little fetching for a woman of her age, Zoli of the Brazen Shield stood balanced atop the pillar, shining sword in hand. With this blade, the crossing guard now pointed at the school side of the Iron River and intoned, "Behold where he comes, the true source of our grief! And his old man." A great roar of astonishment went up from the crowd as they saw two fully robed wizards being hauled bodily down to the riverbank by a hostile knot of armored swordswomen.

"This is unspeakable! An outrage!" Dean Thrumble bellowed as he and his son were chivvied along. "Just let me get my hands free and I'll smite you all with a vast and awesome spell of destruction!"

"Try," Pojandra Foeslayer snarled, giving him an extra shove that nearly sent him tumbling off the bank and into the river. "Won't work while you're wearing those enchanted manacles, though. Took ten of us to get 'em on you, but it's worth the peace of mind."

"Do you mean to kill us?" the dean demanded.

"Hardly," said the leader of swordswomen, one Lt. Vida Chookslaughter. "We just want to *educate* you."

The elder Thrumble drew himself up huffily. "Madam, I am the dean of Overford Academy. I don't *need* an education."

"No, but someone ought to teach you a lesson."

"Good people of Overford!" Zoli called out. "I come before you with a heavy heart. This very day, while I was doing my sadly underpaid job, the water-dragon surged from the Iron River and attacked. I was as shocked as our mayor to see again a beast I'd thought dead. The monster took advantage of my amazement to strike me a mighty blow which threw me headfirst against a tree. When I recovered my senses, the dragon was gone. Alas, so were your children!"

Above the people's cries of anguish, Mayor Eyebright sternly said, "Madam, the town council will be expecting you to refund us a suitable portion of your salary, in view of the insufficient performance of your—"

A small but attention-getting pebble flew from Pojandra's sling and nipped the mayor's hat off his head and into the river. "Shut up, Baldy," she suggested.

"I loved those children as my own," Zoli went on. "Thus I resolved to avenge them. To this end, I sought the services of the greatest wizard in these parts."

"I never saw that woman before in my life!" Dean Thrumble spat.

"Not *you*." Zoli's contempt was epic. "I speak of Master Porfirio. From his wisdom I gleaned the reason for the dead water-dragon's return, and from his hands I received *this*." She yanked a small glass vial from her belt. "Behold the Elixir of Veracity! None whom it touches may speak aught save the truth!"

"And how is the *truth* supposed to kill a dragon?" the mayor wanted to know.

"Yes, do tell," said the dragon. (Such patience and courtesy—that is, the beast's neglecting to devour anyone during the extended parley—were downright odd. However, most of those present were too thoroughly distracted by other matters to remark on it.)

Zoli ignored both the mayor and the dragon. Without another word, she leaped lightly down from the pillar and sprinted the length of the bridge railing to the far bank, where the father-and-son wizards stood captive. Standing before them, she unstoppered the vial with her teeth and poured the contents over Master Thrumble's head before he could react in any way save incoherent spluttering.

"Phew! What's *in* that stuff?" his father asked.

"The doom of liars!" boomed a new voice. There was a second puff of purple smoke and Master Porfirio appeared upon the same pillar Zoli had just vacated. "A brew of my own devising, compounded of the dead dragon's liquefied vitals."

"But the dragon's *not* dead!" the dean and the mayor objected as one.

"I was," the beast in question said, "but I got better. It's a fascinating story, good Overforders, most of which has to do with what's been mucking up *your* river, but I'm not the one who can tell it. Am I, Mayor Eyebright?" it ended on a note of dreadful significance.

The onlookers began to mutter amongst themselves. The mayor, trapped in the midst of a disgruntled constituency, felt fear beyond any that the revenant water-dragon could evoke. Nervously he exclaimed, "Alarmist nonsense! Nothing's wrong with the river."

"No, dragons *always* come back from the dead," someone said snidely.

"We'll see," said Master Porfirio with unnerving calm. He waved his hands and materialized in quick succession a vial identical to Zoli's, a chicken carcass, and a length of thin rope. Anointing the dead bird with the gloop from the vial, he tied it by the feet, held it up before his face, and in a loud voice quizzed it thus: "Are you now or have you ever been a marmoset?"

"Here! How can a dead chicken lie?" the mayor demanded.

"Or tell the truth, for that matter?" someone else asked.

"What's a marmoset?" a third party wanted to know.

"Shush," the fat merchant directed them. "It is likely a wizardly matter. They're always communing with the strangest things. Don't let him hear you questioning his ways or the next dead chicken may be you."

Master Porfirio laid an ear to the fowl's side, then announced, "She says yes! And now . . ." He swung the body overhead at the rope's end and let it drop into the river. When he reeled it out again and the mob saw the horrific changes that had overtaken the small corpse many turned pale, some gasped, a few screamed, and one unsteady soul vomited over the railing.

"Behold the power of the elixir and the fate of liars!" Master Porfirio proclaimed, flourishing the blackened, boil-encrusted remains of the experimental poultry.

Zoli turned to Master Thrumble. "I'm only going to ask you *one* question before I shove you in the drink and we see what the elixir thinks of *you*: What have you been doing to this river and who's been making it easy for you to go on doing it?"

For only one question, it was a doozy, and young Thrumble's reply was worthy of it. By the time he finished rattling through his deposition, most of the Market Day crush had come up out of Overford Town just to listen. Apparently he had never quite mastered the art of summoning demons to transport his alchemical errors to the safety of the Netherworld, as was standard practice among wizards. The one time he tried, the fiend broke free of a defective pentagram and only his father's intervention saved him from annihilation. He never found the nerve to try again. Dumping his "leftovers" into the river seemed like the perfect solution: cheap, simple, and didn't everybody do it? There were some complaints from local anglers over the mounting number of fish kills, but a word with Mayor Eyebright and the complaints vanished. By a strange coincidence, so did the anglers. Master Thrumble admitted to feeling a smidgen of concern when the water-dragon was reported missing-presumed-dead, but soothed his conscience with the thought that it wasn't a bad thing if the stuff he'd dumped in the river had killed a monster.

"Didn't kill it any too *permanent*, though, ha?" someone on the bridge yelled.

"My *son* crossed that river twice a day!" someone on the townside bank added. "If he'd fallen in, your sludge might've killed *him*!"

"It *did* kill him!" someone else cried. "*And* permanent! Did that when it brought the water-dragon back to life and it et him!"

Other parents amid the press now added their voices to the rising clamor. The swordswomen instinctively moved into protective formation around their captives at the sound of a mob baying for revenge, its mildest demand being that Master Thrumble be tossed into the river without delay.

Master Porfirio gazed down upon the rabble and innocently asked, "Why would we want to do that?"

"Because of what you did with the chicken," someone hollered up at him. "*To* the chicken. *Using* the chicken."

"Yeah!" someone else added. "With the magic elixir-thingie."

"Oh. That. No, I don't think so. You see, good people, sometimes when the truth comes to light, it's more than magic: it's a miracle. And so, if all that young Thrumble told us is true, we ought to be seeing a much more spectacular proof of it right . . . about . . . *now!*"

The water-dragon let out a spine-prickling howl. "O, I am slain! *Again!*" it wailed. "The truth has finished me! O woe, alas, alack, welladay——"

"Yes, yes, point taken. Now fall down already!" Master Porfirio directed.

The dying dragon eyed the river uneasily. "Into *that?*"

"Oh, for—!" Raising one hand, Master Porifiro engulfed the swaying monster in an impenetrable cloud of smoke which was, for a change, green instead of purple.

It was rather a lot of smoke, veiling the dragon, the bridge, large shares of both riverbanks, and most of the crowd. People stumbled through the murk, coughing, bumping into things, and calling out "Is that you?" in a generally useless manner. At last a brisk breeze swept in, banishing the thick haze.

One of the town patrol rubbed his eyes, blinked, and declared: "The water-dragon's gone!"

"'Course it is. Didn't you hear that nice young wizard? The truth was spoke and it was the truth that got rid of it once and for all."

"If that's so, I'd like to lay my hands on that Master Thrumble *and* his pa for what they done to our river!"

"Hard luck. Look across the water. They're gone as well, and them female sword-slingers with 'em. Prob'ly run off, and good for 'em."

"Come to think of it, where's that nice young wizard? And our Zoli? *And* our rotten excuse for a mayor?"

"*Ex*-mayor soon enough, you mark my words."

"Can't say I care if I ever see him *or* them Thrumbles again, but what happened to the others? Where did they—?"

Someone standing by the railing on the downriver side of the bridge gave a shout of amazement and joy that brought an end to all other conversations. The people thronged the railing, pushing and shoving in an effort to see what it was that now came drifting slowly out from beneath the shadow of the toll bridge. A volley of wild cheers went up as the raft emerged into full sunlight, Garth Justi's-son at the tiller, all the schoolchildren of Overford aboard.

"Magic's nice," said one onlooker. "But give me a miracle any day. Less smoke."

✧   ✧   ✧

"Can I take this smelly thing off *now*?" Ethelberthina asked. She indicated the patch of water-dragon hide balanced on her head.

"You may," Master Porfirio said, closing the door of Zoli's cottage behind him. "Sorry about the smell, but you know it was necessary. No wizard can conjure a truly effective illusion without some token bit of the real thing to anchor the chimera."

"Sorry for the delay, too," said Zoli. "We had to settle certain matters with the town council."

"And about time." The girl doffed the piece of water-dragon hide and stepped out of the wizard's chalked diagram. She was in such a hurry that she almost upset the scrying basin full of river water which had allowed her to observe the goings-on at the bridge and manipulate the dragon's image accordingly.

"A job well done *takes* time," Master Porfirio recited, ever the academic. "And you should certainly take pride in this one. You're a clever girl, Ethelberthina. Your plan won me back my job, and a promotion to Dean *pro tem*. It won Zoli back the respect of the townsfolk and their offspring."

"*And* a fat raise," Zoli added.

"It also won us all a clean river, now that I've got the clout to organize a massed faculty cleansing spell, and it won you—hmm. What *did* it win you?"

"The right to continue her education," Zoli supplied.

"Nnno. The council told us that her father will lose his job for this, remember? And her own money's all tied up in trust. She can't pay the fees."

"After all she's done for you, you'd charge her *tuition*?" Zoli's hand automatically fell to her sword.

The wizard was rueful. "I'm dean, but I have no power over school finances. Our bursar's a troll—literally. Trolls only understand the bottom line."

"Oh, don't worry about me," Etherlberthina said cheerfully. "I'll be earning my own money, soon enough."

"Indeed? How?"

"By bottling and selling as much Iron River water as I can before you clean it up," she replied.

"Who would want to buy *that* swill?" Zoli asked.

Rather than answer, Ethelberthina inquired, "Would either of you have some dragon skin to hand? Besides this, I mean." She waggled the patch of hide.

Zoli looked dubious, but rummaged through her storage chests. "I'm not supposed to have this," she said handing the girl a limp remnant. "The king knows that armor made from these scales is flexible, light, and virtually impenetrable, so he reserves it for *his* soldiers. He also knows that it's the only edge those clods have over the swordsisters, which is why royal law forbids a freelance female from owning even a scrap of it. But I had to keep this, law or no. It's a souvenir of my first dragon slaying."

"Well, you'll always have your memories," said Ethelberthina, and dropped it in the scrying basin. Zoli said a highly improper word and fished it out with the tip of her sword, only to have the girl smoothly swat the blade upward, sending the soaked bit of hide flying. The scales hit the floor and shattered like thin ice.

Zoli gaped. "The river water does *that* to dragon scales?"

"And dragonscale armor too," Ethelberthina said. "*Now* can you guess who'll buy it from us? Of course we'll get better prices once the river's cleaned up, and we're the only ones with a supply of the old water put by."

"'We'?"

"Well, I'll need help with packaging, advertising, distribution . . . You'd have to quit your job as a crossing guard, Zoli, but you're our ideal sales rep to the Swordsisters' Union. What do you think they'd pay for the Elixir of Equality?"

"Nothing they couldn't recoup once the king's enemies start hiring them wholesale," Master Porifiro muttered.

Zoli of the Brazen Shield laid one hand on the little girl's shoulder. "Ethelberthina," she said, "has anyone ever told you that you're a very *exceptional* girl?"

"Yes," she replied. "But for once it's nice to hear it as a compliment."

Even the ancient Greeks knew it: There really is no business like show business.

This is Kate's first Chicks appearance, though by no means her first sale. She's the author of six young adult mysteries, with a seventh on the way, and her adult work-in-progress, Polar City Nightmare, *will be forthcoming from Orion Press in England.*

... But Comedy is Hard

Kate Daniel

It wasn't my fault I stumbled. Blame the slob who threw his melon rind on the pavement instead of in the gutter where it belonged. These big city-state modern Greeks have no graces left, no culture. The great days of Athens are long past. Which in a way is where the whole affair started, not just with Citizen Melon-dropper.

But start with the stumble. It was embarrassing enough . . .

"Hippolyte! What're you . . . be careful . . . Hades, will you watch where you swing that sword?"

I didn't answer, being somewhat preoccupied with staying on my feet, a normally easy task made difficult by melon rinds underfoot. I'm no acrobat, but I felt like one as I twisted, righted myself, overbalanced once more, and finally steadied myself with my new sword. Called into service as a crutch, the tip of the blade plunged deep into the piece of melon, skewering it neatly.

My impromptu dance had drawn laughter around the agora, which rose to scattered cheers and applause at this point. I hammed it up for the gawkers, bowing and holding up the rind-topped sword as if it were laurel awarded a victor. After a moment I dropped the pose, lowered my sword, and pushed the garbage off the blade with my foot. Traffic in the agora resumed as I examined my pretty new toy for damage. Bronze is hard, but it can still be nicked.

Then a familiar voice spoke behind me. "Brava, my dear. I haven't laughed so hard in ages, certainly not at my own poor efforts. Now *that* is comedy!" It was a musical voice, pitched to carry.

"No, it's clumsiness." Glycera, my fellow Amazon, came forward once my blade no longer posed a threat to nearby eyes, ears, and limbs. She's a square-built older woman, tough as a boot, who wears her armor as easily as an Athenian housewife wears her chiton. "Hippolyte, I don't know what your mother was thinking of, naming you for the Old Queen."

"She probably thought she could get back at her own first sergeant by giving another one a headache in the ranks. Don't you just love being a part of the great Amazon tradition?" I sheathed the sword and turned to face the man who had spoken, doing my best to smile charmingly. Given how embarrassed I was by my awkward salute to Terpsichore, I don't think it worked. "You're Nicomachus, aren't you? I loved your Silenus last year."

"*Did* you?" The grin widened. "I'm glad somebody did. The judges weren't too happy with it."

"But . . ." Before I could say more, another man took Nicomachus by the elbow and steered him away. The borders on the newcomer's robe were wide and purple, embroidered with gold; probably the sponsor, who wouldn't enjoy waiting while an actor discussed the art of comedy with an Amazon warrior-girl. The actor in question directed a helpless smile back at me over his shoulder, confirming my guess.

So did the sergeant's next words. "That's Timaeus, the shipping king. You don't keep that sort waiting."

"But what did he mean about the judges? That was the funniest Silenus I've ever seen!"

"You know that's not how the world works. That Silenus almost cost Nico the prize last year; *way* too old-fashioned an interpretation. Only reason the judges didn't give the wreath to someone else was because he did such a terrific job on the part of the god and, well, he *is* Nico."

"But it was *funny!*"

"So it was funny. That and half an obol will buy you a cup of wine. Goddess, Hippolyte, sometimes you act as if you've never been out of the Caucasus before."

I hate to admit it, but Glycera was right. This was the fifth year I'd been sent to Athens with the tribute party. Some year Athens will get so involved with its own politics they'll forget that old business between Theseus and my namesake, but don't look for it to happen any time soon. My first year I had to miss all the plays in order to stand guard over the offering, especially the gold sheepskin. (No, not *that* golden fleece. That one's just a myth. Ours is real wool, dyed gold because of some prophecy or other.) Standing guard is just for the symbolism. The money's real enough, though, and a heavy tax it is on our people, too.

It's always the junior members of the tribute delegation that pull guard duty, and by my second trip to Athens I had enough seniority to get to the opening comedy. The tragedies are the big show, even at a

Dionysia, but I had no real interest in them. Especially not after the first time I saw Nicomachus. On stage, of course, all you can see is the mask, but the actors take their bows barefaced, and I memorized his. By the second show, I was in love. Well, theoretically in love; I didn't have enough rank for a pregnancy, and I doubt if the Mothers would have approved a comic actor as a father in any case. But he was good.

Good, however, wasn't enough, as Glycera had pointed out. (Goddess, what a name for a sergeant. It means Sweet One in the old tongue.) There are fashions in theater as in everything else these days. The current trend in comedy is political humor; select the right target and you can name your own price to the sponsors. But don't expect me to laugh with the crowd. Call me old-fashioned if you want to, but I prefer traditional humor, with the protagonist whacking prune-faces over the head with a stuffed sausage phallus.

You might wonder what a country girl, even one who's also a seasoned warrior, could possibly know about the theater. Sure, every apprentice sandal maker in Athens thinks he's an expert, and the haeteras really are (they have time to study, during the day), but an Amazon from beyond the Hellespont? Most of my sisters, I'll admit, regard theater as unimportant, something to kill time when winter keeps us close to our fires. But you see, I had an oracle once. Not from the Pythia, a private one. Thallia, Muse of Comedy, spoke to me. She told me to make people laugh.

See? You're laughing already.

But we didn't laugh when word came that the god's favorite comic actor had gone missing.

"Missing? You mean he missed a rehearsal or something?"

"I mean he's missing," Glycera said. Grimly, she pushed through the marketplace crowd, with me following in her wake. "Gone. AWOL from his sponsor and his play and his house. And it looks like it wasn't his idea to walk out."

"But . . . but the dedication was held yesterday! He belongs to the god for as long as the festival runs."

"Yeah. So?" Glycera stopped in front of an attractive house at the edge of the agora. A crowd had gathered in front, spilling into the garden and staring curiously in at the open door. Everyone was busy expressing their own opinions on what had happened at full volume. It sounded, in other words, like any normal gathering of Athenians.

I shook my head. In my opinion, a dedication should mean something, but times have changed. Judges accept bribes, hired claques make more noise than the audience, playwrights trim their poetry to the latest rabble-rousing breeze. With Nicomachus as protagonist, Anaxis was almost guaranteed the laurel. Personally I thought his poetry limped in every foot, a centipede of bad verse. But he was popular, and the sponsor was Athens's latest political darling. It's enough to give democracy a bad name.

The shipping magnate stood in the doorway, a sick expression on his face. Most likely he was picturing his expected crown on another's brow. He caught sight of us and, to my surprise, motioned us forward.

"Thank you for coming. It was kind of your captain to offer your services." He mopped at his brow, although the day was unseasonably cool. "Not that I expect it to do much good. He's probably dead already. Poor darling Nico."

I felt a pang. Peering over his shoulder, I saw why he'd said what he did; there was enough blood in the front room to supply an altar, or even a small battlefield. But no corpse. Most likely the killers had carried off the body. Or bodies; from experience I know even a small person holds a surprising amount of blood, but there were amphorae-worth of the stuff here.

Glycera entered the room and, after a slight

hesitation, I followed. There was no reason to go in, since the entire room was visible from the doorway, and I didn't want blood on my best sandals. But Glycera was the boss. "So why _are_ we here?" I whispered.

"Captain thought it'd make a good impression on the locals. Called it an offering to Dionysus, for the Festival." She poked with her sword tip at a chiton, dyed red by the puddle it rested in. The fabric dripped when she lifted it from the floor, and she let it fall again. "I thought you'd want to help, seeing as how you've been mooning over the guy for four years. We probably won't be able to rescue him, but if we're lucky we may be able to avenge his shade. You should appreciate that."

A soft golden light dawned in one corner, wrapped around a graceful feminine form. It wasn't the first time I'd seen this. My mouth gaped open like a fresh-caught fish, and I gasped more than said "Thallia!" The figure within the cloud of light giggled and nodded.

"Hmmm?" Glycera glanced over at me, apparently unable to see the apparition. "Oh, you mean Nico served the Muse of Comedy. Well, yeah, but a god trumps a muse. It's Dionysus's festival, after all." She bent to examine a gore-caked dagger without touching it. "Strange, the furniture isn't even broken. Just knocked over. You'd expect more damage, with this much blood."

"But . . ."

Thallia giggled again, her finger raised to her lips. The words I had intended to say wedged in my throat, almost choking off breath. It seemed the muse wanted to keep this visitation a secret between the two of us.

"Timaeus is probably right." Glycera dropped to one knee, examining a red streak where something had been dragged through the mess. "Problem is, I don't see how we can find out what actually happened. My guess is Lycus is behind it. With Nico dead, he finally has a change at beating Anaxis."

"But Lycus is nice!" Now that I wasn't trying to draw

attention to Thallia's presence, I could speak. "Everyone raved last year about the victory party he gave for Nico, and Nico wasn't even his protagonist."

"Hippo, you're *so* naive."

I may be naive, but I couldn't believe Lycus was behind Nico's disappearance. For one thing, he really was a sweetheart. A lousy poet, but a nice guy. You'd think verse that cutting would come from a venomous tongue, but oddly enough you'd be wrong. He's just got an overdose of humor in him; give him any subject and he'll find the funny side. Give him a *politician*, and . . . well. He may not be much of a poet, but he knows how to hit the funny bone. Timaeus's political career would sink faster than a leaky trireme if Nico wasn't there to offset the effect of Lycus's new play.

But even if Lycus were as nasty as his most cutting jokes, he couldn't be behind Nico's disappearance. If it were that obvious, why the private visitation from a deity, even a minor one? He was already the chief suspect; Glycera was as reliable as a lodestone in reading public opinion.

Thallia pointed to some footprints leading through the bloodiest part of the room. A small table was overturned beside them, but not one crimson drop marred its smooth surface. It felt staged, like a tragedy, if theater ever dealt with common people rather than gods and heroes. The footprints glowed with a ruddy light of their own. Thallia pointed to them again, demanding, then faded from sight.

The luminous footprints remained. No one but me noticed them, just as no one else had noticed Thallia. And it seemed like no one in the room, not even my own sergeant, could see me. I'd gone as invisible as the Muse herself. Glycera didn't look up even when I spoke to her. I'm certain she couldn't hear me.

The Muses aren't Olympians, but they swing a lot more weight than a mortal. The Muse of Comedy wanted me to find her comedian, that was obvious, so I followed the footprints out the door. No one took any notice. To this day I wonder when Glycera realized I was gone. Sometimes I miss the old battle-ax.

The tracks led away from the door, away from the agora. I had only had the basic course in tracking, but even a six-year-old male-child could have followed these. Here the tracks halted, there they went to tiptoes, a bit further they widened into a lope. Whoever had left them had taken care not to be seen. I didn't have to worry about that; I wasn't on the run. Besides, Thallia's magic still shrouded me. At least I thought it did.

At one point, I looked back. Behind me, the footprints had vanished. I retraced my own steps, searching, and they reappeared, ahead of me. Only ahead of me. I went back and forth a few times, confirming my deduction: the tracks led forward but not back. Thallia, it seemed, *really* wanted me to follow the guy who'd left them. I had a hunch about who it was, but my hunch didn't make any sense.

The spoor led to the edge of town and past it, away from Athens. At first the trail followed the road to Corinth, then it turned down a series of country lanes, each less traveled than the one before. When darkness overtook me, I made a rough bivouac for the night. The footprints glowed, in one direction only, all night long. At dawn I resumed my deity-inspired quest, down another country lane. By this point, I didn't need the glow. There were no tracks on the rough path other than the ones I followed.

It ended at a small tumbled-down farmstead. The war god has plowed this section of the Attic plain time and again; there are dozens of such places to be found, abandoned to chance comers and wild animals. The traveler I sought was here, sitting under an olive tree, plunking idly on a lyre. The lyre was badly in need of new strings. In the end, finding him was rather anticlimactic.

❖   ❖   ❖

"Nicomachus." He looked up when I spoke.

"Yes? I . . . oh, I remember you! The Amazon girl from the agora, the one who appreciates comedy." He grinned, the grin that had charmed me years before, the unmasked grin that invites the observer to share his delight in his own clever performance. I just stared back at him, hand on the hilt of my weapon. A few minutes of this made him nervous.

"Well? I assume Timaeus hired you. All right, you've found the runaway. What now, march me back at sword's-point to Athens? I warn you, I'll just run again. Timaeus is wasting his money; I won't go on."

By this point all I wanted was answers. "Why, Nico? You're the greatest comic actor alive. You've taken the crown repeatedly at the Dionysia, at Corinth, even at Delphi. Sponsors beg you to be in their productions. So what's to run away from?"

"Have you heard this year's play?" I shook my head. "It stinks. Anaxis has always pandered to whoever pays his bar tab, but this goes way beyond that. It's disgusting. Pure hubris. I couldn't be part of it."

"So why not just go to a different playwright? Lycus would have been delighted to get you, I'm sure."

Nico banged his hand against the strings of the lyre, a frustrated sound with no music in it. "I had a contract. I agreed to it before I read the new play, but you don't break contracts with Timaeus. Besides, I doubt if Lycus's play is any better. His sponsor this year is Castor of Piraeus."

"But he's not even a politician!"

"I know. He's a boat builder, a shipper. Timaeus's *real* rival, not for power but for the gold that buys power." Nicomachus dropped his gaze to the lyre in his lap and he started to play a beginner's exercise, not looking at me. "He tried to bribe me to wreck the play. I could do it. Change the timing here, slur a line there, wear a different mask, re-write the part the way I did with Silenus—"

At this he looked up. "That was mostly my own writing, you know. Anaxis wanted to kill me for changing his verse, but since he got the laurel he couldn't very well say so."

I bit my lip to keep from speaking and interrupting the flow, but I felt vindicated. I *knew* that Silenus was too good to have been Anaxis's work.

"Be that as it may," Nico went on, "my life won't be worth a broken sandal strap if I play it straight, and I don't want to play the part anyway. So I bought some pig's blood and set my scene. I should have known it wouldn't fool a real warrior."

"You'd be surprised," I said, thinking of Glycera. "So you ran. Dedicated to the god, and you ran."

"Not from the god! From Castor, yes, from Timaeus, even Anaxis, but never from the god." He got up, lyre forgotten in one hand, and began to pace. "Look, I know you won't believe me, no one else does, but I've *seen* the god. He appeared to me, Dionysus himself. Nico, he said, Nico, go make people laugh. It was an oracle. But it's not fun any more, not when I'm just doing political jokes."

I'd gotten a good grip on my sword hilt when he stood up, but now my hand fell away as my mouth fell open. "Make . . . people . . . laugh . . ."

"I can, you know. I can make people laugh at anything if I want to. But let it be *worthy* of laughter!" He waved his arms, a broad actor's gesture meant to reach the back rows. "Give me decent material, a revival, one of the old satyr plays, something to *work* with! I'm sick of doing topical humor, I want *comedy*."

I looked at Nico as if he were my own oracle come true, which in a way was exactly the case. "I believe you."

"Yeah, we're dying with laughter over here, funny man. Too bad Castor don't have a sense of humor."

Neither of us had heard them approaching. Now we turned to find four men facing us, swords drawn. The leader grinned as they advanced. I didn't much care for the expression. Cutting humor is one thing, but not when it involves real cuts from real swords.

"The two of you planning to run off to Thrace or something together?" The man leered at me. "Can't blame you; she's kind of cute, even if she does wear armor. But Castor wants you dead, comic, and he don't pay us till you are. Sorry to spoil your plans." He didn't look sorry. He looked like a man who enjoyed his work.

The quartet of swordsmen spread out slightly. I shoved Nico behind me, up against the olive tree, and drew my own weapon. "We hadn't made any plans, but that sounds like a good one. We'll send your shades a nice souvenir."

"You think one little Amazon chick'll be able to stop us? They don't teach you girls much sense, do they?"

"No one taught *you* anything, that's obvious." Before the final syllable left my mouth, I was moving, feinting left, drawing the end swordsman out of position, then whirling right as I drew my long knife with my left hand, catching the leader's sword with it while my own sword slid past the guard of the man next to him and on through his body. That one wore no armor. The rest would be more difficult. But common thugs are no match for a trained warrior; they'd made a serious tactical error in speaking at all.

The Amazon sword-and-knife technique seemed unknown to them. Nicomachus, safe behind me, yelled like a spectator at the Olympics. I feinted, ducked, whirled, jumped, keeping myself always between the swordsmen and the actor. A second swordsman fell back howling, upper arm opened almost to the bone. But it was still two against one, and a lucky stroke by the chief thug sliced through the right shoulder strap of my breastplate. I hadn't fastened the side straps securely that morning, convinced I faced only an actor. Glycera would have blistered my hide for such carelessness, and she would have been right. Now the armor sagged sideways, hampering my sword-arm and leaving my right side vulnerable.

Behind the two thugs, a familiar golden light took shape along with a graceful feminine figure. I called out her name, "Thallia!" and I'm still not sure if I meant it as a prayer or invocation or curse. The two hired swords pressed forward, the second man hacking at my head. I parried the blow, turned, took a step, and my right foot came down on something slippery.

Desperately I tried to keep my balance, aware as I did so that the Muse was laughing, merry as a child. My sword almost lopped an ear off the second thug as it swung around wildly. It felt as if I'd done all this before. Behind me, Nico shouted, "Yes! By all the gods, yes, *comedy!* Dionysus!"

And he brought the lyre down on the second swordsman's head. The strings parted with an unmusical *thwang*, leaving the instrument around the man's neck like a halter. Nico ducked under my sword and grabbed one dropped by the first casualty. His opponent, intent on pulling his head free, failed to notice until Nico poked him in the backside. The man limped away at high speed, still wearing the lyre.

I caught only glimpses of the action, as I repeated the same involuntary dance I'd performed a few days before in the agora. Nico laughed like a fool, apparently under the impression it was intentional. I wanted to tell him there was nothing funny about it, as once again I twisted, righted myself, overbalanced, and caught myself with the sword. This time the point sank through the foot of the man facing me, just as his blade found the gap in my armor.

"And *that* finishes *him!*" Nico said, as he followed up with an inexpert cut at the man's neck. The man reeled backwards. Nico's paean broke off as I collapsed.

"Hippolyte! What . . . you can't be hurt!" He dropped to his knees beside me. "Come on, that's not funny. Please, get up. This is comedy. The protagonist can't die in a comedy, the god would never allow it. You can't die, you can't."

Behind Nico, I could still see the golden form of the muse, smiling at me. I managed to draw a breath past the fire in my lungs. "Oh, dying is easy. Comedy . . . now, comedy is hard . . ."

My eyes lost focus, but I could hear Nico calling my name. It almost sounded like a sob. "Hippolyte!"

I didn't die, of course. I came to before Nico had lugged me half a league, his shoulder pressing the edge of my breastplate into my gut. I doubt if he could have carried me much further; he'd spent enough time at the gymnasium to know how to move, but he didn't have much endurance. I've got him on a serious training program now.

He hadn't bothered to take my armor off, which was a good thing as that stanched the wound. It should have killed me, but Nico was right; that wouldn't be funny, and the Muse herself was our sponsor. I healed, quickly and without pain. I've had more trouble with wounds taken in practice.

Since we'd both had an oracle, we decided we should stay together. We turned our backs on Athens and, taking the joke for omen, headed for Thrace. Nico's understudy was a great hit at the Dionysia, we found out later. Castor of Piraeus was so enraged he walked out, slipped (Thallia does love her melon rinds), and fell down the marble steps almost all the way to the stage. I hear the physicians think he may walk again someday. It doesn't do to annoy a deity, even a minor one, and especially not one with a sense of humor

It turned out Nico didn't remember my name after all; Hippolyte was just the only Amazon name he knew. Ah well, he knows *me* now. We make good partners. Of course in Athens women aren't allowed to perform, but this isn't Athens. Besides, we Amazons have never allowed Greek notions to keep us from doing what we want to do. Anyway, this really isn't theater, just a refit of an old satyr play, done right here in the agora. You'll enjoy it, I'm sure, and so will your customers. Like they say, a little song, a little dance, a little vino down your chiton. Comedy, and a headliner from Athens, and all for just two drachmas apiece. Your merchants' association won't find a better bargain. What do you say, eh? Do we have a deal?

You really wouldn't want to annoy Thallia.

One time I wished aloud that someone would do something a bit different for the "Chicks" series. After all, it's a big world with all sorts of cultures, and I do like variety. Kevin's tale taught me that the second part of "Be careful what you wish for . . ." can sometimes be " . . . you'll be very happy when you get it." His work has appeared in numerous anthologies, and according to his web page he does "cool goth stuff." Cool web page, too.

Baubles, Bangles and Beads

Kevin Andrew Murphy

Mbutu spread her hands wide, making her rings wink like the eyes of caracals as she drew forth !num-fire from the stones. "Ai-yeeeigh, little ones! Listen! Listen! Gather round and listen! Hear now a tale from the days when the earth was young, the grass was high, and the men of the Nmboko tribe were still born with monkey tails. . . ."

Folk gathered from the night-market, drawn by the !num-light and the promise of a story. Mbutu waved her hands, weaving the talespell. "Hear now as I tell of Princess Mfara, the most radiant woman who ever lived, whose beauty was like that of the sun, with hair as black as night, eyes clear as diamonds, and teeth like sea-washed cowries . . ."

"That is a dirty lie!" A young man stepped forward from the crowd and stamped the butt of his spear on the hard-packed earth. "Take it back!"

Mbutu paused, unsure for a moment what the dirty lie was and exactly how she was supposed to rescind it. "Her teeth?"

Mbutu grinned weakly, showing her own, which she knew unfortunately to be nowhere near as plentiful or as beautiful as Princess Mfara's, at least if legends were given any credence. "Well, the radiant Mfara's teeth weren't *exactly* like cowries—we storytellers must exaggerate sometimes, you understand. After all, they didn't start out brown with white spots, none of them were loose, and most important of all, her teeth never had snails living inside of them . . ."

The audience laughed, but Mbutu could tell by the young warrior's expression that her jest hadn't improved the situation. "No, storyteller," he hissed, "the *other* lie."

Mbutu grinned wider, showing the places where her teeth had fallen loose like wayward cowries. "The beauty of Princess Mfara? In that I told no lie, young warrior. She *was* the most beautiful woman who ever *lived*. But I know only of the past, not of the present, and perhaps you know of another woman, alive today, whose charms rivals those of the great beauty of ages gone by?"

"*No!*" shouted the warrior, though probably not in answer to the question. "Take back your *other OTHER* lie!"

Mbutu thought back to what she'd been saying, but was fairly sure that the young man would have the same objections—or lack of them—to her mention of Princess Mfara's night-black hair, diamondlike eyes, or radiant glow, which while probably nothing like the sun, hadn't any living detractors to say it was otherwise.

Except for this man. Who had a spear. And the common wisdom of the marketplace, not to mention the morals of a thousand times a thousand tales, told Mbutu that you didn't argue with the guy with the spear. The guy with the spear was always right.

Unfortunately, Mbutu hadn't the faintest idea *what* he was right about. "Eh-heh-heh-heh . . ."

He then turned his back to her, then, much to her surprise, lifted the back flap of his loincloth. "What do you see here, woman?"

Mbutu paused. "A butt? Um, a very nice butt?" The butt of a man holding a spear, who was obviously drunk?

He whirled on her. "*That* is the butt of a man of the Nmboko tribe. And as the Sky God is my witness, neither I, nor my ancestors, have *ever* had monkey tails!" He stamped the butt of his spear on the ground, slapped his other butt, and stood there glaring at her in challenge, and she was not fool enough to contradict him, regardless of what the ancient stories said regarding the ancestors of the Nmboko tribe and their dalliances with Aktebo, the Queen of Monkeys.

That *should* have been the end of it. A warrior had stood his ground, denounced a mere night-market storyteller, and stamped one butt and smacked the other. And as everyone knew, you didn't argue with the guy with the spear.

Unless you were an orisha or a mmoatia. Everyone who heard the stories knew that you didn't argue with gods or faeries either.

At the man's last word, the beautiful blue glass eye-bead he wore about his neck shattered, as if the glassblower had taken it from the kiln too quickly, not allowing it to cure. Yet something was left behind on the string, something black and sorcerous, and Mbutu watched as the dark knot of /num energy uncoiled itself, like a serpent birthing from an egg, pure /num, invisible to the eyes of all but poets and sorceresses, but as both, Mbutu certainly counted. The /num flowed and wavered for a second, then struck in a flash, grounding itself into the warrior's chest like lightning into a tree. At which point the back flap of the his loincloth lifted without the aid of his hands and something long and brown and furry uncoiled itself like . . . well, like nothing half so much as a monkey's tail, like the men of the Nmboko tribe had in ages past, and apparently now well into the present.

The warrior hadn't noticed, or at least, not the tail. He was looking at his chest and the powder of blue glass across the burn of the /num-strike. "You witch!" he cried. "What have you done to my eye-charm?"

Mbutu paused, licking her lips, wondering how to explain that it wasn't her, she wasn't responsible, and pretty as the talisman had been, the warrior had greater concerns at the moment, when a small child, not knowing the wisdom about men and spears, or the dangers of strange magic, reached out and grabbed the end of the tail.

The warrior screeched like a monkey and jumped in the air, whirling about in a fighting stance, only to find a child. The little girl sat down on the ground, pointed at him and wailed, "Monkey!" while bursting into tears, not yet having learned that it was not wise to pull a monkey's tail, no matter how fuzzy and alluring it might be. And when that tail was attached not to a monkey, but a warrior of the Nmboko tribe, such an action was doubly foolish, especially to those who knew the full account of the "The Monkey's Tale" or "Ufaro and the Furry Temptation."

Which Mbutu certainly did, as both storyteller and sorceress, and she took advantage of the monkey-man's distraction to beat a hasty retreat, fumbling wildly through the tangle of talismans and baubles about her neck, trying to find the necklace of the owl spirit, which, if she worked the charm correctly, would turn her silent and invisible, and hopefully not invite the displeasure of Bwillo, Orisha of Owls, for being invoked without a propitiatory offering of fattened mice.

Unfortunately, this was not yet one of her tales, and Mbutu was far less skilled, or at least less well organized, than Gefghen the Storyteller, aka Gefghen the Sorcerer, who would not only have obese rodents and all other appropriate offerings for the orishas, but would also have a far better filing system for his talismans than simply wearing them on necklaces of different lengths. Or perhaps it was just the fact that he was a man, and had never had breasts, and so the stories of Gefghen and his Tales of Tales and Sorceries had completely failed to mention what happened to the necklaces of a no-longer-girlish sorceress who ran from a monkey-tailed warrior of the Nmboko tribe while wearing nothing more than a patterned skirt and a light scarf.

Mbutu dodged around the weaver's booth, past the village well, and through the court of Ozomo, the palm-wine merchant, hearing a cacophony of screeches of "Aieee! Pretty lady! Pretty lady!" which were either the wine merchant's less-than-discriminating patrons or else the hundred trained parrots of Fat Etemboko, the bird-catcher, who ran the shop next door.

Unfortunately, it was night, and the doors of the courtyard, the ones that led out into the desert, and possible escape, were locked and barred. And Mbutu turned and tried her very best to look small and unassuming and hope that the warrior would not notice her behind fifty drunkards, more than half of whom were the bandits that the gates were officially locked to guard against.

Mbutu looked around the bar, at the men and women leaning on the rail behind which Ozomo and his wife ladled watered palm wine from open crocks, hoping to find a warrior of consummate skill and passable honesty, like Temzarro from the Twenty Tales, or Ulata of the Flashing Spear, who, if the tales were to believed, felled twenty warriors before breakfast without even breaking a sweat. Yet aside from the sudden horrible Miracle of the Monkey's Tail, nothing that had happened that night was like anything from the age of legend, when Mfara and Gefghen and Ulata had walked, and Mbutu only looked from one unfamiliar face to the next . . . until she saw the shimmer of a hundred times a hundred brass rings and cuffs accentuating the tall and lithesome form of Talisha, the knife-dancer. Talisha, the scarred, who displayed her wounds and raised cicatrices with as much pride as her skill. Talisha who wore no clothing aside from her bangles and the strips of leopardskin she had cut from one of the children of Osebo, the Leopard, with nothing more than her wrist knives, and that when she was twelve and living in the same village as Mbutu.

Talisha was also known as Talisha the Mad, and while so far as Mbutu knew she had never killed twenty warriors before any meal of the day, or even in her lifetime, all Mbutu needed was for her to kill one, after dinner, and she didn't care one way or the other if she broke a sweat. By the orishas, she wouldn't even mind if Talisha *failed* to kill the man with the monkey tail, just so long as he quit chasing her with the spear.

Mbutu ran behind her. "Bangles!" she hissed, using the pride-name the warrior had chosen early in her career. "Hide me! Hide me and I will pay you well! For the sake of the friendship we shared as girls, hide me!"

Talisha looked back, more than a little drunk, and squinted. "Who—Oh, it is you, Baubles," she said, using the taunt-name she and the other wild girls had given Mbutu when she first apprenticed to old Rashna, the village sorceress, and Mbutu had tried, unsuccessfully, to explain the importance of the many beads of her spirit necklaces. "What trouble have you gotten yourself into now?"

This was answered by a scream of "Witch!" and a responding chorus of "Pretty lady! Pretty lady!" cinching the fact that it had been Etemboko's parrots, or perhaps indicating that Ozomo's wife was not watering the wine as much as she usually did and some man had gotten *exceedingly* drunk, and could now no more recognize "lady" than he could "pretty."

The Nmboko warrior stood in the middle of Ozomo's court, one hand on his spear, the other pointing directly at Mbutu as he cried again, "Witch!" and the monkey tail curled in the air like an inquisitor's crook which had somehow become entrenched in his buttocks.

Talisha stood, her bangles chiming up and down her arms as she stood to her full great height, and she took a drunken step forward as she removed the leather guards from the circular knives she wore on each wrist. "Who is it who is calling my good friend Baubles a witch?" Talisha purred, like a true daughter of the orisha Osebo, and Mbutu was glad because much as Talisha had never been her friend, or even shown any particular kindness to her at all (and in fact, much to the contrary, had often tormented Mbutu until she finally gave up the game as poor sport), Mbutu also had never seen Talisha back down from a fight, or let go of even the slightest excuse to pick one.

The man of the Nmboko tribe stood as proud as he could with the monkey tail kinking his spine. "I am!" he shouted. "Look what she has done to me!"

Talisha looked him up and down, at last pronouncing, "You appear to be a perfectly healthy man of the Nmboko tribe, and I can see nothing wrong with either you or your tail. What did Baubles do? Give you that ugly loincloth?"

The Nmboko warrior screamed and raised his spear, Talisha immediately falling into a fighting stance, and when the warrior lunged, she knocked the spearhead aside with her bracelets with a chime of brass. She then kicked forward with her right ankle-knife, which she had either somehow taken the guard off of or had never put it on in the first place. Regardless, a bright slash ran up the warrior's thigh and down, a long swatch of flesh peeling away from the muscle to dangle from his left knee.

"A pretty mark, monkey-man," Talisha cried. "Let me give you its mate!" She stepped forward with a whip-kick with her left ankle, but he dodged back, then feinted with his spear.

Talisha moved back, laughing. "You will have to try better than that, Nmboko monkey." She shook her shoulders then, making her magnificently scarified breasts shimmy, taunting him. "Come, try to get a piece of this. There's no sport in a little tongue-wagging sorceress like Baubles. Try yourself with a woman who knows how to dance!"

"Witch!" the Nmboko man screamed, utterly confused as to who or what he was dealing with, and lunged again with his spear.

With a shake of her arm and a spin of her bracelets, Talisha caught the head, half of the brass bangles looping about the shaft as it thrust forth, the others protecting her arm from the edge of the blade. She grabbed the wood and held it then, tugging against the Nmboko warrior, then executed another snap-kick, the ankle-blade this time contacting the middle of the spear and snapping it in two.

The warrior-man was caught unaware, and fell directly on his tail, literally, as Talisha disengaged the half-spear tangled in her bangles and tossed it up to catch in the timbers that roofed Ozomo's winestand. "What, all you can offer me is that short stump?" Talisha cried, then leapt over the prone warrior and kicked him upside the head.

He did not move. Not even when Talisha grabbed his tail, pulled it straight, then slashed down with her wrist, severing the furry appendage, leaving the Nmboko man with nothing more than a fuzzy stump of a few inches, like a baboon's, which, if rumor had it correct, many of the Nmboko men still had. Talisha then took the tail and draped it around her neck like a dancer's boa—assuming that on the day the Sky God created the boa, he'd not only forgotten the legs, but the scales as well, not to mention a head—and returned to Mbutu. "An interesting breed of enemy you have, Baubles." She sat down at her

customary place at the bar and took a swallow of palm
wine. "When did you pick up witchcraft?"

"It was not me," Mbutu protested quickly. "I was
telling a story when suddenly—*bang!*—the *!num* flashed,
and the next thing he was wearing a monkey ta—"

Mbutu broke off as a drunken merchant, wearing a
princely dashiki and more necklaces and gold rings than
Mbutu had acquired in all her years as sorceress,
staggered up and put a rude-to-the-point-of-suicidal hand
on Talisha's shoulder. "Talented work, pretty lady," he
said, feeling her many and beautiful scars. "I could use
a pretty lady like you in my household."

Mbutu saw the danger sign. Talisha might be beautiful, but she was beautiful the way a leopard was, and
you didn't put your hands on one like that either. But
the merchant advertised his wealth like a cobra did its
poison, for it was clear that only a fool would kill him,
for only a king would be able to afford the death-price
his family would demand.

Talisha might be mad, but she was no fool, and
knew better than to strike him back. Physically at least.
"Pretty lady?" she inquired, removing his hand from
her shoulder. "It would appear to me that it is you,
not I, who is the 'pretty lady.' Indeed, you have more
necklaces and rings than Baubles and myself combined!"

"Pretty lady! Pretty lady!" shrieked the parrots, and
the merchant took his much beringed hands back with
an offended sniff, resting them proudly on his many
necklaces and tokens of wealth—and Mbutu watched as
a blue glass eye-bead, almost lost in the sea of treasures
about his neck, suddenly shattered, and a flash of *!num*
sunk into the merchant's chest. Which began to swell.
And swell.

The merchant's chest grew, and his waist slimmed,
and his hips grew wider and wider, suited for child-
bearing, while his eyes became as clear as diamonds,
his hair long and black as midnight, and his teeth

became remarkably like cowrie shells. Sea-washed. Without the snails.

The most beautiful woman in the world since Princess Mfara, or perhaps just her reincarnation, looked at her fingers, then touched her face, then touched her breasts, then screamed.

"Pretty lady! Pretty lady!" shrieked the parrots.

The spitting image of Princess Mfara, assuming that Princess Mfara were in the modern age and had taken to wearing men's dashikis, looked at Mbutu and Talisha in horror. "What have you witches done to me?"

Talisha looked at Mbutu, but after Mbutu did not respond, the warrior replied, "We have done nothing to you, 'pretty lady.' Indeed, if anything, you have done this to yourself. By your impudence, you have attracted the attention of a mmoatia, or perhaps even an orisha, and they, not we, have done this to you."

The merchant, or merchant princess, looked at them in horror as again the parrots shrieked, "Pretty lady!" "Oh woe!" wailed the merchant. "What is to become of me?"

Mbutu thought he had an excellent chance of marrying a prince, or even becoming one of the many wives of a less discerning king, but didn't feel it politic to say so. "My friend Bangles and I," she said with a small side-glance to Talisha, to see if the warrior objected to the familiarity, "we go far back. We have had many great adventures and faced many strange perils together." "Great" and "strange" were of course highly relative terms, but when she was seven and Talisha had been eight, it had seemed a great and strange adventure for the village girls to steal the akua doll from Farmer Naniko's gourd patch and put it in the bride hut of the chieftain's son on his wedding night. "If you were to give us three bags of gold and an elephant tusk, I am certain we could find the witch or mmoatia who worked this magic, or perhaps the orisha you offended, and persuade them to restore you to your proper form."

The mention of money, at least, shocked the merchant back to sobriety. "Three sacks of gold and an elephant tusk? Preposterous! Besides which, how do I know you have the ability to do what you say?"

Talisha waved the bloody end of the man-sized monkey's tail in the merchant princess's face. "There was just a man who was upset at suddenly having a monkey's tail like his ancestors and we fixed *that*. I'm certain we can fix your problem as well."

"Though it will, of course, take a bit more time," Mbutu added, looking at the princess's ample chest. "I doubt you would want such . . . an expedient . . . solution."

The princess looked at her, then at her own breasts, then looked away, as if she could somehow pretend they did not exist. "I'm certain I could find cheaper help."

"But not better," Talisha purred back. "And never on such short notice. Though perhaps Baubles here has asked more than you are able to pay? I am familiar with the mercenary trade, and we could settle for what wealth you have on you now, with a sack of gold when we solve your problem. Plus reimbursement for incidental expenses."

The merchant princess looked at her hard. "Half my jewelry now, half later. Nothing more."

"Save expenses," Mbutu added.

The princess paused. "Save expenses," she agreed, then added, "but I expect receipts. And results."

"And you shall have them," Talisha promised.

"Now where," Mbutu asked, "did you get that lovely blue bead charm . . . ?"

Mbutu and Talisha traveled through two more villages, hearing stories of a fat hippo, an ugly stork, and the village braggart whose endowments were now just as grossly exaggerated as he had always claimed. And always there was a blue bead in the tale, one of superlative beauty and finest craftsmanship, paid in trade for one service or another by an unknown and unremarkable young man, most likely a bandit.

"I say a witch is responsible," Talisha insisted, her bangles jangling with the gait of her horse, even beneath the loose cotton robe she wore as protection against the sun, "a witch with a very sick sense of humor."

Mbutu shook her head, wishing she was able to afford a better beast than a donkey. "Witches don't have such power. One curse, perhaps. Maybe two. But that would be it. A witch who did such magic as we have seen would be dead, or at least invalid for months, and in any case, one would never be this capricious—it would cost him too much. Or her—witches can be female as well, you know. But I say it is a mmoatia. Perhaps a whole band. The Otherfolk are known to play such tricks and have a strange . . . logic . . . to the way their affairs are conducted. Mmoatia could definitely do what we have seen."

"Perhaps Spider?" Talisha asked, saying the name of the orisha in hushed tones. "It would fit with the stories you tell."

Mbutu shrugged. "Or Hare. But the orishas seldom involve themselves like this." She speculated a bit more, trying to figure out what manner of magic it could possibly be, and then all speculations died in her mind as they crested the next dune and saw the scene before them: a massacre. A complete and total massacre. A caravan had been working its way across the desert, with horses and mules and camels, except now the sand was dark with blood and bodies lay strewn every which way, mangled and partially eaten, by the teeth of something—many things—huge and powerful.

Mbutu and Talisha paused for a long moment, drinking in the scene, then went down to investigate, a wake of vultures flying up, croaking in protest. Bolts of cloth lay strewn about, along with dried fruit and other trade goods. They both searched in vain for any sign of life until at last Mbutu grew soul-sick and drew forth one of her necklaces. "Oh Abo," she whispered, invoking the python orisha who had blessed the serpentine beads, "if there are any alive here, any at all, show me . . ."

The beads gleamed in the sunlight, and Mbutu let the *!num*-fire flow through them, feeling the tug, as inexorable as the coils of the python, as sensitive as the taste of one's tongue.

For a long while they lay still, then the string snaked west, pointing across the desert, like the head of Abo after his prey, and Mbutu motioned for Talisha to mount up again.

They traveled for hours, until at last they found a horse, lying dead in the sand, yet unmarked, run to the point of exhaustion and death. And beyond it, a set of footprints. They followed, the gray-green beads guiding the way over dunes until at last they found a man lying unconscious in the sand.

Talisha jumped down and lifted his head, giving him water, and holding him when he screamed. Yet then his eyes cleared, and realizing they were neither vultures nor desert ghouls, but instead his rescuers, the man calmed. "Shaka bless you," he croaked, then accepted more of the water.

"Tell us what happened," Talisha said simply.

"Oh, it was terrible," the man said at last. "Our caravan was beset by bandits."

Talisha raised one eyebrow. "What we saw was not the work of ordinary bandits."

The man nodded. "But they seemed so at first."

"Tell us what happened," Mbutu said, *exactly.*"

After informing them of a number of inconsequentials regarding the journey, the price of dates, and the relative profit to be had in the investment therein, the man came to the important information: "And then, as we half-expected, the suspiciously unencumbered group of travelers who had offered to let us share their fire, well, they took out their knives and their swords."

"And then?" Mbutu prompted.

"Our guards took out their knives and their swords."

"And then?" asked Talisha.

"Well, our caravan master, and the head of the bandits, looked at the approximate size of each other's forces, and set down to haggling. Standard, everyday business. Until at last they reached an agreement, and our caravan master ritually cursed them all as being the sons of jackals and evil-minded camels. Nothing out of the ordinary."

Mbutu paused, drinking this in. "And then?"

"And then . . ." the merchant said, shivering in horror, "that's exactly what they turned into. All of them. . . ."

The date merchant was returned to his family in a nearby village, and Mbutu and Talisha were never so heartily sick of the palm-fruits as they were after the twelve feasts in their honor, involving every possible perversion of dates that twenty generations of villagers and date merchants could devise. There were date pastries, date punch, date salad, date bread, and date-stuffed-everything and everything-stuffed-dates, with all options either marinaded in palm wine, fried in palm oil, or both. And there were yet more horrors as the jackal-camels—or jacamals, as they became known—attacked again and again.

Something, obviously, had to be done. If just to save them from the villagers.

"We must kill them," said Talisha. "They are vicious beasts, but they can be killed."

"Are we talking of the jacamals," Mbutu asked, "or the chefs?"

Talisha paused, considering. "The jacamals," she said at last. "We must kill them. Cut them with knives, trap them with traps, poison them with date punch." She pushed the cup away from herself in revulsion.

"No," said Mbutu, differing with the warrior for once, "we must talk to them. Explain the situation."

The knife-dancer looked at her as if she were mad, then at last said, "Wait, are you talking about the chefs?"

"No, the jacamals." Mbutu simply spread her hands, allowing her rings to flash. "I spoke to the stork and I spoke to the hippo. They are beasts now, yes, but very clever beasts, and the sons of jackals and evil-minded camels are very clever beasts indeed. Besides which, they have the hearts of bandits, and so can be counted on to be greedy. If we explain matters to them in the right fashion, we can count on them to follow their enlightened self-interest . . . and ours, as the case may be."

Talisha leaned closer and took another nut-stuffed date, which were as addictive as they were vile, from the tray. "Go on, storyteller. I'm listening. . . ."

The plan was simple: a wedding feast fit for jackals and evil-minded camels. Chickens were stuffed with dates and roasted, then placed with more dates into a goat and roasted, then the roast goat was stuffed into a sheep (with more dates) and that was roasted too, and the roasted sheep was stuffed into a slaughtered ox, which was smeared with date paste and left out to bake in the sun, abandoned at the edge of the date grove along with Mbutu and Talisha, who sat in hammocks suspended from the tops of the palm trees like large bunches of dates.

The smell was truly incredible, especially when Talisha put date pips into her sling and killed three vultures who wished to crash the feast. Others were discouraged, after which one of the jacamals finally arrived, eyeing the traditional village wedding feast, which was complete in its presentation except for not having been stuffed into a camel and set ablaze with palm wine as the finale.

Mbutu rubbed her feathered earplug, sacred to Darshima, orisha of parrots, and called out in something between the howl of a jackal and the evil braying of a camel: "Welcome, brother. This feast is in your honor."

The jacamal sniffed the air. "What poison did you use, sorceress?"

"No poison," Mbutu wailed back, correcting her accent in the strange jacamal speech, "merely chicken, goat, sheep, rotted beef, and lots of dates. Lots of them."

The jacamal sniffed again. "And to what do I owe this courtesy?"

Mbutu paused, wondering how to render the flowery speech she'd composed into jacamal cries. At last she tried: "Honored cousin, I know that the shape you wear now is not the one you were born with. Moreover, my partner and I have a proposition which we both might find equally profitable, ending with you being restored to your proper form, and all of us becoming exceedingly rich."

The jacamal waggled its long and evil ears and twitched its equally long and evil nose, which was doubly horrible, for it combined a camel's buck teeth with a jackal's fangs. "What do you propose, cousin?"

Mbutu paused, realizing she was playing a long shot, but a reasonable one to try. "First of all, payment. I have it from my sources that you and your brothers recently came into some startling wealth, a great number of beads of finest craftsmanship, blue eyes, such as are commonly used to avoid the gaze of a witch."

The jacamal spat. "Fat lot of good it did us. They obviously didn't work."

Mbutu smiled to herself. They most obviously did, for after a long while of sorcerous speculation, she had realized this: It was the eyes of a witch that held his power, and as such, an eye could protect against them. However, if that eye had been stolen *from* a witch, then that eye would be the curse itself, not the protection from it, just waiting for the extra hint of malice to release the curse and aim the strike. For example, an everyday insult like "You fat hippo" or "You sons of jackals and evil-minded camels." Yet there was no point in telling the jacamal that.

Mbutu waved one hand and demurred. "Ah, but the lay public does not know of the eye-charms' defectiveness, do they? And the rest of those beads will still be quite valuable, if just for craftsmanship alone."

The jacamal nodded. "They would. Certainly there'd be enough to pay for our restoration, if you have that power, sorceress."

"Not quite," said Mbutu, shifting position in her palm-tree hammock, "but I know where I can get it. But these beads—may I inquire as to their source? For while I have seen a few examples—and I know they must be quite rare and costly—if more were to turn up all at once, they would lose their value, and I would have a harder time paying for that which you need, as well as the trouble for myself and my partner."

The jacamal snorted. "Not much chance of that. We got them from a mad foreigner, a pale-skinned man from the north, who came through the desert himself with nothing more than a horse and a pack with a king's ransom in beads."

Mbutu nodded sagely. "I see. And what became of this foreigner?" Obviously the man was the witch she'd surmised, and if it had been a death curse he'd laid upon the beads, it was not only fiendishly powerful, but would most likely prove impossible to lift.

The jacamal spat again. "Oh, nothing much. Foreigners are valuable in the slave market, so we just bagged him, gagged him, and sold him to a slave merchant in Embeko." The jacamal gave her an evil look. "Now what was this plan you mentioned involving wealth and power in addition to our restoration?"

"Oh, it is simple," Mbutu said, "let me explain it to you . . ."

The villagers hailed Mbutu and Talisha as saviors when they led the jacamals into town, all meekly shackled with ropes and what chains could be found. Talisha, however, stopped the villagers from stoning them, threatening that violence might break Mbutu's nonexistent spell, and moreover, would damage the beasts' value when they were sold to the King's circus in Embeko.

Mbutu collected the money from the grateful villagers, and didn't feel bad about it at all—after all, they were ridding the village of a group of vicious beasts who were far worse than the bandits they'd originally been. And they were at last escaping the dates.

After which they journeyed to Embeko, where Mbutu told tales of her and Talisha having a fantastic battle with the jacamals, full of /num-fire and flashing knives, until finally, by power of blade and sorcery, they had brought the beasts to heel. It sounded much more impressive, overall, than hanging in a palm tree and haggling with enchanted bandits, but it didn't matter— the jacamals danced and cavorted, pranced in circles, and finally ate a condemned prisoner for the amusement of the King. It really couldn't have gone any better than it did.

Of course, what Mbutu knew that the jacamals didn't, was that so far as she knew, there was no such treasure as the Lifestaff of Shango in the King's treasury, and even if she wheedled herself into the King's confidence as she promised, avoiding a dozen wizards, sorcerers, and backstabbing courtiers, it would be exceedingly difficult to appropriate a sorcerous object which did not exist, or use it to break a fiendishly foreign spell.

Not that the jacamals needed to know that particular fact, or the King for that matter. After all, he'd already paid Mbutu and Talisha lavishly for the jacamals, which were the talk of all Embeko, beating even the story of the miserly shopkeeper who, upon asking his wife if she thought he was made out of money, very suddenly vanished to leave an extremely wealthy widow.

Not that Mbutu and Talisha were doing badly themselves. Mbutu bought a dozen new necklaces, and Talisha new bangles and custom scars, and decked out in this manner, they entered the legendary slave market of Embeko. Mbutu was in paradise—lavishly perfumed and beautiful slaveboys brought her sweetmeats for her pleasure, all of which were wonderful, excluding the nut-stuffed dates, which after the third feast the week before, Mbutu had sworn off of for life.

"And how may the House of Orunmila bring pleasure to you ladies?" asked the slavemaster in his elegant feathered headdress as Mbutu flashed the additional golden rings she had got from the merchant princess.

"Slaves," said Talisha. "We are in the market for a slave. Something male. Something to pique our interest."

"And what might your tastes be?" the slavemaster inquired unctuously.

"Oh, I do not know. . . ." Mbutu fluttered her lashes and looked to Talisha. "What do you think, Bangles?"

The warrior woman laughed. "Oh, let's see them all. We'll tell you what strikes our fancy."

"Of course," said the slavemaster, bowing, "we at the House of Orunmila live only to serve . . ." And then the slaves were brought forth. Some were tall and lean. Some were short and fat. Many were very much to her tastes or Talisha's. But there was still business to attend to.

At last, the slavemaster bowed again, his feathers bobbing like a secretary bird's twin crests. "I see you are ladies of discriminating taste. Perhaps the next might intrigue you."

At his words, the "next" came out—tall, lean, with skin as pale as a frog's belly and hair as red as antelope fur. Talisha looked to Mbutu, and Mbutu inspected the man with the spirit sight. Strong, certainly, and healthy, but foreign as he was, not a witch or mmoatia, or even one blessed by the orishas. Mbutu shook her head subtly, and Talisha said, "Not quite, but intriguing. Do you have any more like that one?"

"I have not yet begun to list his skills and accomplishments," the slavemaster protested.

Bangles waved him away with a chime of her namesake. "It doesn't matter. He doesn't please my sister. But

I like the foreign look. Do you have any others with this pale skin?"

"Another," the slavemaster allowed, and a moment later a fat older man was brought forth, with steel gray hair and a potbelly.

Mbutu shook her head again. "No, not that one either. Do you have any others?"

The slavemaster hung his head. "I'm sorry, that is the last of them."

Mbutu sniffed. "Are you certain? I was so interested in finding a foreigner, but neither of those were quite suitable."

Talisha smiled, showing her leopard teeth. "I am certain that you have goods you are not showing us."

The slavemaster sighed. "All, I'm afraid, that I would feel honorable selling. For foreigners, the only other one I have has been unconscious for weeks, victim of . . . ah . . . let us call it a regrettable accident. We have been attempting to revive him, but I'm afraid we may soon have to call it a loss."

"Bring him forth," Mbutu ordered. "I would like to see everything."

The moment they did, Mbutu knew they had the right man. Not only did he fit the jacamal's description—pale of skin, but with hair black as Princess Mfara's and almost as long, and a nose hooked like an eagle's beak—but he also had the feel of a powerful witch. Yet one with his *Inum* drained down to the lowest ebb.

"He looks sickly," Talisha said. "Are you sure he's not dead?"

The slavemaster waved his hand in the negative. "No, no. He is very much alive. But barely and he has been wasting away."

Mbutu pulled off the least of her gold rings, one without any *Inum*, merely value. "I believe I will take him. As a curiosity, if nothing else. Accept this trinket in payment . . ."

"Ah, sweet lady, but I paid so much more for him . . ."

And so the haggling began. In the end, they sealed the bargain, the man in exchange for two gold rings, a glass necklace, and an ivory earplug. Mbutu sent Talisha to the King's palace to borrow Mumfaro, the youngest and best-tempered of the jacamals, who Mbutu felt vaguely sorry for. At which point they bore away the unconscious witchman and set off across the desert to where Mumfaro knew the treasure trove to be.

After all, splitting the wealth with one bandit as opposed to twenty bandits was much preferable.

The bandits' lair was a ruined caravanserai at a dry oasis, and the treasure was stashed in the hollow of a broken wall—not terribly original, but effective. Talisha brought forth a leather saddlebag and revealed a huge cache of blue beads. Mbutu quickly put her hand over Talisha's mouth before she could exclaim something foolish, like that she'd be the mother's brother to a monkey. Mbutu only took the pouch and laid it across the chest of the sleeping man.

At which point he woke, like a prince from one of her tales. Slowly. Weakly. With lashes aflutter like dying butterflies, never quite opening, and Mbutu had more than ample time to propitiate the orisha of parrots so as to understand his speech. "Welcome back to the living," Mbutu said. "Your treasure has been returned to you. All but a handful of beads. And they've caused quite some trouble, let me tell you. . . ."

He sat up and felt his head. "I'm glad. You southerners should learn to fear a gypsy's curse." He then looked at her, revealing eyes a startling blue, bright as his witch beads.

Mbutu blinked and made a subtle gesture against the evil eye. "What is a gypsy? Some type of witch or mmoatia?"

"I am a gypsy," the man replied, glaring with all the azure balefulness of a peacock's fan. "We are of the Rom. Travelers. I came because I heard your folk valued beads."

"We do," Mbutu replied, "and evidently your people do as well."

"Not so much as you do. And not so much as our freedom," the man said, looking away, and allowing Mbutu to relax her hand. "Slavery is the worst thing in the world to the Rom, and the second worst is stealing from us. To invite the curse of one is to invite the curse of the whole tribe."

Mbutu bit her lip. An entire tribe of foreign witches—all fueling their malice into a single curse. Well *that* easily explained the power they'd been dealing with. Gypsies—hmph! Bad as witches and mmoatia combined. "You are free now," she said, "and you have your beads back. At least most of them."

"Good," he said, then looked at both of them. "Not that I'm ungrateful, but may I ask why you two ladies have rescued me? It doesn't look like you're under a curse yourselves, and I can tell that you are a woman of power."

Mbutu bowed her head. "My name is Mbutu," she said, "but you may call me Baubles." After all, if Talisha was going to keep using it, she might as well make her taunt-name into her pride-name, and there was no one better to start with than a gypsy witch.

"Talisha," said the warrior woman, not understanding the language but obviously understanding it was time for introductions, "Bangles." She chimed her bracelets as explanation.

"I am Davio, of the Rom." He grinned then. "I suppose that would make me Beads."

"Well, Beads," Mbutu said, "Bangles and I have a business proposition for you. There are a number of curses you could end immediately if you felt like it, but there is one in particular—a merchant who is now a beautiful princess—that it might be more profitable to hold off on until we could do it in person. With all appropriate ceremonies. And extra charges. After all, he doesn't *know* it was your curse to begin with."

The gypsy man grinned. "I like the way you think, Baubles. It is good to know the *dukerin* is practiced this far to the south . . ."

And so it went, and many wondrous tales were told, of a widow whose chests of gold and ivory turned to blood and bone, of a King whose fabulous monsters turned into common bandits in chains, of storks and hippos that changed into thin girls and fat men, and village braggarts who remained exactly as they were, for there are some things even foreign witches find too funny to change.

And of Baubles, Bangles and Beads and how they bankrupted the most beautiful princess in the world, leaving her a happy man in the end.

All hail a true Warrior Woman, one who teaches fourth graders by day, writes by night, and has been a Nebula finalist into the bargain! I stand in awe. Her fourth novel, Black/on/Black, has just been published by Baen. And oh my, wait until you see what she's done in this story!

Hallah Iron-Thighs and the Five Unseemly Sorrows

K.D. Wentworth

It was a miserable, sultry day down in the valleys of deepest Findlebrot. What passed for streets, all two of them, were choked with pink dust, pink apparently being the color of choice for most everything in that part of the world. Gerta, and I, Hallah Iron-Thighs, sworn sisters-in-arms, had just escorted a herd of attack goats across the mountains from Alowey. They had been ordered as Queen Maegard the Meek's wedding present to her daughter, the illustrious Princess Merrydot. For once, the bandits infesting the passes had been fairly scarce. We hadn't been forced to kill more than a dozen, hardly a decent workout for my sword, Esmeralda.

In the distance, the Findlebrotian palace rose before

us. It had the unfortunate appearance of being sculpted from icing, then left out in the sun to melt. In keeping with the local color scheme, it was constructed of the most nauseating of pink stone. The turrets were covered with a rounded stucco that dripped with flourishes and curlicues, hardly a warrior's dream for defense. The crenellations were nonexistent. A two-year-old with a battle-ax could have taken it.

Gerta scowled. "I hate this place."

"You can't hate it," I said. My bay mare, Corpsemaker, waggled her ears in agreement. "We just got here. It takes at least half a day to properly loathe a country."

"Well, I hate its smell anyway," she said.

I couldn't argue with that. Findlebrot did have a most peculiar odor, oversweet and noxious as though a perfume caravan had fallen off a mountain and smashed all the bottles in a heap.

"And look at that." She gestured at the pink castle. "It makes me embarrassed just to be close to that eyesore."

"I don't care what it looks like as long as their gold is yellow," I said testily. I flicked my whip at an errant attack goat that was taking aim at a local dog. It had been my decision to accept the Findlebrot run this go-round, though it was very unpopular among our sisters-in-arms. Everyone who came back from Findlebrot went on for days afterward about the locals and their ridiculous official list of "Unseemly Sorrows," any and all of which could be committed without even trying. At the moment, though, our purses were emptier than my favorite serving lad's promises and so we were here.

We escorted the goats and their trainer through the castle portcullis without encountering challenge. Once inside, the smell of perfume grew even stronger. My eyes began to water.

The castle guard, if one can dignify a bunch of sissies tricked up in red dancing outfits trimmed in gold braid with that designation, surrounded us belatedly. Gerta swore under her breath as she gazed down at their beardless pink faces. The head sissy, swathed in ribbons and medals, stepped forward and muttered something about "uncivilized heathens." He fumbled for a hanky and held it to his nose.

My saddle creaked as I leaned toward him. The pasty-faced little turd didn't even top my mare's withers and he reeked strongly of roses. "What was that?" I asked. "I'm afraid my partner, Gerta, here, didn't quite hear you, and her so touchy and all about being left out of the flow of conversation."

Gerta smiled wolfishly and drew her dagger.

He flinched and stepped back. "I said, 'Halt where you stand. Creatures dressed in such a brazen, Unseemly fashion cannot be allowed to offend our liege's eyes!'"

Here we go, I thought and shook my head.

Gerta swung a bare leg over her saddle and leaped to the ground to tower over him. "Who are you calling Unseemly, bucko?"

He averted his gaze from her ample cleavage, located conveniently for his perusal before his nose, and turned an innovative shade of red, somewhere between Ripe Tomato and flat-out Fire. "Findlebrot is a highly moral country," he said stiffly. "Our women are admired far and wide for being the most comely, the most demure, the most delicate and refined. We tolerate none of the Five Unseemly Sorrows anywhere within our borders, but certainly not here at court."

"Yeah, yeah," I said. It was much the same in half the new kingdoms we traveled to, these days. The whole world was turning into the most frightful bunch of stuffed shirts. "Just pay up and we'll be on our way."

He flushed further, tending now toward a deep, true Puce, an unusual achievement for one of his pallid coloring. Perspiration beaded up on his chubby neck. "We are experiencing a bit of a problem with the royal cash flow."

I crossed my arms. "That's what they all say."

"This time, however, it is true," he said. "Three times, our most gracious Princess Merrydot has been betrothed, and three times her intended has been kidnapped by a vicious dragon who lives up beyond the highest pass. King Merwick sent gold to ransom them all, but though the gold disappeared, none of the princes has ever been released. The royal treasury, is, shall we say, destitute."

"Don't give us that rot," Gerta said. "There are no dragons." She raised her chin proudly. "My valiant foremothers across the channel killed them all!"

"On the contrary," he said, "the vile beast is often seen frolicking up in the mountains after dark—flames shooting everywhere. Word of it is keeping trade out, exports in. No one pays us visits of state anymore. The situation is becoming quite desperate." He gave us an appraising look. "Despite your shocking propensity for vulgarity, you two do look as though you might be competent with those swords. I don't suppose—"

"Forget it," I said, waving a fist in negation. "Even if there were any left, we don't do dragons. Send your own men up there."

"That is out of the question," he said haughtily. "Every member of our guard is of noble birth. If they went after the princes, they could very well be killed!"

"I'll just bet." I slid down Corpsemaker's bay side. "Now, about our fee—"

"You will have to wait," he said. "What little is left in the treasury is reserved for essentials such as wrapping paper and ribbon, not to mention satin and taffeta, silver wedding goblets, and those cunning little bundles of rice to throw at the reception. In fact, the royal wedding shower takes place in just a few hours. You cannot imagine how expensive wedding frippery is these days, and of course each time the wedding falls through, we have to resupply. Princess Merrydot, being of a sensitive nature, cannot endure the sight of implements intended for canceled nuptials."

He flicked a bit of dust off his red sleeve. "It will be necessary for you to apply for your fee next year, after the princess is wed, unless—" he waggled his eyebrows invitingly "—you would care to waive it altogether as a sign of good will?"

I drew Esmeralda from her scabbard with a singing hiss. Gerta moved to my side, her sword also drawn.

He paled. "This is a civilized country. Hooliganism will get you nowhere." He snapped his fingers and a hundred more sissies tricked out in gold braid flooded into the courtyard.

Gerta bounded forward, sword raised. "Death to you all!" she shouted, her blue eyes joyously savage. "Hallah, stand back! I wish to kill the first fifty myself!"

I shook my head. Glorious death in combat is still all the rage across the channel where Gerta was born, but my mother, Marulla Big-Fist, raised her ten daughters to be nobody's fool. "Now wait just a blamed feint-and-parry minute," I said.

My partner's eyes blazed with anger. "Where is your pride? No one cheats Gerta Dershnitzel and gets away with it!"

"Hold!" A tiny figure, covered from head to toe in layers of pink lace, drifted toward us across the courtyard. Her skin possessed that classic upper-class pallor and she smelled fiercely of violets. "We would speak with these Unseemly creatures."

"Your Majesty, no!" The head guard fell to his knees, clearly horrified at the prospect.

The princess, for that was who she had to be, stamped her dainty slipper-clad foot. "And why not, Major Duero?"

"J-just look at them!" he sputtered. "They are coarse, vulgar, rude, tall, completely immodest, nay, even—" he lowered his voice "—*bold!* Altogether Unseemly in every way! You must not sully your royal ears by discoursing with such!"

"Really?" She tapped a manicured finger against her

lovely chin. "Perhaps even bold enough to rescue our fiancé?"

"Which one?" Gerta asked loudly, then snorted.

"The lack of a royal bridegroom is a great national tragedy," Major Duero said. "I will thank you not to make light of it."

"Why, all of them, of course," Princess Merrydot said.

Gerta slapped her knee and doubled over with the effort not to laugh. "Won't that make it a bit hard to honor your obligations, there being three of them?"

"Besides that," I said, giving Gerta a hard look, "what makes you think any of them are still alive? I mean, dragons—not that I'm admitting there is such a thing— are not known for the quality of their mercy."

"Well . . ." The princess stared at her demurely folded hands. "We know poor Prince Tristin is alive, as well as Prince Adelbert, because—" Her face went pink as the finest Findlebrotian dust. "We recognize their voices every night when the flames appear and the screaming starts."

"You did a bit of screaming together before they disappeared then?" I asked conversationally. "Auditioning the little rascals, perhaps?"

She stiffened. "They shouted—a little. We only listened." She picked an imaginary bit of lint off her lace overdress. "Obviously, We cannot discuss such a sensitive matter of state here. Meet Us down the road at the Inn of the Five Unseemly Sorrows in a hour."

I frowned. "I smell a ploy to get us out of the castle without collecting our lawful fee."

She shook her head. "We swear upon our sacred honor, this is nothing of the sort." She glanced around. "The Inn—in one hour." Then she walked back across the courtyard, head up, chin set, hardly more than an inch of exposed skin showing.

Major Duero gave us a withering glare. "Now you've gone and upset her, and just before her bridal shower!

We'll have to play hours of those odious bridal shower games to cheer her up."

Gerta and I mounted and left without offering our condolences.

The Inn of the Five Unseemly Sorrows had a warped wooden door that stood open. I grasped the hilt of my sword, Esmeralda, and stuck my nose inside. The room was stuffy and reeked of cabbage and about-to-turn pork. A skinny serving girl looked up from the oak table she was scrubbing without enthusiasm, gave me a horrified look and darted behind a ragged curtain.

Gerta pushed past me and pounded her fist on the table. "Ale!"

The curtain quivered, but no ale appeared.

Gerta, never the shrinking violet, jerked the curtain aside and dragged the poor girl out by the wrist. "We've been on the trail for weeks and we want ale!"

"But I-I can't!" The serving girl hung her head.

I disengaged the poor girl's arm before Gerta broke it. "Why not? We can pay."

She sniffled. "Didn't you read the sign?"

"Read?" Gerta grinned savagely. "Who can read?"

I swiveled my head. "What sign?"

The girl pointed with a trembling finger. "Outside— it says 'No Skirts—No Service.'"

Gerta's mouth dropped open. She reared back and drew her sword with a great rasp of steel against steel.

"Are you crazy? Don't say the S-word!" I snatched the girl out of range. "It makes Gerta really cranky!"

She backed against the wall. "But it's the First of the Five Unseemly Sorrows—An Immodest Woman." She glanced fearfully toward the back room. "My master would stripe me good and proper if I ever served anyone dressed like—"

I covered her mouth before she incited Gerta to full-out murder. "Just bring us some ale, and we'll say no more about this little misunderstanding." I produced a silver piece and waved it beneath her nose. Her gray eyes blinked twice before she snatched it out of my hand.

An hour later, several taciturn patrons had come in and then ducked back out again, apparently unwilling to share the inn with the Unseemly likes of us. The ale tasted like the vats had been used to soak rutabagas, but I was just reaching that wonderful muzzy state a bit southeast of mellow. Gerta was considerably further down the same road. My boots were propped up on the plank table and I was scratching that insistent midback itch beneath my hauberk with the hilt of my dagger, when the princess entered the inn.

"Oh—my," she said unsteadily when she saw us.

Gerta balanced her chair back on two legs and pared her nails with her dagger. "If you have something to say, spit it out."

"It's just that—" She swallowed hard, then straightened her spine. "You are showing your legs so freely, both of you. I've never seen such a blatant display of the Second of the Five Unseemly Sorrows—a Vulgar Woman."

Gerta's chair slammed down on the floor just as her dagger bit into the table.

The princess flinched.

"I'm beginning to think all this so-called Unseemly stuff everyone keeps talking about only involves women." Gerta leaned across the table, palms down, and glared. "Tell me that I'm wrong."

"That would be untrue," she said primly. "We recognize Five Unseemly Sorrows in all." Princess Merrydot ticked them off on her fingers. "An Immodest Woman, a Vulgar Woman, a Bold Woman, a Rude Woman, and a Tall Woman."

"How—interesting."

I've seen grown men faint at the sight of that particularly feral gleam in Gerta's eye, but to her credit, the princess pulled out the bench opposite Gerta and sat down. "I am in desperate need of having at least one of my fiancés rescued, and none of my father's guard are willing to go after them. My bridal shower is this afternoon, the wedding is tomorrow, and there simply isn't a bridegroom in sight. Then I saw you two and . . ."

I motioned to Gerta to hold her tongue. "And?"

"And you're so big," she blurted, then rushed on at the sight of our grim expressions. "Or should I say *tall*, taller than any of the men in our guard. You see, one must be related to our family to serve in the royal guard and Papá is quite—" She hesitated, looked around, then whispered, "untall."

"Lot of that going around," Gerta muttered darkly and returned her attention to the dregs of the dreadful ale.

I held my tankard out for the little barmaid to refill. "So what—exactly—makes you think a dragon is involved?"

"The bones," she said. "They're all gnawed and strewn along the trail up to its lair, not to mention the fearful amount of screaming most nights, and sometimes up on the horizon, one can see fire licking straight up into the sky."

"Sounds like a bunch of snot-nosed kids playing a prank to me," Gerta said drowsily and pillowed her head on her arms. "You got one of those Unseemly things for that?"

She raised her chin. "I believe Prince Tristin, he of the lovely green eyes, and Prince Adelbert, who has the most exquisite cheekbones, are both still alive. I fear poor Prince Rumkin, my third fiancé, is dead, because I never hear his voice. That might be for the best, however, as he was rather unremarkable. At any rate, if you can rescue any or all of them, I—" She hesitated, clearly conflicted, then forced herself to finish. "I will see that you are invited to the wedding!"

"Gee," I said, "just what I've been longing for. I'll break out my best knife sheathe and polish up my mail."

Gerta looked up blearily from the table. "You'll have to come up with serious gold if you want us to stir from this inn, sweetcheeks."

Two bright spots of red danced in Merrydot's ivory cheeks, making her look almost human. "That's Her Royal Princess, the Most Illustrious Merrydot, Keeper of the Sacred Cutlery and the Back Staircase, to you!"

"Whatever," I said. "Okay, here's the deal. Gerta and I will ride up and have a quick look-see, but you have to guarantee double our original fee, whether we find any bits of fiancé lying about or not."

Merrydot bit her lip. "Very well, but you must hurry! The wedding is tomorrow. After that, I have but two days left before my sixteenth birthday when I become an official old maid and therefore unworthy to marry and continue the family line."

"Whoa," I said. "We can't have that."

Gerta just snored.

After the princess left, I hauled Gerta outside to dunk her head in the horse tank. She rubbed her eyes blearily, then stared at me, dripping scummy green water. "Wha—?"

"Wake up," I said. "We're off to see the dragon."

"There are no dragons," she said. "My foremothers—"

"Yeah, yeah," I said. "I know the litany. Mount up."

As dusk fell, we took the only road up into the south pass and found it curiously abandoned. This time of year, there should have been trade caravans arriving one after the other, not to mention messengers, perhaps even a young blade out to court a likely lady. A warning prickle ran up my spine.

Gerta rode with her head sunk on her chest. "I don't feel so good," she said thickly. "I think someone punched a hole in my head, when I wasn't looking, and let all the thoughts out."

"I think maybe you're right," I said. "Stay away from rutabaga ale after this. It doesn't agree with you."

"Yeah." She thumped her heels against her gray gelding's ribs and rode on in silence.

An hour later, we were climbing one switchback after another and were about midway up the side of the mountain when I glimpsed a bright gleam playing along the rocky peak. "What's that?"

Gerta shook her head, then groaned at the excessive movement.

The gleam waxed and waned, waxed again. I stood up in my stirrups. "It looks like flames."

"I don't want to know," Gerta said. She pressed her hands to her aching temples. "Let's bed down here and then tell the princess tomorrow that we couldn't find anything. We can collect our fee and she'll never know the difference."

"That would be Unseemly," I said in my best royal imitation. "Besides, if there really is a dragon up there, don't you want to kill it? I mean, it is a tradition in your family."

"A glorious one," she agreed dully. "I think I'm going to be sick."

"Thanks for sharing," I said.

Half an hour later, we heard sounds echoing down from the rocks. They started low, just a few groans and whimpers, then rose in pitch, ending with a final maniacal scream.

Gerta reined in her gray gelding. "Dragons don't torture their prey," she said. "At least, not in any of the tales my family used to tell. Sometimes they eat you, but that only takes one bite, maybe two. They're not dainty."

"And the meal wouldn't go on night after night," I said. My curiosity was roused. "Three princes would last no more than three days. After that, the dragon would have to hunt."

We found a scrubby pine and tied our horses, then climbed the rest of the way on foot. Esmeralda was comfortingly heavy on my back, but Gerta carried her sword already drawn. The noises continued, but in a different pitch, lower. Tristin or Adelbert, I wondered, or even the unlamented Rumkin?

The sounds were coming from a large cave lit from within. "—you can chain me up like *this!*" a male voice was saying enthusiastically. Metal links rattled. "And then like this and this! Very fetching, don't you think?"

"Go home," said a weary voice that sounded like a cross between a vulture and a camel. "I have told you over and over—I am a vegetarian. I have no desire to eat any of you wretchedly scrawny humans, no matter how crazy you are or how much you deserve it."

"I shall be the Harem Boy, staked out for sacrifice by a Cruel Eunuch. You can be the dragon," the first voice continued eagerly. "You can drop down from the sky and have your way—"

"I *am* a dragon," the vulture/camel voice broke in petulantly.

"All the better!" the human cried. "Chain me to the wall here. Just a few links—please! You know you want to!"

Gerta and I gave each other a startled look. Was this one of the missing princes, or an insane goatherd escaped from being locked down in his family's root cellar? I slipped a dagger between my teeth and motioned for Gerta to follow me up the slope.

Inside the cave, shadows danced upon the wall, distorted and huge. A large bonfire was burning just a few feet away. A dusky pink dragon, about the size of a mastiff, sat turning a spit full of squash and eggplant.

Gerta shuddered. "By the gods, I hate zucchini!"

"Shut up!" I whispered, craning my head for a better look.

"If you don't want to play Harem Boy, then how about—"

"Oh, give it a rest!" another voice, also male, broke in. "If he doesn't want to play, I'll chain you up again myself."

"You are both vile, despicable knaves!" a third voice put in, full of ringing overtones. "Though I will not live to bask in poor sweet Merrydot's presence again, I thank all the powers that ever were she will not be exposed to your depravity."

"Put a sock in it, Rum-Punch!" the other two said in unison. Someone giggled. There was the sound of a brief scuffle.

Stranger and stranger. I slid my back along the rough wall, Gerta at my heels. Fifty feet beyond the dragon, three figures moved in the shadows and light gleamed off a quantity of metal. A pile of treasure caskets lay nearby.

"Besides, you've already had your turn, Bertie," the voice continued. "I want to play Cabin Boy, the victim of desperate Pirates. You can be the Pirate King and lash me to the mast!"

The dragon sighed, then tested a winter squash with an extended claw.

I straightened up, stepped into the light, and cleared my throat. All four figures froze, the three humans, and the dragon as well. "Princes Tristin, Adelbert, and Rumkin, I presume?"

"Thank goodness you've come!" the diminutive dragon said. "I thought these three were going to eat me out of house and home."

A handsome young man darted forward, hair brown as mahogany, eyes green as the first leaves of spring. "Mind your tongue, dragon. No one asked your opinion!"

The dragon removed a steaming eggplant from the spit. "You will take them away, won't you?" it said to me plaintively.

I hefted Esmeralda. "You will permit it?"

The dragon rolled its golden eyes. "I will positively dance for joy. Name your price, old thing. I'd pay all I have to be rid of them!"

"You weren't torturing them?"

"They were torturing me!" it said.

"But, then, what are all these chains for?" I asked.

"They're left over from the cave's last tenant, my maternal aunt," the dragon said. "In her day, they were the latest in dragon chic, but now that clanky stuff is so passe. I'm trying for nice clean lines, you know, a much more modern look."

"No!" the young man cried, rushing forward to throw himself on his knees. "Don't make us go back! You don't know what it's like down there! *This* is Unseemly and *that* and *that*! Nothing I do is right and they keep making me memorize lists of rules. Nobody in all of Findlebrot knows how to have fun! Would you believe—" He lowered his voice. "They don't even play Hide-the-Thimble there? The princess looked positively shocked when I suggested we retire to her bedroom to get acquainted. Everyone is so proper and serious and—"

I turned to Gerta. "He does have a point."

Firelight glinted off her blonde braids as she nodded.

"And you?" I gestured to the second figure with Esmeralda. "Back there in the shadows. Come out where I can see you."

A second young man shuffled forward, shorter than the first, as fair as the other was brown, and owner of the exquisite cheekbones which Merrydot had mentioned. He was swathed in chains and very little else.

"Nice outfit," Gerta said.

He blushed. "My father made me come to Findlebrot," he said petulantly. "I didn't want to. Everyone down there is a sodding bore!"

"Mmmnph!" someone said from the deepest shadows. "Mmmmnphhhh!"

"What's that?" I said.

"Oh, that's just Rum-Punch," the first prince said. "He can't talk very well at the moment. He has a sock in his mouth."

I scowled. "Well, take it out!"

Upon his release, a red-faced Prince Rumkin hastened forward. He was shorter than the other two, rounder of face, with soft myopic gray eyes. "Arrest these two wretches!" he cried. "They are traitors to my beloved Merrydot! When they saw I would not be coaxed into running away, as they both had, they knocked me on the head and kidnapped me. They wished to stop Findlebrot's alliance to my father's kingdom, even though either one of them could have wed Merrydot themselves and prevented it."

"Bummer," I said.

"You don't know what I've suffered." He glared at them. "Having to watch their sordid little games night after night, while poor Merrydot was doomed to pass her sixteenth birthday unwed and die an old maid."

"There, there," Gerta said awkwardly, because there seemed nothing else useful to say.

"Gosh," I said, "what to do, what to do?" I stared off into space helpfully. "The lovely Merrydot must have her prince, and soon, but she only needs one." Adelbert and Tristin hung their heads. The dragon munched thoughtfully on a roasted zucchini.

"Wait!" cried Gerta. "I am getting an idea!" She closed her eyes and pinched the bridge of her nose. "Give me a minute!"

I sagged back against the wall of the cave and studied the hilt of my sword. Could use a good polishing, I thought. I rubbed the embossed elephant's trunk with the hem of my tunic.

"We'll only take back one of the princes for the wedding!" Gerta looked at us all triumphantly. "The other two will return to their own kingdoms—but how will we ever pick which one?"

"Gee," I said, "that is a problem."

"I will go home," Prince Adelbert said abjectly, "if you're sure it's really necessary."

"And I." Prince Tristin hung his head. "But I'd rather just stay up here and go on having fun, if it's all the same."

"No can do, sonny boy," I said. "This noisy male bonding stuff is creeping out the rest of the kingdom. All the jumping around the fire, howling at the moon, and chaining each other up has got to go. Otherwise, the royal guard is going to find its nerve one of these days and come up here to check things out."

"How true," the pint-sized dragon said. "And I long to have my nice peaceful cave back to myself again. How will I ever summon the energy to grow to a properly terrifying size with all this racket?"

"As for you, Prince Rumkin," I said, "I'm afraid you will have to keep the details of this unfortunate experience secret."

He threw his pudgy chest out. "And why, pray, would I do that?"

"Because, your highness, if you keep quiet," I said, "Gerta and I will tell everyone you had just worked free of your bonds, slain the dragon, and rescued the other two princes seconds before we arrived. We'll return the gold to the king and you'll be a hero."

"And if I don't?"

"Then we will tell everyone that you were tied up like a sausage by choice, playing nasty macho party games with your two lunatic soul mates here, while poor Merrydot languished in the valley below, doomed to go to her grave a virgin."

He paled. "But that would be a damnable lie!"

"So it would," I said affably, "and, for the record, Gerta and I are quite good at lying. We've had lots of practice."

He ran spread fingers through his sandy hair. "But it all sounds so—dishonorable, so downright unseemly."

Gerta nodded sagely. "He's just the man to help rule Findlebrot," she said in a stage whisper.

"So, Prince Rumkin," I said, "what will it be?"

Prince Tristin dropped to his knees. "Rum-Punch, play the hero, please! My father would kill me if he ever found out what I'd been up to. He frowns on the whole concept of harem boys. He'd marry me to someone even worse than Merrydot in a second!"

"Me too," said Adelbert. "I promise we'll back you up every step of the way, have songs sung in your honor, make feasts in your name." His lower lip quivered.

"And there's always the chance that Merrydot will choose one of these scoundrels over you," I said, "all things being equal."

Rumkin scuffed his boot in the pink dust. "Oh, all right," he said in a low voice.

"Say, old things, on your way out," the dragon said, "could you dump those ridiculous chains down the nearest ravine? I can't look at them another second. They're so incredibly tacky."

Prince Rumkin and Princess Merrydot were married scant hours before she turned sixteen and exceeded her expiration date. Princes Tristin and Adelbert hung out at the castle long enough to back up Rumkin's story, then set off for home, shoulders slumped. Fortunately, no one in Findlebrot ever realized they were pining for one more round of the Whipping Boy and the King instead of marital bliss with the luscious Merrydot.

The weird screaming up on the mountain, the ominous fires, and clanking of chains ended. No more gnawed bones were strewn along the high trails and there were no more royal abductions, although I later heard reports of an excessive amount of broiled squash rinds littering the heights.

True to her word, the princess paid Gerta and me handsomely, though the bulk of our fee came to us in the form of surplus wedding gifts. I suppose we'll eventually find a use for the silver candle-snuffers and jewel-encrusted toilet paper cutters. It's the thought that counts, as they say.

The most elegant reward for our exploits, though, Merrydot kept secret until her wedding reception, where she announced to one and all that henceforth only Four

Unseemly Sorrows would be recognized throughout the kingdom.

That's why, in Findlebrot, it is no longer a sin to be Tall.

Sarah informs me that she "has just finished her fourth SF novel, The Quiet Invasion, *and will go on to write her fifth, if nobody stops her. When not writing, she sings, dances, does tai chi and plays the hammered dulcimer, but not all at once." To which I wish to add, in view of the following story: Arrrrrrh!*

Miss Underwood and the Mermaid

Sarah Zettel

As told by Captain Latimer of Her Majesty's privateer Nancy's Pride *for the general edification of all Their Majesties' subjects by land or sea.*

First, let me say, she was not the kind of woman one normally saw in the Debauched Sloth. No mother who produced that straight spine and those squared shoulders should have permitted her daughter to know that dim, smoky, dockside tavern where unmarried men with open shirts and braided hair mingled freely with women of the Queen's navy, and the Queen's privateers.

For all that, the young lady in exquisite, but wholly modest, green silk walked a straight and determined line.

She seemed wholly undeterred by the silence that fell like leaden weight around her. Without pause she approached the table where I sat with, it must be confessed, Jimmy Harte, an amiable, ample and generous lad employed by the Sloth's mistress—and occasionally by her customers. The stranger looked right at Jimmy and I swear before Goddess, her eyes flashed with a cold blue light. Jimmy stumbled to his feet, splashing beer and mumbling excuses, and retreated.

Neither event warmed me to this person.

She turned those eyes to me, and I saw they were huge, ice blue and judgmental in her fair-skinned, rich woman's face. After the barest instant, I found I had to drop my own gaze to my beer. This also did not encourage my favor toward her.

The young lady cleared her throat. "You are, I believe, Captain Latimer, of the Queen's privateer, *Nancy's Pride?*"

I raised my gaze and straightened my own shoulders. "I am, and you, Miss, are interrupting my personal business."

I saw it then, the light shining beneath the blue. Without a doubt there was power here. *A witch, then? With those manners and that Dress? Whoever heard of a prudish witch?*

"Then I must apologize for my actions, which without my knowledge or intent have been rude and an affront; but I must say, I believe that when you hear me out, you will both forgive and understand the reasons for those actions, as I am on an errand of both delicacy and urgency."

"And you, Miss, were obviously traumatized by a grammar book in your youth."

The quip failed to put her out. Uninvited, she sat, and her spine did not bend an inch with the act. As there was no immediate prospect of a brawl, or a shooting, the noise around us gradually returned to its normal levels.

The young lady raised her voice. "I wish to hire your ship, your crew and yourself."

I looked again at her clothing in all its silken splendor, and the diamond and sapphire necklace around her throat. "My ship has a letter of marque and reprisal," I said, a touch reluctantly. "My commission is to capture, burn, sink, or destroy all of Their Majesties' enemies by sea. I can take no other work until the war is over."

That took her back for all of one heartbeat. "What would you say of a personage who accosts one of Their Majesties' ships? Abducts one of Their Majesties' officers? Would you say this personage could indeed be considered an enemy to the peace and security of Their Majesties' kingdom, territories, and possessions?"

I did not like the turn this was taking. "I would be hard pressed not to."

I would not have believed it possible, but she actually sat up straighter. "Then, Captain Latimer, it is my duty to tell you of the work of one of Their Majesties' greatest enemies by sea, a cunning, ruthless and destructive enemy, one who terrorizes at will, and who is also magnificently rich."

All at once, you could have heard a pin drop in the tavern. All my sailors looked at me, as wolves might look upon hearing the words "wounded deer nearby." My own monetary hunger rolled hard through my privateer's blood. Glowing eyes and prudish Miss or no, this woman had word of a prize.

I wiped at my mouth before I could start drooling, something this woman would surely consider uncouth, and tried to reassert my powers of reason. "What enemy would this be, Miss . . . ?"

"Cecilia Underwood," she answered primly. "As to the enemy, you have perhaps heard of the King's ship *Magnificent*?"

I choked on my own breath. The *Magnificent* had set out early in the year five to cruise the northern waters and protect Their Majesties' shipping. As a

King's ship, the frigate was crewed by men and captained by one Jack Tremor, a young fellow but a prime seaman by all accounts.

Six months later, the *Magnificent* returned to the Kingdom, a broken hulk. The ship foundered off Whitefish Point, and only one sad wretch was pulled from the water. No matter what the doctors and wizards attempted, all he could say was, "Go and tell her he will marry the mermaid. Go and tell her he will marry the mermaid."

"Captain Jack Tremor is my fiancé," said Miss Underwood. "Your enemy is the mermaid."

Very slowly, I set my tankard down. "Your enemy is the mermaid, perhaps, Miss Underwood, as it was your fiancé who was stolen. My enemies are all mortals, and dry-skinned ones at that."

Miss Underwood did not bat an eye. "She is rich."

Damn the woman! My blood sang as I thought on all the treasure that went to the bottom of the sea: ingots, plate, fine jewels, not to mention the wealth in pearls that grew down there of their own accord. All for the taking. The Queen's ships were bound to assist the King's, as the King's were the Queen's. The *Magnificent* had been foully attacked, an officer dragged away, to all that wealth, chests of it, casks overflowing with it. . . .

I wiped my chin. Reason made a last, desperate bid for victory. "How could we find the mermaid, Miss Underwood? She is said to be a secretive creature."

Again, the light shone behind her eyes. "I will find her, and her treasure, for you."

Reason collapsed, beaten. I lifted my gaze to my sailors, standing still as statues around the tavern. "What say you, good women?"

The storm of cheers, defiance and approval threatened to raise the Sloth's roof. In the midst of it all, Miss Underwood sat and quietly smiled.

❖   ❖   ❖

A fortnight later, Nancy's Pride was ready to sail. Miss Underwood arrived at dawn on the appointed day. It took four of my crew to lift her sea chest and stow it for her. My first lieutenant, who hated passengers, was for once not put out that her cabin was commandeered. Miss Underwood could have had my cabin, if she'd desired it, as long as she took us to the mermaid, and the mermaid's riches.

So, with the breeze freshening from the southwest and an ebbing tide, I gave the order to weigh anchor and make sail. Wind caught the canvas, filling it proudly. Ropes and timbers creaked and Nancy's Pride slid forward from the bay toward the open sea. I turned to Miss Underwood, whom I allowed beside me on the windward side of the quarter deck, as a courtesy. I saw, with a start, that she smiled the same smile she had in the tavern when we had accepted her mission. Discomfort stirred in me, overriding my greed for a moment. I wondered, was this really the proper reaction for a woman whose love had been kidnapped by a mermaid? Then, I wondered why I had not thought of this before.

Miss Underwood turned to look at me, her eyes shining with gentle amusement. I feared that all I thought was plain in my face, then I feared her speaking those magic words "she is rich," and chasing my fears away.

"Would you care for a cup of coffee, Miss Underwood?" I blurted out. "It was an early start for you this morning."

She inclined her head politely. "Thank you, Captain, but no."

"Tea then, if you prefer? Or wine against the chill?"

Her smile both broadened and gentled. "Again I thank you, but I believe I shall retire."

An important point reached my conscious thought. "You have not yet told me what our destination is."

Miss Underwood looked forward and her eyes

narrowed. "The course you are on will be satisfactory at present, Captain." Without in the least minding the pitch and roll of the ship, she walked down the quarterdeck ladder and disappeared through the hatch.

I blinked. In fact, I would swear I'd never even saw her sway the smallest bit, despite the strange, weaving course she walked across the deck. The strange course, as if avoiding something only she could see . . .

A captain must never collapse to her knees on the quarter deck, pounding the boards with her fist and cursing herself for ten times worse than a fool. It is bad for her authority.

I settled for bellowing. "First!"

"Captain?" Miss Sherman bounded up the ladder and saluted smartly.

"Pass the word for the ship's carpenter." I did not say why. I did not wish it generally known I wanted to find out how much cold iron we had on board.

The next ten days passed without incident. Any incident. Even aboard a tight, happy privateer there are cases of drunkenness, falls, minor disagreements that flare up into brawls. But not this time. Nothing happened to keep any hand from her work, and they worked cheerfully. Never a cross word or a mild curse. For the first time in twenty years of sailing, I heard sailors say "please" and "thank you" to those of their own rank. I'd finger the nail I'd taken to keeping in my pocket and consider issuing them generally, but I confess, I liked it. As unnatural as it was, it made for a remarkably pleasant change.

Miss Underwood herself kept to her cabin, only coming up once or twice a day to take a turn on deck and stare straight ahead of us. Each time, I would ask her what course to set and each time I would receive the same answer. "This one is most satisfactory, Captain." Then I would ask whether the normal precautions against mermaids should be instituted and she would say, "Not at present, Captain," and I would have to be content with that.

In the middle of the morning watch on the eleventh day, I sat in my cabin drinking my first pot of coffee and going over the charts. Miss Sherman knocked on my door.

"Beggin' your pardon, Captain," she said brightly. "But Miss Verity reports there is a sea serpent."

I did not spit out my coffee. I swallowed. "A sea serpent?"

"Yes, and a most prodigious big one, she says."

I squinted at my First. Miss Sherman's eyes were lively and full of her native intelligence. She simply did not see any reason to be alarmed. It was then I concluded things had perhaps gone too far.

"Very well, Miss Sherman. Beat to quarters and clear the decks for action fore and aft. Have the great guns and all the muskets loaded directly. I shall follow you up."

"Very good, Ma'am."

She vanished, and I got to my feet. With great effort, I blanked my face of all expression. I would not, I could not, appear before my crew wearing my fear. Only when I was certain I had succeeded did I leave my cabin.

On deck, I found my orders being carried out, merrily, as if for a target competition. The unoccupied crew leaned on the rails and grinned at the creature casting its shadow over our deck. Its dripping head reared higher than our mainmast, its fins spread out broader than our spritsails. It bellowed and sound and stench rolled over us. In the next instant, it bent its great, pale neck and swooped down on us.

"Raise weapons!"

Those of my crew who had armed themselves lifted their muskets. The creature must have been acquainted with guns, because it pulled back abruptly and had the nerve to look affronted.

I opened my mouth to give the command to fire, when the air stirred behind me.

"I would not recommend it, Captain," said Miss Underwood calmly. "Its hide is too tough for such projectiles. You will only succeed in angering it."

As if in answer, the creature shook the sky with a fresh bellow and dove straight down. Something smashed against the hull, knocking us all ahoo and causing every hand to clap hold of ropes and rails. The crew's unnatural calm vanished. It takes more than a spell of bemusement to remove the fear of hull breach from a sailor.

Miss Underwood, of course, did not move an inch.

"Can you suggest a remedy, Miss Underwood?" I gasped, pulling myself upright.

Her blue eyes were thoughtful, but without light. "Have you anything you believe exceedingly hard I might throw, Captain?"

One third of my mind considered the phrasing of the question and the nature of the person in front of me. This was neither the third that was gibbering in terror, nor the third reminding it that captains did not gibber on deck. "Miss Sherman!" I barked. "Tell Miss Barton to jump down to the galley and have Cook roust out some of the month-old biscuit. Handsomely now!"

I turned my attention to ordering the hands to take up the canvas, to mind the wheel. The serpent erupted from the water. Its great, fanlike fins battered at the waves, rocking Nancy's Pride and almost swamping us. The thing opened its mouth in a grin I took to be idiot glee and reared back, ready to strike.

Miss Barton arrived and saluted. She handed me a rock-hard ship's biscuit which I handed to Miss Underwood, who thanked me. Like any sailor, I would happily show the chips in my teeth from such objects, and I firmly believed nothing could be harder.

Miss Underwood's eyes glowed intensely blue. She drew her arm back and hurled the biscuit at the sea serpent's head. It smacked the creature right between its eyes.

The serpent bellowed in gargantuan pain. Cheers

arose from the crew. The monster slipped slowly beneath the waves.

"All sail!" I shouted. "All sail, now!"

Still laughing and cheering, the crew obeyed. *Nancy's Pride* leaned against the wind and sped forward.

I turned to my passenger. "Miss Underwood, a word with you, if you please."

Once in the great cabin, I turned to face her. I had to keep myself from clutching the nail in my pocket.

"Miss Underwood, were you aware we would meet this . . . creature?"

"I suspected something of the kind might happen, yes," she said coolly. "I thought perhaps Scylla and Charybdis, but I was mistaken."

"Can we expect any similar troubles?"

"I do not believe so. I think she will wait for a direct assault before she attacks again."

"I see," I nodded. "Miss Underwood, I fear I must be direct. Exactly who are you?"

For a moment those blue eyes glowed and I feared for my safety.

But the glow subsided. "So difficult to bespell someone in their own place of power," she shook her head. "I had hoped the lure of riches would be enough to lull you. I see that in this I was also mistaken." She met my gaze. "Obviously, I cannot give you my true name. Let us just say that I am a person of some importance in the Seelie court, and that the mermaid has stolen something of value to me, and destroyed one of your King's ships while doing so. I could not travel to reclaim him in my own form and under my own power, as the mermaid would sense that leagues away and strike me down at her leisure. Hence, my need for this disguise, and your services."

"And who is Jack Tremor?"

Her eyes did glow then, cold and dangerous. "Mine."

"I see." I felt curiously little fear now. Perhaps it was her acknowledgement that she did not have me in the palm of her fairy hand. "One thing I wish to make perfectly clear, Miss Underwood. If I determine you are unnecessarily endangering my ship and my crew, or forcing my people to act contrary to my direct orders, I will have you thrown in irons."

At that, I had the sweet satisfaction of seeing her blanch. "I understand you perfectly, Captain. Now, will you excuse me please? We are approaching the mermaid's demesne and I wish to be ready."

I bowed politely. "By all means, Miss Underwood."

Miss Underwood left me there. When she was gone I passed the word for the blacksmith, deciding I might do well to order up some additional precautions for this voyage.

Back on deck, the normal order of things has reasserted itself, including the crew's fairy-wrought unflappability. Miss Verity steered a straight northeast course, both sea and sky were as clear as one could wish and from the feel of things, *Nancy's Pride* made a good seven knots. Still, I could no longer be easy. I paced the quarter deck, aware that my First watched me with amused patience.

"Miss Sherman, let us beat to quarters and crew the forward guns. I should not like the next serpent to catch us unawares."

"Aye, aye, Captain." She grinned at the prospect of good sport and turned to bellow out my orders to the appropriate crewmembers, who repeated them up and down the deck. The drum rolled to beat to quarters.

Even under the sound of running feet and the insistent drumbeat, I heard it. A rumble from deep below the ship, like thunder originating from the ocean rather than the sky. Miss Sherman's cheerfulness faltered and something like real concern showed on her face.

I opened my mouth, trying to think of something captain-worthy to say, when a great jet of water

fountained from the waves to leeward. The sea split open.
From the depths rose a great, grey whale, a living wall
between us and the horizon, smelling powerfully of very
old fish. It regarded us with one baleful eye.

On the whale's back perched the mermaid. The blue
and green scales of her tail shimmered in the sunlight.
Sea weeds and sea flowers twinned in her green hair.
Her, ah, feminine endowments were bare to the world.
Beside her sat a man in a naval uniform much bedrag-
gled from overexposure to salt water. Where the mermaid sat as calm as a cat or a queen, he seemed
uncertain as to what to do, blinking and bobbing his
head in all directions like a man being introduced to
too many people at once.

Fine-looking cove, though.

I summoned all my lung capacity. "Ahoy the whale!"

The mermaid answered, her voice ringing clear as
a bell over the sounds of wind, wave and whale. "What
do you mean, Mortal, addressing us in that fashion?"

Well. "Madame, that is a King's officer next to you.
As a servant of the Queen, I must demand his return."

The whale snorted. A gout of fishy-smelling water fell
across the deck, and consequently across me.

"I think perhaps we have just been insulted," I said
to Miss Sherman.

"I think so, ma'am. Shall we give her a gun?"

"No, I think . . ." My sentence trailed off. Miss
Underwood had appeared on deck.

The prudish miss was gone. This was a warrior. A
breastplate of bronze and silver encased her proud torso.
A golden, plumed helmet covered her head. Her legs
were bare, except for the greaves covering her, quite
probably perfect, knees and shins. She carried a silver-
tipped spear. I could not miss the fact that the fretwork
encircling the helmet's brim looked remarkably like a
crown.

A person of some importance, indeed.

"The man is mine!" Her eyes flashed and her voice

rang and I wondered that I had ever had the nerve to raise my voice, to her, to this.

She also seemed no longer occupied with my crew. Smiling insensibility was fast being replaced by incredulity descending into wonderment and into fear. "Miss Sherman, ready all guns. Miss Chapwick!" I lifted my voice to the rigging. "Haul in the main top gallants. Handsomely now!" All hands sprang to their work, fear replaced by reflex. Quite suddenly no one seemed to mind the whale and the mermaid, or the warrior fairy.

The mermaid, however, was not so easily put off. "Jack Tremor is my lawful prize! You shall not steal him from me!"

"I will reclaim my own!" Miss Underwood hurled her spear with all the force she had used to hurl that biscuit.

The mermaid roared, as did her whale. The animal arched into the air like a sea bird. The spear shot under it. The whale hit the water with an enormous splash, sending salt water sheeting across our decks.

Miss Underwood also took to the air. I was not surprised to see a pair of gossamer blue wings spread from her shoulders. She beat the air, flying swift and sure toward the mermaid and her resurfacing whale. I also saw that the spear was back in her hand.

The mermaid called out something harsh and incomprehensible. The waters roiled. A monstrous, slime-covered tentacle rose from the water and lashed out at Miss Underwood. Miss Underwood circled us and emitted a piercing shriek. All at once the air was alive with raptors; eagles, falcons, hawks. They poured down from the clouds, savaging the tentacle.

I was just wondering whether I should order a broadside, and if so, which target to make, when a new voice caught my attention.

"The ship ahoy!"

My gaze dropped to the water. Captain Tremor had obviously lost hold of the whale in the fracas and now bobbed in the waves on the leeward side of *Nancy's Pride*.

"Miss Verity, a rope for the captain, if you please."

The rope was dutifully lowered, and Captain Tremor was hauled, dripping, onto our deck. Out across the water, the tentacle had somehow become entangled, and Miss Underwood, a bolt of glowing gold and blue against the sky, let out a peal of savage laughter.

I turned my attention to the drenched man in front of me. "Captain Tremor, permit me to welcome you aboard the *Nancy's Pride*. I am Captain Latimer."

"Delighted to make your acquaintance, Captain." Despite the dampness of his condition, Tremor gave me a smart salute and a most appealing smile.

I sent immediately for blankets, and brandy, and directed Miss Fletcher, my personal servant, to take Captain Tremor down to my cabin where there were some dry things that might do for him until his uniform could be cleaned. Miss Fletcher took Captain Tremor neatly in hand and I turned my attention back to the battle royale.

The mermaid seemed to have summoned a wealth of seabirds to assist her now, and the raptors screamed and clawed at gulls and albatrosses. Blood fell in a red rain onto the rolling sea. The whale had a bad gash in its side and Miss Underwood had blood on her bright spear.

"A little more sea room, Miss Verity, I think."

"I should think so," she muttered under her breath, and I knew the fairy veil had been truly stripped from my crew.

The mermaid raised her arms. A wave lifted out of the water and swung like a club at Miss Underwood who managed to back-paddle (back-wing?) just out of its reach.

"Captain Latimer?"

Captain Tremor stood at the foot of the quarterdeck ladder. He now wore the blue jacket, trousers and white shirt I keep in case . . . similar situations might arise.

"Do come up, Captain." As he did, I called for coffee. While we settled ourselves, a large, damp chunk of unearthly flesh dropped onto the deck.

"A mop and bucket, Miss Verity."

"Aye, aye, Captain."

"May I ask, Captain Tremor," I began, sipping hot coffee and wishing I smelt a little less of second-hand fish. "How you came to be embroiled in the affairs of these . . . persons?"

He smiled again, dropping his gaze to his coffee. "I am afraid, Captain Latimer, I am a victim of an old story. You see, my father became lost in the Great Forest and . . ."

I saw at once. "And was given shelter in a mysterious castle for the night. In return for the hospitality, he promised to give his host the first thing that greeted him upon reaching home?"

"Just so." Captain Tremor drank some coffee with evident relish. "What greeted him was myself of course, and I was informed of the bargain upon reaching my thirteenth birthday."

I nodded in sympathy. A hoarse cry of rage tumbled across the deck. Heavy waves slapped the hull. A shadow, which seemed to come from a leaping whale, fell momentarily across us.

"Well, my feelings had not been consulted in the matter," Captain Tremor went on, "and I took it rather hard. I've never been one of those clever fellows one reads about in the histories of such matters. I confess I ran away to sea, hoping to escape my fate. I seemed to have done so, until my twenty-third birthday and my first command. You are aware, perhaps, of the care one must take in waters frequented by the mermaid?"

I nodded. The wind carried screams and shrieks to us. I surmised Miss Underwood and the mermaid were hurling imprecations at each other in their native tongues. "I mostly cruised the far southern waters where such things are not as common, but I had heard. One must not use proper names on deck, that sort of thing."

"Indeed, yes." His handsome face grew grave. "If one calls out a real name, such as 'James' the mermaid might rise from the water and say 'give us James,' and so you must, or your ship is lost. Consequently, one must call one's crew such things as 'lamp' or 'bucket,' 'old shoes,' and so on. Unfortunately, one of my men forgot this most sensible rule, and called me by my proper rank. The mermaid," he gestured toward leeward with his cup, "rose from the water and cried, give us Captain!'"

"I attempted to explain to her there was a prior claim on my personage, but it was to no avail. I had to accompany her or the ship would be wrecked and my men lost." I looked at him with renewed respect. A captain who held his men's life above his own was not merely a pretty face. There was honor and a spine underneath. I felt absurdly pleased.

"Unfortunately, due to my crew's mistaken attempts to reclaim me . . ." He shook his head.

"Incoming!" cried Miss Verity, and we instinctively ducked our heads as a fairy spear shot across the deck, falling into the waves to windward.

When we straightened, I noted that the sky had darkened perceptibly, and I knew in my bones the glass was sinking fast. Miss Sherman bellowed the orders to take in the sails.

I drained my cup, briskly. "Well, sir, I must ask you, what are your particular wishes in this matter? The ladies," I decided to use the word in its loosest possible sense, "are likely to finish soon, and the winner will most certainly try to lay claim to you."

Captain Tremor sighed. "Yes, I'm afraid you are correct. I will tell you quite honestly, Captain Latimer, I have no wish to go with either of them." My heart warmed within me at this, but I hope I only managed to nod gravely. "But I do not see how it can be helped."

All blue sky was not hidden behind dark clouds. I regarded them with a pursed mouth as, in the distance, the mermaid laughed out loud.

"It would seem at the moment the mermaid has the advantage." I frowned. "I believe she and Miss Underwood, the one who flies there, are closely related."

"Indeed. They are both of the fair family."

"Mmm." I considered certain events, as well as the uncommonly beautiful man before me. "I believe we may safely say both are Their Majesties' enemies. The lower there kidnapped you and took a considerable number of lives. The higher—" The mermaid let out a piercing scream just then, cutting off my words. "The higher attempted to enslave you, which is clearly against the law." I tapped my chin. "I would be for making sail immediately and leaving them to each other, but my crew was brought out here with the promise of a crack at the mermaid's treasure. We are a privateer, you understand Captain, and while I have no wish at this time to assist Miss Underwood—" Lightning flashed overhead. "I must pay my crew."

"If it would be of any assistance," said Captain Tremor, "I know where the treasure is. There is a sea cave beneath an island not far from here. She took great delight in showing all its contents to me."

Now, I let myself smile. "It would be of great assistance, Captain. If you'll just give directions to Miss Sherman at the wheel, we can get under way at once."

He regarded me for a moment with a mix of emotion playing across his features. "With all due respect, Captain, do you not fear pursuit, from either the mermaid or your Miss Underwood? The mermaid easily subdued a ship of the line . . ."

He was, unfortunately, correct. I regarded the combatants out across the choppy, darkening sea. Miss Underwood glowed in the remains of the sunlight like a living bolt of lightning, surrounded by her birds of prey. The mermaid reared up on her battered leviathan, raising her hands to call up the waves and bring down the storm.

Whatever I did, it would have to be done quickly. If I gave my crew too much time to consider whom we were attacking, they would believe we could not win. Even when engaging mortal foes, belief in your abilities is critical.

Belief. Perhaps if the crew could be induced to believe differently about these ladies. Perhaps if they could be shown they were not all-powerful, but rather, were something quite different . . .

"Miss Sherman," I called. "Pass the word for the blacksmith, and tell her to bring the precautions we arranged." I faced Captain Tremor. "Captain, I must ask you to indulge me. I am going to attempt to disarm Miss Underwood, but to do so I will need to get her attention."

He bowed gracefully. "I place myself entirely in your hands, Captain Latimer."

As beguiling as that image was, I had no time to reply properly, for at that moment Miss Johnson, our blacksmith, along with the cook and her assistant, appeared. Between them they wrestled one of the galley's great, cast iron soup kettles up the ladder. It had been modified so that its lid was attached by means of a sturdy hinge. A lock for firm closure had also been provided.

Captain Tremor looked at me quizzically.

"When one has a fairy on board, one never knows what one is going to be obliged to store," I said. "Miss Johnson, place the kettle behind me and be ready to slam the lid." Then, I turned from him to the combatants.

"Miss Underwood!" I bellowed. The fae queen's attention turned abruptly toward me, the glow in her eyes hitting me like a solid blow. I staggered, but did not fall. "You cannot win! For if the mermaid does not prevent you from stealing away Jack Tremor, I most certainly shall!" At my side, Captain Tremor drew himself up straight, proud and unafraid.

"Upstart mortal!" cried Miss Underwood. "You have no power here!"

She hurled the spear toward me. I stayed stock still as long as my nerve held. Then, I slid sideways.

The spear fell into the iron kettle with a great, ringing clang. Miss Johnson slammed the lid over the top and shot home the bolt on the lock. Trapped, the spear banged madly about, seeking escape and causing the heavy kettle to shudder. Miss Johnson and Cook understandably backed away.

"No!" screamed the fairy. She dove toward the quarterdeck. Biting my lip, I reached for my pistol, but a new noise split the air, as I hoped it would—the rude, raucous laughter of the mermaid.

Miss Underwood screamed incoherently and turned in midair, descending on her damper cousin like all the wrath of Heaven. The fairy wrapped both her hands in those seaweeded, golden tresses and pulled hard. The mermaid screamed and slapped uselessly at the fairy's hands.

"Miss Sherman," I said. "Encourage the whale to leave."

"Aye, aye, ma'am!"

Miss Sherman gave the order and the great guns fired, filling the air with smoke and stench. The balls skipped across the water, bruising flukes, trimming tail and shuddering the great flanks. This iron attack convinced the poor, beleaguered beast that it had finally had enough. It arched its mighty back and vanished beneath the waves. Miss Underwood shot into the air a moment before the whale vanished, hauling the mermaid with her by the hair. The mermaid screamed again and clung to her rival's arms. They rolled over and over in the air, struggling with one another, slapping, biting, and letting out the most piercing of shrieks.

"Cat fight!" shouted one of my crew.

"Get 'er girl!" came the cry from one of the foremast hands.

"That's the way! Slap that pasty face!"

"I've a shilling says the one with wings can take her!"

"I'll take that bet, Chips!"

Someone chuckled, someone guffawed, someone howled, watching these two great queens of the fair folk rolling about like jealous serving boys fighting over some seawoman's affections. The crew's laughter rang across the waters, sliced through the wind and waves. It poured forth until even Jack Tremor joined in. I added my own mirth to the din with the greatest satisfaction.

The pair of them froze in midair, the mermaid's tail wrapped around the fairy's waist. The fairy's hand in the mermaid's hair and her free arm drawn back to deliver a ringing slap.

The merriment of my crew redoubled at this splendid tableau. Several of the women in the rigging had to clasp the ratlines and masts to keep themselves from falling as they shook with their laughter.

The air around the fabulous pair shimmered and I blinked. Instead of a winged warrior and a mer-queen, my streaming eyes made out a bone thin girl of about ten years suspended by a pair of limp, flower-petal wings hanging onto a thing that looked more like a boiled haddock woman than a seductive ruler of the sea.

They looked at us, they looked at each other, they looked down at themselves.

And, oh, Goddess, how they did scream.

The winged girl dropped the haddock woman and flew for the horizon. The haddock dove beneath the waves, and did not reappear. I laughed again at the sudden thought that the whale might be waiting for her in order to discuss its terms of employment.

"That was wonderful, Captain Latimer." Captain Tremor's eyes shone with mirth and delight. "Nothing short of wonderful. However did you think of it?"

I laid a hand on his firm, square, young shoulder. "Belief, Captain Tremor," I said, "I have learned, is all-important in matters of magic. We believed they looked ridiculous, and for that important moment, so did they." The clouds were clearing and the breeze freshening all around us. "Of course, I was praying the entire time that their vanity was as real as their beauty was false."

"You are a marvel, Captain Latimer," he said, with his admiration plain on his open face. "I hope you will tell me in more detail of your voyage. Perhaps when we have a moment to ourselves."

I let my self be warmed by the young man's earnestness. "First, Captain Tremor, you must guide us to that sea cave, or my crew will be more put out than either one of us would care to deal with." I smiled over my deck and my seawomen. "After than, I do believe you and I shall have all the time we need."